Bitter Passage
Thunder from Above Book 2

By
Tracy Van Gorp

PublishAmerica
Baltimore

© 2011 by Tracy Van Gorp.
All rights reserved. No part of this book may be reproduced, stored in a retrieval system or transmitted in any form or by any means without the prior written permission of the publishers, except by a reviewer who may quote brief passages in a review to be printed in a newspaper, magazine or journal.

First printing

All characters in this book are fictitious, and any resemblance to real persons, living or dead, is coincidental.

PublishAmerica has allowed this work to remain exactly as the author intended, verbatim, without editorial input.

Hardcover 978-1-4560-3080-3
Softcover 978-1-4560-3081-0
PUBLISHED BY PUBLISHAMERICA, LLLP
www.publishamerica.com
Baltimore

Printed in the United States of America

I dedicate this book to you, mom (Sharon).
Thank you for all your help in getting this story ready for publication.
This was my favorite to write of the trilogy.

Mom!
I love you.
Thank you for all you have done for me.
Tracy

THE CHARACTERS

Skiringssal (Vestfold) and Ragnarr (Iceland):

Lord Valr Vakrson - Jarl (Chief) of Skiringssal
Lord Rafn Vakrson – "The Raven" – Warlord
Lady Seera – Rafn's wife and Peder's sister
Lady Kata Vakradottir – Rafn and Valr's sister
Dagstyrr – Rafn's best friend and husband to Kata
Joka – Warrior Woman
Systa – The Seer and Joka's sister
Father Duncun – Christian Monk
Esja – Head Servant Woman
Agata – Maid
Leikr – Warrior
Hachet – Warrior
Fox – A young man under Rafn's protection
Yrsa – Young woman rescued by Seera from slavery

Dun'O'Tir (Fortress by the Sea; in Pictland):

Eorl Airic – Ruler of Dun'O'Tir
Lord Peder – Heir to Dun'O'Tir and the King's soldier
Jakob – A scholar
Iver – Peder's lieutenant and best friend
Berthor - Blacksmith
Father Albert – Priest
Isibel – maid

Skahi (Iceland):

Bekan – Leader of Skahi
Rakel – Bekan's daughter
Kale – Rakel's betrothed
Hadde – Dwarf
Amma – Rakel's grandmother
Marina – Rakel's mother
Father Leo – Priest
Danr – Warrior
Vikkar – Warrior
Onnar – Warrior

Seyois (Iceland):

Ari – Leader of Seyois

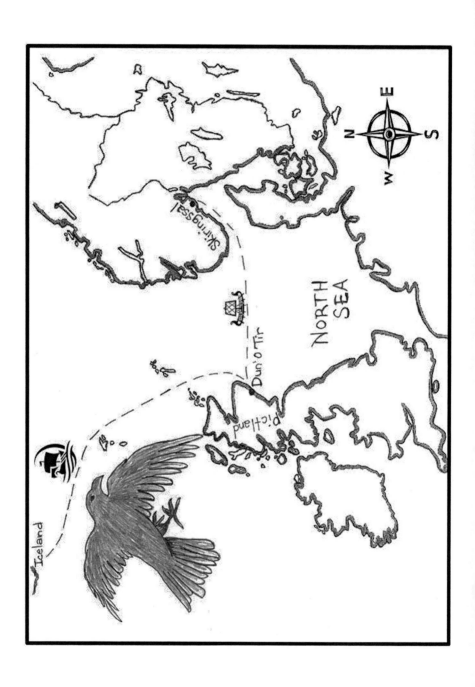

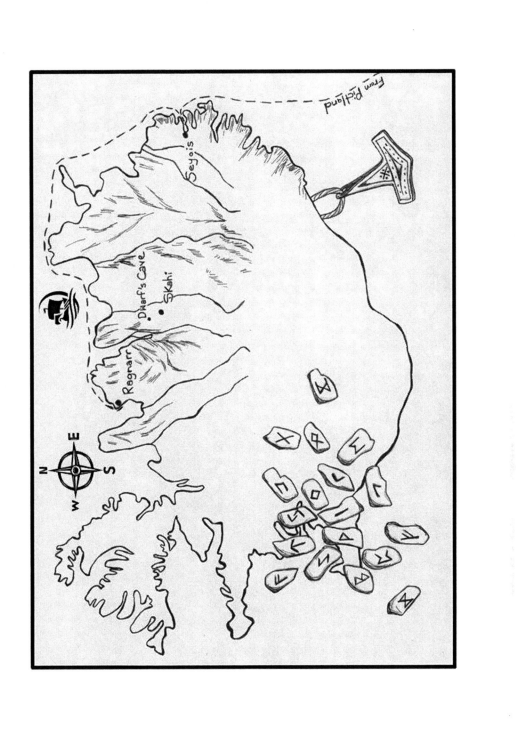

CHAPTER 1

In the night Systa crept off to sit in her small cave. She sat silently as she shook the runes between her hands. The runes were made of animal bones on which she had carefully sketched symbols used by her people. She breathed her life into the runes so they might help her find the answers she sought.

Haunted had been her dreams lately and she needed to find some answers. She stopped the movement of her hands and brought them, while still closed over the runes, to her mouth and pressed them against her lips.

With a soft prayer she tossed them across the cave floor in front of her. She closed her eyes and willed calmness to travel through her before she dared to open them to see what the runes would tell her. She leaned over the scattered bones to study them.

She read them carefully… and knew what the next step must be.

It was time for Joka to know the path that must be taken.

II

Joka had fought, and fought well. Her hand clenched in memory of the sword she'd held. It had not tasted flesh as she had hoped, but a life had been taken by her hand.

Her gaze moved around her small cottage as she reached for the hilt of the dagger on her belt. She rubbed it with reverence. Its short blade had been the one she'd used to kill the warrior.

Joka sat down on the pallet of her bed and held her hand in front of her. She could still see the blood that had poured over her fingers before the rain had washed them clean. Her hand fell to her side.

Her sword would be wetted, this she vowed. She had fought well with it. Her dance had been everything she'd dreamed it would be. None could doubt she had the right to claim the title of warrior.

It had only been a few days since she'd gone to find Rafn Vakrson, Warlord of Skiringssal. He was husband to Seera, the woman she'd rescued from a blizzard, after she'd escaped the clutches of the one-eyed man who'd raped and flogged her.

With the help of Joka's sister, Seera healed and birthed her son in the high mountain meadow they called home.

Then one night, after the Raven had searched many months for his wife, Systa had sent Joka to lead Rafn to his wife and son.

Hwal, the giant man with the missing eye, lay dead in a valley that had taken her two days on foot to reach. Rafn had left him for the scavengers.

Smoothing the wrinkles from her woolen trousers, she stood to face the door. On the other side she could hear the voices of the two men. Rafn's voice was deep and clear, but it was the other's that caused Joka to hide within her dwelling.

She began to pace across the wooden floor, her irritation growing. The sunlight outside the window beckoned and Joka was itching to escape.

Outside the door, at the front of the cottage, she heard Peder, Lord of Dun'O'Tir, laugh. Her heart quickened at its easy sound.

She stepped to the window in the side wall. She could make it through, she thought. She was determined.

She peeked out the window and was satisfied the men wouldn't see her. She lifted first one leg, then the other, and slid through the opening. Her feet touched down with no sound to alert Peder and Rafn as they sat around the corner.

Joka wandered out into the forest behind the cottage she shared with her sister and as of late with the Lady Seera and her son. A soft breeze rustled the leaves and carried a sweet scent of flowers. Quiet as any hunter, she stepped with care along the dirt path. A squirrel that sat munching on a fallen nut beside the trail did not look up to watch her passage. She slowed as she heard the trickling of the stream.

She breathed in a sigh of relief at her successful escape. As she bent at the water's edge her thoughts turned to her sister's words of the night before.

BITTER PASSAGE

Systa wanted them to leave. To journey with Seera and her husband back to Skiringssal, the large trading village set on the waters of the Vik. It was a place where many lived, and the best warriors trained. But Joka didn't believe they would allow a woman to train with them, even if she'd already proven herself a warrior.

She had not believed they would leave their secluded mountain hideaway so soon. She had grown to love the independence it had offered her and her sister, but Systa had argued that it was never intended to be a permanent home. The goddess, Freyja of the Vanir, had only led them there to help Seera when she was in need.

Joka had known this and had understood it, but it was still hard to walk away to return to a world where men dominated. Memories filtered through her mind to catch her in its claws. She would not forget the images of her father beating her mother until she could do nothing more than weep at his feet.

When Systa became a woman, he turned his fist on her and Joka had known that it was only time before she too would receive his wrath. When she had turned sixteen he came for her. He beat her only once, for she would not allow him to touch her again.

That night as the bruises started appearing on her skin, she'd quickly and cleanly taken his knife from the table by his bed and killed him while he slept, plunging it through his heart. As he lay in death she had stared down into his scarred face and smiled. He would not hurt any of them again.

A movement in the bushes brought her back to the present and she drew her knife from her belt. She searched out the danger. She was alert and cautious even as the bushes parted to reveal that it was Seera's brother, Peder.

The man made her uneasy and she wasn't happy at his intrusion. She had failed to leave him behind. Somehow he'd seen her and followed. She frowned as he headed toward her. She glanced to the side to see if she could hide before he reached her, but she dismissed the idea as cowardly and she had no intention of being thought of as such.

She held her ground, but she kept the knife raised in front of her and he eyed it with caution.

"I am no threat Joka." He tried to put her at ease, even as he wondered at her hostility.

"I have but to believe your word?"

"I have yet to earn your trust. I understand it will not come easy, but I wish you no harm."

"We will see, lord," she said. With reluctance she slipped the dagger back into the sheath she had attached to her belt.

"We are ready to leave." He motioned back towards the meadow where the others waited.

Joka nodded. When Peder realized that she would not go before him, he led the way back to the cottage. Rafn was helping to secure the baby onto Seera's back, while Systa was going over all the packs they were to bring. Joka walked over to her.

"Go we must, to the home of the Raven," Systa said quietly so that only her sister could hear. "Our destiny is with the one whose son into this world we helped bring."

"I have always trusted in your visions. I will follow your wisdom as I have always done."

Systa smiled in acceptance of the pledge her sister made and began to put on her pack. Joka sighed in defeat. It was time to leave this place. Perhaps it was as it should be. What warrior hid from the world because they were too afraid to be a part of it?

She would not.

III

They only had two horses and Seera was helping Rafn to secure what packs they could to their backs. The five of them would walk, not ride out of the mountains. Seera was both happy and sad to be leaving this place. It was here she had given birth to her son. It was also where she had come to learn a lot about who she was.

It pleased her that the sisters were coming with them. She hadn't wanted to say goodbye to them, they had taught her so much and become as close as family to her. She sensed Joka had reservations about leaving, that she went because her sister believed it was the path they must take.

Seera did not know what the Seer's visions had shown her, but she was happy that it meant they would be together.

"Are you ready my love?" Rafn looked down at her and the love reflected in his eyes was enough to give her the courage to leave. Hwal was dead, the threat gone. She could walk out of this hidden paradise and know that she was safe.

She could also feel confident in the fact that the one-eyed giant would no longer harm her. She would take with her the things Joka had begun to teach her about being strong enough to defend herself.

"I am ready to go home." She responded to his tender look, with a smile that spoke her happiness.

Seera had been too afraid to ask Rafn about the time they were separated, of the things he did to find her. Systa, through the magic of her inner sight, had seen that he had torn the world apart in search of her. The Seer had spoken of the death he'd left in his wake. Joka had scolded her when she had turned from Systa's word. Joka demanded that Seera understand that the world was one of violence and death was a part of that.

She had come to believe the warrior woman was right. She would accept what had to be and not dwell on it.

They had spent the previous night outside under the stars and she had slept in Rafn's arms with their son curled beside them, the warm summer breeze soothing them with its sweet scent. Now her son slept soundly on her back in a carrier that Systa had helped her make.

One of the horses nickered and Seera looked up to see that Peder was loading the stallion. Seera went to him. He smiled when he saw her approaching and she was so very grateful that he was there. They had always been close, but had become even closer after their mother's death. They had leaned on each other for comfort and support. It was something that was not so easy to stop once started.

"You came all the way from Pictland to help my husband search for me."

"Though you are now wed, you are still my sister. Where else did you expect me to be?" He leaned in and whispered in her ear. "Besides, your husband was in bad shape, and I could not leave him."

Seera's eyes widened. She had known it would be so, but to hear Peder say it made it real. That he had given Rafn his support was a generous thing. "Thank you brother."

"We have become friends," Peder said. He glanced over to where

Rafn was speaking with Joka. "I also have learned to respect him."

"I am glad." She hugged him and with his gentle touch wrapped her into his arms, so not to wake his nephew whose tiny face was pressed against her shoulder.

"He will be a strong boy," Peder said. She stepped back to see Systa approaching.

"Go we must or late it will be." Systa placed her hands on her hips as if she were scolding them. Her face held a smile and her eyes shimmered with a knowledge that was for her alone.

"It is time," Rafn agreed and began to lead his family from the meadow. Joka had shown him a path that was far easier than the one they had taken to get there. It would take them on a more direct route to Skiringssal.

IV

Rafn led with instructions from Joka, while she preferred to take up the position at the rear. Peder led his horse ahead of Joka and he kept glancing over his shoulder at her. She was a woman he couldn't figure out. She was fiercely independent, but that did not disturb him. It was that she chose to place herself alone that left him baffled.

He didn't know her history, but something must have caused her to become the woman she was. She had marked herself as a warrior. She wore a blue tunic, with dark brown trousers and a lighter brown cloak. She had braided her hair into two braids, one down each side of her face, rather than a single one preferred by his sister.

She was not a soft woman. Her muscles were as solid as any of the men he'd fought with, and she walked with the stealth of a hunter. So quiet were her footsteps it was easy to forget that she was behind him… and yet he could not.

She had a savage beauty he had never seen before. She was so different from the ladies of the court he'd known. There was no coyness to Joka's actions, only truth.

And the truth was that she did not like him, and for some reason this knowledge irked Peder. He would have liked them to be friends, to learn the mystery that was Joka. He was impressed by her strength.

Peder remembered with awe her display of skill when she'd fought against Hwal's man on that rainy night when Rafn had killed the one-eyed giant. She had been fearless and determined. Her technique needed practice, but he had no doubt she would achieve excellence.

He looked back again to where, not far behind, she walked. Her eyes shifted around their surroundings, trying to detect any signs of danger. She carried a spear in her right hand, her fist gripping it tightly and was ready to spring into action at the slightest movement.

Her face showed no emotion. She had kept her distance from him since arriving at the meadow, as if it displeased her to be too close.

Peder had decided early on that she didn't care much for men, but she had not been as hostile with Rafn as she seemed to be with him. She had been formal with the warlord, but it was somehow different with Peder. Something about him made her angry.

They traveled for most of the day, only stopping for brief breaks to allow Seera to nurse the baby and clean up any mess he'd made. They ate quick meals at each rest and then continued until night began to creep through the trees to steal their light. The first night Rafn located a sheltered overhang up against a cliff wall which offered them some protection.

"We will spend the night here," Rafn said. "Peder would you build a fire, while I try and catch something fresh to eat."

"I will come." Joka joined Rafn and was prepared to argue. He simply nodded his head in acknowledgement before they slipped down a small animal trail.

Peder watched them go before turning to his own task. Systa had already managed to collect some wood and dumped it at his feet. It startled him, which caused her to laugh. A tinkling sound that set his nerves on edge.

"Thank you," he said. She turned to help Seera with the baby. Peder's unease, about this woman who was said to predict the future, grew. If Joka was a mystery to him, her sister was even more so. She had this gleam in her silver eyes that made him feel that she was not all there, that a part of her was somewhere else.

Peder turned to the task of building a fire that would burn hot and long. By the time Rafn and Joka returned with two hares each, the fire was ready to cook the meat. Joka and Systa suspended the rabbits over the fire without skinning them first.

"When they have burned to a crisp, then the skin is pulled back and the meat inside will be cooked and tender." Joka spoke to him as if he was a child and he wasn't sure he liked that. He was a soldier in service to King David. Who was she to speak to him as if he knew nothing?

He grunted in acknowledgement, but he offered no reply. He went instead to see how Seera was doing. The baby had finished feeding and lay asleep in the crook of her arm.

"May I," he asked as he sat next to her. Seera handed him the baby and he held him in his arms like he was the most delicate thing in the world. Peder traced a finger lightly over his small perfect features.

Peder took one of Orn's hands in his and marveled at how tiny the hand was against his own. The baby shifted in his arms and managed to release one of his legs from his blanket to kick at the air.

"He will be a strong one," Peder said.

"He is bound to be with a father and uncles such as he has." Seera laughed and it made him feel good to see her so happy after months of fearing that she was dead.

"I will find great joy in watching him grow." He looked up then to see that Joka was scrutinizing him across the fire where she was tending to their supper. She had an odd expression on her face, but she turned from him as soon as their eyes met.

"I hope that you will visit often." He returned his attention to Seera.

"As you will come to Dun'O'Tir, and soon I hope, for father will want to met his grandson and see for himself that you are safe."

"I will come soon."

V

They left with the first light and Seera was as impatient as Rafn to get home. She had been gone too long from those she loved and she wanted to see them all again. She had worried most about Kata. The last time she had seen her she had just been stabbed and left for dead. She had not known if she lived or died until Rafn had found her and set her mind at ease.

Finally, after days of travel, Skiringssal came into view and Seera was more than willing to quicken her pace, for that night she would sleep in her own bed.

They stopped at mid day to rest the horses and feed Orn. It was then that Seera realized that Joka was not pleased to be reaching their destination.

"Are you alright?" Seera went to sit with her away from the others.

"I am fine." Joka leaned against a large boulder, picking at a piece of bread in her hand.

"You are very quiet and I thought perhaps you were not as happy as I to be reaching the village."

"It is not my home," Joka said. "I have never been to this place. It holds no special feeling in my heart."

"Why did you come with us?"

"Systa said that we must follow your husband." Joka scowled as she looked at Rafn. It had never been a secret that Joka didn't trust men.

"I for one am glad. You are my friend and I would have missed you had you stayed."

Joka glanced at Seera and something softened in her eyes. "I too value you as a friend and parting would have saddened me."

A smile streaked Seera's face in a mischievous grin. "Besides, who would teach me to fight?"

"I would not want you to stop your training." Joka gave her one of her rare smiles before sighing in resignation that they would go to Skiringssal, where destiny awaited them both.

"Let us go and we can sup in the Great Hall tonight." Rafn's thick voice urged them onward. Even Joka's steps became lighter.

VI

Systa watched them all very carefully. She saw each of them clearly in a way no other was capable of. Each of them was special.

Rafn had a fiery soul. He'd been touched by the thunder god, Thor. Systa had seen that at once and would have known even if she had not heard the stories. She felt the energy in the very air around him change as he passed. He left behind a hidden spark that reacted with the life pulse of the earth.

Systa kept a close eye on him. Her future was tied strongly to the choices he would make…that she would see that he made.

There was something deep in her dreams that she had sensed, but was yet unclear. He would lead her to it, of this she was sure.

Her gaze moved to Seera. A smile came to her. Seera had become like a second sister. Her heart was gentle. Even the pain and humiliation she'd been forced to endure had not taken her spirit from her. She was strong, but in a different way from Joka. Her sister had chosen to fight back at the world's cruelty, against everything that had hurt her. Seera did not allow it to haunt her dreams, to shape her into the hard woman Joka had become.

Systa spotted Orn squirming on Seera's back and went to relieve her of the burden. The child fascinated her. His future held great things and he would be important. She cooed to the baby in a soothing tone that quieted him.

She chuckled when she noticed Peder glance yet again at Joka, and her sister pretending not to notice. Joka kept her face hard and focused on the path ahead of them.

The Seer had not seen Peder's future. She sensed it was tied somehow to the same one waiting for all of them, but she was not sure. He was a strong man, with a good soul. He didn't fight against the world as Rafn did. He strived instead to claim a fluid union with it, embracing life rather than battling it.

Yet there was still a restlessness that was undefined. He followed a different god. Perhaps that was why he was harder to read.

Systa's eyes narrowed when she finally thought of Joka. The sister who had saved them from the clutches of their father, from a village that would have ground them into the mud without a second thought.

It was something that Systa hadn't had the strength to do, but she had known that Joka would. That she would stand up and break free from the grasp of the place that held nothing good.

Joka's future held something that scared Systa. There would be a moment that she would tumble towards a violent end. There would be a death, she was certain of it, but she was not yet sure whose. Only that it would come.

The answers lay in thick shadows that she had been unable to peel back and see through. Perhaps because of her love for Joka she couldn't see it clearly. Maybe she was too afraid of what she would see.

She shook such negative thoughts aside and focused on the first step of their journey.

It would start for them all once they reached Skiringssal. Fate would be set into motion and Systa was most anxious to see it unfold.

CHAPTER 2

The guards on duty noticed them long before they reached the town. A crowd waited to welcome them home and a cheer went up when all spotted Seera among them. They had all come to love the wife of their warlord and had feared her lost. By the time they had reached the gates to the compound word found its way to Valr and he waited with Kata at his side.

As soon as Rafn's sister saw Seera she ran forward and the two women embraced each other with tears in their eyes.

"My heart feels relief at seeing you safe," Kata said as she stepped back to make sure that Seera was whole and well. Her eyes clouded before she asked, "And the baby?"

"He is strong and healthy." She turned and beckoned Systa forward. The Seer had insisted on sharing the burden of carrying Orn.

Kata's eyes brightened with joy as she accepted the baby into her arms. She held him so that she could stare down into his perfect face. Valr came up beside her and his hand reached out to smooth the hair on the baby's head. Seera didn't miss the brief flash of grief that crossed his face before he hid it.

"He looks like his father." Valr managed a smile for he truly was happy for his brother. Rafn had told her of Valr's wife, Geira, dying after birthing their stillborn son. She had cared for Geira and would mourn her loss.

"His name is Orn." Each looked at her in surprise and gratitude. Orn had been their younger brother and was still in the forefront of their memories.

"He was the best of us all," Valr said. He met Rafn's face and was pleased to see the pain was gone from his eyes. "I am glad brother that you have found your wife and son. It is good to see the storm within you at rest."

"I wouldn't have found her if it had not been for these women." Rafn beckoned to the two women who were strangers to the Jarl of Skiringssal. "I would like you to meet them brother for they are very dear to my wife."

"I would be most pleased," Valr said. He glanced to Systa first and then his eyes roamed to Joka. His gaze lingered on Joka with curiosity until Peder stepped beside her. Valr smiled at the action, though the woman scowled at both men.

"This is Joka," Rafn said. "And her sister is Systa. They kept Seera safe until I could find her."

Joka's eyes narrowed even more. Seera, seeing that the warrior woman's defenses were on alert moved next to her. "Let us find somewhere to rest our feet. Then you men can talk all you like. I for one am tired."

All three men looked at her. Valr was the one to answer. "Yes, of course. Supper will be served soon and you must all wish to refresh yourselves before then."

Rafn left with Valr and Peder to bring the horses to the stable, leaving the women to themselves. "We must find a place for you to sleep," Kata said to the sisters. "There is a vacant dwelling on the edge of the village. The occupants have recently returned to the home of their birth and no one has yet claimed it."

"Fine it will be, and thank you we do," Systa said before Joka could say anything.

"Come and I will see you settled."

"I will leave you then so that I might rest before supper," Seera said. She took the baby back from Kata and left her sister in-law to find accommodations for the two women.

II

Kata left them in a dwelling much larger than their cottage had been. There were two rooms, so each would have their own bed, and a main living space that held a table and chairs and a hearth.

Joka went to the room that was to be hers. It was small, but serviceable. The bed didn't have blankets, but Kata promised to send some before they retired for the night. An empty trunk sat against the wall beneath a window and Joka began to place her things within it. Her weapons she arranged in the corner of the room.

She did not feel settled, as Kata had put it. She felt out of place. Her first impression of Skiringssal was that it was large. She had never seen a village that spread so far, or a port that held so many longships. She was both impressed and wary of such a place.

She had seen at once that a compound had been built around the Jarl's family dwellings, and those of their closest companions. In the center was the Great Hall and to its side was another building that Seera had said was the kitchen. There were two stables within the walls, one for the Jarl's family and another for the warriors.

Along the fortified walls stood many guards, all steel eyed warriors ready to defend to the death if needed. As they had made their way through the trading village, a large group trailed after them, cheering for the safe return of one they obviously loved. Many had turned to gaze at Joka and she'd felt their curiosity grow as they wondered about the woman who dressed like a man and carried the weapons of a warrior.

Had she not walked with their warlord, they may have asked, but thankfully they kept their distance and she'd been able to proceed. More than one man had stared at her with an interest that went beyond simple speculation. She'd hardened her face and refused to acknowledge them and she would certainly show no fear.

Systa had been just as quiet, but she had studied the crowd as intently as they studied her. Joka returned to the main area of the dwelling and sat at the table with Systa.

"Is good this place, but stay we not here." As Systa spoke she seemed to be looking within herself at something that Joka couldn't see.

"You said we were to come here." The only reason she had come to Skiringssal was that her sister had told her that they must. She began to feel uneasy.

"Come, aye." Systa's eyes widened. "Must follow the Raven to where he flies. Not long will he be here."

"Where will he go?" Joka watched a spider scurry up the wall and return to a large web in the corner of the thatched roof.

"A new land calls to him, and we must help him hear."

"And if he does not?"

Systa leaned forward, a slight madness pinching her face. "Then make him we must."

III

Peder finished brushing down the horses before he went to the warriors' longhouse to clean up. He changed into a fresh dyed green tunic and brown trousers. He left his weapons stored by his bed, but fastened a single knife to the belt he wore around his waist. The hide shoes he wore came to his ankles and he had but to slip them on. He didn't care for buckles or laces as the women preferred.

On his bare arms, just beneath the short sleeves, he clasped the twin arm bands that Rafn had gifted him after he had married his sister. They were made of gold and had intricate etchings of serpents upon them.

He thought of Joka as he dressed. Thinking again how different she was from the women at King David's court. She was not a Christian as he was, but followed the Old Norse religion. She and her sister worshipped the goddess Freyja, who was one of the Vanir, a lesser god of Asgard.

How did one speak to a woman that did not welcome the attention of men? And why did he care so much that she didn't like him?

Too often he found his mind wandering to Joka. He needed to clear his thinking and return his thoughts to securing a voyage home. His father would be anxious to hear word of Seera, so he could delay no longer in bringing him the news.

He would ask Rafn to arrange something on the morrow as he'd been too long from his duties at home. Peder stepped outside and was welcomed by a pleasant breeze that helped clear his thoughts. Or so he thought until he found himself stopping Kata to ask her where she had sent the sisters.

Before he knew what he was doing he approached Joka's dwelling. He almost turned away, but the Seer opened the door and saw him. A smile that told him that she knew exactly what was in his thoughts washed over her face. He almost hated that she could see his feelings so clearly.

"I have come to escort you both to supper," he said as formally as he could muster. Joka came out the door, dressed very similar to him, except that her tunic was sleeveless and paler. He had to contain a smile when he noticed the knife on her belt.

Joka sneered at him. "We could have found it ourselves."

"Be not rude sister. Glad we be for his company." Systa shot her a glare that made her shut her mouth against any further protest.

He offered Systa his arm, knowing that Joka would not take it. The Seer slipped her hand around his arm and allowed him to lead her back into the compound they had only had a glimpse of earlier. Joka followed behind, a guarded expression on her face as she watched the man that made her feel so uneasy.

The Great Hall was crowded when they arrived, but Peder led them through it with ease. Though this was not his home, the people respected him and made a path to the head table for him and the women. Seera had made sure places for them all had been reserved.

Peder helped Systa sit in the seat across from Kata, but when he turned to do the same for Joka she narrowed her eyes and he held up his hands in defeat. He watched her sit next to Systa, leaving the chair on her left open for him.

He felt reluctant to take the seat, knowing how she felt about him, yet he did not want to be any other place. He had become a contradictory person because of this woman.

Systa had taken charge of the baby so that Seera could enjoy her meal. Peder had seen her try and protest, but the Seer wouldn't relinquish care of Orn. She muttered to the baby and seemed to find joy in his hands reaching out towards her.

Peder ate in relative silence and was content to listen to the conversations around him. He was in a sullen mood and wished to be alone. And he would, as soon as he had asked Rafn about securing passage home.

After supper was complete and the servants had cleared the tables, Peder realized he'd been putting off his request and knew that he could wait no longer.

Clearing his throat he looked to Seera. "Sister, you are safe and happy, and I could not be more pleased. Long have I been from home and father waits for my return."

He felt Joka turn a steady gaze on him, but he didn't look at her. Perhaps he would see pleasure in the knowledge that he wouldn't be around much longer, perhaps she felt nothing at all.

"Peder, what is it you say?" Seera lost her smile.

"I must return to Dun'O'Tir," he said. "If for no other reason than to let father know you are safe."

Rafn lowered the ale he'd been drinking. "I will arrange a ship to bear you. When would you like to leave?"

"Tomorrow, if that is not too soon?"

"It will be done." Rafn took his wife's hand in his and turned her face so that she looked at him. "Soon will I take you to Dun'O'Tir. Soon you will see your father and Peder again."

"You are right." She turned to speak to Peder. "It is selfish of me to want you to stay. Dun'O'Tir is where you belong."

"Tomorrow then," Rafn said. "Hachet will take you."

"Tomorrow," Peder repeated and forced himself not to look at the woman who sat to his right. He didn't have to see into the icy blueness of her eyes to know that she would not be saddened by his departure.

IV

Joka couldn't stand the noisy hall any longer. As soon as Rafn and Seera took their son to bed, she found her excuse to leave. She didn't look at Peder as she rose from the table and found her way to the door.

Though the sun had set, the air was still warm when she left the compound and found a path that led up the hill. At the top she found that she could look out at the ocean and see the longships that lined the harbor. One of them would take Peder back to Pictland the next day.

She knew she should be glad that he would be gone, that he would be far enough away and no longer haunt her dreams. He made her nervous. She knew that he desired her, and that such an emotion was dangerous. It would be best to never see him again.

But, the fact that she was not happy to see him go confused her. He was a man and men could not be trusted. This she had always known. This is what had hardened her and made her independent. To give one's self to a man was to give up that independence. She could never relinquish that freedom to anyone, even if her body betrayed her by being drawn to Peder.

Dangerous!

When he sailed with the tide, she would take up her sword and she would turn to practicing her skill. Her feet would dance and the blade would sing, and once again she would become centered. Discipline and strength would keep her from faltering.

It was but nature's baser instincts that controlled her emotions. She was no animal. She had a choice whether or not to succumb to the weakness of her body. Rutting and getting with child, trapped by the will of a man was not something that would ensnare her.

Her will was her own.

And yet did her heart beat faster as she glimpsed the lord of Dun'O'Tir walking along the shore below. He didn't see her for which she was grateful and she slipped back into the shadows.

V

The hustle and bustle of the crowded streets had quieted. Shops had been closed for the night, ships secured and men and women alike were safe within their homes. A soft breeze blew in off the water carrying the scent of salt and the aura of mystery. The moon reflected across the water becoming distorted by the slight waves that kept the sea from being still.

A dark shape moved beneath the water's surface close to shore. Peder tracked its movement until it dived deeper and disappeared beneath the wooden pier.

Guards were posted on the docks to prevent theft from the ships that anchored for the night in Skiringssal's harbor. He had spoken with Hachet before coming to the docks to confirm they would leave with the morning tide.

Peder's attention was drawn to someone hidden in the shadows. He touched the hilt of his dagger as he tried to see who it was. An older man hobbled from the darkness beside one of the shops. He had a bad limp to his left leg. His face was pox marked with scars and had eyes too small for his head. Gray hair hung thinly on his head and was in need of cutting.

A scraggly beard covered the man's jowls and hung half way down his chest. His stomach was potbellied and soft. He was staring at Peder whose scowl told him that he didn't want to hear what this old man had to say.

"I know them." The man whistled through a mouth that was missing its front teeth.

"Who?" Peder questioned and the man stepped closer. Peder was a good head taller than the man who had to look up to meet his eyes.

"The sisters," he said. Peder noticed the redness in his eyes and the stench of mead on his breath.

"Say what you have come to say, or leave me be." Peder scowled at the foul smell that rose from the man, as if he were already a corpse rotting in the ground.

"Dangerous they are." The man stepped back and looked to the darkness deep within a stand of trees close to the village edge. He seemed to search it before continuing.

Peder looked also to the trees as a strong wind blew out of them. It was oddly warm and violent and was gone the next moment.

"The witch is always watching," the man warned, "And the other… she is worse."

Peder drew his dagger and held it to the man's throat. "Don't play games with me." The man's eyes widened in surprise at the threat and proceeded with caution.

"I have seen you with them," he said. "You should not turn your back on them. The witch's powers are harmful, but her sister uses a sword when she has no right."

Peder's defenses rose with his anger. "If you speak of Systa and Joka, they are friends of my sister, who you must know is married to the warlord. They are under his protection as well as mine." Peder drew his knife back so the man had a chance to step away.

"You are a fool." The man spat on the ground. The sound of his voice was becoming irritating to Peder. "She killed her own father. She stabbed him with his own knife while he slept. You have been warned."

"Go now, before I call one of the guards to dispose of you." Peder watched the man slink back into the shadows.

Again the wind grew violent inside the trees. Peder could have sworn he saw the darkness shimmer. An uneasy feeling settled around him that he couldn't dismiss. It was illogical, but his gaze was locked to something within the trees that he couldn't see.

Somehow the man's words sank deep. "She killed her own father."

Could it be true? Had Joka slain her father? What would drive a person to do such a thing? Not for a minute did he believe Joka would give him the answers.

CHAPTER 3

Peder said a private farewell to Seera and was gone with the morning tide. Seera watched from her favorite spot on the bluff overlooking the village and harbor. She had left Orn with Kata so that she could watch her brother disappear on the horizon.

She felt they hadn't spent enough time together since their reunion, but duty called him home. She couldn't fault him for leaving, as she knew their father wouldn't want to be kept waiting for news of his daughter. A part of Seera had wanted to board the drekar with Peder so that she could see him herself.

Soon, Rafn had promised. For now it was just good to be back in Skiringssal where life could once again be normal.

When she could not see the longship on the horizon any longer, she turned to head back to the village. She really should find the sisters and make sure they were adjusting. Joka in particular seemed very edgy.

Seera had no trouble finding the dwelling on the edge of town that had been given to the sisters. She knocked on the door and Systa answered.

"Come, waiting have I." She beckoned Seera in. She entered into the main living area and took a seat at the table.

"Joka is not here?"

"Gone along the river bank, has she," Systa said. "Find she must a place to train. Men's place does not welcome her."

"I could speak with Rafn," Seera said. "Certainly he wouldn't object to her using the training field."

"Might he, but Joka yet not ready. Much pain past has brought, and not all has been forgotten."

She nodded in understanding. She had no idea what haunted Joka, what had hardened her so, and she would never ask. She would honor the woman's need for privacy.

"Good is your heart." The Seer reached out a hand to lay over Seera's. "And sad brother is gone."

"I will miss Peder, but we have been apart before. We have different lives now and our paths lead us in opposite directions."

"Not so far are your trails." Something glinted in her silver eyes, some knowledge that she knew that Seera did not. "See him soon you will."

"Tell me what you see."

"Soon enough all will be revealed." That was all she would answer, but she gave into the question that rested in Seera's eyes.

"Believe I that your brother's destiny lies with your own. I think soon will he be with us again."

II

Within a break of trees, Joka found a secluded spot along the river. There was a clearing, large enough for her purpose, where she could be alone, away from the watchful eyes of the others.

The ground beneath her feet was soft and spongy. No rocks or fallen branches littered the space. The gentle gurgling of the river was soothing. A faint breeze swept by offering its fingers in cooling relief of the intense heat. She took a breath and reached a hand over her shoulder.

From the sheath on her back she drew her sword and held it in front of her. She balanced her feet and she steadied her breathing as she called to the goddess, Freyja, for strength and patience. She would not be denied the right to be a warrior, and both those qualities were needed to be successful.

Focusing her mind and body she sliced the sword through the air. She felt the power of the blade through the hand that held it. The sword was a bit too large for her, but she had learned to compensate for its size by using both hands. She alternated between slicing it downward and then bringing it backwards and up as if to cut her opponent open from below.

Her feet touched the dirt only lightly, leaving barely a mark of their passing. She found the center inside of her. Finding her calmness she let it drift over her until it had reached out to her fingertips. With another breath she narrowed her eyes and focused on the spot before her, seeing everything around her, but not allowing it to distract her.

She forgot about Peder, of the pull he had on her emotions. She forgot that he had left that morning and she wouldn't see him again. She pushed from her heart the unwelcome pain this knowledge caused her.

Instead she became a dancer, partnered with the blade, and moved in perfect unison with the object that empowered and emboldened her. Gone were the uncertain future and the painful past. All that mattered was the here and the now, the graceful movements of the dance.

The air seemed to part before her. She could feel her pulse quicken with satisfaction. Somehow her deadly motions had grace.

III

Rafn and Valr sat outside the Jarl's dwelling, not wanting to be cooped up inside the Great Hall on such a fine day. Valr's latest visit to King Harald hadn't gone well.

Valr snarled. "His greed increases. He asks far too much from the people. And the ones who can't afford to pay he has beaten or tortured."

"And what does he ask of us?" Rafn felt his defenses rise.

"Not more than we can afford, but higher than we have ever paid before," Valr said. "It is only his fondness for me, and perhaps his fear of you, that keeps him from reaching too deeply into our lands."

"I long to live in a land where you do not have to answer to a King." Rafn looked out through the open gate to the ocean beyond, and thought of the freedom it offered.

"Some days I do too." Both brothers were deep in their contemplation over the King's growing greed when the young man who would have been brother-in law to Orn, was spotted heading toward the gate.

"It is a longship, my lords." Fox came running into the compound to inform Rafn and Valr of the ship that was headed their way. "It is one of ours."

"It would be Dagstyrr returning," Valr said.

Rafn received the news with eagerness. He stood to follow Fox back down to the docks. "We will speak further on this matter," he said to Valr over his shoulder.

He was almost to the harbor when Kata caught up to him. She looked flushed from running to catch him.

"I would meet him alone," he said. She stared at him in shock.

"He is my husband."

"And you will have him to yourself soon enough, but I would speak with him first."

Kata nodded in defeat, understanding why Rafn wanted to talk with Dagstyrr alone. When last they'd seen each other, Rafn had been in bad shape. He'd almost died from the wounds he'd received on the battlefield, but even worse was losing his will to live when he'd begun to accept that he would never find Seera. He pushed everyone away from him, including his best friend.

Not wanting to be plagued with Dagstyrr's concern, Rafn had sent him away on the trade route. He regretted doing so and wanted the chance to apologize.

Rafn watched as the longship was secured, anxious for Dagstyrr to disembark. He looked for the red hair that surely would stand out amongst the dark heads around him. Dagstyrr jumped from the ship and went to stand before Rafn. The concern had not left his eyes in the weeks he'd been away, but Rafn's reaction to it had changed.

"I am glad you have returned safely," Rafn said. They clasped hands to arms in greeting.

Dagstyrr studied him, searching for answers he wouldn't ask. "I am glad to be back. I have missed my wife."

"As she has missed you." Dagstyrr was quick to notice how easy Rafn smiled.

"If she missed me so," he broke his scrutiny to search out his wife, "then where is she?"

Rafn watched the men as they began to unload the sacks and crates of trade goods. He didn't look at his friend as he spoke. "I asked her to wait for you in the compound."

"Why?" Dagstyrr was on instant alert at the seriousness of Rafn's tone.

The warlord turned to meet Dagstyrr's gaze. Rafn was surprised to see the dark circles beneath his eyes. New lines had been etched into their corners in the short time he'd been gone. Rafn's gut tightened from guilt.

"So that I could apologize for sending you away," he said. "I was lost even to myself and I could not stand your pity."

Dagstyrr looked shocked. "I didn't pity you. I feared only that your grief would not let go."

Rafn turned from the dock and the two men started towards the compound. "I know that, now that I have been able to look back on my actions."

Dagstyrr continued his close observations. "You have found yourself again."

"That is not all I have found." Rafn smiled and the light that touched his eyes told Dagstyrr what he needed to know even before he spotted Seera walking towards them at Kata's side.

Dagstyrr's eyes widened. He went straight to Seera and hugged her. "I am most happy to see you."

"How about me? Your wife!" Kata attempted to sound miffed, but a smile stretched wide across her face, even as she tried to pretend she was offended by his lack of a greeting.

"I am more than happy to see you." He scooped her up and kissed her, until she had to push him away and straighten her skirt. Her face turned red with embarrassment.

Dagstyrr turned back to Rafn. "You must tell me all that has happened since I have been gone."

"Later, after you have spent time with your wife. Then I will let you meet my son."

"Son?" Dagstyrr's smile grew even wider. He was sure he had never seen a man look more pleased with himself than Rafn. He felt the weight of worry lift from his shoulders. With the heavy burden gone, his steps became lighter and his easy nature returned.

He lifted Kata once again into his arms and carried her towards their dwelling. Rafn's laughter followed them and it was very good to hear.

IV

Systa tossed in her sleep, caught in dreams of the past. She was again that thirteen year old girl, barely a woman. She'd received her menses, but she was still much a child. Her father had begun to beat her. She had begged Joka into silence but it killed her sister to watch from where she hid in the shadows behind their bed.

The Seer shook in memory as a dark shadow loomed over her. Stark eyes filled with evil stared down at her. His breath soured with mead and a rotten tooth. A calloused hand reached for her.

Systa bolted awake and struggled to sit. She clutched her blanket against her as these images came sharply even to her waking mind.

A violent shiver of fear that echoed that of the first time a man of the village desired her. His name if she recalled was Avetorp, a man with eyes too small. Her father had given her to him. She couldn't rid the memory of his loud laughter, or how it made his soft belly shake.

Avetorp had not cared that he was a grown man three times her age. That he was older than her father. He had used her cruelly despite her being a virgin. She had remembered not to cry, recalling it had always been worse for her mother when she cried.

Her breathing became rapid and tears trailed down her face, as she also remembered that her mother had taken her own life not long before Systa had become a woman. She had been beaten and raped so many times that her mind had gone. In the end she no longer saw her daughters when they came to her, but sat with a blank stare looking at something only she could see.

Systa pulled the blanket closer and tried to focus on the room she was now in, the room in Skiringssal where she had come with her sister.

The shaking wouldn't stop. The dream had been too clear. She could still feel his rough hands on her skin, his warm breath against her breasts. She ground her teeth in desperation to gain control. Her breath became too painful to draw in.

It had been him! She had seen him talking to Peder the night before he left. She had hid within the dark protection of the trees and known it could be no other. Avetorp's face was imbedded in her memory. He was older, had less hair and walked with a limp, but it was him.

She had not been able to hear his words, but whatever was said, Peder hadn't liked it. She had found great joy when Peder had pulled his dagger on the man.

He should have used it.

Systa knew that he would spread his lies, his hate. She knew that if given the chance he would hurt another girl. Systa felt a surge of anger grip her.

She had ways of dealing with him. She was no longer helpless. She didn't have the power of the sword, but she did have power.

Systa smiled insanely as she realized what she must do.

V

A yell went up near the edge of the village, close to the harbor. Rafn ran down to see what the commotion was. A crowd had formed outside a clump of trees. Many faces turned to him as he walked by.

Hachet was there before him and came to report. "My lord, a dead man has been found."

Rafn stepped into the shade of the trees and knelt down to examine the body. He looked to be a man about sixty. His hair was gray and thin, matching a long beard. His eyes were frozen in horror as if just before he died he'd seen something that had scared him.

"I have checked and he has no wounds," Hachet told him.

"He was not killed then." Rafn looked around the area and saw no other tracks besides the ones that were made by Hachet. He frowned at the oddity. There should at least be evidence of the man's passage.

He felt a strange sensation flood him. He looked again at the man's expression and wondered again if he'd been scared to death.

Rafn knelt down next to the body to look more closely at him. "Perhaps his heart gave out. It is not uncommon in one his age. Does anyone know who he is?"

"I have seen him before." Hamr came forward. "His name I believe was Avetorp. He comes from a village north of here. I have been there only once and that was more than enough for me. It is a foul place, dirty and in a shambles. The women are treated as slaves and the men drink too much so I did not linger."

Rafn looked back at the dead man. "Get someone to burn the body," he said to Hachet.

"Aye my lord."

Rafn left Hachet to clean up the mess. He turned to head back to the village when he spotted Systa in the crowd. Anger held her face captive as she stared at the dead man. Pain mixed with hate in her eyes and he was shocked to see such fury in the woman. Had she known the man?

Systa's gaze shifted to Rafn. He saw something powerful shimmering in her eyes. He had felt the effects of the gods often enough to recognize it in another.

She turned away and melted back into the crowd before he thought to question her.

VI

Systa found Rafn on a bluff overlooking the ocean and docks. He was alone, as she knew he would be. She quietly approached him, having taken only a few steps when he turned. She smiled at his quick alertness. She continued even when his eyes narrowed in suspicion.

She stepped to the spot next to the large man and though she felt small beside him, she was not afraid of him. She knew the way of his heart. He never used his strength without reason, and never against a woman.

"Calm the wind that the sea blows in," Systa said. She looked out at the ocean that stretched to the horizon. "Never seen I such an impressive sight."

"It is a magnificent view." He studied her with wariness.

"Many drekar I see, but absent are the Knarrs." Systa observed the line of ships anchored below.

"Knarrs are used for long voyages of exploration and trade, far from our shores," Rafn said. "Sometimes they come to our port, but we haven't had need of any of our own."

"Build one you must." The Seer's sharp gaze turned on him. He felt a shiver of premonition at her words.

"We trade along a route that keeps us close to shore. We don't need…"

She cut him off before he could explain. "Hear not its call?" The silver in her eyes glittered with flecks of a deeper color, reminding him of dark slate.

"What are you speaking of?" The power in her eyes shifted and grew stronger. He could feel an answering pull deep within where Thor's storm lay sleeping.

Systa looked at him in wonder. Certainly this man could feel the strength of his future, the pull of the forces that would lead him. How could he not?

Something of her thoughts must have reached her eyes, for he became very still. "What have you seen Seer?"

"Your destiny."

Rafn reached for the small iron replica of Thor's hammer that hung around his neck. He clasped his hand around the symbol of his god and drew in a deep breath.

"And what is that?"

"Know you will when time is come." Her reply was vague and unsatisfactory, but she didn't elaborate. She turned to leave, but not before she added, "A knarr must you build. Your hands will strong it make. Start you must, soon it be complete."

She left him to stare after her, wondering what she meant by her words. What did she see that he did not?

The waves hitting the rocks below called to him with their comforting music before washing back out to sea. Rafn looked out to the horizon and did feel something, a sense that he belonged out beyond it.

VII

The next day Rafn began what Systa wanted without really understanding why he felt compelled to listen to a witch. He sent for the supplies he would need, but the oak trees that would be used for the ship he would allow no other to chose.

He had helped in making drekars before, and the method to making the knarrs was similar. They both used the clinker method.

But the knarr differed in many ways. It wouldn't be long and sleek, or built for speed the way the drekar was. It would be short and wide, and not shallow in the draft. It would sink too deep to navigate through the shoals with the ease the drekars did.

It was meant for long sea voyages, and built for the rough waters. The knarr had a single mast, like the longships, with a sail that was stitched in the typical cross-hatched pattern, but it couldn't be taken down as on the drekar. It was permanent.

Lastly, the knarr had very few oars. The center of the boat was open so that cargo and livestock could be carried mid ship. The stern and bow had decks. Below them were spaces that could be used as sleeping quarters and protection from bad weather. It was on these decks that the few oars were placed, so the men could use them when pushing from port or entering it. The decks were higher off the water and therefore the oars were used in a standing position rather than sitting as one did in the drekars.

Rafn had the supplies brought to a clearing close to the docks that had been used for shipbuilding before. Word spread quickly that the warlord was planning on making a knarr.

Rafn wondered what fueled his blood into making the ship. It wasn't simply because the Seer had told him to. Deep inside something was speaking to him. He didn't know to what end his work would lead, but he trusted that it would be revealed, as Systa had promised.

He told Seera of Systa's words which she accepted without question, which surprised him. He realized then that she believed in Systa's magic. It amused him to learn that his Christian wife would trust in such a pagan belief. It was the first change he had seen in her since they had returned home and somehow he knew it wouldn't be the last.

Over the days that followed, Rafn chopped down his trees and set them aside. Men walked by in curiosity to see their warlord, not on the training field, but doing the hard labor of a common man.

He brushed off their offers of help and bent to the task that he felt must be done by his own hands.

Systa watched often from a distance, her smile filled with knowledge. She knew what was to come. Though she had yet to tell him what it was, he continued to work on faith that something important lay ahead.

Valr came to the clearing one day when Rafn had begun cutting the oak trees into the planks he would need to begin the keel.

"Why do you work so?" Valr came to stand beside his sweat stained brother.

"I can't explain what I feel in my soul, only that it is strong. When I look to the horizon, I know it is where I should be."

"This is your home."

"It is where I have always been," Rafn said. "Skiringssal holds a great part of me, but I sense that I must leave it."

Valr's face hardened in concern. He ran his hand over his smooth jaw. "Why?"

"Changes are happening all around us. You have seen them yourself. You told me of the King's growing greed and the fear of those under his rule."

A large eagle lifted into the sky from a nearby grove of trees. Its screech carried to them as it glided on the wind, heading westward above the jagged rocks along the shore.

"I have," Valr said.

Rafn's eyes widened with excitement. "What if we can have something more? What if we left all that we know behind and head to a new land, to a land that is filled with promise and freedom?"

"Freedom of what? You are already the most respected warrior in our lands." Valr fought to understand what it was his brother sought. Rafn was a man who could command an army and whose men followed him without question. He was the Raven who his enemies feared and his people admired. What was it he wanted?

"Freedom to be more, my brother. To become more than a warlord, trapped by the will of his people."

The eagle dove from the sky in a sudden swoop, its claws reaching for something beneath him.

"You have never sought anything else."

"I have never felt the need," Rafn agreed. "But this past year has changed me."

Securing its prey the eagle flew up once again, a rodent trapped in its talons, and disappeared into the trees. Rafn looked back to his brother once it was gone.

"You have been through a lot, first losing our brother as we did, then having your wife abducted and the months of search not knowing if she lived. It is bound to have an impact on any man."

Rafn smiled. The gesture was something that hadn't always come easy to him. It had been hard earned.

"A profound impact," Rafn said. "I can't keep from dreaming. It is not something I have done much of, but now it is a part of me."

"Then all I can do is support you in your quest and hope you find what it is you seek."

Rafn wiped a hand across his sweaty forehead. "I appreciate it. To what end I know not where I go, but your support means a lot."

"We are brothers, it will always be so."

So Rafn continue to work through the long days to build a ship that would lead him from the only home he had ever known, to a future that was nothing more than a dream implanted by a woman who could see such things.

CHAPTER 4

Peder stood on the battlement looking out as the sea crashed against the rocks below. He felt the cool promise of fall against his face. He drew in a deep cleansing breath, trying to shake off the agitation that had claimed him since returning home a month ago. He turned to peer down into the courtyard to see his men dispersing for the night. He knew he had worked them hard that day, but still he smiled at their weariness.

He had been attacking his duties with a vigor that had those around him wondering at the cause. As far as he was concerned their speculations would continue to go unanswered.

He looked back to the sea that separated him from the woman who returned each night to his dreams, a woman who didn't look at him with warmth. Peder ran his fingers through his hair in agitation.

He was a lord, in service to King David. To act moon-eyed over a woman was beneath him. He could have his pick of a number of beautiful women who batted their eyes when he walked past, or giggled behind their hands as they watched him on the training field.

Lacing his hands at the back of his head in frustration he shuddered at how these women bored him. He wanted more than a woman who thought of nothing but marrying well and securing a place in society. Once or twice he'd met one with more intelligence, who possessed desires of her own. His sister was such a woman. He had yet to meet one that sparked the same kind of interest in him as that of the warrior woman.

Clouds hung heavy in the sky and Peder smelled the promise of rain. The guards on duty walked the wall passing him, but he paid them no heed. The castle gate had been secured tight for the night and all was well in the fortress by the sea.

Peder sighed.

He was restless. He didn't know its cause, but he couldn't remain still for long. He was waiting for something that he could not define. His life at Dun'O'Tir didn't hold his heart as it once had. His father sensed it, as the Eorl had been watching him closely since his return.

Peder turned for the ladder and climbed down. He crossed the courtyard and headed for the keep. He stopped short of the keep's doors and turned instead for the chapel, knowing at this hour it would be empty.

A few candles had been lit by worshippers and supplied the only light to soften the darkness. A large wooden cross hung above an altar. Rows of well worn wooden benches lined either side of the small chapel, leaving a center aisle.

After checking his boots to make sure he didn't needlessly track in mud, Peder walked to the front. He lit one of the candles before taking a seat on one of the front benches.

He wanted to say so many things to his God. He needed to speak of the turmoil within his heart, the waywardness of his soul but his words remained unspoken.

Airic entered the chapel. Peder saw his approach out of the corner of his eye. The Eorl went first to light his own candle, then sat down next to Peder. The two sat in silence for some time before Airic finally spoke.

"You have been troubled, my son, since your return from Skiringssal." Airic folded his hands in his lap and Peder was startled to realize how much he had aged. Deep were the lines etching his face. His blond hair had turned white. Why had he not seen these changes immediately upon his return?

"I had hoped that you wouldn't notice," Peder said.

"It has been plain enough to see that you have been deep in thought."

Peder noticed his father held a gold cross on a chain between his hands. Recognizing it as his mother's, his gaze returned to the low burning candle.

"I suppose you are right."

"There is a restlessness in you that has never been there before. It makes me curious."

Peder turned to look at his father and saw concern shadowing his face. "I have been questioning many things."

"You do not feel as you once did about Dun'O'Tir?"

Peder felt he owed his father nothing but the truth. Airic had always been a fair man, honorable and trustworthy. He could give him no less than the honesty he had always given his children.

"I have always known that my place was here, that my duty was to this land, to you and to the King."

Airic rubbed the gold cross with his fingers, seeking comfort from it. "But that has changed?"

"I have not sought to change it. A part of me still feels the loyalty I owe Dun'O'Tir, and I will not falter in that, but I also feel I have lost some pivotal connection that once bound me to the only home I have ever known or wanted."

"You want to be somewhere else?" A frown formed between Airic's brows, darkening the circles beneath his eyes.

"It is not that clear. I seek something that I can't define, or understand."

"This search torments your thoughts?"

"Among other things," Peder said. He made no mention of Joka. He kept his feelings about her closed to any other.

Airic grew quiet as he sat considering all his son had said and tried to decide on the best way to reply.

"Dun'O'Tir is only a place of stone and mortar walls, built upon a large rock. It is a home I have enjoyed throughout the years, but what makes it so is not the buildings, it is the people that dwell within."

Peder nodded in agreement. Many happy times were imprinted in those very walls. "The people are important."

Airic continued. "Home could be anywhere a man makes it. It is what's in your heart that keeps you tied to a certain place. Here is where I loved your mother. Her memory is what ties me to these cold walls and makes them warm."

"I also have memories of mother that have everything to do with this place." He looked at his father and wondered where his words were leading. One of the candles on the altar sputtered and died, sending up a thin trail of smoke.

"As does your sister, and yet she found a home somewhere else."

"She found love. It is Rafn she can't do without, it has nothing to do with Skiringssal."

Airic smiled at his quick understanding. "You are right. Her home is wherever her husband is, which is my point."

"And what exactly is that point father?" Peder ran a hand through his gritty hair, noting it needed washing.

"That even though you are heir to my title and lands, I do not want that to be what guides you. A man must find his own destiny. He must follow his own heart."

Peder stared at him in surprise. "You think I should leave?" He had never thought that his father would tell him to turn from the duty that bound him to Dun'O'Tir. His heart quickened at such a possibility and he tried to squash the sudden longing to be free.

"This is only a castle. It can't keep you warm at night, or make you laugh with pleasure. It will not share your dreams, or be your partner in life. Those are the things that a man must seek and be true to. Only then can he make a home."

"Is this your subtle way of telling me to marry?" Peder laughed but his attempt to lighten the mood was forced.

"I do not ask you to marry until you find that woman who fulfills you. I have never wanted my children to marry for duty, only for love. That is what your mother and I shared. It is what she would have wanted for you."

"You say I should follow my destiny and leave?" His palms became sweaty at the idea and it disturbed him how much he wanted to accept what his father proposed. But was it right?

"Aye," he said, and with that simple answer he released Peder from any obligations he felt he had to lord and land.

"You would release me from my duty, for that I am speechless. Though the truth is I have no idea where I am supposed to go."

Airic laid a hand on Peder's shoulder. "You will son. In time you will know."

II

Peder crept silently through the bushes. His lieutenant and oldest friend Iver was only steps behind him. The woods rose around them as they followed a fresh deer trail between the trees. The sun found its way through the canopy of leaves to wash over the two men. Peder tried to ignore the heat and motioned Iver forward.

They had not gone much further when Peder held up his hand to signal they should stop. Around the next twist in the trail was a full grown deer, a large buck with an impressive set of antlers upon its head. He stood perfectly still as if he sensed he was not alone.

Peder gripped his spear and signaled Iver to do the same. Iver moved up beside him and waited for Peder to take the lead. Peder waited. Once spooked the deer would run and there would be no catching him. The timing had to be perfect.

The animal began to relax and bent to drink from a shallow stream that had found its way across the forest floor. The buck turned enough to present Peder with a clear path for his spear.

When the timing was perfect Peder's spear sailed through the air, followed a second later by Iver's.

Peder's spear sank deep into a vulnerable spot on the deer's neck. He pierced a vital vein and blood spurted out as the surprised animal fell to its knees. Iver's spear penetrated deep into the buck's side. The animal toppled sideways and even with death upon him, maintained its grace.

The deer was not yet dead and Peder couldn't watch it suffer. He boldly approached the buck and finished the job by slashing his knife across the deer's neck. The life went out of the deer's eyes and his legs stopped kicking.

"It was a good clean kill." Iver smiled in excitement.

Peder shrugged. "Perfectly executed."

"Do you remember when we were boys?" Iver laughed. "We would sneak out into these woods, determined to be mighty hunters."

A smile touched Peder at the memory. "I remember we failed a lot. We were lucky if we managed to bring back a squirrel."

"It amused our fathers," Iver reminded him. For it had. They'd been only eight at the time and so anxious to be like the men. They had watched for hours as the men practiced with both sword and spear.

"We vowed that one day we would prove our worth," Peder said.

"And so we have." The dusty haired man that had been his friend through the years, from small boys to men, chuckled.

"It was bound to happen." Peder laughed. "We practiced day and night until we were so exhausted we could barely walk."

"I remember we had a lot of fun." Iver leaned over to pull his spear from the buck's side as Peder reached for his own.

"We did." Peder smiled, "And got into much mischief."

"Which amused our fathers even more." Iver's eyes lit with pleasure at their youthful exuberance. Many things had happened since then. They had become men as nature and culture intended, and had taken their places as leaders of the soldiers of Dun'O'Tir.

"How is your wife?" Peder asked. "Is it not getting close to her time?"

"It is." Iver smiled with a different kind of joy. His wife was expecting their first child. "Perhaps it will be a boy."

"One to follow in his father's footsteps?" Peder punched him in the arm.

Anticipation gleamed in his friend's eyes. "It is something to look forward to. What of you old friend? When will you stop breaking hearts and chose a wife?"

Peder laughed as he knelt to tie the deer's legs together. "When I find the one who will keep me challenged. I do not want to grow bored."

An image of Joka came unbidden to his mind and he had to force the smile to remain on his face. He pushed the warrior woman's image from his thoughts and turned instead to the deer.

"Come we have a deer to get home." He stood and brushed off his hands. Dirt was embedded beneath his nails and he thought of a much needed bath.

Iver went in search of a sturdy branch, which they secured to the front and back legs of the deer. They carried it between them and made their way back along the trail to the main road that would lead them back to the castle.

As they travelled the heat intensified until sweat poured off Peder's brow and stung his eyes.

III

The next day turned out to be another hot one and Peder wished that the wind would blow to cool the air. Maybe then his arms and legs wouldn't feel like they were weighted down with iron, making every movement a real effort.

Peder walked across the courtyard as he made his way to the corner of the castle which housed the blacksmith's forge. A heavy steam billowed from its opened door and the heat of it hit Peder with a blast as he reached the stone building.

Peder sucked in a breath, hoping for fresh air, but received only the thick foul stench that billowed from inside. He went from the heat outside to the unbearable sauna of the forge.

The blacksmith, Berthor, worked undisturbed by the black air and the smell. Peder braced himself and entered further. His mood did not improve as the temperature continued to climb.

Berthor looked up and was surprised to see Peder there. He stuck the blade of the sword he'd been working on into a vat of water, bringing forth a fresh wave of steam.

"Lord Peder, I was not expecting you this morning." The man turned to face him.

Peder pushed a damp lock of hair from his eyes. "I am sorry to disturb your work."

"It is no bother. It is always a pleasure to see you." Berthor rubbed his dirty hands on the leather apron he wore.

"I have need of your talent."

"Anything my lord." Berthor took a cloth from his work bench and wiped his forehead.

"I want you to make a special sword for me," Peder said.

"There is a problem with the one you have recently paid for?" A worried expression came to the blacksmith's face.

Peder smiled. "None at all, your work is always excellent. This sword is not for me."

"For your father then?"

He shook his head and wondered if he were truly going insane. "It is to be for a woman."

"A woman!" The man looked shocked to say the least, but Peder ignored the man's widened eyes and continued with his request.

"It will need to be a bit lighter and shorter than the ones you usually make." Peder envisioned how he wanted this sword to look.

"Why, my lord, would a woman want a sword?" Berthor's expression was almost comical and Peder had to contain the urge to laugh, as he thought of Joka's desire to be accepted as a warrior.

"She is no ordinary woman. She is a warrior and has skill with a blade to equal many men. But, the sword she wields was not made for her hand and is much too large. She would do better with something that would flow easily with her movements."

"A woman warrior?" Again the man was surprised, but Peder offered no explanation.

"Can you do this for me?" He snapped with irritation, because of the heat or the man's questions, was anyone's guess. Berthor stiffened in response to his master's sharp tongue.

"I will see it done." He lifted his chin in pride.

"Good. I would also like the hilt to be made of gold and etched by the hand of an artist." The heat was turning unbearable, forcing him to take shallow breaths as his lungs began to burn. How did the smith stand it?

"My cousin is a fine artist."

Peder nodded at the man's recommendation. "Then you will handle it?"

"Aye, my lord."

Peder nodded a goodbye and pushed to escape the stifling atmosphere of the forge. He drew in a deep breath, but outside the day's heat didn't offer much relief. He needed to cool off.

He entered the keep and proceeded into the great hall where servants were busy preparing for the evening meal. It was a lot cooler within the stone walls, but he had thoughts of something better.

He beckoned one of the maids and ordered her to bring up buckets of cool water and a tub. A cold bath had worked wonders the day before and it would allow him to clean up before sitting down for supper.

The maid and two others hurried to complete the task and soon Peder was relaxing in the cool water. It was welcome relief. He found a bar of soap that had been left for him and began scrubbing his sweat stained skin and sand colored hair until he was clean and refreshed.

There was a knock at the door and a blond head peeked in. It was Isibel, the maid he'd summoned earlier. She was fair and beautiful, and his mind turned to other thoughts.

"I have your drying sheets, my lord," she said.

"Come in." He beckoned her to step further into his bed chamber. He didn't embarrass easily, so he hadn't bothered with a privacy screen.

Peder watched the woman come forward and look at him coyly from beneath lowered lashes. Without much time spent on thought, he stood up in the tub and stepped out. Isibel stared at him in surprise.

She handed him a drying sheet with which he half heartedly dried himself. When she would have turned to leave his hand snaked out and grabbed hers. A smile betrayed her willingness, but he knew she would succumb to his wishes. He'd had her before, though it had been some time ago.

He pulled her against him and kissed her. She responded with eagerness as he lifted her and carried her to his bed.

She was blond, like Joka, but she was soft and pliable where the warrior woman was hard and sculpted to perfection. Peder was startled he would make such a comparison. He groaned when thoughts of Joka aroused him. He sought to find release in the woman who was as different from the one he could not forget, as day was from night.

It was false satisfaction, and even as the maid slipped contented from the room, Peder lay back unable to feel at ease.

IV

Far to the north and west, among mountains that spit fire and fertile fields that would one day be forced to yield to bitter winds and ice, sat a man of very short stature. He was hiding within a cave, staring out at the girl and her father who had ridden close to his home.

The girl was beautiful, more accurately described a woman, though a maiden still. She had deep red hair that made her stand out in any crowd. She was a flower among stones in the company of the hard looking men that traveled with her and the man who she had the misfortune to call father.

The short man sneered in contempt at the girl's father who believed himself of great importance and kept his people on the edge of fear. The man who'd wielded and threatened to use a whip against the short man and would have if the red haired beauty had not seen to it that he escaped.

She was feisty and brave, but the short man knew he shouldn't have let her place herself in such danger. He should have denied her help and faced the man.

He hadn't been as brave as she and he had let her hide him in a wagon filled with straw that had been headed out to a nearby farm. He had waited until the cover of darkness allowed him to slip from the wagon and then he fled into the forest.

He had missed their friendship these long years he'd hidden in the mountains, sustaining his hunger with the animals he snared and the fish he caught in the streams.

Now she was there, so close that he could see the weariness on her face from being trapped in a life that didn't allow her to spread her wings and fly.

If only he could run out to greet her and convince her to flee with him into the embrace of the cliffs that could engulf one so effectively.

Yet what could one short man, barely able to hold a sword, much less wield it, do against men who'd gained their hardness as Viking men, preying on the helpless. For though he had heard stories that there were those Vikings that followed an entirely different code of honor, he had never seen it in these northern lands.

The friend, who had been lost to him long ago, turned her head and looked in his direction with an expression on her face that made him wonder if she'd seen him, or somehow sensed he was nearby.

She frowned as her eyes scanned the rocky hill, but she did not see the entrance to the cave which he'd hidden with brush.

She turned her horse and followed her father. The short man, longing for an end to his loneliness, stared after her for a long time.

CHAPTER 5

Joka ignored the snickers of the men as she walked by. She kept her face hard and unreadable, but inside she seethed with anger. They thought her a joke for daring to tread into their domain. They couldn't admit that a woman could be a warrior as effectively as a man. Their overgrown egos wouldn't allow that a woman had the ability to be strong.

Joka continued to dress as a man, in tight fitting trousers and a sleeveless tunic. In a sheath across her back she carried her sword. The one she had stolen from her father after she had killed him. The sword she had used to fight Hwal's man by the run down cottage in the mountains. With the rain pelting down on her and making the ground slick beneath her feet, she had fought and won, even though it had been her dagger that dealt the killing blow, not her sword.

She had proven herself a warrior and would gladly prove it again against any who dared to enter the training field with her and spar. Let them see her well placed foot work and how she made her sword sing sweetly as it sliced the air.

She would gladly prove her talent and her worth.

Yet on the one occasion she had tried to entice a man to practice with her, she had brought about such laughter from the men that she'd not asked again. And now, they chuckled in amusement each time she walked by. Only when Rafn was about, did they keep their laughter to themselves. They knew she was his wife's friend and he looked favorably upon her for saving Seera when she'd been lost and injured in the mountains.

Gladly she would prove.

They would not let her. Instead they made crude suggestions to her and invited her to their beds. She sneered in answer to their male urges. Joka wondered if a man could see much past his manhood.

She had often caught Rafn looking at Seera with tenderness, or touching her gently with his hand and she knew that perhaps there were some rare ones that did treat their women with care. These revelations would make her think of Peder and she would get angry with herself for such weak thoughts. Never would a man touch her.

Never!

She left the men behind and walked past the kitchen on her way to Seera's dwelling. A group of women were outside washing dishes in large water filled basins. Their laughter and gossiping stopped abruptly and they all turned at once to stare.

Joka gritted her teeth to keep from speaking out. She could accept the men's teasing far more than she could accept the women's cruelty. They didn't understand her need to fight. She wanted to give them all a good scolding about how women shouldn't bow to a man, that they could learn to be self sufficient, self important. Strong!

She knew she was missing so much of what women thought. She had never led a normal life. Living as she did on the fringes of a village controlled by ruthless men who treated the women no better than they did their cattle.

Skiringssal was not such a place. She could see that easily enough, but her thoughts were biased and she was too stubborn to get past what she had always believed. Perhaps she needed to learn as much as she could teach.

Seera had expressed a desire that Joka continue to train her, but since returning to Skiringssal they hadn't had the chance. Seera's duties kept her busy as did her son. Joka saw little of her. It was why she searched her out.

She came to Seera's dwelling and knocked on the door. She waited for a reply but none came.

Joka sighed.

Maybe she would go instead to watch Rafn working on the ship. She had heard he'd finally consented to Dagstyrr's help and even that of his brother. The Jarl didn't have as much freedom to spend his days building a ship, but he was seen in the clearing whenever he could.

Joka found her way down to the docks and to the clearing. She spotted Seera there with Orn. The baby slept peacefully on her back as she sat on a log with Kata watching the men work.

Seera looked up and saw her. She waved a hand to beckon Joka over.

"I have not seen you for days," Seera said. "I am glad you are here. Please join us." Joka sat beside Seera.

"Have you eaten?" Kata asked. "We have plenty of food left." She reached for a basket to her left and began to drag it closer.

"No, thank you. My sister won't stop feeding me. I fear she thinks I will get too thin."

"She knows how active you are." Seera stretched out her legs being careful not to wake Orn.

"The ship looks good. It must almost be finished." Joka nodded to where the men worked.

"Rafn says only a few more days of work and then they are going to test to see if it's seaworthy." The warlord appeared on the ship's deck. He bent over to straighten a rail and hammer it into place.

"And then?"

Laughing Seera met Joka's gaze. "Rafn says he awaits your sister's direction on that."

"She is full of secrets." Joka shook her head. Her sister hadn't even shared the vision with her. It was frustrating.

"But she claims that Rafn is to sail to a new land, is that not so?" Kata asked as she leaned over the food basket. She dug out a slice of bread and a piece of cheese. She placed the cheese on the bread and took a bite.

"She has told me no more than him. She tells me only that we are to follow where he leads."

"You will go?" Seera asked Joka.

"I must." She fiddled with the knife she had strapped to her leg.

"I am beginning to think that an adventure awaits us all. Rafn has never been more excited than he is right now. I like seeing him like this."

"So do I," Kata said. She lifted her gaze to watch her brother.

"Will you come Kata? Certainly Dagstyrr will not want to stay behind when his best friend sails from here."

Kata glanced at Seera before answering Joka's question. "I admit we have talked about it, and Dagstyrr very much wants to join him."

BITTER PASSAGE

Seera's smile spread across her face. "I dared not hope that you would come. I had not wanted to be separated from either of you. I am glad it will not be so."

II

Rafn had been working nonstop for several weeks and finally the ship was complete. He stood back and assessed his accomplishment. Dagstyrr and Valr stood by his side and he had to admit he wouldn't have completed it so quickly if it weren't for their help.

"It is done, we only have to take it out on the water and see how it fares," Valr said.

Rafn rubbed his hand along the side, feeling the smooth wood with his fingers. His pulse quickened with expectation. He was confident about their workmanship. "It will float, and it will sail."

"Of course it will." Dagstyrr stepped back to better study the craft.

"Come then, Hachet and Leikr have gathered a hundred men to help us test the ship. They wait only for our word." Rafn led them to the group waiting along the shore. He gave his signal and men took positions along both sides of the knarr. Using logs on the ground, they rolled the ship into the water.

They launched the knarr from a small dock adjacent to the clearing. All hundred men went aboard, and still there was room to carry more. The sun reached through the clouds, touching Rafn's face. A strong wind rippled across the sails.

Rafn stood in the stern and shouted out orders to the men to row them clear of the harbor and out into the deep waters of the Vik. The wind tugged strongly at the sails, bringing a smile to the warlord. The sail was strong. Upon his request his own wife and sister had stitched the seams. He believed if the ship was built by their hands, then it would see them safely across the dangerous waters that would take them to this new land.

His destination was yet unknown, but he could feel it in his dreams. He grabbed onto the idea as strongly as he'd fought in any battle. He drew in a deep breath of the salty sea as his thoughts turned heavy with memories. He hadn't had need to fight since that day in the mountains when he faced the one-eyed giant, Hwal. Thor had been with him that day, as surely as the god had back when he was twelve and their village had been attacked.

He had been but a boy, but he had killed with the power of a man, led by the hand of a god. His reputation had grown through the years as he had fought against those who sought to destroy him and his family.

After their parents had been killed, their uncle Gamal had taken them in and raised them. It was he who had taught Rafn and Valr the finer points of wielding a sword. He had been a good teacher, a strong leader. Upon his death Valr had been made Jarl, for he possessed the same qualities as their uncle.

Rafn was different from his older brother. A storm had been born inside him on that fiery morning when he was twelve. It was constant within him. He used the thunder when he fought. He would gather its strength and wield its power. His enemies saw it and feared it. His people felt it and were in awe of it.

Yet Rafn had not felt at peace. He was always restless and ready to strike. It had only been with his little brother Orn that he could center himself and find a measure of calm. But Orn had been taken and sacrificed by his enemy to the god Odin.

Rafn felt the sting of his death still. Had it not been for the love he found with Seera he would have lost a part of himself, which he almost had when she'd been taken from him by Hwal. Rafn had given into the violence of his soul and attacked without mercy through the lands of his enemy in search of her.

He would have become a hardened man if he hadn't found Seera and their son. The only way to have survived the grief and the pain would have been to shut off any feeling.

Rafn's mind returned to the present as he stared out at the choppy waters and felt the strength of their dark depths. It was a mistake to underestimate the power of the sea. Only a fool believed he could control such strength. It took skill and courage to ride the waters of the ocean, and only with proper respect could it be done.

Rafn felt the change inside of him. He had found the peace that his soul sought, and for the moment the storm lay dormant. He wasn't fooled into believing it was gone. He knew it never would be, as he knew that someday it would awaken again when he was in need of its power.

For now he let himself dream of the future. A future he had never imagined he might seek, but longed to claim all the same. He would take his family and those with a desire to follow and head north.

He didn't know how he knew that he had to head north, only that he sensed it. When they were done testing the ship, he would seek out Systa. He would ask the Seer where it was he was to go. She knew his destination. She had always known.

It was time that Rafn did also.

The wind caught the sail and Hachet steered the ship expertly. Those on board cheered when the sail didn't rip, and the ship stayed afloat. Rafn had known that it would, for the gods themselves had guided his hand in its creation. There was a path he was to follow and nothing would stop him from taking it.

Dagstyrr moved to stand beside him. "It is a success. When do we leave?"

"In five days."

"Five days." Dagstyrr smiled.

III

Joka was in the woods where she went to practice often to hone her skills. They would be leaving in five days. Rafn had announced it after they had tested the seaworthiness of the knarr.

She had felt a thrill of excitement pass through her at his words. She hadn't wanted to remain in Skiringssal. She'd been unable to feel at home in this place. It was an impressive trading center, with many dwellings built in rows, and a large compound built behind fortified walls that housed the leaders. The warriors were fierce and dangerous, ruled by a strict hand.

Would the warriors continue to adhere to such a strict code when their warlord was no longer there to guide them? She could only image that they would, as Valr was still their Jarl and he was remaining behind.

Still, she hadn't felt at ease since coming to Skiringssal. She was always on the defensive, waiting to see what would befall them. It wasn't a good way to live and she would happily put Skiringssal and Vestfold behind her.

Joka held the sword confidently in her hands and brought the blade parallel in front of her. She didn't look at the blade, but kept her gaze fixed on a spot in front of her where she pictured an enemy would stand.

She started the dance that always eased her tension. Her focus never wavered as she created music with the blade, as she brought it through the air in imaginary thrusts and lunges. She also pictured how she would block an oncoming blade.

She was so lost in the power of her movements that she didn't hear the approach of another.

"Impressive," an intruding voice cut into her focus and her foot missed a step.

Instinct took over and she had her knife in her hand and threw it with force. Only the acknowledgement of who it was altered her aim at the last moment before it took flight. The knife sailed through the air and stuck in a tree beside Dagstyrr.

"Did I do you wrong, that you would wish me dead?" he asked.

"If I wanted you dead, you would be." Joka's tone left Dagstyrr knowing that she was deadly serious. She eased her sword into the scabbard secured to her back.

"I had not meant to intrude. I was just wandering by and noticed you. Your moves are very graceful and precise. I admit it stunned me."

"Why, because I am a woman?" Resentment soaked her words as she yanked her dagger from the tree.

"Nay. Peder told Rafn that you fought well. That he saw you kill a man with courage and skill."

"He did?" Shock replaced her anger. She slipped her knife back into the sheath on her leg.

"Aye. I didn't doubt his words, but I had not spoken to him myself so I didn't know what he meant until watching you just now."

"You think that women can't be strong?" Her eyes narrowed.

"I don't think that at all," Dagstyrr answered. "I have seen how strong women can be. Is it not they who come close to death each time they birth a child? They are the ones who keep Skiringssal running smoothly the way it does. They make sure the food supplies remain high, the work organized and done. We men would be best to remember all that they do."

"Yet all you have mentioned are domestic things. You don't talk of women's bravery on the battlefield or with a sword."

"It is not done, I admit, but I am not saying that women can't be strong in battle. I say only that the men do the fighting because the women are too valuable to lose. Men can't have children. They can't feed them from their bodies when they are born."

"Warrior, you have different views then the men I have known. My experience with men is that they think of women as property, to be treated with less respect than the horses they ride. This I have seen and lived with, do not tell me it is not so."

Dagstyrr was startled at the venom in her voice. "I don't deny that there are men who feel that way. But these men are not in Skiringssal. Valr and Rafn would never allow such behavior to happen within their rule. Certainly you have seen that in your time here."

"I have seen. Yet still I am frowned upon for dressing as a man, for carrying a weapon—for using it. The men laugh at me, the women disapprove. They are not so open to free thought as you may think."

"I am sorry if you have not been welcomed. You are different, it may take time for people to change the way they have always thought. In time I must believe they will come around. My own wife thinks very highly of you."

"She is strong like Seera. They make up their own minds and I admire that in a person. As for the rest, I will be leaving shortly and they matter not."

"I think you are the strongest woman I have ever met. I doubt that you have become the person you are because you care what others think."

Joka shrugged. "You are right. I don't."

Dagstyrr smiled and it put her at ease. He was friendly and easy to talk to. It surprised her that she could speak so easily with a man. She could see the charm that must have drawn Kata to him.

"There is a goodbye feast tonight in the hall. You must come. Kata and Seera would want you there."

"Perhaps I will."

"Good, then I must leave you to your practice."

Joka watched him go and decided she no longer felt like practicing. What she needed was to bathe if she was to go to the feast. She had not eaten in the Great Hall since the night before Peder had left. She preferred the quiet of her dwelling to the noisy atmosphere of the hall.

That night she would go, for soon they would sail.

IV

Rafn found Systa waiting for him on the bluff overlooking the harbor. As he joined her she turned and smiled at him with a look that bordered on insanity.

"Good is it that you have come."

"In just a few days we will sail. North I will head, but I must know to where I go. You know Seer. You must tell me now."

"Yes north is good and to the west. Follow will we the trails of others. To a land known as Iceland, to a land that holds new hope."

"Iceland?" Rafn nodded in sudden understanding. "I should have guessed."

"Aye." Systa grinned.

He ran a hand through the black strands of his hair, trying to tame it in the light wind that teased it. "Others have left to settle in Iceland."

"Room for more there is."

Rafn studied the petite woman who looked at him out of silver eyes that held many secrets. He didn't doubt that she saw more than she was telling him. Yet he did not want to know more. Let the future unfold as it happened. He would meet each surprise it offered.

"Come, they wait to feast with us." Rafn offered Systa his arm.

She took his arm and they walked together to the hall. Seera was already there with Kata and Dagstyrr. Surprisingly even Joka sat across from Valr.

Let the feasting begin, and then he would board his ship with his family. Rafn promised Seera they would stop at Dun'O'Tir for a week before heading for their new home. She missed her father and brother and wouldn't forgive him if he didn't grant her this wish.

It would be good to see Peder again. He had much to discuss with his brother-in law.

V

Systa had led Joka to a thick part of the forest, far enough away from the village that they wouldn't be disturbed. She had ordered Joka to build a fire and as her sister did this, she searched the ground for sage.

BITTER PASSAGE

It was a purifying and cleansing herb, with silver fuzzy leaves, that when added to the flames of a fire it would burn a cleansing smoke. It was something that most did not know. They thought only to use it as a tea and to add flavor to food.

Systa needed its cleansing smoke. She had to purify herself before she left in the morning. She mustn't taint the ship that would carry them to a new life. She had killed a man, though she had done so by magic instead of by her hands.

She couldn't feel sorry for the momentary insanity that led her to take his life. He had brought forth such haunting memories that she had been unable to think, only feel.

Systa remembered the look of horror that had seized the man. She had worked her magic and planted within his mind unnatural images that had him running in circles to escape them.

The images possessed him so strongly that he manifested them in flesh. Or at least he thought he was seeing something real. Even though it had only been in his mind, he'd been so petrified that his heart had stopped.

She hadn't thought her conjuring through. She had meant only to scare him. She had not thought him so weak that he would die of fright. After all he had done to her, she couldn't be sorry that he was gone.

He would have spoken ill words against the sisters. Would have told anyone who would listen of how Joka had killed their father. Of the powers that Systa possessed and he feared.

No, she had not minded killing him. She had smiled with pleasure as she had walked from the cover of darkness and stared down at him as he lay on the ground clutching a hand to his heart.

He had met her eyes, had seen the power she had spun still reflected in their silver depths. He had understood and had wet himself in fear. She had smelled the acidic odor rising from him as he died.

Such blackness on her soul could not be left. She didn't want to bring bad luck with her on their voyage. She had to make it to Iceland. She had to make sure they arrived safe.

"The fire is ready." Joka said. The flames licked at the air beside her.

Systa joined her sister beside the fire and began sprinkling the sage leaves into the flames. A sweet scent was emitted as the smoke rose and washed over the sisters. She beckoned Joka to step closer and she brushed the smoke over them both.

"Deep make your breath." Joka sucked in a breath to Systa's satisfaction.

"Cleansed we must be," Systa told her and Joka understood. It was a ritual they had done many times.

When the cleansing ritual was complete, Systa moved on to the next task that had brought them into the woods.

"Goddess, call I for your wisdom." Systa raised her eyes to the sky and spoke to the unseen.

"Goddess, I ask for your strength," Joka said.

"Guide us. We who are your children." Systa continued as the smoke thickened and wrapped around them like a cloak.

"Teach us, we who are humbled before you," Joka said.

"Dance we must." Systa led Joka in a circle around the fire. Power guided their steps and energy filled the air. They had evoked Freyja and she had heard.

Systa danced for the goddess's protection. She danced so that their voyage would be blessed. She danced because she gave herself over completely to the goddess and in her power she drew strength.

Tomorrow, it would begin.

CHAPTER 6

Seera was organizing the trunks they would be bringing on board the ship. Fox had taken the first of them down to the docks and she was now awaiting his return.

Seera once more peered into the dwelling now void of their things. It had been her home for only a short time, but it held many memories. She would miss it, as she would miss Skiringssal and the friends she would leave behind. But she had survived leaving Dun'O'Tir and she would survive this too.

Seera closed the door and stepped outside to wait for Fox. She was startled to find Yrsa, the former slave girl she'd rescued from Hwal the previous year, waiting for her.

"Yrsa," Seera said. "It is good to see you. We have had so little time to talk since I've returned."

"You have been busy my lady."

"It is no excuse for my neglect, and here I am leaving once again. This time I am afraid I will not return."

"It is why I have come to speak with you my lady," Yrsa said. She fidgeted nervously and Seera patiently waited for her to speak. She was just happy that Yrsa now spoke to her. There was a time when she would speak only a few words. As a result of the cruelties she had endured as a slave, she'd withdrawn into herself and Seera had feared she would never return to her normal self.

Yrsa had been Hwal's slave for two years before Seera had managed to release her from her prison in Ribe. Though Seera's own escape had been thwarted by Drenger, the man who'd taken Seera as a slave, Yrsa had made it into the care of Rafn and was given passage upon the drekar he had hidden nearby.

Before the day was done, he'd also rescued Seera, but not before Hwal, upon Drenger's request, had whipped her to teach her a lesson. It was the first time Rafn had seen Seera. In desperation Seera had killed Drenger, though it had been Rafn's right. Rafn claimed her then, not as a slave but because he'd admired her courage.

They found love when they had not expected to. Seera wouldn't change any of the past, for it had led her to Rafn. She would have changed Yrsa's torture at the hands of the one-eyed man who'd taken her when she was only twelve. The girl looked up to meet Seera's gaze and must have come to some decision. She spoke with more confidence.

"I would come with you, my lady," Yrsa said. "I would leave Skiringssal and make a new life in Iceland with you and Lord Rafn."

Seera was surprised and pleased. "You wish to go?"

"Aye."

"May I ask why?"

"You and Lord Rafn have always been good to me." She looked over her shoulder in the direction of the harbor. "And Fox is going. He has asked the warlord already."

"Fox?" Seera's eyes opened wide. The admission was more a shock than Yrsa's request to go.

"Aye, my lady. We have become friends. He is very kind and I don't want to part from him." Color washed across Yrsa's cheeks as her hands twisted in her dress.

Seera smiled in understanding and pleasure to know that Yrsa could find love after everything that had happened to her.

"I would be most pleased to have you along," Seera said. "I will get Fox to come for your things when he is finished with mine."

Yrsa impulsively hugged her. "I will help you care for your son. I would be very careful with him."

"Of course you would and I know no one better to help. I am sure to need it on the long voyage. Go now and pack what you wish to take as we will soon be leaving."

Yrsa nodded and ran off towards the longhouse where she lived with the other unwed women.

II

Valr was down at the docks helping Rafn with the last minute loading. Cattle, sheep and horses were already on board, being cared for by some of the farmers Rafn had convinced to go with them. Many families had decided to uproot and leave with Rafn. It was a chance of a better future for those men who were second born and therefore wouldn't inherit their father's farmlands. Others just wanted to leave behind the King's greed, as he continued to take more from them than he should. Then there were those who wanted to go for the adventure of seeing a new land and for the chance of making a new life.

There were about one hundred and fifty men, women and children waiting on the decks for their warlord and his family to board.

Valr stood facing Rafn, who was both excited about his voyage and saddened by leaving his brother behind. The two of them had been together, ruled together, for many years. After their parents were killed, they had made a new life for their family. With the help of their uncle they had rebuilt Skiringssal. They had built the fortified compound around their homes and people had flocked to Skiringssal to build a new town outside its walls.

Through the years it had grown until it became one of the largest trading posts in the Viking world. Those who fell within its rule had never known hunger or fear. The warriors of Skiringssal were fierce and were successful in keeping their enemies from their gates.

Their uncle, Gamal, had been a fair Jarl and Valr had followed his example. It was why Skiringssal was so successful. Why those who dwelled there were all family and had great respect for those who ruled.

But Rafn was leaving them, their mighty warlord who had always kept them safe. Hamr was being left to lead the warriors in his place and he had a strong arm and smart mind. Rafn was confident that he would do well. Rafn didn't regret his decision to leave. He knew his destiny lay north in a place that was said to have fertile land for the taking, even though leaving Valr was hard.

Parting with his brother was difficult for Valr as well. Not only was Rafn leaving with his wife and son, but Kata and her husband were going as well. Even Fox, the boy who would have been family when Orn had married his sister, was going with Rafn. Leikr and Hachet would always follow where Rafn led. Valr didn't begrudge their wish to stay with the man who had always been an inspiration to them.

"You take care of yourself and all our family that goes with you," Valr told him. "I wish only that you find a safe place and that you are happy."

"I will take care of them brother," Rafn promised. "And this is not goodbye. We will see each other again. That I vow."

"Aye we will. Let it not be too long."

Rafn drew Valr into a brotherly embrace before stepping back to allow Seera to come forward.

"I will miss you, my husband's brother." Moisture shone brightly in her eyes. She hugged him with her usual spontaneous affection. Valr was overwhelmed by emotion. He placed a hand on the head of his nephew as he lay asleep in Yrsa's arms.

Kata pushed forward with tears streaming down her face. She choked on a sob. "I wish you were coming with us." Her embrace was fiercer than the others had been. His arms tightened around her. Their family had always lived as one and it was painful to be severing that close tie.

Valr spoke to Dagstyrr over Kata's shoulder. "Take care of her."

"I will see to it." Dagstyrr took Kata's hand and led her away.

Joka and Systa stood back watching the emotional display of affection as each said their goodbyes. When it was done Rafn ordered them onto the knarr. Seera and Yrsa boarded first. Fox, who was already on board, helped the women onto the ship. Kata followed closely with Dagstyrr, but Rafn hung back. He would board last.

Joka stepped onto the plank that led to the ship and looked back over her shoulder. She nodded to Valr before she stepped on board. Systa paused for a moment and turned to Valr. A mysterious smile touched her face as she looked at him.

"Come, when no choice is left but to follow the raven." She winked and followed her sister. Valr and Rafn exchanged a glance and Rafn lifted his shoulders in a shrug. The Seer always talked in riddles.

"Go, while the tide is still with you," Valr said. Rafn turned from him to walk the plank to the boat. Valr went to the ropes that held the ship to the dock and unraveled them himself.

Rafn moved to the stern of the ship and watched as the men rowed the boat away from the wooden pier out into the waters of the Vik. Once out in the open they unfurled the sail and the wind caught it and took them even further from Skiringssal. Valr stood on the dock and the brothers watched until the distance became too great to see each other.

III

Peder was at the King's castle. It was in the southern part of Pictland a few days journey south of Dun'O'Tir. He'd been in chambers with King David all morning. It had been an exhausting debate about the problems they were having with Celts in the area.

The King was forceful in keeping his lands and pushing out those who thought it rightfully theirs. The King's soldiers were well trained tough men. What the King had needed to know was if Dun'O'Tir had been having any problems with the rebels. Peder had little to report because there'd been no unrest in the Eorl's lands.

"Glad I am to have you back with us," King David said. He beckoned a maid over to pour them more wine. The goblets they drank from were made of gold and gaudily decorated with rubies. They were surprisingly heavy and Peder couldn't understand their appeal. "I am to expect that your sister is safe?"

Peder nodded. "She is, my lord. She is back in the care of her husband. She has given birth to a fine son."

David smiled. "A son! That is good to hear. Will she be visiting Dun'O'Tir soon?"

"Rafn has promised to bring her as soon as he can. My father is most anxious to see her and his new grandson."

"If she has time, please tell the Lady Seera that the Queen would like to see her." David took another sip from his goblet.

"I will pass her the message." Peder placed the heavy goblet back on the table. "I am afraid I must ask your leave your majesty. I have a long ride ahead of me and my father expects me to return as soon as possible."

"Of course." The King rose from his high backed seat. "Do not be so long again from my court."

Peder stood as well. "I will try not to be. Though, I should let you know that my father has given me leave from my duties for a time. I am not sure where I shall be in the coming months."

"Leave from your duties?" The King stared at him in shock. "Whatever for?"

"To search for answers," Peder said. The King had always been close with the Eorl of Dun'O'Tir and by extension had great respect for his son. He could easily order him to fulfill his duties to King and country, but he did not.

"I will miss you." David put a hand on Peder's shoulder.

"And I you, but I will see you again."

"Then I wait expectantly for that time."

Peder left the King in his chamber and shut the heavy wooden door behind him as he stepped out into the hall that was filled with banners and shields. He made his way down the steps and out into the courtyard.

He was on his way to the stable and his horse, when a man stopped him. He recognized him as Lord Kent. The man was a dour fellow, best described as a pompous fool. He held himself in higher esteem than did those around him. Peder plastered a fake smile on his face and greeted the man.

"It has been awhile Kent." Peder tried not to show his irritation about being delayed.

"It is a pleasure to see you again Peder." The man smiled like a fool as if the two of them were the closest of friends.

Grin and bear it, Peder told himself.

"What can I do for you?" Peder asked, thinking that he might as well get it over with.

Kent's face beamed with excitement. "I wish to inquire about your sister. How does she fair? I have not seen her at court."

"Seera is in Skiringssal with her husband." Peder tightened his jaw to refrain from laughing at the absurd expression that marked the man's face. It was if he'd eaten something sour and not to his liking.

A stunned stammer escaped when he began to speak. "I had not known that she married."

"She has wed Rafn Vakrson, Lord of Skiringssal and younger brother to the Jarl." Peder made sure pride laced his words so the man knew he was pleased with the union.

"She married a Viking warlord?" An unmanly squeal marred his voice. Peder had to grit his teeth to keep from showing his distain.

"Oh yes, he is an impressive man. I have seen how fierce he is with a sword in his hand." The man's eyes bugged out. Perhaps it would dissuade him from inappropriate thoughts of another man's wife when he had the mental picture of that man with a blade.

Kent's face smoothed into one of confusion. "She is happy with this arrangement?"

"They are much in love. Further reinforced by the son she has given him."

"Dear Lord." Kent shook his head. Without another word the man wandered off in a daze, contemplating this unexpected news.

Without a moment's hesitation Peder retrieved his horse and left the King's castle before anyone else had an opportunity to stop him.

IV

Joka stood stiffly as the ship moved along at its slow pace. She had never been on a ship before. Many had come and gone from the small village where she had lived as a child, but she had never been allowed to board one. Systa had gone below to the sleeping quarters that had been given them and slept peacefully, undisturbed by the motion of the ship.

Joka wasn't so comfortable with it. It was going to take some getting used to. She looked to the starboard side of the ship and saw Kata hanging over the railing again. The poor woman had been throwing up since leaving Skiringssal four days ago. She hadn't been able to stay in the rooms built below the deck. She claimed it made her feel worse, and she needed to be on deck where she could breathe the fresh air.

Kata had told her she often felt ill from the constant motion, but she had never felt quite so horrible. Never had it driven her to the point of vomiting. Dagstyrr stayed close by, a worried expression on his face.

Joka watched as he moved up beside her and slipped an arm around her waist as she leaned over to empty more of her stomach into the sea.

Children played in amongst the grown-ups. They laughed with delight at being on the ship. The animals in the center hull weren't quiet. Many voiced their displeasure at being forced to travel in such a manner. Joka supposed they would have to get used to it as well.

She glanced back out to the ocean that stretched before them. Early that day they had lost sight of land. They were now on the North Sea heading for the castle Dun'O'Tir, that was said to be built on a large rock overlooking the sea. She'd heard it was an impenetrable fortress.

Joka's stomach clenched. Dun'O'Tir was the home Seera had grown up in, the home where her brother still lived. There was no avoiding seeing Lord Peder again. Her only comfort was that Rafn said they would only stay a week. Then they would head north along the coast of Pictland, before turning west.

She could be around him for a week. Certainly his duties would keep him busy, making it easy to avoid him. The sun dipped low on the horizon and a sharp wind blew off the water. Joka pulled her cloak tighter around her, but remained where she stood.

V

Peder walked from the blacksmith's forge, carrying the new sword wrapped in a leather cloth. Once secure behind closed doors he uncovered it and pulled it from its sheath. A shiver of premonition ran down his spine. What had possessed him to have a sword made for Joka? His intent was to send it on a ship bound for Vestfold and have it delivered directly to her in Skiringssal. He gripped the hilt of the sword and knew he would not send it.

He would keep it until the time was right to present it to her. He didn't know when that would be, but he couldn't send it anonymously on a ship. He wanted to see her reaction and more than that he wanted to see her yield it.

Peder slipped the blade back into the sheath, which was made of hard leather, with a strap that would fit diagonally across her chest to hold it to her back. It was an exquisite sword, fit for a nobleman. Yet he would give it to a woman. Not one of noble birth but one with the heart of a warrior.

"Stop thinking of her!" He would drive himself mad with his thoughts. His King would laugh if one of his soldiers was undone by desiring a woman to the point of losing his mind.

He placed the sword in the corner of his bed chamber and strapped on his own weapon. He would go to the training field and work his own men until they could no longer walk from sheer exhaustion. It wouldn't be the first time since his return to Dun'O'Tir.

A knock at the door drew his attention. "Enter." His command was sharp. He felt a touch of anger to see the maid Isibel. In his frustration he had called her to his bed too often. It had been a mistake that he had been slow to acknowledge.

When she entered his chamber she was quick to smile at him and he saw the moon-eyed affection in her brown eyes. He had vowed that he would not take her to bed again. She was beginning to develop feelings for him and he needed to stop them before things got out of hand. He was wrong to give her such hope. He could never marry her. It had nothing to do with her being a maid and him a noble. He simply felt no love for her.

He was usually more careful to select women that understood the rules. That accepted they could never be more than a lover. He had erred this time. In his desperation to erase Joka from his mind he had sought comfort in Isibel. Because she was too young, she had romantic notions of love. Perhaps she dreamed of marrying him and what that would mean to her, never having to serve others again.

"My lord," she said as she carried in a tray. "I had thought you might be hungry."

Isibel placed the tray on the table in his room. Usually he took his meals downstairs, but on occasion he did enjoy the solitude of having his food brought to his chamber. The bread still steamed and must have come directly from the oven. There was cheese and fruit as well as some sliced cold meat placed on the platter.

His stomach growled in hunger. He sat down at the table and looked at Isibel. She watched him with an eager expression, but he ignored the plea in her eyes that he might invite her to stay.

"Thank you for your foresight," he said. "I need nothing more."

A look of disappointment crossed her face. He had kept his words emotionless and straight forward. His words had sounded gruff even to him, but he couldn't help it. He would not feed her delusions.

"Aye, my lord." She no longer smiled as she backed from the room.

He finished his meal in silence and deep thought. When he was done he went in search of some unlucky recipient to drag onto the training field. He thought of Iver.

When he reached the courtyard a shout went up from one of the guards on the wall. Peder looked up to see the man waving him over. Peder quickened his pace and climbed the ladder two rungs at a time.

"What is it?" he asked.

"A ship, my lord."

Peder climbed from the ladder to stand beside the guard. He looked out to the sea below and saw a large knarr headed in their direction.

The sail bore the unmistakable mark of the raven. It was Rafn's emblem and usually marked his drekar. He had not been expecting his brother-in law so soon. That was surprise enough, but to see him arriving in this large ship rather than his sleek double headed longship was a shock.

"Inform my father." He turned from the sight of the ship to slip back down the ladder and to head for the gate.

He was on the beach waiting by the time the ship anchored close to shore. A small boat was lowered into the water and a group made their way to the beach. Another shock kept Peder very still as he watched their approach.

He had made out Joka at once, sitting beside his sister. Her face was stern and her eyes cold when they met his. No pleasure crossed her face to see him, but even so he was mesmerized by her and a thrill of excitement coursed through his body.

CHAPTER 7

He was on the beach waiting. She kept her emotions from her face and forced herself not react to the way he was staring at her. Hachet jumped from the boat and pulled it up onto the shore. Dagstyrr and Rafn climbed out to help him.

Rafn reached for Seera's hand and helped her to the sand. She went into Peder's arms and the man's face warmed at the sight of his sister. Rafn turned back to the boat to help Yrsa, the girl who was vigilant in her care of his son.

Peder reached out a hand to touch the baby's face, which caused Orn to become still. He looked up into the face of his uncle as if studying him. Peder's smile widened.

"He looks round and healthy," Peder said.

Soft easy laughter washed from Seera. "He should, he does nothing but eat."

"As he should if he is to be a man like his uncle." Peder chuckled and the sound made Joka fidget with unease.

"You mean his father." Rafn corrected as he locked hands to arms with his brother-in law. "It is good to see you again."

"I am pleased you are here." He glanced down at Seera. "Father will be most excited to see you."

"As I am to see him."

Joka jumped from the boat and helped Systa out and noticed that Kata looked quite happy to have her feet on solid ground again. Joka couldn't blame her. The voyage so far had not been easy for her. Peder's easy timbre drew her attention back to him as he spoke.

"Please tell me brother-in law, why you sail on such a ship?"

Humor sparkled in Rafn's dark eyes. "I will tell you all once you place a mug of ale in my hands."

"I can do that. Come."

"I have a request to ask?" Rafn said.

"Please ask. I will do what I can."

"There are families aboard the knarr, including children. I would ask permission that they be allowed to set up tents outside the castle walls so that they may have a rest from the confines of the ship."

"Yes, of course. I am sure Hachet could see to it while you and I go find somewhere more comfortable to speak."

Rafn turned to speak with Hachet for a moment and then he and the others followed Peder up to the castle.

Joka took in her surroundings. She tried to look everywhere at once, except at the back of the man who caused such disturbing emotions within her. Against her will her gaze slipped to the handsome man who led them up the hill to the castle gates.

She caught Systa watching and knew the smile of amusement she wore was because of Joka's predicament. She ignored her sister's all too seeing eyes. What did it matter that she found the man attractive? She wouldn't allow such desires to rule her. She was far too disciplined to succumb to such unwanted feelings.

She wouldn't give her body to this man, or allow his hands to touch her.

When the castle's gate appeared Peder stopped to look back. For a moment their eyes met and Joka scowled. Before he turned away, something flashed across his face that puzzled her.

II

Peder led his guests into the keep and to the great hall. They were met by the Eorl. Airic ignored the others and went straight to Seera.

"I have worried about you, and missed you," Airic said to his daughter. Tears slid down her face as she allowed him to draw her into his arms. She sobbed in his embrace.

Peder watched and understood how worried their father had been. He'd been relieved when Peder had returned with news that she was safe. He had aged in his son's absence. Worry had driven him half mad until his son had come home. He had longed each day since to see Seera with his own eyes. Only Peder's promise that Rafn would bring her as soon as he was able had kept Airic from boarding a ship and sailing to Skiringssal himself.

"It makes me so happy to be here Papa." Seera stepped from him and beckoned Yrsa to her. "There is someone you must meet."

Airic's eyes lit when she presented him with his grandson. He took the baby into his arms and held him so that he could get a good look at him. "Strong he is and rightly so," he said. Orn reached out and gripped one of his fingers, causing the Eorl to smile with happiness.

Isibel came into the hall then and the Eorl beckoned her over. "Show the women to the guest chambers." Her eyes flicked to Peder who avoided her gaze.

"Aye, my lord." The maid gave a slight bow and then led the women to the stairs.

"I can find my own way," Seera told the girl. "Direct the others to where they are to go."

"Aye, my lady." She nodded and led the other women from the room.

"I will see you later Papa." She hugged him once more before she also left the hall so that the men could be alone to speak more freely.

Another servant was beckoned and told to fetch some ale. The men took a seat at the head table. Once before these four men had sat together as they did now. On that day Rafn had not asked, but demanded, Seera's hand in marriage. Only Rafn's obvious love for his sister had kept Peder from flogging him.

Through the months that Peder had searched for Seera with Rafn, they had developed a close friendship. Peder had come to respect the man that was known by many as The Raven, the feared warlord of Skiringssal.

The servant brought an ewer of ale and mugs to drink it with. The men sat back to enjoy their drinks as another servant brought in a tray of food for the men to enjoy.

"Now tell me Rafn, what you are up to. You travel with more than just warriors. Women and children are with you." Peder raised his mug and took a drink of the ale while waiting for an answer.

A smile that Peder could only describe as being laced with mischief tugged at Rafn's mouth. His eyes held a dreamy look that Peder had never before witnessed in his brother-in law. "We are going to Iceland," Rafn said. Peder's eyes grew wide with surprise.

"Iceland? Whatever has possessed you to go there?"

"If I told you that Systa has seen my future and has counseled me in my decision, would you think me mad?"

"Once perhaps I would have thought so, but I have met this woman who claims to be a Seer and I would not discount her claim."

"Good, because she has made me a believer and I am being called to this new land. I can do nothing less than answer."

Airic, who up until then had sat quietly beside his son, spoke up. "Perhaps this is the answer to your unrest, my son."

"You think so?" He searched his father's eyes and saw the encouragement in them.

"I do."

"Care to explain brother-in law?" Rafn raised an eyebrow in question.

"I have been restless since returning to Dun'O'Tir. I have often taken my discontent out upon my men on the training field. Many have complained." Peder laughed and Rafn smiled in amusement.

"I have released him from his duties to Dun'O'Tir and recommended that he find what it is he searches for."

Rafn studied Peder. "You are most welcome to join us on our adventure. Seera would be delighted to have you along. My men already know you. They speak highly of you and they would be honored by your presence."

Despite trying his best, Peder couldn't help but think of Joka. If he went along he would be close to her. He had not missed the look on her face. She hadn't been pleased to see him again, but that made little difference to him. He had only to say yes to Rafn's offer and they would be forced together whether she liked it or not. He found pleasure in that knowledge.

"I find the idea most intriguing. How can I refuse such an offer?" A heavy weight lifted from his shoulders as he spoke.

"Let's drink to our future then." Dagstyrr raised his mug and the others joined him, each with their own hopes for the future.

Peder's connection to Dun'O'Tir had already been lost. He felt no sadness at thoughts of leaving it behind. His father he would miss, but they would see each other again. He would make sure of that.

"Iceland then," Peder said. Hope flared with vicious flames inside him. He prayed he wouldn't regret his decision.

III

Joka followed the stairs back down to the great hall. She'd bathed and changed into a fresh tunic and trousers. She ran her fingers through her loose hair, having left it down so it could finish drying. The others were already seated in the hall when she arrived.

A place had been left for her beside her sister. As she approached she met the Eorl's gaze and saw the curiosity there. The hall was filled with those from Rafn's ship as well as those from Dun'O'Tir.

She walked between the benches until she came to the head table which had been placed beneath one of the narrow windows. Somehow it didn't surprise her that Peder sat directly across from her, or that he had risen to greet her.

"I hope your journey went well." Peder was polite, but he didn't offer her his hand. He was learning to keep some distance between them.

"Father, I would like you to meet Joka of Vestfold." The Eorl had also risen and he had no misgivings about offering his hand.

Peder watched her closely and she could tell from the expression on his face that he fully expected her to ignore his father's upturned hand. She let her face soften when she turned to the Eorl. She held out her hand and allowed him to take it. He raised it almost to his lips but stopped short of touching her skin.

"It is a pleasure to make your acquaintance," Airic said.

Joka felt Peder's stare, and ignored it. "As it is to make yours, my lord."

"Sit please and enjoy the feast that has been prepared."

Joka did as the Eorl bid and managed to eat even with Peder's continuous glances her way. Kata sat to her left and she spoke with her to avoid being led into a conversation with the man who sat across from her.

Kata was still not feeling that well and wasn't able to eat much, Joka took note and halfway through the meal she suggested that Kata go and rest. Hearing this, Dagstyrr agreed and led her from the hall.

Joka should have realized what losing her companion would mean. She turned to speak with Systa who sat on her right, but she was helping Yrsa with the baby.

Feeling trapped by the inevitable she met Peder's intent gaze. A smile slid across his face when she finally acknowledged him. He was quick to draw her attention before he lost his chance.

"Are you looking forward to reaching Iceland?" he asked.

"Yes." Beneath the table she gripped her hands together and couldn't understand why they were slick with sweat.

"Do you still practice with your sword?"

She concentrated on keeping her voice even. "Every chance I get, but there is nowhere on the ship to do so."

"I don't suppose there is," he said. "Please feel free to use the training area while you are here."

Joka wasn't quick enough to hide her surprise and knew he was aware of it. Still the shock filtered through her. The men of Skiringssal had never allowed her to use their training area. She hadn't expected the lord of Dun'O'Tir to feel any different. Peder studied her far too closely, watching her reaction.

"You do not wish its use?"

"I would, my lord. I was not permitted use of the one at Skiringssal." She clamped her mouth shut at having said more than she'd intended.

"I see."

She cursed his close scrutiny. "It mattered not as I need no other to train with. I am perfectly capable of teaching myself."

"You have done a fair job so far," he said. Again she failed to suppress her surprise. She wasn't used to such praise.

"No one will keep you from my area. It is open to all who wish its use it."

Joka sensed he could see her discomfort and found she could only nod, unable to verbally express her thanks.

IV

Later that evening, shortly after Joka had retired to the bed chamber given her, a knock sounded on her door. She opened it to find a young man, dressed in short baggy pants and a green tunic. She had seen him earlier in the hall speaking with Peder. Seera had greeted him with warmth and called him Jakob.

Joka couldn't imagine why he would be calling on her. "May I help you?"

"I am sorry to disturb you my lady," he said. "Lord Peder asked me to deliver something to you."

"I am no lady, you may call me Joka." He simply nodded.

Instead Jakob held out a leather wrapped object that was slightly longer than the length of her arm. She looked at him in question. "This is for you. He told me also to tell you to be at the training area at dawn. If you need any assistance finding it I am to show you where it is."

Joka took the object from him and she felt the power of it even through the cloth. Jakob bid her goodnight and slipped away before she had a chance to question him further. She closed the door and walked to the bed.

She placed the object on the bed and stared. She was almost too nervous to open it, which made no sense at all. Certainly any gift from Peder she would return at once. She wouldn't allow herself to keep it. What would that say to him?

She gently drew back the cloth to reveal a beautiful leather sheath. She touched it with light fingers and traced the design up to the golden hilt that peeked out the top of it. She could just see the top of the metal that made up the sword that was attached to it.

She held her breath in anticipation. She allowed her hand to close around the exquisitely etched hilt and drew the sword from its sheath. She held it in front of her and gasped in appreciation at the perfectly crafted sword she grasped in her hand. A tingling sensation shot up her arm and her eyes opened in excitement.

She ran the fingers of her left hand along the cool metal and felt the power of the sword reach out to her. She tested the sword with her right hand by bringing it through the air. It was lighter than the sword she was used to. It was also smaller, as if it had specifically been made for her hand.

Joka realized with a start that it had. Peder must have hired the blacksmith to cast this sword for her. Why would he present her with such a gift?

She should make him take it back. She knew that was the right thing to do, but she wanted this sword with a desperate greed. It had been hers from the moment she had touched it and she couldn't part with it.

She didn't have that kind of willpower.

A rare smile appeared on her face. She had the urge to laugh, but the moment was too sacred. She had never even dared to dream of owning such a weapon. It could have been made for a king, but it was made for the hand of a woman. She knew of no noble woman who would carry a sword and so she knew beyond doubt that Peder had indeed intended it for her.

What would he expect in return?

That question should have frightened her, but the sword kept her locked in its power. She could think of nothing else but how it felt in her hands.

Tomorrow she would practice with it. She knew that sleep would be elusive as she waited with little patience for the dawn.

V

Systa dreamed that night of the force that was leading her to Iceland. She had felt it before but not as strong as she did that night. It was the first time it had become clear to her that the power she felt was from another person. Not one who saw the future, but one who had been touched by magic.

Concentrating on the connection to him, she was overwhelmed by his emotions. She felt his loneliness and ached to reach out to him. She had never felt a soul so pure. It was surprising and calming all at once.

The man's purity rippled across the expanse that separated them, making her feel a part of him. He did not know she was there with him. He had no sense of their connection.

How she wished he did. His loneliness echoed her own so much that she knew that they were the same. Magic filtered through him and touched the deepest parts of him.

She felt the link slipping from her as she ascended into wakefulness. She reached desperately to keep hold but she was thrown awake in sudden shock. She shivered from the chill of the chamber she'd been given.

BITTER PASSAGE

It was a dark and cold place. Even the thin light that filtered into the room through the narrow window didn't bring warmth. The stone walls were hard and uninviting and she couldn't feel the wind through them.

She did not like this place. It didn't feel right. It lacked some fundamental spirit that she was used to feeling. She was too far from the ground. She was separated from the pulse of the earth that had always brought her comfort.

She disliked this place.

CHAPTER 8

The sky had barely begun to lighten when Joka dressed. She made quick work of her hair as she created a braid to hang over each shoulder. She wrapped a wool head band around her forehead and slipped on the short hide boots and clasped them closed.

She strapped her new sword onto her back and her excitement grew. What powers did the sword possess?

She peeked out through the narrow window in her room to see the sky just beginning to redden on the horizon. It was time. She found the stairs and made her way down. She startled a maid who looked like she had just crawled from bed.

"Sorry," Joka said.

"Would you like anything, my lady?"

Not wanting to have to waste time explaining once again that she was not of noble blood, she dismissed the girl. "No, I am good."

The girl continued on her path to the kitchen and Joka wondered for a moment if she should stop and eat. She decided she had no appetite.

She made her way into the courtyard and was surprised to see Jakob standing just outside the keep door. He looked as awake as he had the night before when he'd delivered the sword.

"My lady, Lord Peder has asked me to show you to the training area."

She groaned. "I could have found it myself. And I told you last night that I'm not nobility, you don't have to address me so formally."

"Yes, I remember you mentioning it," Jakob said. "Come."

Joka followed him across the courtyard to the area set aside for practicing and training. The space was empty and she turned to Jakob.

"Thank you for your assistance, I will be fine now," she said. She hoped that he wasn't intending to stay and watch.

"Then I shall bid you good day." Jakob bowed and thankfully left.

Joka tread into the area that had always been reserved for the men alone. She felt a thrill of power to be allowed its use. She would have smiled but for the solemnity of the moment. She walked to the center and drew the sword slowly from her back.

She held it in front of her and the mornings first light reflected off the blade. She breathed in to calm her rapidly beating heart. She said a quick prayer to the goddess and closed her eyes to focus on the center of her being and to push all other thoughts from her mind, save for that of the sword that she gripped.

"I knew you would be early." A deep voice penetrated the stillness she was trying to maintain. She opened her eyes to find Peder standing before her, dressed only in trousers and boots. He was shirtless despite the chill on the morning air. He clutched his sword in his hands.

"I didn't expect you." He raised his eyebrows in question to her comment.

"Didn't you? I sent you an invitation last night with Jakob, did he not deliver it with the sword." His eyes flicked to the weapon she held possessively in her hands.

"He told me I was to come here at dawn. I understood that as an invitation that I was allowed to use this place."

"You did not expect a partner to spar with?"

She was trying hard to hide her surprise, but she knew her eyes betrayed her. "I have never practiced with a partner. What man would spar with a woman after all?"

"I would gladly be that man." He moved closer to her with a devastating smile that she really had to ignore to keep her calm.

"You don't worry that your men will make fun of your choice of partners?" Sweet goddess this was her chance, her chance to show another what she was capable of.

"Are you afraid, Joka, to fight me?" He moved in closer and when he spoke his face was but inches from hers. He had a challenge in his eyes that she couldn't ignore.

"I'm not afraid."

"Good." He stepped back and brought his sword in front of him. They stood facing each other for a moment as if evaluating the other.

Without a word the sparring started. Joka took the first lunge and Peder stopped it easily. Joka breathed in slowly, trying to find strength from deep within to help keep her focused. She could not embarrass herself in front of this man.

Her dance began as it had countless of times, but this time was different. This time another moved with her. Back and forth their swords clanged against each other. The sword was alive in her hands as if it had become an extension of her arm.

Her feet moved in silent steps, his followed and led. Each stopping the others moves and the dance became more frenzied.

She was good Peder thought as he deflected her sword with his own and was thrilled each time she stopped his. He became aware of a crowd growing at the edges of his vision. He kept his eyes on her. He could almost read her mind and predict where her next swing would land.

It was becoming frustrating. He knew how to stop each one of her lunges. Metal rang against metal in a perfectly timed song. She tried harder. He didn't let up. Sweat poured down his chest and dampened his hair and it was a distraction that she couldn't afford.

Her face hardened further and her lunges became quicker. Her movements were far more graceful than any man he'd ever seen fight. Her body moved with fluidity and control and he knew that she would do well on any battlefield. Yet there was much she still needed to learn. Things he would gladly teach her.

Joka saw the moment something changed in him. The second that she knew she would be bested by him. She was powerless to stop him when his next move caught her off guard. The tip of his sword found an opening and she felt it press lightly against her side. His control was faultless.

"You are good woman," he said. She scowled at him. "Do not be discouraged."

"I am not." She pushed back from him and brought her sword down quickly only to be stopped by his.

"I can teach you many things if you let me?" he said quietly to her when their hilts locked and they were drawn close together.

"Why would you do that?" she asked.

"All warriors need to train, even the best continue to learn and hone their skills," he replied.

"I am a woman."

"I am all too aware of that." His voice could only be described as seductive. It put her on the defensive. Something hot flashed in his eyes and she stiffened against it.

Growling she pushed him back. A smile of enjoyment crossed his lips. "Why do you wish it?"

"Because you are good Joka, but with some proper training, you could be great. I for one would like to see that."

Joka was stunned by his words. None had ever praised her so, or encouraged her to try harder and to become better. She wanted what he proposed. To be a great warrior!

"Teach then." She brought her sword up.

"First thing, you must learn is to watch your opponent's eyes, never his sword." He waited for her to make her move.

She did as he said. She kept her eyes locked with his and had to fight against the desire she saw growing in them. She looked past that to see the man she fought.

II

Seera went to stand next to Rafn and Dagstyrr where they watched Peder and Joka. Seera shook her head at Rafn's amusement.

"What point is my brother trying to make?"

Rafn looked down at his wife and laughed. "He is only daring to do what no other man has."

"And what is that?"

"To see exactly what this warrior woman is made of."

"And how is she measuring up to the men's critiquing?" She scowled in disapproval of the eager crowd. Joka was her friend and she didn't want her being used for the men's entertainment.

"They are no longer laughing at her," he said. He nodded towards the group of men who had come with them from Skiringssal.

Seera studied their faces and realized her husband was right. They were impressed by what they saw. Joka was proving herself to these men who had dared to snicker each time she walked by.

Seera turned her attention to the two sparring. She could not hear Peder's words, but she realized he was giving her instructions and she was listening. That was an accomplishment in itself on her brother's part.

"She is doing well then?"

"Extremely well." Her husband's words brought a smile to her face.

"That is good to hear," she said.

"You think so wife?" Rafn looked down at her.

"I do." She smiled up at him.

"Peder has fallen hard," Dagstyrr said. The couple turned to him and caught the amusement that crinkled the corner of his eyes.

"What?" Seera looked from one man to the other and saw her husband's eyes light up.

"You are right my friend, I should have seen it." Rafn roared with laughter.

Her attention snapped to Peder and tried to see what they did. A inkling of what they saw began to form as Rafn spoke.

"Your brother desires Joka."

She looked to the couple locking swords and realized there was a visible tension between them. Peder's eyes never left Joka. Yes, she could see it, something alive in his eyes that she'd never seen before. She gasped in surprise.

"Poor Peder," she said.

"Why do you say that?" Rafn put his arm around his wife's waist and pulled her close to his side.

"Because Joka hates all men," she said.

"You think she will not return his affections?" Dagstyrr lost his smile and glanced at Joka.

"I don't believe she will. She has been quite adamant that no man will ever touch her. It is why she has learned to protect herself. She would be nobody's victim."

"Peder would not hurt her," Rafn said.

"No he wouldn't, but Joka doesn't know that. She sees all men the same."

"Poor Peder," said Rafn and Dagstyrr at the same time.

III

Joka's breathing was labored, as was Peder's. At once they ended what had been an intense sparring match. It left Joka feeling exhilarated like she never had before and a bit confused by the man who stood before her.

"I thank you, my lord, for your instructions." She spoke formally and knew that it irritated Peder. "And a sincere gratitude for the sword."

"It was my pleasure." His emphasis on pleasure had her on guard once again. She became aware then of the crowd watching.

Peder enjoyed her shock at seeing that so many had witnessed their sparring. He could tell by the men's faces that they were impressed. They hadn't expected that a woman could fight so well. Even without training she had proved herself. Once she had finely honed those skills, she would be a sight worth seeing.

Joka noticed Seera and headed for the one person in the crowd who she felt comfortable with. Peder followed on her heels. She nodded to Dagstyrr in greeting before turning to her friend.

Peder witnessed the smile that had touched her face when she had acknowledged Dagstyrr. They were friends and that came as a surprise to him. It was good that the other man was married to a woman he so obviously loved, or Peder would have been jealous.

"You did well," Dagstyrr said.

"Thank you," she answered with pride.

"Come Joka, let us summon you a bath." Seera took her arm. Joke did not look back as walked away.

It didn't stop Peder from watching her. His blood pumped fiercely as it had never done before. Their match had been at once a release of his sexual frustration and the beginning of a much deeper feeling that could not be redirected so easily.

"You enjoy challenges my brother-in law." Rafn slapped Peder on the back. Peder looked at him in confusion.

"What?"

"Certainly you could have found one more willing to warm your bed." Peder turned to stare at Rafn as his meaning became clear. He shrugged.

"I thought I'd been subtle."

"Dagstyrr's eyesight is far too keen."

Peder looked at Dagstyrr and smiled. "So it was you who found me out."

"She is a beautiful woman," Dagstyrr said. "Probably slit your throat while you are sleeping, but beautiful."

They all broke out laughing. "Isn't that the truth," Peder said.

"But you are hooked anyway aren't you my friend." Rafn slapped him on the back.

"So help me God I am." He lost his smile and looked to where the women had disappeared.

Rafn and Dagstyrr exchanged a knowing glance as they also left the training area.

IV

Iceland was a place where people had come to seek the freedom that was too hard to obtain in the lands of their birth. Many had already made a life for themselves on its fertile lands.

The red haired girl stared out her window at the lands beyond the limits of the village her father had built and now ruled. She was lonely and sad. She wanted to seek the freedom that others had achieved so easily, yet had been denied her. She wanted to escape from under her father's rule.

Her dreams haunted her even when she was awake. Of a place she had yet to see, but one that offered her the fulfillment of her hopes. It was all she could think of.

Someday she would reach out past those dreams and seize what she could, when her courage was strong enough that it would not fail her. When her father's eyes were not so watchful and she could flee without fear of capture.

It would happen. She vowed that it would.

The sun disappeared and the land turned to darkness. The red haired girl drew her blanket tightly around her. She fought against the sudden assault of fear that the shadows always brought.

It was this fear that kept her locked more securely than any lock upon her door. Fear of what those shadows hid.

She was a Christian woman and should not believe in spirits in the dark, of Frost Giants in the cold hearts of the mountains and certainly not in trolls lurking off the forest paths. Yet Amma's words haunted her in the nights when storms blew down from the mountains. She could almost hear icy voices in the howling winds.

Laughter rose outside her window. Her heart clenched with a greater fear than that of imaginary forces.

The man's laughter was not born of joy, but of malice. He had cornered an unsuspecting slave girl. One of those her father had brought on a ship from Vestfold. The girl would get no help from the men who turned a blind eye to the man's actions.

It happened so often that no one but her paid it any heed. The girl's whimpers filtered through the closed shutters of her small room. She wanted to go to the frightened girl's aid, but fear paralyzed her. She was a coward and she hated that about herself.

Tears came to her eyes at the brutal sound of their coupling. The girl's cries were silenced with a slap of a hand against her. Grunts of violent pleasure grew louder until the man reached his climax.

The red-haired woman began to tremble. There were far worse things than evil spirits in the world…

…there was the man her father would force her to marry.

CHAPTER 9

The maid Isibel filled a bath for Joka behind a privacy screen in her bed chamber. She felt uncomfortable having a servant wait on her like this. The maid didn't seem to enjoy it any more than Joka did.

She kept shooting Joka a look of hostility. The maid was easy to ignore. She stayed out of the small woman's way until she finished setting up the soap and drying cloths. It had been Seera who'd insisted on the bath. Joka would have been content to find a private stream somewhere.

It should have pleased her that Seera and her family thought so highly of her, but she had grown up a poor girl in a small village where women were treated with scorn. She had become fiercely independent since her escape from the place of her birth. Such independence ruled her and being waited on felt wrong.

She watched Isibel leave before she undressed. Joka stepped into the hardened leather tub and began undoing her braids. She washed her hair and scrubbed her skin and had to admit the bath felt nice.

She sat back and relaxed in the water's warmth. When it began to cool she climbed out to dry herself. She was just wrapping the drying sheet around her when Isibel returned carrying a tray of food.

Joka realized that she was indeed hungry after her workout with Peder. She watched as Isibel, with little care, dropped the tray on the table.

"Lord Peder asked that I bring you something to eat. He said your appetite should be plenty worked up by now." Bitterness laced her voice.

"Thank you for bringing it to me." Joka tried to be polite but this woman's attitude was annoying her.

"Is it true that Lord Peder gave you a sword as a gift?" Isibel's eyes narrowed and it was plain to Joka what the woman thought of such a gift.

"He did."

"Why would he do such a thing?"

She shrugged. She felt no need to explain anything to this maid. In truth she wasn't sure why he had and she didn't want to examine it too closely.

"He thinks of you as a man then?" Isibel brightened at the idea. Her anger had to do with Peder then. Joka wondered if the two had some sort of a relationship.

"I don't claim to know what he thinks."

"I will leave you then to eat." Isibel left and Joka breathed easier. She had no patience for jealous tantrums.

She was leaving soon. At the end of the week she would return to the ship and gladly sail to Iceland with Systa and Seera. She would make a new home for herself and Peder would be far from her.

It would be a good thing, because she hated how he made her feel. He could be a very frustrating man and she found herself always on the defensive with him.

Her stomach rumbled. She sat and ripped open a piece of warm bread. She bit into it and was sure she had never tasted anything so good.

II

Joka went for a walk and found her way to a bluff that looked out at the ocean. She could no longer see Dun'O'Tir and she felt her tension ease. It was a relief to find time alone before she was forced to spend days on the sea trapped with so many others. She needed to spend time in the open spaces while she still could.

She felt herself relax. Her longing for solitude was finally fulfilled and her sheer enjoyment of the moment made her too exposed. With her guard down she failed to hear the horse that approached.

Peder was out riding. Needing a break he slid from his horse and hobbled it. He rolled the stiffness from his muscles and was immediately alert when he sensed that he was no longer alone. He crept through the bushes to find Joka staring out at the ocean.

Her eyes were closed and her face at ease. She looked so content. It changed her somehow, made her seem younger, more vulnerable. It pleased him to see her so.

She must have sensed him for she turned and her eyes hardened as they found him. He regretted that.

"Joka," he said. He moved towards her, because he could do nothing else when she was near.

"My lord," she said. He wanted to reach forward and smooth the frown from between her brows.

"I wish you would call me Peder."

"No." She lifted her foot as if to step back, but never moved.

"Why?" His gaze shifted to her lips. Even pinched as they were, they were lush and enticing.

"It is too familiar."

"Would that be so bad a thing?" He lifted his gaze to her thick lashed eyes. For all her hardness there was an appealing femininity to her. He moved closer to her and was sure she would move away, but she stubbornly held her ground.

"Yes," she said.

Peder watched her for any reaction to his presence but could see none. She blocked him out completely. She was so good at that. He wanted to unhinge her. Show her what he could make her feel.

Without stopping to think of the wisdom of what he did, or her reaction, he leaned forward and kissed her. For a moment he imagined that he felt her respond before he felt the dagger that she pressed against his throat.

Peder pulled back and stared down at her. Damn, could she feel nothing at all but hate for any man?

She spoke with such iciness. "You have no need of me for that. You have Isibel." Joka almost choked on the words. Why had she said that? She sounded like a jealous wench.

"Isibel?" Peder looked at her in confusion and then understood. Her face still betrayed none of her emotions so he couldn't tell if it had been a jealous statement or one of contempt. He supposed it was the latter but hoped it was the former. "I admit she was once a lover, but that has ended."

"It matters not to me." She tried hard not to feel pleased by his admission that Isibel no longer shared his bed. She clenched her teeth lest she betray herself with a smile.

"You are good at not caring, aren't you?"

Joka refused to answer his question and simply shrugged her shoulders in reply. He clenched his fists. Damn her for making him feel such a fool. Why did he want so much for her to like him? And why did his heart clench whenever he looked at her. It wasn't as if she'd encouraged him in anyway. Quite the opposite, she had let him know just how she felt about him, and it was not favorable.

"I will go then," Peder said. "I won't force myself upon you."

Joka had mixed thoughts about seeing him walk away. She sensed that she'd hurt his feelings somehow and a part of her felt guilty.

The ship to Iceland couldn't leave fast enough. It would be good to put distance between them. Certainly then her heart would remember how to beat normally again.

III

Seera entered Kata's bed chamber to find her still lying in bed. She'd run into Dagstyrr in the courtyard and he'd been worried that Kata still felt ill even though they'd been off the ship for many days. Seera promised to check on Kata.

Kata struggled to sit up. Seera went to sit beside her, adjusting a sleeping Orn in her arms. "Let me help"

She fixed the pillows behind Kata's head. Seera noticed the platter of untouched food on a bedside table.

"I have no appetite in the mornings," Kata said. "Dagstyrr would feed me in hopes that it will make me feel better and doesn't believe me when I tell him it won't help."

"Are you with child?" Seera watched her friend's pale face.

"I think that is the most likely answer." Kata's eyes shifted to the sleeping baby. "I have not bled in two months. The sickness I feel is enough to confirm it."

"Yet you have not eased your husband's worries by telling him." Seera chuckled.

"I had wanted to be sure. On the ship it could have just been motion sickness. It has been four days since we have been on board and it has only worsened. I think I can safely give him such news."

"Then do so soon. The poor man is beside himself with worry."

"He has been hovering. Though telling him I am pregnant is unlikely to change that, as such news will only make him become more protective."

"It is what men do. The women do the work of carrying the child, while their husbands can only stand back and watch. Feeling useless unnerves them so you will have to show patience."

The women laughed at that. Their mighty husbands could after all be vulnerable. It was something worth seeing.

Orn let out a sudden howl as if he'd been battling a monster in his dreams. Both women looked at the baby and were visibly stunned. He was usually so quiet. Orn kicked his legs to free himself of the blanket that held him prisoner. Seera lifted him so that she held him out in front of her.

"Is there something you need my son?"

Orn stopped his wrestling as soon as he was free of the blanket. He looked at his mother with wide green eyes and both women laughed.

"He will be just like his father," Kata said.

"Then it will be I who'll need a lot of patience." To Orn she said, "Would you like a little cousin to play with; another boy to get into mischief with?"

"Dagstyrr would want a son."

"All men want sons, but I would love to see Rafn with a daughter."

"Can you imagine how protective they would be with daughters?"

"They would be impossible to live with."

IV

Peder returned his horse to the stable and spent time brushing him down. He could easily get a stable hand to do the work for him, but he found the task very relaxing. He was starting to doubt whether or not he should really leave Dun'O'Tir. He was restless, but was that any reason to leave his responsibilities.

If Joka would warm to him in any way he knew his uncertainty would vanish. Without a second thought he would follow her to the ends of the earth. Did that make him a fool? He saw her again as he had first seen her.

It had been raining and Rafn had been locked in a battle to the death with the man who had dared to harm Seera. It had not been Peder's fight and he was forced to stand back and watch. He remembered how his hands had twitched with the need to be useful. To take out his own revenge for what Hwal had done to his sister.

A badly cast spear had landed beside him and he'd twisted around to find Hwal's warrior returning. He'd had no time to react. Joka had engaged the man before he could.

He had been shocked. He recognized her beauty at once. It was haunting and wild. Rain had soaked her and plastered her clothes to a body that was firm and muscular. He had never seen a woman's body that was so strong. She was more woman than any he had ever met.

He'd been impressed by how fiercely she'd fought. He'd not wanted to interfere in her fight. He had stayed close enough that had her life been threatened he could end the man's life at once. The warrior had not bested her and she had taken his life with courage.

It had left a damning effect on him.

Peder turned at the sound of someone approaching him. Isibel had managed to enter the stables and make it to his side before he was aware of her. He frowned at his lack of awareness.

"What do you want woman?" He had little patience left for this small irritating nuisance.

"I came to find you, my lord." Her musical voice which had once been appealing now it grated on his nerves.

"Speak quickly, then be gone." He spoke harshly and this time she did react to his cruelty. He felt ashamed at having spoken so to her. It had been his own selfishness to bring her into his bed. He made an attempt to soften his tone. "I am sorry, I have much on my mind."

This brought the smile back to her face. "I heard Jakob speaking to one of the other servants. He said that you were leaving. Is it true?"

"It is," Peder said. "I have decided to join my sister. I have an interest in seeing this new land to the north which the bards in the King's court have so recently begun spinning stories about."

"Will you return?" She looked up at him with eyes that reminded him of a doe. When they began to mist over he had to look away.

"That is yet to be decided."

"Don't go, my lord." She whispered and he had to strain to hear her words. "I would miss you."

Peder lifted her chin so that he could once again look upon her face. He saw a woman who was so very young. He recognized that she had foolishly grown to love him. Again he cursed himself for allowing it to happen.

"Isibel." He tried to keep his voice gentle. "Find yourself a boy with a good heart and marry him, for you deserve that kind of happiness."

Isibel looked at him as if he'd given her a death sentence. The hurt was plain to see. "But..." she began to protest but he held a finger to her lips.

"Do not say it." He sensed that she was about to tell him how she felt. "Save it for that boy you will one day call husband."

Tears spilled down her face. He thought of bringing her into his arms and comforting her, but that would only make it worse. Instead he watched her turn and with a broken heart she ran from the stable.

V

Peder left the stable to find Rafn in the area where they had set up temporary dwellings. Children ran amongst the tents chasing each other and the few dogs they had brought with them.

One small boy raced by him and would have collided with Peder had he not reacted quickly and caught the boy before he tripped. The boy stared up at him and smiled and Peder could see that his front teeth were missing. That told him the boy must be about six, the age when children began to lose their teeth.

He spotted Rafn talking with Dagstyrr and Hachet just past the rows of tents. He made his way to his brother-in law's side. "You need any help?"

"Not at all," Rafn said. "Hachet has everything in such good order the rest of us are rarely needed."

Hachet smiled at the compliment. "I do my best my lord." To Peder he said, "That was an impressive display that you and Joka showed us all the other day."

"She is good isn't she," Peder said.

"I admit I was surprised. None of us really believed she could use a sword with such ability."

"I have never seen anyone more graceful." Dagstyrr spoke up to add his opinion.

"I trust the men will treat her differently from now on," Rafn said. Peder couldn't tell if it was meant as a question or a command.

"She will most definitely be shown more respect." Hachet nodded.

"I am glad to hear it," Peder said.

"Does she know that you are joining us?" Rafn asked, for surely Peder's reasons for going had a lot to do with her.

"I saw no reason to inform her."

"You want her to be surprised?" Rafn chuckled.

"I don't believe she would care either way."

"Not warming up to you?" Dagstyrr asked.

"Warm is not the word I would use to describe her feelings towards me."

"Completely immune to your charms is she?" Rafn elbowed him in the side making him flinch. His brother-in law forgot his own strength.

"I'm pretty sure she doesn't think I have any."

"I have another matter I need to discuss with you before we sail." Rafn quit teasing Peder and turned to serious matters.

"What is that?"

"I was unable to find a willing blacksmith to join us."

"And you wish me to see if one of mine might be interested in making the trek?" Peder asked.

"I would indeed."

Peder dismissed himself and went in search of Berthor. The man was young and unmarried. He might wish to leave his father's forge and search out a new life elsewhere. It was certainly worth a try.

CHAPTER 10

The morning came with unexpected warmth that had everyone in good spirits. Systa stood with Joka on the beach as the men continued loading the last of the supplies and animals onto the ship.

Berthor agreed to leave Dun'O'Tir and join Lord Rafn on his quest. Joka guessed the blacksmith was close in age to her. He also had the exuberance that came with youth. An adventure into the unknown was enough to spark his interest.

Joka looked up the hill to Dun'O'Tir for the tenth time since coming down to the beach. Systa glanced at her with a knowing smile.

"Come he will when time to go," Systa said.

"I don't know of who you speak."

"He comes for you," she said even as Joka spotted Peder heading down the hill towards them. She glanced away in case he caught her staring at him.

Peder walked passed her without a glance and went straight to Rafn who was guiding the first people into the small boat that would take them out to the anchored knarr. Rafn smiled in greeting and the two exchanged words that Joka was unable to hear.

The first load of passengers headed out to the ship and Joka hung back watching. Seera and Yrsa joined the sisters. The young girl was proving to be a good nursemaid for little Orn.

Systa cooed to the baby when he was brought close, which brought a stream of giggles. The Seer's face lit with motherly pleasure and Joka wondered if her sister ever had the desire to have a child. She had never shown any interest towards men, even though her hostility didn't match

Joka's, Systa had her own bad memories to hold her captive.

"Starts our adventure," Systa said.

The women were on the last boat to leave. Seera wanted to wait for her husband. Kata was sitting down on a log close by, with Dagstyrr hovering nearby, waiting until the last to board the rocking vessel. Seera had shared the news that Kata was with child and that Dagstyrr was likely to fuss over his wife the entire journey.

The Eorl of Dun'O'Tir came to stand with Seera and took the baby from Yrsa's arms. "I will miss this little one. He has already taken my heart."

Tears showed in Seera's eyes as she hugged her father. "I love you Papa, don't forget that, even though I am far away."

"I will not. Yet I find it hard to say goodbye to my children. It will be lonely here without either of you to keep an old man company."

"I know Papa," Seera said.

Joka's gaze sharpened on Airic and was sure she'd misunderstood his words. He didn't possibly say that both his children were leaving. That made no sense. Peder would still be there. She looked at Peder who was still with Rafn. He was a man that looked quite pleased.

Joka turned to her sister to find Systa watching her closely. "He comes he does, for he can't stay away."

Joka was too stunned to reply. She wasn't possibly telling her that she would be forced to spend this journey on the same ship as Peder. That he would be there in the shadows haunting her through the entire voyage.

The ache inside confirmed her worst fear. He would be there whether she wanted it or not.

II

Peder stood with Seera as they watched Dun'O'Tir disappear on the horizon. He held her hand in understanding of what it meant to actually be leaving it behind. It was the home of their childhood, the place where memories of their mother still connected them to her. It was where their father would continue to stay.

He knew that Seera was please he had joined them. It made the going easier to be together. She had not mentioned Joka, but certainly if Rafn had guessed his desires then Seera had as well. She let the subject lay unspoken between them, for which he was grateful.

Joka had kept her distance since they boarded the knarr. She stayed on the opposite side of the ship with Systa. He had erred badly when he'd tried to kiss her before winning her trust. Now he had no idea if it could even be earned. He had decided to come anyway, because to never see her again was far worse than being hated by her.

III

"How is Kata?" Rafn asked Dagstyrr who had come to join him on the starboard side of the ship.

"I've convinced her to lie down in our sleeping compartment and get some sleep. Systa gave her something to ease the morning sickness."

"And how are you my friend? Do you anticipate fatherhood with excitement or dread?"

A genuine smile came to Dagstyrr's face. "How could I be anything but excited? Perhaps I will have a son and our boys will grow to be as close as you and I."

"I would like that. A nephew."

"The sky has become thick with clouds." Dagstyrr motioned and both men looked to the sky that promised rain.

They followed Pictland's coastline to the north, but Rafn predicted tomorrow they would leave it behind. There would be two sets of islands they would need to pass before reaching Iceland. A great deal of time would be spent on the open water, which could be treacherous if they ran into bad weather.

A group of children were laughing as they bailed the water that collected in the bottom of the knarr. It was something that needed to be kept up so the ship would not reach a point where sinking was a threat. The children enjoyed the task of filling the buckets and dumping them overboard. They made a game out of it, trying to see who could fill and dump their water the fastest.

Rafn laughed and Dagstyrr followed his gaze to the children. There was a time when both men would not have paid attention to their play. Fatherhood made them more watchful of the youthful antics taking place onboard the knarr.

"I suppose this means we are getting old," Dagstyrr said.

"Nay, we will be old when our children have made us grandfathers."

"That's when we'll be ancient and decrepit."

"I will never be decrepit. My wife shall have no complaints."

They smiled with the pleasure of two men who were satisfied with their lives and the women they loved. Rafn looked to the horizon as the sun began to set and knew that the future was his to grasp.

IV

Peder had not been able to sleep. Rafn had offered him one of the sleeping rooms below deck but Peder had declined. He figured the women and children would make better use of it. He was content to sleep on deck with the other men.

The air off the water was cold, but he barely noticed. He had his cloak and a heavy wool blanket to wrap around himself to keep the worst of the wind out. It was not the cold that kept him awake, but thoughts of a future he was no longer in control of. He had always known his place in the world. He had always known his duties and his home.

Now he was cast upon the mercy of an undefined future in a foreign land. It was both exciting and terrifying. Peder was trapped in these thoughts when Joka came up on deck. He had noticed that she didn't like being below for long. Preferring as he did the fresh breeze that being on deck offered.

They had left land behind at dusk and had yet to come upon the first set of islands that they would pass. The sky remained heavily clouded but rain had yet to fall. It would though. He could smell it on the air and knew by morning they would get wet. The spaces beneath the deck should offer most of them protection. He had confidence in Rafn's men to see them through the coming storm.

Peder's gaze stayed on Joka as she walked to the railing and stared out at the blackness beyond. She pulled her blanket tighter around her as a sudden gust of wind blew off the water. Impulsively, for around her he had no control over his actions, he went to stand beside her.

She acknowledged his presence with a slight nod and the two simply stood there for some time before she broke the silence.

"How do you maintain a northerly direction when the clouds are too dense to see the stars?"

"Hachet, the man working the steering ore on the starboard side, has what he calls a sun stone. The stone changes color depending on which direction it is faced. One of the colors means north."

"So as long as one knows the correct color you can always find north." Joka avoided looking at him as she spoke, and instead stared out in the direction that the ship sailed. It was encouragement enough that she was speaking to him and Peder knew he'd better not do anything to scare her off again.

"Yes," he said. "Have you sailed much?"

"This is the first ship I have been on."

"I would not have guessed."

"There were ships that came to the village where I grew up. Mostly fishing vessels, but at times a drekar would come into port. I thought them the most magnificent things with their dragon heads rising from both sides."

"Your father never took you out on one?" He wanted to know more about this woman, anything that she was willing to tell him, but he felt he had gone too far when he mentioned her father, for a fierce look came to her eyes. It wasn't the cold hard stare he'd become used to, but one full of fire and hatred. She surprised him when she answered.

"My father did not own such a fine ship. He wasn't a warrior with noble blood who had pledged his allegiance to any Jarl. He served himself and was loyal to no one. All the men of my village were the same. The only time they were not asserting their strength was when the warriors sent by King Harald came to collect taxes.

It was the only time I had ever seen them defer to anyone and afterwards they were always in a very bad mood. As if they knew that they would never be as strong as those men and as a result the women usually paid for it when the warriors left."

Joka glanced at him as if she had forgotten he was there and knew she had said too much. It caught her off guard that she had opened up to him and the coldness returned to her eyes and he was shut out once again.

And still she stayed by his side in silence and they each watched the black waves as the ship sailed through the water. Her words caused Peder to think back on the strange man who'd approached him that last day in Skiringssal. His words echoed strongly in Peder's memory.

Had Joka really killed her father? Somehow he didn't believe the answer to that was a simple one.

The knarr rocked gently. A soft spray blew up from the sea and Peder felt its salty moisture on his lips. Peder realized he felt happy in that moment. He was a long way from winning Joka's trust, but she stood with him of her own accord. Had even opened up to him, if however briefly.

Somehow it was enough...for now.

V

Systa came up on deck when all but a few slept. She had to weave her way past men sleeping in every corner in hammocks. The warrior Leikr was working the rudder oar and nodded as she passed by. She smiled but continued on her way.

A few drops of rain began to fall. Their icy wetness was refreshing and she lifted her head so she could feel them on her face.

The dream had come again and woken her from her sleep. There was a vague sense that another like her was out there. She had felt the cold stone walls of his home that was somehow a part of the earth itself. It had taken her some time to realize that he was within a cave.

She'd been able to smell the dampness of a thin trickle of water that ran down the back wall of the cave. The strong scent of moss touched her from where it grew on the surrounding rock.

The walls of the cave were ragged and sharp, but for one side that had been chipped away at until it was smooth. A faint drawing had been etched onto the surface, but Systa hadn't been able to make it out.

Rabbit was roasting on a stick above the fire. It had been skinned and the raw meat was being turned so as not to burn. Its aroma was so strong that her stomach had rumbled.

She had focused on the blurry shape that sat before the orange flames and could not bring it into focus. It was him. The loneliness that seeped from him was so strong she had cried out in agony in her sleep. His face was nothing more than a blur that still swam before her vision.

His soul was so warm and pure, so beautiful. She'd reached with desperation to join with him, but a barrier kept them apart. He didn't have the power that she did. He didn't know she was there and could not welcome her into him.

They would meet in the flesh one day. This she knew with certainty. She had but to wait until he came to her.

A sudden shiver ran through her as a dark image formed. It was not something anyone else could see, but it was a bad omen for it spoke to her of death.

Joka's face flashed before her. Her sister was angry with rage and blood covered her blade, the same one Peder had given her. Although its power was strong it didn't appear to be helping her sister who was visibly weakening.

An unknown danger was before her. Systa tried to see through the shadows to the threat, but the darkness held her back.

VI

In the mountains of Iceland the short man sat crouched in his small cave, a fire burning inside the opening. He had wrapped a fur around him for warmth as he listened to the cries of the Frost Giants as they howled down the mountain bringing with them a bitter storm.

It came as freezing rain that chilled him. He threw more wood on his fire and watched as the flames leapt up. It kept him safe from the Giants that dwelled in the highest peaks of the mountains.

The dwarf felt most lonely at these times when he was trapped inside his cave. At least when he wandered the hills collecting his plants and setting snares for small animals, he could keep his mind distracted. He glanced to the back of his cave where racks had been set to dry the variety of plants and roots he had spent hours collecting during the summer.

Most were medicines, others were herbs to flavor his food. He didn't know why he had need for so much, but it was fear of the loneliness that kept him busy. He was not a hunter, his legs and arms were too short for him to learn the skills needed. He had not developed the strength to thrust a spear, hold a sword, or the arm length to cast an arrow from a bow.

But he did know magic. It had woven itself into his life at a young age. There had been an ageing witch that had taught him before Bekan, the village leader, had converted to Christianity and forced all those who dwelled within his village to do the same.

BITTER PASSAGE

The witch had not obeyed him and continued to sacrifice to the Norse gods. Bekan had tied her to a post and built a fire around her. She died in agony as fire seared her flesh and the smoke robbed her of her breath.

The dwarf had hidden behind the red-haired girl who'd been his companion. She'd stood stiffly and emotionless, even though the short man had known that she was scared. Bekan was her father and a cruel man. He thought to use the new religion to bring the people more firmly under his rule.

There was a monk who lived in the village and had a hand in Bekan's conversion. The dwarf had never liked the priest because the man had stared at him as if he were something evil.

The priest had told Bekan that the short man, with his stubby arms and legs who had grown no taller than an average man's waist, was nothing more than a spawn of the devil and not welcome in God's kingdom. He'd advised the leader to execute the dwarf in the same manner he had the witch.

The red haired girl had heard them talking and she'd warned the dwarf in time. She hid him in a farmer's wagon and he'd stayed there until he was well away from the village.

With only a small pack of supplies and a fur to keep him warm, he hurried on his short legs as fast as they would take him and disappeared into the mountains. He was met by the shadows that lurked in the forest. The ensuing loneliness was hard to bear.

He suddenly looked further into the depths of his cave. Uneasiness gripped him and he felt something that he could not explain, a sense that there was something in the darkness that he could not see.

That he was being watched.

CHAPTER 11

Joka could no longer see in the distance the last set of islands they had sailed around. As the morning progressed, all that was visible were threatening dark clouds and violent waves.

The gentle rain that had come and gone, gave way to a tempest. Fighting against the strong winds, the women scrambled to the lower decks with the children.

As the ship creaked and moaned, Joka watched as two men climb up the mast. They struggled to tie the lowered sail so the wind would not get in under it. Joka held her breath as they fought slick ropes and rain that felt like ice chips when it stung exposed skin.

The rocking boat threatened to knock the men from their perch and Joka let out a sigh of relief when having completed their task their feet once again touched the deck.

Rafn yelled orders and men appeared with buckets. Not wanting to be trapped in the stale dankness below deck, Joka went to help.

Dagstyrr appeared, his hair plastered to his face, and shoved a bucket into her hand, which she took and bent to the task of bailing. Large waves reached high and spilled over the rails to pool in the bottom of the ship.

Day turned to night as they worked without pause. As the men grew weary, the women began to work alongside their husbands, brothers and sons. Joka felt a sense of wonder at how they worked together.

"They follow your lead." Peder had to yell to be heard.

The ship tilted and he had to fight to find his footing on the slippery deck. He managed to stumble to the rail and dump his pail of water over the side, only to have the wind throw it back in his face.

Joka laughed as a sputtering Peder tried to wipe the water from his eyes, a useless effort with so much rain. His blue eyes met hers and locked. Something clenched in the vicinity of her heart.

Screaming above the wind she strove to reclaim the humor. "Perhaps you should pay attention to the direction of the wind."

"With this ever changing wind, that is good advice."

The ship rose up the next wave only to drop suddenly down the other side of it, rocking the boat sideways.

Joka slipped on the wet wood and reached for the rail, only to miss and fall into Peder. Strong arms wrapped around her.

She heard his voice close to her ear. "Perhaps it is time for you to rest."

She pushed from him and found her own footing. She stared at him in anger. "Have you rested?"

A smile touched his face. "Nay, I haven't."

"Then why should I?"

Peder lifted his hands in defeat. "I meant no offense."

The knarr dropped again, leaving a sick feeling in Joka's stomach. This time Peder was knocked off balance and landed in her arms. Her own unsteady feet gave way and they landed together on the deck.

Peder stared down at her in shock. She shoved at him to get up. Laughter shook through him as he rolled to the side and lay on his back beside her.

As they both stared up into the rain, Joka thought with relief that it was lessening, even as the man beside her continued to laugh.

She pushed to her feet and reached a hand towards him. With a firm grip she yanked him up.

He was close, very close, and as his eyes flicked to her mouth she was certain he was going to kiss her. One moment, then two passed and neither moved. The smile slipped from his face and he took a step back.

Without a word he grabbed his bucket and returned to the job at hand.

The storm lasted midway through the night before it died and the wind dropped completely. The sky cleared to fill with millions of bright stars. The last of the bailing was completed and men and women alike dropped down where they were and slept.

Peder led Joka to a free spot beneath the deck and coaxed her into lying down. She was too exhausted to offer him any resistance. He found her a dry blanket and draped it over her.

She knew she should protest but her muscles ached and her mind had gone numb hours before. She hadn't been completely unaffected by Peder working beside her, as it had left her more off balance than the storm.

"Sleep." His whispered order worked its way through her muddled mind. She was going to refuse, but the blanket he rolled and placed beneath her head was so comfortable that before she knew it sleep claimed her despite her stubborn desire to deny him.

II

Peder lay beside Joka and watched her. She was peaceful when she slept. Her face was so smooth and he longed to reach out and feel the softness of her skin. Her damp hair had turned into a mass of curls. Moisture still glistened on the ends of her eyelashes and her cheeks.

She looked as if the storm had swallowed her and then spit her back out. He thought she had never been more beautiful. A fool he was indeed, but not to be drawn to her would be even more foolish.

When he had first seen her among the men with a bucket in her hand he had been shocked that she was not safely below deck with the other women. Then he realized that she wouldn't be. Not her. She would be angry that he even thought for a moment that she should be in the safe confines of the sleeping compartments.

He'd felt pride in her as she worked beside the men and he saw more than one man stare at her in admiration. They were coming to respect this warrior woman. As the storm raged on Joka was not the only woman to brave the storm. The men were quick to accept their strength and their presence by their side.

It was an insight that Peder had failed to notice before. That perhaps it was not such a new thing for women to work beside their men.

Joka shifted in her sleep. Peder stared at her and understood that what had started as desire for her was quickly growing into a feeling he was not familiar with, but he was coming to recognize as love. If only he could reach over and wrap her in his arms.

Not with this woman could he be so forward. He still remembered the cold steel of the dagger she had pressed against his throat when he'd kissed her back on the cliff at Dun'O'Tir. Yet in recent days she had relaxed around him. There had even been laughter. Could he hope?

Peder knew it was still too fragile a thing to risk touching her. Damn, this woman had him bound in a string of knots that he had no way of untying. He didn't pull her into his arms as he wanted, but his eyes closed content just to be beside her.

III

Joka slept soundly for a few hours before the nightmare hit. It was more of a memory really. One she hadn't had in a very long time. She had mistakenly thought herself immune to the fear of the past.

She was just a girl again crouched in the corner of her dwelling. Her father had come in and grabbed her mother by the hair and dragged her outside. His words trailed back to reach her and she cringed because she was at an age when she'd just learned what they truly meant.

"The King's warriors are here. One has requested you. Tonight you will warm his bed."

Joka had cried and Systa's arms wrapped around her in comfort. "Hush, if father hears he will be mad," she had whispered into Joka's ear. Joka stopped sobbing but she couldn't control the tears that wet her face.

Sometime later her mother had returned and her father followed her inside. He was angry, very angry. His fist struck out and hit her mother. Then he began to kick her and his foot found the tender parts of her body until she cried for him to stop.

He never did.

Systa dragged her further into the corner, behind the bed they shared. She could hear the rats that crawled behind the walls. Their claws scratching on the floor seemed to grow louder, distorted by the memory of a child.

Before he left he beat her mother until she lost consciousness. The girls had crept from the shadows and gone to help her. She was too heavy to move. They had tried, but they were yet too small. Systa put a pillow beneath her head and a blanket over top of her.

Joka had stared at the door her father had left through and sent her dark thoughts to find him. Thoughts of how she hated him, how she wished him dead. The tears dried as she vowed someday that he would get what he deserved.

They were such dark dangerous thoughts for a girl to have.

Joka woke suddenly and sat upright still caught in the snares of her dream. Peder came instantly awake beside her and she was confused by his presence.

Concern shone in Peder's eyes. He reached out in comfort to touch her face with his hand.

Joka drew back at once. She stared at his hand as if it were a living serpent meant to harm her.

"Don't," she said.

"Are you alright?"

The claws of the past still clung to her. She needed to climb free of its embrace. She averted her eyes lest he saw too much. "I'm fine."

"Joka…"

"No," she cut him off. He had no right to ask about the things that she meant to keep private.

His expression remained worried and she hated his concern. It made her feel…well she just didn't know what… nevertheless, it made her nervous. She got to her feet and realizing they were just outside the sleeping compartment used by Systa she opened the door and disappeared behind it.

Peder was left to stare at the closed door.

IV

Kata was miserable. The storm had her so queasy that she couldn't keep herself from continuously vomiting. Blessedly the winds had stopped and the ship swayed only lightly now. She had argued with Dagstyrr to allow her up on deck so that she could get some fresh air to help her feel better.

She looked up to see the sun rising on the horizon. With the darkness creeping back to allow the morning light, everything seemed less frightening. Dagstyrr stood by her side and kept glancing towards her to make sure she was fine. He meant well but she wished he would go find something else to do.

The animals in the open hold had quieted. They had been forced to stand through the storm. There'd been no room for them in the spaces beneath the stern and prow decks. She had seen Rafn checking on them earlier to make sure they had fared well and he'd seemed pleased when he'd left them.

She turned to see Seera climbing up on deck with the baby and Yrsa. Her sister-in law spotted Kata and joined her. Orn gurgled gleefully in Seera's arms as if there had never been anything to worry about.

"You alright?" Seera asked.

"Better now," Kata said. "How did Orn manage through the storm?"

"It didn't even frighten him." Seera laughed. "Much of his father is in this one. He probably thought it was entertainment for his benefit."

"A little warrior already." Dagstyrr rubbed Orn's head. The boy reached out a hand and grasped his uncle's finger. He brought it to his mouth and bit down and even without teeth caused a little pain.

"Ouch!" Dagstyrr yanked his finger back. "I might still need that, little warrior." The baby giggled with delight in discovering a new game even as he reached to grab Dagstyrr's finger back.

"We will stay with Kata." Seera said to Dagstyrr. "I'm sure there are things that need seeing to."

"I believe I am being dismissed." He looked at his wife with the pretense of being shocked.

"I'm fine, go." Kata touched his face and tried to smooth the worry lines from the corners of his eyes.

"A man knows when he's not wanted. That's fine, I'll leave. But don't overdo yourself. Don't forget to rest."

"I won't."

They watched Dagstyrr walk away before Kata spoke again. "Thanks for that. He was barely giving me room to breathe."

"Once we are settled he should improve."

"I hope so," Kata said. She turned to Yrsa, "And how did you manage the storm?"

"It was frightening, but Fox came and checked on us often enough that he put me at ease."

"The two of you have grown close," Seera said.

Yrsa blushed. "Aye, he is a good man. He is so gentle and kind."

"He is that." Kata nodded. "It pleases me that he has found happiness with you. He was sad for so long after losing his family."

"He misses them still," Yrsa said.

"Then it is good that he has you to talk to."

"Let me take the baby." Yrsa held out her hands. "I would take him to see the animals now that they are calm."

"He would enjoy that. Thank you," Seera said. She handed Orn over to his nurse and was grateful that Yrsa had become so close to the baby. It was a great help to Seera.

"Come sit." Seera motioned Kata over to a wooden box that had been secured to the deck.

The two women sat together and looked around the crowded ship. There didn't appear to be much damage. Kata watched as two men climbed the mast and began to unfurl the sail.

The wind had remained calm and failed to catch the sails with the strength that was needed to propel them forward. Kata looked to Rafn and saw that he was frowning.

V

"We won't go far without any wind." Rafn paced back and forth. Lines of concern wrinkled his forehead at this turn of events.

"Certainly the god Loki is playing his tricks upon us. First winds that are too strong and now none at all," Dagstyrr said.

"Hachet!" Rafn yelled to the man who kept the ship in order. "Collect the least tired of the men and set them to rowing until the wind picks up."

"Aye my lord."

They watched as a dozen men picked up the oars and began to use them. The oars worked differently than the ones in the drekars. The deck was higher off the water and the oars longer. Instead of sitting to row, the men had to walk two steps forward and then pull the oars towards them while stepping back.

With the oars working and Hachet taking up the position at the styri, the steering oar that was used as a rudder, they were slowly under way once again.

"The winds through the night were mostly from the west and therefore I figure we have been blown off course towards the east," Rafn said.

"And what will that mean to finding our destination?"

"If I am correct, we will come upon the eastern coast rather than the southern."

"I will keep my gaze to the east then." Hachet declared.

CHAPTER 12

After about a week of travel they finally spotted what they believed to be Iceland. They had to turn their direction to the west as Rafn had predicted to reach its eastern shores. As they got close enough to get their first good look at the landscape they were met by a welcome sight.

Fjords that looked so similar to the ones in Vestfold that they at once felt like they were coming home. They traveled in closer to shore and turned north following the coastline until they spotted a village which they could reach by veering into an inlet.

A good size port had been built in the inlet for which they were grateful and they were able to bring the knarr right up to the docks. They were met by hundreds of curious people.

Rafn ordered that everyone stay on board until he had requested permission to come ashore. Rafn took Dagstyrr and Peder with him and left Hachet in charge of the ship.

A man stepped forward to greet them. He was a large man with a lot of facial hair, but he had kind eyes. It was to him that Rafn walked.

"You are Jarl?" asked Rafn and the man smiled.

"We have no Jarls here. We have a counsel of men, of which I am a representative, and have been appointed leader of this village."

"And what do you call this village?"

"It is Seyois," the man said. "I am Ari. Traders are most welcome here."

"Thank you Ari, but we are not traders. I am Rafn Vakrson and we seek free land to settle on."

A rumble went through the crowd at the recognition of Rafn's name.

Ari's eyes grew large in surprise and he had to clear his throat before he could continue.

"The Raven?" Disbelief and awe laced his question.

"Some have called me that," Rafn admitted. "It is who I am in battle, not the man who has travelled far from his home. I am simply in search of a new place to settle."

"You are warlord of Skiringssal, your brother is the Jarl there…what need do you have for a new home?" Ari stared at him with a stunned expression.

"Even lords get tired of answering to a King."

"It is just that most of us here are common folk. We are farmers, fishermen, masons, blacksmiths and such. We do have our share of warriors, but none from among the highest nobility."

"I hope you will not hold that against me."

"You will have to understand that the laws here are different from the lands of our birth. We do not answer to a King, Jarls or even warlords."

"I don't come here to change that. I am not a conqueror, but an explorer. I wish only to live in peace."

"Those words are strange coming from a Viking warrior such as yourself, who has been the subject of many stories of war."

"I am only fierce when it is demanded of me. I do not seek it out. I defend my own to the death if necessary, but I have no squabble with innocent, peaceful people."

"That is good to hear."

Ari's glance shifted between the two men that stood at Rafn's side. Dagstyrr smiled to ease the man's worry.

"These are my brothers-in law. Dagstyrr has always acted as my second in command and is now married to my sister. The other man is my wife's brother, Lord Peder of Dun'O'Tir."

"The fortress by the sea?" Again the man's voice was touched with awe. "We had not thought to have such noble men amongst us."

"As I said before, we are peaceful travelers and wish only to find somewhere yet unsettled to make a new home."

Two men joined Ari and were introduced as Hvalr and Olef. "Stay my lords, feast with us this night and we will draw you a map to a place that has not yet been claimed. It is good land to the north and should be to your liking."

"We thank you for your hospitality and we accept your invitation gladly. We have women and children aboard that grow weary of the ship."

Ari looked at the large knarr and smiled. "All are welcome."

II

Ari and the other villagers went out of their way to produce a feast worthy of a king. Rafn's reputation was known by everyone. The warriors who guarded and defended the village of Seyois each had to meet the mighty warlord of legend.

Seera walked at his side with their son. It gave the people a glimpse of the man behind the stories, the man who was simply a husband and father. It made him more approachable and many found their way into his presence that night. Seera had to restrain a laugh at seeing her husband so flustered by all the attention.

Joka caused an altogether different kind of stir when she left the ship. She kept her head high and her face hard. She would not give up her tunic and trousers to make these people feel more comfortable. She went among them as she would any other. Her sword she kept strapped to her back and her dagger remained on her belt.

Systa was with her. They were a contrast, the two sisters. One small and soft, the other tall and solid, but each was deadly in their own way. Joka used strength and skill, but Systa had magic on her side. Any would be foolish to cross the woman many had labeled a witch. One thing the two women had in common was beauty.

More than one man turned his gaze to the sisters as they strode amongst them. Yet the women held themselves apart and the men sensed they were not so easy to approach.

The feast had been set outside. The great hall was too small to accommodate the large number. It was nice to be out in the warm air as all too soon winter would have them trapped within the confines of their dwellings.

Peder who'd been hanging back watching how Joka was received by the villagers, moved up to join her and Systa. "Their leader has invited us to join him. Seera would want you there as well."

"Come we will." Systa answered for Joka was scowling at him. Peder wasn't sure what had happened, but the fragile peace they had briefly found on board the ship was gone. Ever since the storm had passed Joka had distanced herself even more than she had before.

She'd been avoiding him as much as she could on the ship. He'd not had the opportunity to catch her alone, finding no chance to speak with her. Perhaps she was on the defensive because they were among so many strangers, but Peder sensed it had far more to do with him.

He led them to the table where Rafn, Seera, Dagstyrr and Kata were already seated. Yrsa was there as well with the baby and the boy Fox was seated beside her. Peder had been seeing them together more and more often. They looked at each other in a way that made Peder jealous. It was silly, really. Why would a strong, confident man as he be jealous of the boy and girl. They were barely sixteen.

Ari rose from where he was sitting, his eyes full of appreciation for Joka. Scowling, Peder introduced the sisters to him before sitting down to their meal.

Servants came forward with platters of food that were set before them on the long wooden table. Mugs of ale were passed around. Peder made sure he was seated beside Joka even though she was ignoring him, but she was too close to their host for his liking. Ari's interest was far too obvious and Peder found his teeth clenching and his appetite gone. When Ari spoke, Peder's irritation grew.

"May I ask why a woman would carry a sword?" Ari asked what many had been curious to know since she'd walked off the ship.

"And why should a woman not be able to carry a sword?" Joka asked. Peder could see the tensing of her body and the defiance in her posture. Ari laughed in response.

"I see no reason why one shouldn't if she chose to do so," Ari said. "I have just never met one who wanted to."

"Now you have," she said. Peder felt the sharp cut of her words.

"I would like to see you use it." Ari's invitation was blatant, putting Peder on the defensive. Peder met the man's gaze. He sent Skahi's leader a silent challenge.

"She uses it extremely well."

Two stallions might look at each other as these two men did and Joka was not impressed.

"Come sister," she said. "The night is late and these men bore me."

Peder looked suddenly at Joka and for a moment their eyes locked. He saw clearly that she was angry. More to the point she was angry with him. He had acted like he had a right to be jealous, and he didn't have to be told that she didn't approve.

She stared at him long enough to get her point across before standing and leaving the bench they shared. Systa rose as well and the sisters melted into the crowd.

Peder was still stunned when he realized everyone was watching him. The entire table had gone quiet. It was only when Ari burst out laughing that everyone's expressions eased.

"She is quite a woman," Ari said. His eyes lit with amusement.

"Yes she is." Peder forced a smile.

Peder looked to the other end of the table to find Seera staring at him with sympathy, confirming that she did know of his feelings. Peder just shrugged at Seera's silent inquiry. It was beyond him to make Joka like him.

Peder raised his mug and drank deeply. He would just have to accept that he'd lost his heart to someone who would never give hers to him.

III

Joka had found a quiet spot away from camp, on the shore a short way from the docks where the knarr was anchored. It was dark but for the thin slice of moonlight that reached her. She was not afraid of the dark for it had often hidden her from the true cruelties of the world.

She found a boulder on which to sit and grabbed a handful of rocks as she sat. One by one she tossed them into the water and watched them disappear into its shadowy depths.

She was restless and confused. Being around so many unknown people always drained her. She preferred solitude and found comfort in the silence that wrapped its way around her. She could only faintly hear the festivities that would likely last until early morning.

She ignored the cheerful laughter and concentrated instead on the waves that washed up beneath her feet. It was a sound that at once comforted her. Even the wind that threaded its way through the trees behind her put her at ease.

She longed for the seclusion of their mountain cottage that had offered them everything they needed and kept them hidden from people. That was the real problem. She would forever feel uncomfortable around others. It was a curse that had lived with her since childhood. She had been incapable of making friends as a child. She was so different from the other little girls, and the boys thought her a freak for being too much like a boy herself.

She recalled there was one boy in particular who had been nasty to her. He hated that she had held her own with him. It had irked him to be bested by a girl. Then she had turned into a woman and he had grown to hate her even more.

Kale had been his name, she recalled. He had once tried to catch her alone and being like all the other men of the village, sought to use his strength to rape her. She had been prepared for him though. She had kneed him so hard between his legs he'd been unable to walk properly for days. He'd been outraged but had not admitted to anyone the real reason why he was limping. He had vowed he would seek his revenge someday.

It had been an empty vow, for he had never been given the opportunity, as Joka's father had beaten her and his strength had been far greater than Kale's. She had been secretly watching as the warriors trained. She had practiced using a stick in place of a sword. She had not been courageous enough to pick up her father's sword and face him. She had waited until the night when he'd passed out from drinking too much mead.

Her mother was already dead. It was not so hard to pick up his knife off the table and stick it through his heart. Taking her father's newly forged sword, she and Systa had disappeared that night and had never returned to the place that had spawned their nightmares.

A twig snapped behind Joka making her surface from her memories. She jumped from the boulder and turned with her dagger already in her hand.

Her arm lowered when she recognized Systa. "Thoughts too deep," Systa said.

"Aye, I was allowing memories to trap me. It is good you have come so that I do not sit here dwelling on them."

"Good man is Peder." Joka stared at her and wondered why she would bring up the lord's name.

"He is but a man, and I have no need for such." Joka knew her words were sharp but Systa had never flinched from Joka's anger.

"Fear him you do."

"I fear no man."

"Fear your heart he will steal."

"It is something I will not allow to happen."

Systa said nothing more. Joka would have to work through her own pain. Only then would she come out the other side and find that loving Peder was not something to fear.

IV

The red haired young woman hid within her room. She had a hard time keeping the tears from her eyes. Her father had just given her the news that she had been dreading. It would seem that her wedding would be next week. Her life would take the next turn and it was beyond her control.

She was perhaps too much of a dreamer. She wanted a marriage based on love, like in the stories told by the skalds. She wanted a man to look at her and she wanted to grow weak in his gaze.

Was it so much to ask to have a man who was both friend and lover, protector and confident?

The tears came then. It was not weakness that set them lose, but frustration. Her father would make her marry the man of his choice. A man she despised and feared. He had lusted after her since joining their village two years earlier. He had small eyes that never held any emotion other than cruelty.

Somehow he had won her father's trust. Perhaps it was because he let her father believe he could order him to do whatever came to his mind.

He had somehow made her father believe that it was his idea that they should marry. It was a nightmare that she was trapped in. She was desperate to claw out of the darkness to discover the light that she could almost reach.

It was there. She felt it in her dream. That dream that carried a hope for something better. Somehow she saw in her future a faceless man. This man was strong and confident, serious but full of passion and tenderness.

The red haired woman shook her head in despair. It was nothing more than a fantasy created in her mind. There was no man with whom she would find comfort and love. There was only the monster she'd be given to.

He would be cruel in their marriage bed she had no doubt of that. He was rough and violent. She recalled that night beneath her window. That he'd chosen that spot on purpose she didn't doubt, because he wanted her to fear him.

She wiped the tears from her face as she spotted her image in a standing mirror that stood in the corner of her room. The white around her hazel eyes had turned red.

She could not stay. She couldn't allow that man to lay his hands on her. Perhaps her dreams were falsehoods, but they encouraged her to do what she had to. She would leave that night when everyone lay sleeping.

Nothing would stop her flight. Nothing! Not even her fear of the darkness. She didn't want to dwell on that, for if she did it would control her and she couldn't allow that to happen. Not if she was going to escape the fate her father had planned for her.

She would not marry Kale!

"Rakel," her mother called as she entered her room. "My daughter, do not cry so." She came to her side and sat with her on the bed. Rakel went into her mother's arms and wept. She drew comfort from her mother's familiar presence.

Her grandmother, Amma, came into the room then. She sat on the other side of Rakel and took one of her hands. Rakel looked down to see the contrast between her smooth hand and Amma's wrinkled and withered one; young and old.

"Marina," Amma said to her mother. "We can't allow this to happen. Rakel deserves more than to be given to that sniveling man. Have you not seen the women he uses? They are beaten to near death half the time."

"What can we do?" Her mother looked defeated. "Bekan will not listen to me. He chooses not to see the kind of man Kale really is. He has been seduced by power and Kale's willingness to do his bidding."

Amma reached out and wiped the tears from Rakel's face. "You are so beautiful child, in body and spirit. I can't allow my son to give you to the likes of Kale. We must make sure you escape tonight."

She loved her grandmother. She always knew the way of Rakel's heart. She would miss her terribly, as she would her mother. She looked from one woman to the next. The ache that came to her chest was almost enough to change her mind.

"Do not think such things," Amma said as if she'd heard the thread of Rakel's thoughts. "We know you love us and we will miss you as surely as you will miss us, but you cannot stay. I have no wish to watch that man beat the life out of you."

"Take only what you must." Her mother spoke up. She hadn't been sure her mother would agree because she was far more afraid of her father than Amma was. Perhaps it was because Amma had borne him and as his mother felt no fear.

Rakel was not close to her father. There had never been any love between them. Bekan had always wanted a son and her mother had given him only one child in all the years they had been married. There had been complications with Rakel's birth that had left Marina unable to have any more children.

Perhaps that is why he had taken Kale into his confidence so easily. It was possible that Bekan was trying to create in Kale the son he never had. In marrying his daughter Kale would become family. The son he should have had.

Rakel cringed at the thought of Kale coming to her bed. Of being made to endure year after year of marriage to him. No matter what spirits lurked off the dark forest paths or deep within the mountains, she would run. She would face giants, trolls, even a dragon to be free of her fate.

"Come child, we must move quickly," Amma beckoned and she knew that now would be her only chance to gain her freedom.

CHAPTER 13

The next morning, with a map supplied by Ari, they were back on board. All they needed to do was follow the coast north and then west until they came to an inlet that Ari had marked on the hand drawn map he'd given Rafn. Much of Iceland had already been claimed by those who had come before them, but Ari assured them that there was a large area of land yet unsettled.

Ari had also promised to mention to the council of men about the new arrivals and have marked in the records that this area now belonged to Rafn and his men. As soon as it was convenient Rafn would need to appear before the council and apply to join it. It was something that would have to be done, but not one that Rafn was looking forward to.

He suddenly wished Valr was with them. He was far better at diplomatic relations than Rafn. Rafn knew how to be a warrior. That was where his strength was, not speaking to a bunch of men. He would need to seek Peder's help. Peder had been trained all his life to take over the running of Dun'O'Tir. He certainly had skills that Rafn sorely lacked.

Seera stood beside him and she slipped her hand into his. He smiled down at her and once again felt lucky he had found her. "How are you fairing?"

"I have no complaints husband. I have been enjoying our adventure and am as anxious as you to see this new land we are to call home."

Rafn pulled her into his arms and kissed her on the head. "I want only to find a safe place where you and our son can be happy."

"We will be happy as long as we are with you." Seera smiled and her green eyes reflected the sun that hung directly overhead.

He thought of the god Thor, whom he had always worshipped and realized he had not thought of him in awhile. He had made a sacrifice to the god before they set sail, but the storm that Thor had placed inside of him was now quiet. Not gone, he knew it would never be that, but it slumbered for the first time since he was twelve.

It had something to do with finding the peace he now enjoyed with Seera and their son. He tightened his grip on Seera, remembering how close he had come to losing them and he never wanted to feel that desperate again.

Seera must have sensed his thoughts for she lifted her head so she could see him and touched his face. "It will be alright my love."

"It will be," he said. He truly wanted to believe it. He was still too much a warrior and a part of him wanted to rebel against such tranquility. It was hard for one who had always lived by the sword to accept that life could be so simple. Here in the wilds of a new land he hoped to find what he searched for. Yet instinct also warned him that it was not going to be easy.

Something lurked just beyond his scope of understanding. He would not share his fears with Seera. She didn't need to worry about something that may only be in his imagination, even if he somehow knew that it would prove not to be.

He caught her gaze. "Come wife, Hachet can control this ship. Let us spend some time alone."

"I would not object to that." Her eyes lit with the promise of passion that had not been fulfilled of late. In her arms all worries would vanish and what was between them would be all that mattered.

They slipped quietly below deck to the sleeping compartment that was theirs. Yrsa and Systa were watching Orn, and as Seera had just fed him, he would be fine for some time yet. Seera closed the door behind them and went into his arms.

II

Joka had watched the tenderness between Rafn and Seera, and noticed as they snuck below deck. She understood and a part of her was jealous of the ease at which Seera went to Rafn's bed. She trusted him. What must it be like to trust a man with both body and soul?

BITTER PASSAGE

Sharp images flashed uncontrollably in her mind of her father, in plain sight of the girls, forcing her mother. He was usually drunk and rough. Joka had never seen anything that brought joy.

It had been the same for every woman in the village. Men groped them at will and never paid much attention to privacy. Women simply had to endure the best they could and give up any pride that they might have had. Joka had not seen that they had any and such degradation was something she had no desire to endure.

Systa had been given to entertain more than one man by their father. Joka was sure that was when she had started to learn the power of seid magic. It gave her some measure of control. It was not long before the men she'd been forced to spend a night with would be violently ill the next day. The men soon understood that Systa was the cause and though they couldn't prove it, they stopped asking for her.

Joka had no such magic so she had turned to strength to be her protector. She knew that no man or woman in that village would save her from the same fate as the other women. She would have been traded to men, or forced to marry a man like Kale.

It was good that they had left when they did. It was good that her sword sang in her hand and she was not afraid to use it.

Thank the goddess who had led them. A feast in her honor was needed once they were settled for she would not be forsaken.

Joka's attention was drawn again from her memories to find Peder standing beside her. She hadn't even heard him approach and silently cursed her lack of awareness. It was dangerous to feel so comfortable that she failed to pay attention.

"It will not be long now," Peder said.

"Nay." She stiffened in response to his closeness.

"Have I done something wrong?" His question surprised her.

"You have done nothing." She would not turn to face him, even as he leaned in closer to her.

"I thought we had at least found friendship, but you are back to hating me?"

Joka steeled herself to speak the words that she needed to say to make him go away. She felt the lie in them even as she spoke.

"I don't hate you lord, I have no feelings one way or the other for you." Despite her best efforts she met his gaze and saw the hurt reflecting in them. Damn it why did he pursue her? What was in it for him?

"I see." His eyes clouded over and she felt him retreating from her. She should have been glad, but a pain grew in her chest that she had never before experienced. "Is it too much for you to just be my friend?"

"I am not so good with friends." The words were out before she could stop them and she wondered why she felt compelled to tell him.

Peder stared at her for a long time as if he was trying to see past her defenses and she found this very unnerving. She had no wish for him to see her vulnerabilities. Why was she finding it hard to breathe?

"I would be a good friend, if you would just give me a chance," he said. He didn't wait for a reply, but left her to stare after him wondering why he tried so hard.

III

Night came and the knarr continued to follow the coast line that was leading mostly to the west. It didn't go by unnoticed. Three men on horseback spotted its dark shape on the horizon.

They turned their horses inland and headed for the village of Skahi. Once they were safely within its limits, they went to find Bekan with their news. They found him in the great hall with his future son-in law. He was not in a good mood when they went to speak with him.

"Have you found my errant daughter yet?" he asked.

"No sir, we have not," answered the warrior Onnar.

"Then what are you doing back."

"We have seen a ship on the horizon," replied the warrior named Vikkar.

"A ship?" Kale glared at them. "We have seen ships before. You have stopped your search for Rakel because of a ship?"

"It was a large knarr headed west. I thought Bekan would want word of it at once."

"Traders?" Bekan perked up at the thought. He loved to trade. He had a collection of exotic things that had been brought from the far reaches of the world.

"If they are traders they will journey up the river to find us," Kale said. "What is important now is finding Rakel."

"She is just a woman." Danr scowled. He thought it a waste to expend energy looking for this woman, even if she was Bekan's daughter. There was also a part of him that understood why she had fled and hoped that she would succeed.

Kale sneered in anger but he was not foolish enough to confront the large warrior. Danr was a deadly fighter and as fierce as they came. Kale had no hope of ever being as skilled a sword fighter as Danr. It considered it unwise to anger the man.

Danr stayed in the village of Skahi by choice, not because he feared Bekan as the others did, so Kale swallowed his objections and cursed silently. The man irritated him and he hoped one day he would be in a position to teach Danr a lesson.

"Continue the search for my daughter." Bekan waved his hand in dismissal.

"We will go once we have eaten," Danr said. This seemed to satisfy Bekan but Kale was far from being appeased.

"Rakel will be found, she can't survive on her own," Bekan tried to console him. "The wedding will happen as soon as she is brought back here."

"Good." Kale scowled and Bekan leveled him a look that warned him not to push him.

Kale left the great hall and made his way to the warrior's longhouse. He was reluctantly accepted by the other men with whom he shared the housing. Most didn't like him. He was considered a poor swordsman and none understood why Bekan had given him such respect.

The truth that none of these men knew was that Kale's warrior training had been limited. He was not of noble blood as the other warriors who had come from Vestfold. He hid that fact from them. Back in the old country the entire warrior class was made up of nobility. It did not mean that all warriors were rich, for not all noble houses were as esteemed as others.

Those from the higher ranking noble families tended to be leaders. These men were the warlords and the Jarls that had always ruled over the common folk and carried out the orders for the King. One of common blood had to prove themselves through many tests to be allowed to become a Viking. In this new land the rules were different. Lords did not rule, though old prejudices still existed. Those with noble blood still thought themselves better. Kale knew he would never measure up so he did not admit his failings to the other men.

They sensed it all the same. They treated him with scorn. They spit on the ground before him, taunted him on the training field when he did poorly. What did they expect? He had grown up in a village where the men spent their time drinking and cavorting. They had been farmers and fishermen. The few warriors amongst them kept apart and generally didn't stay long before they sought a better posting.

Most headed for Skiringssal in hopes the great Lord Rafn would train them and invite them into his circle of warriors. Just the name of that man had come to grate on his nerves as he heard story after story about the Vakrson brothers.

Such a man as the Raven would never have welcomed him. It was why he had gladly left the dirt poor village which had spawned him. It was this embarrassment that was his greatest shame.

Blessedly the longhouse was empty. It was still early and many of the warriors were out looking for his promised bride. He didn't believe they did so for him, but knew it was because Bekan had threatened them.

Curse that wench of a woman. She had too much spirit and the thought of beating it out of her delighted him. She needed to be put into her place. It was something that Bekan had failed to do, but Kale would not.

IV

Rakel hid within a hollow dug beneath a tree. She had come so close to being discovered. It was only the appearance of a ship on the horizon that had turned the three warriors back to Skahi. As she had cowered in her hiding place she had heard them speaking of it.

Only once she was sure they were not coming back did Rakel crawl out in the open to catch a glimpse of the ship before it disappeared. It was heading west. Perhaps they would pull in to shore at some point and she could ask them to take her aboard.

It was a slim chance, but she knew she couldn't make it on her own. She wanted to believe she was strong enough, but she didn't have the skills to hunt. She had only a small woman's knife on her and it would not do her much good in her attempt to survive.

BITTER PASSAGE

Once decided, despite the dark that loomed there, she headed deeper into the mountains. She felt fear blossoming when the shadows first appeared. Within those shadows hid wild beasts and evil spirits. Amma had told her so. Her grandmother remembered the old ways before her father had decided the path of Christianity was the way to keep his people in line.

He used the new religion as a weapon, but Rakel had found comfort in the words of the Lord taught by Father Leo. The priest himself was a stern man who Rakel had a hard time trusting, but his words about God's son and the teachings that Jesus had brought to the people had wrung true to her.

She was young when she was baptized and had no memory of the Norse religion they had once followed. Since she was a small child Amma's words about the evils of the pathless forests had scared her.

Such fears were hard to put aside, but they must if she was to escape. She looked back the way she had come and knew she was not safe staying in one place. The warriors wouldn't allow night to slow their search and they certainly would not fear the dark paths of the forest or the spirits of the mountains.

Neither could she afford to let such reservations slow her step. Deeper she went until the trees rose on all sides and only a touch of the stars peeked through the thick canopy of leaves above her.

Her pace quickened. She mustn't think, only move, and move fast. She was so determined to be brave that she failed to hear the noises that rose around her or notice the person who watched her from the path ahead.

A small shape stepped out from the darkness and startled Rakel. She opened her mouth to let out a scream, but some self preservation warned her. Any number of warriors might be close by and something told her that the figure on the path ahead was not one of them.

Whether it was wise or not, she stepped closer before she took the time to think. The figure became clearer and Rakel's mouth opened in shock. Before her stood the dwarf she had known as a child, but who was now clearly a man. A short man, but a man!

"Hadde," she said. She spoke softly, afraid to speak too loud.

"It is I Rakel," he said. "There are warriors ahead, come. I will hide you where they can't find you."

"Thank you." She almost wept with relief.

Hadde led her up a steep cliff. They followed not a path, but went from rock to rock so they left no sign of their passage. A sheer stone wall appeared before them and Hadde led Rakel towards it. He pushed aside a bush to reveal an opening to a cave that she never would have seen.

"It is large enough for both of us." Rakel crawled inside to find, not a large cave, but one that was cozy. It was indeed big enough to hide them both without them being cramped.

"I have longed that we would meet again," Hadde said. He pulled the bush back into place. He lit a few candles to give them a bit of light but told her it was not safe to light a fire until he was sure that the warriors were gone.

"I had thought you long gone from this area." Rakel stared at him in wonder. They had once been friends and she had never thought to see him again.

"I have made a home for myself here." Hadde swept his hand to indicate the area around them.

"All these years alone?"

"Aye." He nodded. The solitude of those years reflected so starkly in his eyes, it made her heart ache.

"You must have been lonely."

"Aye."

They stared at each other for a long time and Rakel could not imagine what kind of bravery it took to live alone.

V

Systa stood at the rail of the ship and watched the dark land that slipped by. Earlier she had felt a really strong connection to the man. He was close. She knew it without a doubt. In the mountains that they passed was his cave.

The wind swirled around her, catching her hair in its fingers and caressing it as a lover might. A soft spray blew off the ocean and washed over her face. She breathed in the salty scent and felt the power of the sea as it gently rocked the ship.

So very rarely in life had she felt excitement, but at that moment it had blossomed in her. She marveled at the oddity of the feeling inside of her. Systa reached out with her mind and found the man. He was in his cave as always. He was stirring a pot of steaming stew over his fire.

There was another…

She was shocked by this. Always before when she'd reached out to him he'd been alone, his loneliness eating away at him. It was not so strong now. In fact she felt his happiness.

What had changed?

Someone else moved in the space next to him. She couldn't make out a face, but she knew it was a woman. Reflected clearly was her copper hair, deepened even more by the flames of the fire.

She had not expected this.

Images of the future flashed before her eyes. The man and woman were running through the mountain paths. Men were chasing them. The woman was scared for her life. She was desperate and hurting.

She feared a man. He would hurt her if she was caught.

Systa knew that this must not happen. The man stumbled and the woman helped him stand. Her shape towered over his. Systa found this odd. The man seemed so much smaller than the woman.

At once she realized the man was a dwarf.

A dark cloud loomed over them and she willed them to continue. For both their sakes the men must not catch them.

They must run to the raven. He would see them safe.

CHAPTER 14

They reached the northeastern point of the inlet Ari had directed them to. A large flat area of pasture land spread before them, perfect for their livestock and their crops. They could build close to the water and have the mountains behind them. They would be able to hunt the wild game within the forested hills. The mountains also offered trees that could be used to build their village.

Rafn was delighted by this new land that was so much like home that they had no problem envisioning a future that could be enjoyed by all. A dock would need to be built, but for now they needed to bring the knarr as close as possible to shore. He navigated them to a spot where they could bring it almost to land and only had a small stretch of water they would need to bring the small boat through.

He immediately ordered his men to work. Rafn and Dagstyrr consulted with the men and a place was chosen close to where they had brought in the ship. It was decided it was a perfect place to build a dock therefore the village would need to be just behind it.

Over the next few weeks the spot of land was transformed. Trees fell to axes and three longhouses were built, one to house the single men, two to house the families and the single women. Rafn, Dagstyrr and Peder each built their own dwellings. They were set apart from the longhouses, but within the circular wall that was being built around the village for protection. Rafn couldn't help but believe that such a defense was necessary. No one argued against his wisdom.

A Great Hall was also built. It was not as grand as the one in Skiringssal, but it would serve its purpose as a meeting place for all.

A kitchen was built adjacent to the great hall. Stables were built for the horses and a training field was chosen outside the walls.

The town quickly emerged and soon the land closest to the village was sectioned off and equally divided among the men who would farm it. Each family and single man got a portion of the land, including Rafn, Peder and Dagstyrr.

Peder helped with this task for which Rafn was grateful. Peder was good at settling disputes and the people easily went to him with their problems. He was as much a natural as Valr when it came to such matters and Rafn wouldn't have coped as well without the man's expertise and support.

In time people would start to leave the longhouses and build outside the compound walls, but for now there were only a hundred and fifty of them and it was decided all would stay within its protection.

Ragnarr, which meant the power of the gods, was chosen for the village's name. Rafn stood on the walls and stared out over the land. For a moment something stirred deep down in his core. He tensed in anticipation... but it stilled once again.

II

Joka, who often went out hunting, returned late one night with a deer thrown over her shoulder. As soon as she entered the half finished walls of the village, women came running out to relieve her of her burden. They would take it, skin and butcher it, after which they would dry the meat and store it for the winter.

Joka was tired and dirty and wanted a bath. She found her way to the longhouse and the room within that she shared with her sister. She found herself a clean tunic and a drying sheet, as well as some soap and left to find her favorite spot to bathe along the nearby river.

At this time of night it should be private enough as most people were gathering in the great hall for supper.

She was almost to the opening, which would soon be fitted with a gate, when Peder walked in from the darkness beyond. He seemed almost surprised to see her, as she had been avoiding him for weeks.

"Joka," he said at once. His eyes lingered over her in an almost possessive way that made her scowl.

"My lord."

"It is dark, where do you go?" The concern in his voice irked her.

"I go to bathe. The dark does not concern me."

Peder stared at her a moment with his mouth agape, as if he'd forgotten how to speak. Perhaps she shouldn't have told him of her plans. She imagined he was now picturing her naked, causing her face to flush and was consequently glad of the dark.

"And you seek to be alone."

"Aye."

"Then I will not keep you." He turned to go but looked back after only taking a few steps. "I will see you at supper?" It sounded like a wishful plea and Joka found herself feeling generous.

"I will be there after I have washed." A smile betrayed his eagerness.

Joka found her way easily along the river bank to a spot behind a low hill. It offered the privacy that she sought and she undressed before stepping into the cold water.

She clenched her teeth. It was too cold to linger so she quickly washed and dried herself. After donning her fresh tunic and pants, she wrapped her cloak around her against the evening chill and headed back to the great hall.

The hall was already filled when she entered. When she went to the head table she found the only vacant spot was beside Peder. Sighing in acceptance she sat down.

"You have had much success hunting." Peder grabbed the opportunity to engage her in conversation.

"The forest is thick with game. No one has inhabited this area and therefore the animals are still plentiful."

"We must make a point not to over hunt so close to the village."

"That would be wise," she agreed.

Rafn and Seera sat across from them and Joka met her eyes. "Have you settled into your new dwelling?" Joka asked her to avoid Peder's next question.

"I have. My husband has been generous in his building and given us four rooms, a large area with a table and a hearth, and three rooms for sleeping." Seera looked to her husband with a smile. "I fear he plans a big family."

"Orn needs brothers and sisters." Rafn smiled as his gaze fell on his wife.

"I shall see what I can do." Seera leaned closer to quietly speak to him, but Joka heard the promise of passion in her words.

"It would be my pleasure to help." Rafn's whispered words also reached Joka. It was hard to stop the pang of longing to have such a connection to another person.

"There is much love between them." Peder spoke into Joka's ear. "They do not hide it."

"I'm glad they don't." Peder met her gaze and she found it hard to look away. A flutter started low in her stomach and it frightened her.

III

Kata and Seera sat beside the water and watched the men build the large dock that would serve as a port for their village. It was all coming together so nicely that Seera was amazed at the efficiency of the people.

Little Orn sat on the ground between the women playing with the rocks that littered the shore. Kata's stomach had grown and the morning sickness had blessedly stopped. It seemed to Seera that she now had more energy.

"I thought I would be more homesick than I have been," Kata admitted. "There is something about this place that captures the soul."

Orn laughed as a seagull landed on the beach close to them. He reached a hand toward the bird, but it flapped its wings and backed away before flying off. Orn watched it go and was delighted by its clumsy display as it flew overhead.

"Everyone seems happy." Kata rested a hand on her stomach as she spotted Dagstyrr carrying an armload of wooden planks.

"It is true, there has been very little fighting," Seera said. "Our husbands and brothers have done a good job keeping things in order. The people respect them and that has certainly helped."

"At the mention of Peder." Kata raised her eyebrows.

"What of him?"

"Joka doesn't seem to like him very much." She chuckled. Seera reached for Orn when he teetered sideways and almost fell over.

"I have begun to wonder why he persists so much." Seera balanced her son and let him go again to continue with his play.

"He does seem truly taken with her. It has not escaped anyone's notice. It has also been obvious that she doesn't welcome his attention. I know the people have been talking about them."

"They have?" Seera was surprised. She hadn't heard anything.

"Yrsa has moved among the women easily and has overheard the gossip in the longhouse when Joka is not there. They can't understand why she scorns a man such as your brother. He is very handsome and strong. The unwed girls giggle about him."

"It has always been so." Seera laughed. Kata joined in the laughter and neither woman saw Peder's approach until he was standing behind them.

"What is so amusing?" he asked.

"Nothing at all brother." Seera looked up at him but had a hard time keeping a straight face.

Peder scooped up Orn. The boy reached out to touch his uncle's face and Peder tickled the boy making him giggle. He threw him into the air and brought on more squeals of delight. Finally the boy squirmed to be free and Peder placed him back on the ground. Orn returned to his mound of rocks.

Peder sat on the log beside Seera and both women waited silently for him to speak. "You are happy sister?"

"Very much so."

"I am pleased. It is very different from Dun'O'Tir here." He glanced back at the circular wall that surrounded the village. Even now guards were on duty.

"It is different from the castle we grew up in, but similar to Skiringssal. Not as large mind you, but what Skiringssal must have been in the beginning."

"We should have brought a priest." Peder turned his gaze out to the water.

"You have something to confess brother?" Seera teased.

"I miss the chapel at Dun'O'Tir," he said. "It was a good place to sit and work through my thoughts."

"There is no reason we can't build a chapel here. Certainly when the traders go out, we could ask them to find a monk willing to come back with them."

"It would not be hard."

Kata sensing that Peder had a need to talk alone with his sister rose to her feet. She picked up Orn and told them she was taking him back to find him new clothes as he had managed to soak through the ones he wore.

"Thank you," Seera said. They both watched her leave before she turned back to Peder. He seemed even more sullen than he had a moment before. She waited patiently for him to explain what was on his mind.

"It is very quiet here," he finally said.

She placed her hand in his. His grip tightened. "I have noticed that also. I admit I enjoy it."

"I do as well. It reminds me of Dun'O'Tir at night when everyone is asleep and only the guards walk the walls. I used to enjoy that time of day."

"You miss it."

"In some ways I do, but not enough to go back." Peder picked up a stone and tossed it out on the water.

"You left Dun'O'Tir because of Joka." She finally broached the subject that she had avoided these past weeks. "Yet she shows no sign of returning your affection."

"She doesn't." He ran his free hand through his messy hair. A gesture he'd often made through the years. Seera watched the pain that reflected in his eyes. Joka had him turned inside out and he was helpless to do anything about it.

"I am sorry brother. She is a beautiful woman. When she allows you to see past the walls she has built around herself, you can also see that she is a good woman."

"What is wrong with me Seera? Why can't I just walk away?"

"It is called love. It is not so easy to turn your back on such a strong emotion. It comes of its own accord and traps you. When that love is returned it is a good thing, but when it is not…"

"It is hell."

IV

Systa sat on the floor within the partitions of her sleeping area. She held a bag in her hands and slowly opened the string that held it closed.

She poured into her delicate hand the runes that she kept within.

Each piece in her hand was made of bone and had one of the rune symbols etched carefully onto it. She had used these many times when she sought to see the future. They weren't always needed, but when she sought something specific they helped her see more clearly.

She'd been dreaming of late and she couldn't make sense of the images that flashed within her sleeping mind. It made her uneasy when things were not clear to her. She didn't like surprises. She had always been prepared for what lay in the shadows of the future.

She had always seen. Even when she was small she had been given images of things that always came true. She had known her father would beat her even before he first laid his hand upon her. She knew the first man she would be forced to lay with and it had come as no surprise that he would not be gentle, but would be quick then fall into a drunken stupor.

But Systa's strongest vision had been about Joka. She had known that Joka would not fall victim as the other women had. She had known that Joka would kill their father and rightly so. She had dreamt of Joka as a warrior woman, meeting men in battle and taking many lives before the killing had stopped.

And the strongest vision of them all had been of a battlefield when Joka came face to face with a man from the past. This man was weak and angry, seeking some kind of vengeance that had remained unfulfilled.

This battle had yet to take place, but it would be here in this new land. This she had seen very clearly. Yet that inevitable moment when Joka faces the man wasn't clear beyond the initial locking of swords. Lately she'd been shown a little more. A weakening before the shadow thickened.

Systa remained frustrated by this shadow that would not dissolve. She had not been able to see her sister's fate. She worried about what that might mean. That it could mean Joka's death.

A chill ran through Systa. She gripped the runes more tightly between her hands and closed her eyes.

"Goddess, show me," she pleaded. "Reveal what hides in shadow. Let light shine upon the darkness. Show me."

She rolled the runes and bent over them to see what they would tell her. She studied them carefully. She saw very clearly there was death and she shivered again. She looked more closely but the runes would say no more. They wouldn't let her see within the shadow of death. They would not tell who it was that died.

Fear gripped her tightly. Was it premonition or concern for her sister that prompted this sense of doom?

What did the shadow hide that it did not want her to see?

V

Rafn stood outside the village. The sun was just dipping over the western horizon and had turned the sky into a wash of orange and pink that reflected across the rippling waters of the inlet. Only a thin scattering of clouds marked the sky overhead. Construction was going well. He could not be more pleased with the people's enthusiasm and efficiency of the work done.

He saw Seera slip through the gate. She wore an apron-dress that was a rich green color and contrasted sharply with the creamy white smock she wore beneath. Her hair was loosely tied back from her face and when she spotted him she headed in his direction.

It amazed him that he could still become so entranced by the mere sight of her. He could not imagine a time in the future when they'd been married so long that she failed to ignite that spark of passion.

"My love," she said as she came to stand beside him. He took her hand in his and caught how the sun changed the emerald green of her eyes into a deeper hue. He brought her hand to his lips and tenderly kissed it.

"Where is our son?'

"Yrsa has taken him."

"She is a very attentive nurse," he said.

"Orn has grown to love her and I am pleased."

"You have time to walk with me?"

"I do." She smiled when Rafn took her hand and led her north along the shore until they were well away from the prying eyes of others.

He turned then to face her and brought her into his arms. He could feel the fullness of her milk filled breasts where they pressed up against his chest. It reminded him again of his desire to have more children.

Rafn's hand caressed Seera's face. It still amazed him that such a love was possible. It was a wonder how such a love could make a person feel so differently within.

Strong were the memories of the battles he had fought. The thunder had echoed loudly through his soul until they beat as one. Such a constant rumbling had always kept him restless. His sword had become an extension of himself and he wielded it better than any other he had known. It was not mere boastfulness that made him believe such a thing, but the power that Thor had left within him.

Yet Seera had come along and counteracted that constant need for action, and brought contentment to his heart. Rafn leaned forward and kissed his wife, this woman who had saved him far more profoundly than he had saved her.

She reacted to his touch and his kiss deepened as his desire grew stronger. He lowered her onto the soft sand beneath them. Perhaps this would be the night that another child would be conceived.

Soon all thoughts were washed away in the purely instinctual sensations that swam through his body as he felt her flesh pressed against his.

CHAPTER 15

Rakel had been hiding in Hadde's cave for weeks now. They had seen her father's warriors come and go along the forest paths below. Hadde insisted she stay hidden while he crept out each day to set his traps and brought back whatever they had caught through the night.

They mostly ate rabbits and lemmings. Hadde also knew a lot about plants and so he never came back empty handed. He knew what was edible and what was not. He created soups that were the best she had ever tasted.

They did not go hungry but her fear remained sharp. Each time a pair of warriors was spotted she would realize that she was still too close to her father to be free. She needed to leave the safety of the cave and put distance between her and Skahi.

"I can't stay here," she told Hadde one night as they finished the last of the rabbit stew.

"But you will be caught if you leave." He pleaded with her to stay. He had been alone too long and he didn't want to return to that isolation so soon. Rakel understood this.

"Come with me Hadde. You needn't stay here any longer." He stared at her as if he had not thought that a possibility.

"You would allow me to go with you?" His voice was choked with emotion.

"I can't leave you. We are friends are we not?"

"Aye, we are friends."

"Then let us leave now, while darkness hides us," she said. He peered out of the cave to the thin slice of moon that hung in the sky.

"I will go with you, but first you must allow me to do something. You must not interfere or speak until I am done," he warned.

"Alright." She was curious what he would do that required such seriousness.

He gathered to him a small iron cauldron and some dried plants and what looked like small animal bones. There were other things that she could not identify, but she did not ask what they were. She remained silent as he had instructed and simply watched as he first boiled the water and then began adding each item one at a time.

Softly he chanted words that she could not understand. She felt a twinge of fear at hearing the power in the words. She was a Christian woman, but she had always sensed things that her faith could not explain. She knew there was more to this world than what the eyes could see.

His words reached out to her and enveloped her in its magic. What had been fear turned to calm and a sense of safety causing her to stare at him in awe.

When his words were done he looked at her and she saw a strength that belied his size. Somehow she knew everything would be alright.

"What did you do?" she asked in a hushed voice.

"I set a spell that should cloak us for a while. It will not last more than two days before its power is stretched too thin to be effective. Hopefully by then we will have travelled beyond your father's watchful eye."

"Thank you for what you do."

"Once you saved my life," he said. "It is only right that I do the same."

They each donned a pack of supplies and crept out into the night. They traveled as fast as Hadde's short legs would allow. Rakel was amazed at his speed as they left the cave in the distance.

For days they traveled deeper into the mountains. They stayed to the mountain passes that took them into the high ranges and then down closer to the valleys. They slept in caves and under cliff ledges. The first few days they didn't risk a fire, but soon they became so cold they had to seek its warmth.

They ate of the provisions they carried, not stopping long enough to set snares. Soon they would have to, but they kept moving as long as their supplies lasted. Water was not a problem as the mountains were littered with streams and waterfalls that kept their water flasks filled.

BITTER PASSAGE

When they were finally forced to stop, they spent five nights in a large cave close to a pool that was fed by a waterfall. Hadde set his traps and they were able to restock their supplies.

They kept heading west, in the direction she had seen the ship sail. It was still her hope that they would find where it had pulled into port. She didn't know the land in which they traveled, or if there were any villages that lay ahead. It was a single minded purpose that kept them going, nothing more.

Winter would come all too soon. They could feel it even now on the night air. It would hit the higher elevations sooner so they needed to be out of the mountains into the lowlands. Death walked behind them and it must not catch them.

II

Kale woke to someone rapping at the door of the dwelling that Bekan had recently given him. It was a relief to be out of the longhouse. He grabbed his head. It ached from over indulging in drink the night before. He pushed away his blanket to discover his body still tangled with that of the slave girl he'd taken to bed.

He pushed her from him but she did not wake. He had forced her to drink as much as he had. She would probably be passed out for some time. A large bruise had appeared on the left side of her face where Kale had hit her.

Kale grabbed the blanket and wrapped it around him before opening his door. A young boy stood there and would barely meet his eyes. Kale scowled in annoyance. "What do you want boy?"

"Bekan would see you in the stables." He told him quickly then turned and ran before Kale could cuff him.

Kale went because it served no purpose to anger the man who allowed him to remain as his right hand. He went to the stables and found Bekan saddling one of his best horses. Packs lay waiting on the ground beside him.

Danr was there also, his horse ready to head out. Kale pulled his cloak tighter against a sudden chill. He raised his eyebrows in question when Bekan turned to him.

"You are going with Danr," he said.

"What?" Kale failed to hide his shock.

"You are not to return without my daughter. Get on this horse now if you still wish to have her hand in marriage."

Kale didn't miss the smirk that came to Danr's face. The warrior was enjoying this far too much and he would pay for it, this Kale promised.

"It has been weeks, men have looked in all directions. Where do you expect us to look?"

"West," Bekan told him, "And while you search for my wayward daughter, I want you to find out where that ship that passed here has gone."

"It may have gone anywhere." Kale looked at him in disbelief. "It may have simply been passing by on its way somewhere else."

"It may have, but there is also a lot of unclaimed land to the west. They may have settled there and I need to know before the council is to meet again."

"Aye." Kale tried to hide the anger in his voice. From the sharp expression that Bekan shot him he knew he had not succeeded.

Despite his wish to remain, Kale followed Danr into the mountains. They kept to the paths until they ran out and then followed the animal trails. Danr was good at navigating and kept a fast pace.

The worst time came when they stopped for the night and Kale was forced to sit at a fire with Danr. They spoke very little for which Kale was grateful, but he felt as if Danr was constantly evaluating him. It grated on his nerves and kept him in a foul mood which seemed to further amuse Danr.

When they finally found Rakel he would drag her back to Skahi by the hair, and once the monk said the words that bound them in marriage, he would make her suffer. The taking of her body would satisfy him greatly. She was a woman of undefined beauty, but he promised she would find no pleasure when wed to him.

It was how all women should be treated. The men of Skahi failed to understand that. Their wives smiled far too often and the children laughed more than they ought to. If his father had taught him anything, it was that the fairer sex was meant to be kept in their place otherwise they would begin to think that they could be their equal.

He knew one such woman. He remembered her all too well; Joka, the woman who had brought him to his knees. He had not been able to make her pay. Her, and the witch who was her sister, disappeared one night and the next day their father was found slain in his bed and his sword missing.

What use was a sword to a woman? That Joka had dared to take it he had no doubt. If he recalled she had even begun to dress like a man. It was why he had cornered her that long ago day, to remind her that she was a woman and what that meant.

Joka had surprised him by nearly rendering his manhood useless. He had promised to make her suffer greatly for that. It angered him still that he had not been able to fulfill that promise.

But he would not fail to punish Rakel. No wife of his would think herself equal to the power of a man. She would learn the lessons her father failed to teach her.

She would learn.

III

Rakel and Hadde finally climbed a ridge from where they could see to the ocean. They no longer traveled at night, but during the day so they could see more clearly. Rakel guessed it would be another four days, with all the ups and downs of the trail, to reach the edge of the mountains.

Rakel had never been so tired in her life. She was afraid at any moment that her legs would fail her and she wouldn't be able to continue. If it were not for Hadde's encouragement she would surely not have made it this far.

That night they slept on the ridge so that they could sit and stare at the sea. It was such a welcoming sight as it offered freedom, if only she could reach it.

They built a fire and huddled in close. It was not long before they succumbed to fatigue. Sleep had robbed them of common sense and neither thought what building a fire on a ridge would mean. At such a height the fire would be seen far into the distance.

It would not be so hard for someone to see such a beacon. Perhaps it was fate that led them to make such a mistake. Maybe it was the spirits that dwelled in the mountains. Who could say what their mistake would cost them.

Rakel slept soundly, but Hadde tossed restlessly throughout the night. Strange dreams filtered through his sleeping mind, but they were confusing images that had no basis in reality. Close to morning the dreams finally set him free but not before leaving him with a clear picture of a woman.

The woman possessed silver eyes.

Hadde woke feeling tired. He rubbed his eyes in an effort to rid them of their itchiness. Rakel remained asleep and he sat for a moment watching her. She looked so peaceful. The serious look that was always present on her face had eased. He'd never seen anything so pretty.

He had always loved her. Not as a man to a woman, but a brother to a sister and they had often played together as children. They had both witnessed the death of the witch in the flames that long ago day that had changed his life.

She had risked herself to see that he didn't follow the old woman into the fire. He'd been afraid as he'd run to the mountains and hid, but his fear had not been for himself, but for her. Worry had eaten away at him that she'd been caught and punished in his place. He had watched for days for another large bonfire.

It had not come and so he had crept further into the embrace of the cold stone walls that sheltered him from the wolves who circled below. He had been only a boy when he'd been cast out on his own. He had come to accept that it was the will of the gods that kept him alive.

For what purpose he had never known, until he had seen Rakel running into the mountains with a pack on her back and a fearful look on her face. From the height of his cave he had seen the horses headed in her direction.

It became clear then why he still lived, knew that he was meant to save her. It was a fair trade. He would risk anything to see her safe. He would travel as far as she wished to go to see her find the happiness that she deserved.

He did not have a sword, but he had faith that they were being led by a greater force. He trusted that something waited at the end of their journey. They just needed to stay ahead of the wolves.

Rakel stirred and looked up at him. A smile touched her face. She sat up and stretched before seeking the sight that had enthralled them the day before.

The day was clear and the icy blue waters reflected the warmth of the sun. He saw the hope spring into her eyes.

"We shouldn't linger."

"Nay," she agreed. "It would be a mistake to forget that I am still being hunted."

"They will not catch us." Hadde hoped his words weren't proven false as the seriousness returned to her face.

"Promise me," she said. "That if my father's warriors catch up to us that you will run and hide. They don't know you are with me and if they take you back my father will recognize you. He will not have forgotten the fire he intended for you."

He shook his head. "I won't leave you."

"I will not be killed. My father has other plans for me, but you are not safe."

"You fear being caught. These past weeks I have not wished to pry and have respected your silence. But, please, tell me now. What is it that your father intends for you that you would risk death."

"Death would be kind compared to what he wants of me."

"Tell me."

"There is a man who came to Skahi two years ago. He is a violent and cruel man who has no respect for women. He has wormed his way into my father's confidence and my father has given him much power. My father would give me to this man in marriage, but I will not go to such a fate."

Hadde stared at her in sudden understanding of what drove her on their mad flight. She feared this man more than her father.

Hadde took her hand between both of his. "It will not happen." Again he hoped his promise would not prove false.

They scattered the remains of the fire and doused it with water from their flasks. The path they took was thankfully downhill so they were able to make good time. They continued travelling not knowing how far behind danger lurked.

IV

Systa knew that the man who Joka was to face was within the forest in the nearby mountain passes. More, she had seen that he was chasing the dwarf and the woman who travelled with him. He must be stopped and Systa knew just how to do it.

Within a cave that she had found not long after coming to Iceland, Systa sat in front of a large black pot. Her chants were swept away on the breeze that blew in through a hole in the roof of the cave and out through a large opening. Energy vibrated in the air around her and began to swirl into a mini cyclone of blue and green.

She faced the swirling wind and a bit of madness sparkled in her eyes at the power that surged forth from within. She was connected with the earth, could feel its pulse beneath her feet.

A witch they may call her but she was simply a daughter of the earth itself. She felt the essence of every living thing around her as she used her magic and her connection to the world. With a sharp command the wind stopped moving in a circle and blasted out through the cave opening and into the forest.

Systa's heart beat rapidly as the power continued to hold true. Every part of her body pulsed and echoed. If any had been there to witness her conjuring, they would have said that her silver eyes had turned a light shade of purple.

She spoke words that would not make sense to anyone not versed in the practice of the seid art. She kept herself connected to the energy of the life force that surrounded everything around them. She saw through the layers of mere sight, to depths far beyond the visible. She saw into a distance that others could not see.

Then she smiled.

She had seen in the vision the two men along a mountain trail a day's ride from Ragnarr. Mounted on horseback they would easily catch the other two who ran on foot ahead of them. She would need to slow them down, give the others a chance to make it to the safe domain of the Raven.

A few short words and she commanded the wind. It obeyed her command as it crept through the shadows until it was almost upon the two men and then it grew into a tempestuous whirlwind that tore at the trees.

V

Kale stopped short as a vicious wind came out of nowhere. His horse balked at the sudden disturbance. Kale fought with the reins to keep the horse from throwing him and bolting. Danr, who was a much better rider, was beside him and having more luck controlling his beast.

The strange wind ripped leaves and branches from the trees and blew up a wall of dirt that soon choked the two men.

"This is witches work," Danr sneered as he brought his horse around and demanded that Kale follow.

The tumult didn't stop but seemed to follow them as they retreated back the way they had come. Danr continued to mutter about witches and magic.

"There is no such thing as magic, no matter what a witch may claim," Kale yelled at his traveling companion.

"Believe what you will, but this wind is not normal."

As if to strengthen Danr's words the wind became more violent, until the two men had to shout to be heard and the animals became more spooked. Danr forced his horse along a trail that led higher, but the wind climbed with them. Getting off the horses when it became too steep to ride, the men coaxed them on.

After what must have been an hour and two more changes of trails, they were high enough that they had left the wind behind them. Kale stopped and gasped for breath from their excursion. It had not helped that they had been breathing dust for the last hour.

"We've outpaced it." Kale breathed deeply, his hands braced against his legs.

"Nay," Danr looked at him in all seriousness. "The witch called back her beast." Kale wanted to deny the man's words, to tell him he was an idiot. Yet as he looked back down the small animal trail they were on, he could see the wind standing in place, swirling in an agitated circle as if waiting for its prey to return.

The analogy made Kale shiver.

Back in a cave that they could not see, a silver eyed woman with white hair laughed.

CHAPTER 16

The thick clouds rolled in over the village of Ragnarr. The wall was completed and the gate fitted and locked while the people slept soundly within. The guards worked in shifts and remained on the walls throughout the night. They had all been trained by The Raven himself. They were fierce and deadly men and those in their protection felt safe.

By late afternoon the rains had started and everyone stayed indoors, except for those unlucky men whose turn it was to stand guard. The other men were gathered in the great hall discussing things that needed to be completed before winter.

As for Joka, she had no wish to stay cooped up with the women in the longhouse. She had no use for their gossiping, so she braved the rain to find her way to Seera's dwelling and was thankful she found her there.

"I welcome you," Seera said. "I had thought I would have to take Orn out into the rain in search of company. I am glad you thought to save me the trouble."

"I couldn't stay in the longhouse," she said. A scowl spread across her face that caused Seera to laugh.

"They are not so bad once you get to know them."

"They don't seem inclined to be friendly," Joka replied.

"You can be a bit intimidating my friend." Seera motioned her over to the table and poured them some of the tea she had just finished brewing. Enjoying a hot drink was a comfort on such a cold day.

"I know." She understood she was not approachable. She had made herself so and found it hard to change. It was just that the women represented a world she had never been a part of, so it was hard to know how to fit in.

"In time you and they will find the way. Once you learn to relax amongst them."

"You truly think so?" Joka raised her eyebrows in doubt.

"You are a good woman. I have been blessed that you and I are friends. Even with Kata you have relaxed, and believe it or not, these women are not so different."

"I suppose that is true," she said. "I just can't help but see myself through their eyes. I am a woman who behaves like a man, but is still a woman."

"There has never been any doubt that you are a woman. You can't hide your beauty beneath men's garments."

Joka looked at her in surprise. She didn't think of herself as beautiful. Women were supposed to be soft and sweet, and she was anything but. She did not fit into most people's view of beauty.

"Your wildness and strength offer a new and exciting kind of beauty. The women are aware of how the men react to that."

"I have no interest in their men." Joka looked startled.

"They are aware of that also and perhaps it has made them even more curious. They have no need to be jealous of you, but the unmarried ones who have noticed my brother's charms have not failed to see his attraction for you."

Joka looked up at Seera and saw the underlying question beneath her words. She wanted to know what lay between her and Peder.

"I do not encourage him," she said.

"I don't say you do, or even that it would be wrong if you did."

"You think I should?" Joka felt her heart catch in her throat and her defenses rising.

"That is not for me to decide," Seera said. "Only you can know what is in your heart. I am sympathetic to my brother's feelings, but I don't place them above yours."

"I..." she searched for the words to explain the emotions that warred within her. They confused and bewildered her. Had they been so obvious to Seera?

"He is a good man," Seera spoke calmly when Joka felt anything but. Seera waited patiently for Joka to confide in her, but she wasn't sure she could. What Joka felt was too raw and she had never opened herself up to such vulnerability.

"I don't doubt what you say," she managed to say. "He just needs to understand I have nothing to offer him."

"You are sure?" asked Seera. Joka scrambled to hide the turmoil that was seizing her. It scared her. He scared her.

"I..." she couldn't find any argument that made any sense. She didn't like that. Didn't like how Seera was trying to make her look at her own heart.

Just then Rafn opened the door and came in, dripping water on the floor. His hair was plastered to his face and Seera laughed at the sight of him. She got to her feet and brought him a blanket.

"Do you have any of that tea left for me?"

"There is plenty left."

Joka felt suddenly like she was intruding and got to her feet. "I should be going." Each looked at her as if they had forgotten she was there.

"There is no need to rush off."

"I have things that need doing," Joka reassured her and ducked back out into the rain. She started back towards the longhouse, but she was not yet ready to return there.

She stood instead in the rain, halfway between Seera's dwelling and Peder's. She tilted her face up to the rain and enjoyed the feel of it on her face. She held her arms out as if to embrace it and was almost caught off guard by someone approaching.

She lowered her arms and opened her eyes to find Peder staring at her. Something inside wanted to betray her and answer the longing on his face. Fear made her defenses shoot up and desperation brought forth her anger.

"Why will you not go away?"

II

Her words hurt and it caused his anger to flare. He could do nothing right around this woman, nothing that would cause her to look at him with anything but hatred. Damn her for making him feel this way.

The rain came down heavily as Peder faced Joka and he wanted nothing more than to kiss her. But the last time he'd attempted that she'd put a knife against his throat.

Without any way to release his growing desire for her, he turned to anger instead. He looked at her and his eyes flared. She must have had a sense of what he felt for her hand went to the hilt of the knife she wore on her belt.

"You are the most infuriating woman I have met." Peder yelled through the onslaught of rain.

"Because I don't simply bow to your wishes as any other woman would so gladly do?" She slung back at him.

Peder clenched his fist at his side and willed control that was hard to maintain in her presence. "I don't know what you think I want Joka. If you had allowed yourself to get to know me even a little, you would know I am not a man who wishes to bend women to my will."

"And what is it you want, my lord?" She spat the words at him as if he was the enemy. How he wished she would see him differently.

Joka stared him down. She wouldn't take a step back, even when he moved closer to her. She wouldn't allow him to see fear in her eyes. Not fear of him, but of the feelings that she had for him. Feelings that she had trouble controlling. How she wished she could just get rid of them. To return to just hating all men equally.

Things had not been so simple since Peder had come into her life. He challenged her at every turn. He treated her like no man ever had and yet she had treated him with nothing but scorn. And still he sought her out and continued to watch her with a look on his face that told her he was waiting for something she was incapable of giving.

Wasn't she?

The anger fled his face and opened up to a well of feelings that had no place to go. Her defenses faltered when his voice cracked with emotion.

"I just want to love you." He watched her for any kind of reaction, but her face betrayed nothing. Her eyes remained locked to him and he couldn't see what was inside of her.

He turned from her as the rain came down harder and the wind picked up forcibly. He meant to leave her standing there stunned at his declaration. She couldn't believe him. Her heart raced in betrayal of her oath to never let a man touch her. Yet he had, not the physical contact that scared her, but on a much more intimate level, he had touched her heart.

"Wait!" She screamed into the wind and thought for a moment that Peder had not heard her.

He stopped and turned back to face her so suddenly that she almost collided with him. His face had hardened and his eyes were cold.

"I can't keep doing this," he said. "I can't hope for something that you are not able to give me. I will leave you alone Joka. I will give you what you want."

For a moment he thought he saw something soften in her eyes, but it was hard to tell with the rain washing down her face. He would not do this anymore, would not ache for her.

Peder would have walked away then. Had every intention of leaving her behind and never speak to her again. But she stopped him with one word, a name…his name. She had never said his name before and it sounded so sweet coming from her lips.

"Peder," she said again.

He met her gaze and saw her defenses drop. Saw the shield that kept her safe from the world slide from her eyes until he could see right into her soul. His heart stopped beating for a moment at the intensity of the emotions he saw within her.

"I don't want you to leave," she said so softly that he barely heard her above the wind.

The rain didn't let up as the two stood staring at each other for what seemed an eternity, but was really only moments. Each waited for the other to make the first move, and Joka knew that he would not. She had turned him away too many times. It was up to her now.

As the invisible wall that had always kept her safe, crumbled around her, she felt fear like she had never known before. She was at once vulnerable and excited by what she dared to do.

She went to him, because if she didn't, then she would lose him and she truly did not want that. She went to him because beneath it all she had come to love him.

Joka stood but inches from him, barely able to catch her breath. She met his eyes and saw his love, saw his desire and she could do nothing other than answer it. She brought her mouth to his and kissed him.

It was all Peder needed to act. He drew her into his arms and kissed her fiercely. Too long had he kept his hunger locked within and there wasn't anything that would stop him now. He crushed her against him and with the rain washing over them both his tongue sought hers. He heard her gasp and he felt himself harden.

It was only a matter of steps to the door of his dwelling. He scooped her up into his arms and carried her to the door.

Joka couldn't think, could only feel. She didn't fight him when he picked her up. Though she was no small woman, he did so as if she weighed no more than a child. He was at his door in three large steps. He kicked it open and carried her in.

The door slammed shut behind them and Peder set her on her feet. He pulled her into his arms and continued to kiss her. Her heart raced and she was finding it hard to breath. She placed her hands against his chest, but she didn't push him away. She didn't want him to stop. What a contrary woman she was, but she felt weak to his will. And the goddess help her, she did not care.

She felt him unclasp the clip on her cloak and it fell away. He stopped then to step back long enough to remove his soaked tunic. His chest was wet with moisture and she couldn't keep her eyes from the perfection of his hard muscles.

His hands sought her belt and it soon joined her cloak on the floor. He reached for the bottom of her tunic and slowly brought it over her head. Before she could think to stop him, she was standing exposed to him. His eyes roamed over her as his hands continued to remove her clothing. She let him, for she was far too nervous to do it herself.

Peder sucked in a breath at her beauty. She was more perfect than he had imagined. He was correct in his assessment that nothing about her was soft. She was toned with shapely muscles and a hard flat stomach. His eyes trailed up to her breasts and a smile spread across his face. There was something about her that was soft after all.

He pulled her against him and looked down into a face that could, it seemed, show desire.

"I am a virgin." She blurted out. His eyes widened in surprise.

Her words were enough for Peder to find his control and ease his grip on her. "I had thought…" he began.

"That I hated men because I'd been forced into their beds," she finished for him.

"I did think that."

"It is far more complicated than that."

"I could stop," he offered even though he would have a hard time doing so. He could never do anything to harm her.

Joka was touched deeply by his words. That he would stop if she asked him to. He was so unlike the men she'd grown up around. This was only the final proof of that. Hadn't he already shown her in so many ways that he was honorable to the core? It was what she loved about him most.

She wanted to discover other reasons to love him. She found she could only answer him truthfully. "I don't want that."

His mouth found hers ready and willing and she let him guide her to the bed. He loved her with tenderness and caring that left her with no doubt of how he truly felt for her. They joined and he brought her to a pleasure that she had never known could exist. A large piece of her soul began to heal and the frightening memories of her childhood started to fade away.

III

The rain sounded almost musical on the roof of the longhouse. The women sat in groups close to the hearths that supplied heat to the building. Systa did not sit among them but within the privacy of her sleeping area. She sat cross-legged on her bed softly humming a tune.

A smile came to her face as she saw something within that only she could see, something that made her very happy.

"Love finds and strengthens, warms what has always been cold," she said quietly to herself.

She laughed as she twined a finger in her hair. The silver of her eyes sparkled with hidden knowledge. It was pleasure that she felt now. She was pleased for her sister and the leap that she had allowed herself to take.

It was time that she let her love for Peder show. For it was in that love that Joka would find what she needed to survive.

She lost her smile as darker thoughts entered. The shadow still lurked in her vision. It taunted her with its malignant curse of what she could not see.

She snarled in defense of the evil she felt. Joka would need all her strength to fight it. Her head snapped up suddenly and she looked through the walls that hid her from the storm and saw something that made her eyes widen.

Something was coming!

IV

Hadde's dreams were haunted by strange images and confusing sensations that had him tossing restlessly. There was something there. It was as if another person was in his head with him and it made him feel uneasy.

He could almost sense the men that followed them. There were two of them, but how he knew this he could not say. It was as if someone had planted the image in his mind. The unmistakable tingling of power washed over him, yet he had not used any magic. It was around him in the forest and had wormed its way into his thoughts.

Twice he woke to stare into the darkness that surrounded their small camp. Rakel lay undisturbed beside him. The first time he woke he thought he saw a strange glowing light on the trail behind them but it disappeared almost immediately.

He managed to drift back to sleep, but it was not an easy slumber. Strange emotions swept through him. Again he felt the presence of another that made no sense.

In the hour before morning an image came to him of a beautiful woman sitting before a cauldron of steaming liquid. She was petite, with long white hair even though she was young. It was clear that the power he felt was coming from her. He had never felt magic so strong in his life. He watched her wearily for a moment before she looked up and met his eyes.

He was startled by the contact. Her silver eyes bore into him as if she had known he was there. "Waiting for you am I." Her voice echoed through him, causing him to wake immediately.

He sat trembling as he felt their connection slip away. Surely it was just a nightmare. It couldn't be real, could it? The old witch that had taught him had spoken of strong magic. Of things he had never fully understood.

It was not beyond the realm of possibility that one with magic had called to him. Yet he didn't feel comforted by that thought, or by the image of the silver eyed woman that continued to appear in his head.

What did it all mean?

Hadde looked over at Rakel as she began to stir. Her eyes began to flutter and he knew that soon she would be awake. He peered up at the sky that was just beginning to turn lighter as the sun began to peek over the horizon. The sky was clear and the air was crisp. He breathed it into his lungs in a hope to clear his thoughts.

It did not help.

CHAPTER 17

Joka woke to the sound of soft breathing beside her. She was startled at first until she remembered where she was and what had transpired. Peder lay sleeping on his back with his face turned towards her. Stubble showed on his face and she had to stop herself from reaching out and touching it.

She was not ready for him to waken. She wanted to look at him while he was unaware. The blankets had been pushed down below his waist and her gaze moved over his chest. A soft covering of hair grew across his upper chest then narrowed to a point that ended not far from his naval. Another line of hair went from his naval to disappear beneath the blanket.

She knew where it led and she was almost embarrassed as she remembered exactly how well he had used that part of his body. She flushed at how much she had enjoyed it. She had not thought it possible to feel such emotions.

Peder's eyes opened to meet hers and she hoped her cheeks were no longer red. He turned on his side so they faced each other and each stared and searched for the right words to use at this fragile moment.

"Are you alright?" For a moment she wasn't sure how to answer for suddenly her world had turned upside down and her ordered existence had crumpled.

"I think so." Confusion wrinkled the skin between her brows. He touched her face and she felt relaxed from the gesture.

"Marry me," he said. Before she could respond he kissed her.

"I can't." She sat up and tried to leave the bed but he stopped her. Not by force but by a simple touch.

"I love you Joka. I want you for my wife." She looked over her shoulder to meet his eyes and she saw the desperation in them. She realized he didn't trust her feelings. That he expected her to leave.

She turned to face him and brought her mouth to his. The kiss was filled with the same passion it had before. He responded to it as she knew he would and he moved her beneath him. She let him cover her with his body and even ran her hands down the length of his back.

She wanted him. There was no denying it, now that she'd had a taste of what he could make her feel. Not just the simple desire of her body, but the much stronger emotions that captured her heart.

They shared those feeling in a way that words wouldn't satisfy, with touch and feel, and a blending of their bodies. When morning finally came they both lay exhausted.

It was some time before they woke again and, Peder would not let his question go unanswered. "Will you be my wife?"

"You are a Christian and we have no priest here." It was an excuse and he knew it.

"Then we will marry according to your beliefs. It matters not to me," Peder replied. She tensed and withdrew from him.

"Why must we marry?"

Peder stared in amazement at the woman who had just given herself so completely to him. "After what we have just shared, can you still deny you have feelings for me?"

She climbed from the bed and this time he let her. She began to pull on her clothes and for the moment he just enjoyed watching her.

"Is it not enough that I have come to love you?" Joka met his gaze and saw that her words pleased him. Yet he persisted.

"Then marry me."

"I will not marry you. Not by a priest or a holy man. I would remain free."

Peder crawled from the bed to join her. He pulled on his trousers and faced her. She had a stubborn set to her mouth. That same mouth he had enjoyed kissing not so long ago. He leaned in and did so again and was satisfied she didn't stop him.

"You are a stubborn woman." He ran his hands up and down her arms, but they remained stiff.

"I don't want to marry."

"Then we will not marry," he gave in, "But I don't want to fight. If you allow me to love you, I will be satisfied with that."

A smile eased the hard expression from her face and he had to stop himself from grabbing her and returning her to his bed. It had been a long night and she was still new to such passion. He had to remember not to be too overzealous.

He took her hand and lightly kissed it. "Have you practiced with your sword lately?"

"Not as much as I would have liked." Her eyes sparkled with understanding of where his thoughts were leading.

"Midday on the training field."

"I will be there."

Peder drew her into his arms and gave her one last kiss that left her unsteady on her feet. If she didn't leave now she would be tempted to stay and though it was a most pleasing thought she needed some space to clear her thoughts.

Joka opened the door to leave only to find herself face to face with Rafn who in surprise raised an eyebrow. His gaze shifted from her to the half naked man standing behind her and he failed to hide a smile.

"My lord," she said and quickly left without looking back. Blessedly she didn't stagger on legs that felt as if they would not hold her.

Peder greeted Rafn with a satisfied expression. Rafn laughed despite his best efforts not to. "It would seem she is not so immune to your charms after all."

"Perhaps, but she still has a long way to go in trusting me."

II

Joka went back to her longhouse and disappeared behind the screen that separated her sleeping area from the others. She found Systa sitting on her bed waiting for her. A knowing smile streaked her face. She stared at Joka through silver eyes that told her that she knew exactly what had transpired.

"What is that look for?" Joka rolled her eyes.

"Glad am I sister." Systa laughed softly. "Time it was to go to him."

"Oh Systa," Joka plopped down on the bed beside her. "Things are not so clear as they were yesterday."

"Happy are you?" Systa shifted so that she was sitting crossed legged and facing Joka.

"I am almost too afraid to admit that I am." Joka frowned. "The more I let him in, the farther it is to fall."

"You not think he will catch you?"

"I don't know anything," Joka admitted. "Is it foolish to let myself feel such things? My body still tingles with the memory of what we have done and I have not managed to keep him from invading my heart."

"Sometimes a fool must we be."

"You think so?"

"Maybe you just have to let yourself fall." Systa became serious. Joka saw something dark form behind her eyes that made her stiffen with suspicion.

"What is it sister, that you see." She narrowed her eyes, trying to see past Systa's defenses.

"Not yet sure am I." Her gaze had shifted away from Joka to something deep within her.

It made Joka uneasy.

III

They met on the training field as promised. Joka had cleaned and changed before heading outside the village walls to the field. Peder was already there when she arrived and for a change he appeared to be a very content man.

They met face to face and she slowly drew her sword. She held it before her and smiled confidently. She had been secretly practicing the lessons he had taught her and was anxious to surprise him.

And that she did. From the moment their swords locked they were equally matched in skill. He had strength, but she had swiftness and accuracy with each placement of her sword. He couldn't help but feel proud of her, especially once people stopped to watch.

The crowd grew and this time Joka was aware of them from the beginning, but she chose to ignore them. She kept her eyes locked with Peder's as they sparred back and forth. The sword he had gifted her had become truly hers, an extension of herself that she controlled with ease. It was perfectly balanced to her height and strength making it easier to maneuver.

"I must really thank you again for this sword," she whispered as they drew close to one another.

"A warrior must have a weapon that amplifies his or her skill."

"And you thought to give me such a weapon?" Their swords clang together in an almost perfectly timed rhythm that had her blood pumping.

"I wanted to see what you could do." She glimpsed the heat in his eyes when they were but inches apart. "I am not disappointed."

It was true that she was more than he had hoped for. The more they sparred the greater his passion grew. He wanted her with an intensity that was not lost on her. Even those who stood nearest had a sense of the heat that was rising between them.

Their feet moved in a perfect dance as they created music with the touch of their blades. One did not outshine the other, but rather they shone together.

Joka didn't want it to end but if it did not they wouldn't find the privacy that was needed to satisfy the other excitement that was growing within her, for something just as physical but of a completely different nature.

Peder sensed this raw desire that shimmered through her. It reflected in her eyes and he had but to answer it. This dancing with their swords was just foreplay for what they both really wanted.

Yet neither would be the first to lay their sword aside. So they continued in their sparring as the crowd grew even larger.

Seera and Rafn had come to see what the excitement was all about and Rafn laughed at what he saw.

"He never lets up, does he," Seera sighed.

"Perhaps," he smiled down at her, "But you did not see her sneaking from his lodge this morning."

"What?" Seera was shocked. She had spoken only yesterday to Joka and...perhaps what she had said had been enough. Seera laughed with Rafn.

"Love always finds a way." He reached for her hand with a tenderness they both shared.

"I had not thought you so sentimental my husband." She spoke quietly as she leaned in closer to him.

"I will admit to nothing," he whispered in her ear.

In what seemed to be a mutual agreement, Peder and Joka dropped their swords and stood panting. The only thing that kept them from reaching for each other was the dozens of people watching them.

They sheathed their swords and joined Seera and Rafn. "You are getting really good," said Seera. Joka smiled in response to her compliment.

"If none of you mind, I will absent myself to go change." Peder spoke but his eyes remained on Joka.

"My lord," she said and watched him leave.

"I go as well." Rafn raised Seera's hand and kissed it briefly before heading down to the nearly finished docks.

The women looked at each other and Seera smiled. "I am glad that you have come to trust your feelings for him."

"I…" Joka began but she was too confused to find the words.

"Go," Seera said. "He waits."

Joka went through the gate and discreetly made her way to Peder's dwelling. The door had been left ajar and Joka entered. Peder stood inside and as soon as she took her first step in he grabbed her hand and pulled her to him. With his foot he kicked the door closed giving them the privacy they desired.

IV

"We are almost there." Rakel spoke with weariness. She wasn't sure how much farther she could travel. Her feet ached and she dreamed of soaking in a hot bath. The dirt had worked its way deep into her skin and she felt filthy. She had always been meticulous in her grooming and she had never gone this long without washing her hair before.

Before they found people she would have to find a stream to cleanse herself. She had seen the smoke rising in the distance and she hoped it signaled a village. She would seek sanctuary there and hope that the leaders of the village were kinder than those in Skahi.

Rakel added more wood to the fire and rubbed her arms to will warmth back into them. It was so cold. The heat of the fire was barely enough to keep her teeth from chattering.

Hadde was off searching for plants to add to his stew. She had lost sight of him in the trees. It was not long before he returned carrying his treasures. He had a smile on his face when he sat down beside her.

"I found something that you will find most pleasing."

"What?" She perked up at the gleam in his eyes.

"If you follow that path to the end, you will find a mineral pool." He pointed down the trail he had just returned from.

"I was just longing for a bath."

"Go," he said. "While I make supper you go and enjoy yourself."

Rakel was on her feet with her pack in her hands before he could finish. "It would make me feel so much better."

Rakel almost skipped down the trail she was so excited. She found the pool easily enough. Its sulfurous smell reached her long before it came into view. She stripped and stepped into it, realizing this was much better than the stream she had hoped to find.

It was almost a sinful pleasure to feel so relaxed. The heat seeped through her muscles and eased the ache she had felt. Even her feet felt renewed. Only a short time ago she had thought she would never feel warm again. How blessedly wrong she had been.

She dug through her pack to find the soap she kept wrapped in a piece of wool. She scrubbed her skin until it glowed anew. She worked up a good lather in her hair and when she was finished she felt like she was ready for anything. It was exactly what she had needed.

With a smile on her face she went back to their small camp. Hadde laughed at her childlike joy. He handed her a bowl of stew and she ate hungrily.

Tomorrow they would reach the settlement that they were sure was just beyond the mountains. It would be close to the sea, a good place for a ship to pull into port.

Hadde took his turn at the mineral pool before they crawled beneath their robes for some much needed sleep. Sleep did not come easily to Rakel. Freedom was almost hers, if she could just make it a little further.

She eventually feel into a restless slumber and when she woke she felt a premonition that her luck was about to fail. It was still dark, with only a faint softening in the color of the forest around her to tell her it was early morning.

Hadde slept soundly in his blankets and she tried not to disturb him as she went to relieve herself behind some bushes. The feeling of unease grew stronger as she readjusted her clothes. The forest seemed oddly quiet and she had this very strong urge to flee.

Hadde woke suddenly and jumped to his feet. He had the look of a startled deer when his eyes met hers.

"The silver eyed woman said we need to run," he said. She didn't understand what he meant. What woman?

"Hadde?"

"Now, we must go. The wolves are closing in." He started to gather up his things and scatter dirt on the fire.

"You are scaring me." She turned to push things into her own pack.

"You should be," he said. "If we don't go now they will catch us. There is no time to delay."

She argued no further and threw her pack on her back. With a quick glance back along the path they had come they left their campsite. Hadde pushed himself as hard as his short legs would allow. Rakel could have gone much faster as she was a very good runner, but she would not leave Hadde behind.

Near noon she heard the sound of horses' hooves and she looked at Hadde as they both realized they wouldn't make it.

"I slow you down," Hadde said. "You need to leave me behind."

Rakel looked around in terror. She didn't want to see her friend fall victim. These men were after her and they were not aware of him. It wasn't fair that he pay her price.

"Hide," she said. "Go deep into the trees and hide in as small a place as you can find. Stay there until it is safe. Come to the village when you can."

Hadde nodded in understanding. It was the only way. She had no chance to outrun her pursuers if she slowed her steps to keep pace with him. He ducked into the thick bushes, where not even a trail could fit.

Satisfied Rakel ran like she had never done before. A single minded determination to reach the settlement whose smoke they had seen drifting into the evening sky. It was close, she could feel it.

And more importantly, the men would follow her and Hadde would be safe. She was relieved to see the trees open up before her and she found her way into a flat meadow. Across the field was the village she had been heading for. A wooden circular wall enclosed the settlement.

The horses were close now. As she turned and saw them for the first time, they saw her as well. Her eyes widened in shock when she realized one of the men was Kale.

His eyes narrowed in hatred as they fell upon her. Fear quickened her steps and she ran for all she was worth. She ignored the ache in her legs and prayed to God that they not fail her.

"Damn you woman. I demand that you stop at once."

She ignored his command, and ran even as she felt his horse closing in on her. She was almost there. She could see people down on the docks and the guards on the wall.

She was almost there…but she was not going to make it.

CHAPTER 18

An alert went up as soon as the woman ran out into the fields. Two men on horseback raced from the trees shortly after. Rafn, Dagstyrr and Peder had their weapons in hand and were on their horses before the woman had made it halfway across the field.

The men were almost on top of her by the time the three men, followed by a dozen other warriors on foot, headed out the gate. The woman was looking back over her shoulder in fear as the man in the lead kicked his horse to move faster. He was almost close enough that he could reach down and grab her.

Rafn had no intention of allowing that to happen. The man on the lead horse seemed unaware of their sudden presence, but the larger man saw them at once. He hung back and didn't reach for his weapons. At least he had some intelligence.

The other man was too foolish to pay attention to his surroundings. His focus was only on the woman whose steps faltered when she saw Rafn.

The man reached down to grab her but Rafn's command came out harsh and deadly. "Halt."

The man sat straight in his saddle and for the first time focused on him. His eyes widened for a moment in fear before he became angry. The other man rode in close to him and pierced him with a look that impressed Rafn.

"Don't be stupid," he told the other, who was now scowling in annoyance.

The men pulled their horses to a stop while the woman disappeared into the group of warriors that brought up their rear.

Rafn's spear lay casually across his lap, but his grip was firm and if provoked he would be ready to use it. The larger man eyed the spear and understood. The men on the walls had raised their bows and were ready to let loose their fitted arrows. The large man's gaze roamed over the growing crowd of warriors and was smart enough to know the odds were not in their favor.

"What goes on here?" Rafn demanded. Dagstyrr and Peder had moved to either side of him, each with a spear in hand.

"I want only the woman," the foolish one said. "You would be wise not to stop me."

Rafn raised an eyebrow in amusement. He could cut this man in half without effort, who was he to make such a threat. Rafn's lack of fear caused the man to hesitate.

He became aware of the other warriors that stood waiting for their warlord's command. Rafn swore the man trembled.

"Forgive his rashness," the large man said. "He speaks without thought." He glared in contempt at the foolish one and Rafn realized there was no love lost between the two.

"Why does this woman run from you?"

"She has run away and her father wants her returned."

"No!" screamed the woman. She moved to stand beside his horse. "You can't allow them to take me back. I beg you for your help."

"Shut up woman." The foolish one moved to strike her but Rafn moved his horse closer and grabbed his arm.

"Touch this woman and it will be the last thing you do," Rafn warned. He let go of the man's arm and was satisfied when he drew back.

"I am Danr Ketillson. Warrior from the village of Skahi." The large man introduced himself. "May we sit and counsel."

"I am Rafn Vakrson and I will agree to counsel."

Danr's mouth dropped in surprise. "Warlord of Skiringssal?"

"I was," Rafn admitted. "Let us go to the great hall where we can discuss this further." He turned his horse around and led the others to the gate.

Danr leaned in to the other man and Rafn heard him say, "You are lucky he did not slit your throat for your stupidity." The other man's face went white and he must have been thinking the same thing. Good, let him be afraid.

"Bring the woman," Rafn said to Dagstyrr.

Dagstyrr got off his horse and took the woman's arm. Her fearful eyes remained focused on Rafn.

II

Rakel went with the fierce Viking who'd been ordered to escort her into the village, but it was the other one that held her interest. She had never been to Skiringssal and didn't know this man's name, but when Kale had heard it his face turned pale. This man was the one who could help her. She just needed to convince him.

Once through the gates they were joined by a couple of women. Rafn who had turned his horse over to a young boy went to speak with them. They followed him back to where she stood.

"This is my wife, Lady Seera, and my sister Lady Kata. Go with them and they will care for you while I speak with these men."

"Thank you." The men left and Rakel turned to the women. Her arms and legs were still shaking from more than exhaustion.

"My lodge will offer privacy." Seera brought her to one of three dwellings that had been built away from the longhouses.

Once inside Seera beckoned for her to sit at the table. "My husband wants you to tell us what these men have done that has caused you to run away."

She looked from one to the other before speaking. "I beg your understanding, my lady. The smaller one, his name is Kale. He is an evil man. He is cruel and violent."

"He has hurt you?"

She took a deep breath to steady her nerves. "Not yet, but he will once I am forced to marry him."

"Marry?" Seera suddenly understood what this woman feared.

"My father would force me. He does not care that Kale beats the women he takes to his bed." She twisted her hands in the cloth of her dress, wrinkling the wool. When Seera noticed her nervous habit Rakel tried to steady her hands.

"You fear him?" Kata asked.

"All the women do," she said. "But for me it would be worse. As his wife he has promised to beat me into submission until I learn my place."

"Then we will not send you back," Seera said. "Our husbands will keep you safe."

Rakel began to cry. "Thank you both." Her voice cracked between her sobs.

"Hush now," Seera said. "Come rest in my bed until Rafn summons us."

Rakel took her hand and let Seera show her to the room where she could nap. She was sure she would be unable to rest but as soon as her head touched the pillow she was asleep.

III

"What claim do you have on this woman?" The Raven demanded of him. Kale stared at him and tried to keep himself from showing fear. It would be foolish to cower in front of this man.

"She is my betrothed."

Rafn's eyes narrowed with suspicion. "This is why she runs from you?"

"The woman doesn't know her place." Kale tried to keep his patience, but it was barely controlled. "She needs to be taught a lesson."

The famous warlord stared at him as if he were a mere annoyance that needed to be dwelt with swiftly. Kale clenched his teeth to keep from showing how that irritated him. He had yet to meet a warrior who did not look at him with contempt. If he had the skills, he would show them all.

"Peder, take our guest outside and keep him company while I speak with the other one." Kale shifted his gaze to a blond man that was as intimidating as the warlord. What were these men of lordly rank doing in Iceland anyway?

"My pleasure," Peder said. He stepped forward to lead him outside. Peder smiled when Kale sneered at him.

They stepped out into the sun and for a moment Kale had to squint against its sudden assault. For a moment he failed to notice the woman who suddenly appeared before him until her hiss drew his attention.

"Black is your soul. Its foulness corrupts." Systa snarled and Peder was surprised by the pure hatred that had come to her eyes.

Kale was just as surprised, not by the hatred, but by the fact he recognized her. "Witch," he spat. He stepped towards Systa and she bared her teeth as if she were a wild animal that had been cornered by a predator.

"Leave you must, you pollute the very air we breathe." Her growl rose in defense. Peder moved to step between them but another beat him to it.

Kale felt the hard iron of a sword press up against his chest. He looked up the length of the sword to the person who held it. What he met were icy blue eyes that held loathing and contempt. What he didn't see was fear. She'd always been so bold.

"Joka," he said in eager anticipation of her sudden reappearance into his life.

"Touch her and you will die." He didn't doubt that she meant it. Yet he smiled in pleasure for he had dreamt often of the woman whom he had failed to repay for the insult done to him. He had never thought to get his chance.

IV

Joka could not believe this twist of fate. It could only have been the trickster god Loki that had led this foul piece of filth back into her life. She held her sword steady and pressed it just a bit harder until she drew a trickle of blood.

Kale's eyes hardened in anger. "How dare you woman." He screamed at her. "You will pay for that."

Joka was aware of Peder moving closer and of the knife that appeared in his hand. She caught his eye and shook her head, warning him back. She also saw Rafn and an unknown man step from the great hall.

"Don't threaten me Kale. Unless you have acquired a considerable amount of skill with your sword since last we met." If it wasn't her imagination she could have sworn that the unknown warrior chuckled.

"He has not," the warrior said. This won a glare from Kale.

"Make no mistake then," she said to Kale. "I for one know how to use the weapon I hold. I will find great pleasure in giving you a demonstration."

Peder smiled with pride and she was pleased by that. "She does not lie," Peder told him. "I have seen her skill."

Kale's nostrils flared in fury as he was faced on all sides with men that could best him. That Joka boasted that she could do the same was too much. He would not be insulted by a woman.

Joka's grip on her sword didn't waver. She had never thought to be faced with this reminder of her past, but she wouldn't allow him to affect her. She was a warrior now and he had best be aware of that.

She would enjoy bringing him to his knees once again. A smile came to her face as she thought of how to do that. He would understand fully that he was not wanted here.

"Kneel," she said. She hoped that the men wouldn't stop her. Peder and Rafn exchanged a look before the warlord nodded to give Joka his approval. This won another smile from the stranger.

"I will not." He whined which did nothing to prove his manhood.

"Now or I will show you just how sharp this sword is." She fed off the power that she felt from belittling this scum.

She saw the concern in Peder's eyes but was grateful he kept silent. Kale grew angrier as she grew bolder.

"She has killed in battle," Rafn said. "I promise you she is capable of doing what she says. No man here will stop her."

Kale's gaze turned to shock as he looked at the warlord. They would let this woman kill him and do nothing. He realized with dread that they could force him to do whatever she wanted.

"Now!" she said again.

Full of hatred he lowered himself to his knees. He kept his eyes locked with Joka. If he did not hate her before then he certainly did so now. Joka couldn't find it in herself to care.

"You will pay for this."

"I would very much like you to try." From the corner of her eye she could see that Systa smiled with approval and that Peder did not.

V

Fox had been sent to summon the women before the start of Joka's confrontation with Kale. Rakel was just arriving with them when she saw what had drawn such a crowd. Her eyes widened in surprise when she saw Kale kneeling on the ground glaring in contempt at a blond woman who held a sword against his chest.

Seera and Kata were equally stunned. Seera went quickly to Rafn's side. "What is going on?"

"Joka is explaining to Kale what will happen if he ever returns here again." Rafn smirked with amusement that caused Seera to shake her head.

"Is she planning on killing him?" Rakel asked the man she'd been told was Seera's brother.

Peder looked down at her and she saw clearly that he was not finding any of this as amusing as the other men were. His concern was for the woman. "I think she is just trying to humiliate him."

"She is brave," Rakel said.

"Brave and foolish." Peder spoke quietly and she wasn't sure if he had meant her to hear his comment.

Rakel found herself feeling a moment's satisfaction that a woman had brought Kale to his knees. She instantly liked this woman who showed no fear. She knew that the men did not think much of Kale, but he had always asserted his strength on the women where he couldn't on the men.

It was comforting to know there was at least one woman out there that was stronger than him. The man beside her moved.

"Alright Joka," he said. He laid a hand over top of the one which held her sword. "You have made your point. I think we should have Hachet and Leikr show him back to the trail they followed out of the mountains."

For a moment Rakel thought that the woman was going to ignore him, but she nodded in his direction and stepped back from Kale. She slid the sword into the leather sheath she wore on her back. It was the first time that Rakel realized that she was dressed in warriors clothing. Somehow it seemed fitting.

Kale scrambled to his feet. "This is not over." It was then that he noticed Rakel. His expression turned feral. He was angry and he needed someone to receive that anger and without a doubt she knew that she was his intended target.

"Come, Rakel," he said. "We are leaving."

"She stays." Rafn ordered and Kale knew better than to challenge the Raven of legend. No man could survive against him.

Kale looked from one man to the other and knew he would be forced to leave without her. They meant to protect her. Now was not the time to get her back. He would have to retreat and come up with a plan.

"Danr." He looked to the warrior who was still smirking at Kale's unmanning.

"I'm staying also."

"What?" This was more betrayal. "You answer to Bekan!"

"I answer to no one." Danr growled at him. "It is best that you and he both understand that."

"You are most welcome among us," Rafn said.

"It would be my honor, my lord."

Kale screamed at him. "Then may you fall to some hideous death."

Rafn beckoned two warriors forward. "Show him to the path." The two men each grabbed an arm and dragged him through the gate. "Someone bring his horse."

A third warrior appeared with Kale's horse. It seemed they would not let him have his mount until he was beyond the village.

"You will all regret this." He was forced at the point of a sword away from the village of Ragnarr.

Rakel was finally able to breathe easier, until she remembered that Hadde was still in hiding along that same path that Kale would be taking.

"My friend is still out there," she said to Rafn. She quickly explained about Hadde and how she told him to hide until it was safe to proceed to the village.

"Dagstyrr, follow Kale's trail and look for this Hadde."

VI

Systa felt a strange foreboding as she watched the warriors drag Kale from Ragnarr. A deep feeling of dread caused her to grab for her throat in an attempt to once again breathe normally. A dark shadow of premonition filled her vision.

That he was the man from the past that would meet Joka on the battlefield had finally become clear to Systa. A man from the very village they had grown up in. She had known that it would be so, but she had not seen the face as Kale's. She should have guessed. He had been the foulest of the young men and he truly had hated Joka.

Systa felt frightened by the images that flashed before her. They were things that the others did not see. They remained unaware of the Seer's growing panic.

Joka would face Kale and only one of them would win. Their blood streaked bodies were clear in her mind. The sound of their swords clashing echoed like thunder in her ears. Each of them held anger deep within and this charged their movements.

Only one of them would live but Systa could not see which one.

Peder's angry voice pulled her from her nightmare and she turned to stare wide eyed as he turned to Joka. His face was tight with fury.

CHAPTER 19

"What the hell did you think you were doing?" Peder screamed at Joka as soon Kale had been escorted from the village.

Those standing around looked at him in shock. Peder was never one to raise his voice. Most began to creep away as the onslaught of his fury exploded.

"You know exactly what I was doing?" Joka screamed back and refused to be intimidated by him.

"You think it wise to humiliate him in such a way?"

Seera and Kata exchanged worried looks with Rafn who simply told them it was not their place to interfere. Danr could only stare with obvious interest at the couple.

"I do not fear him, he is weak."

"You may not fear him, but even a weak man can get lucky." He moved towards her until there was barely any space between them, forcing her to look up at him. This infuriated her.

"He would need to get close first."

Danr turned to Rafn and asked, "Who is that woman?"

Rafn turned a hard stare to the young man. "She is his." So simple a statement but it also held a threat.

Peder went to grab Joka's hand but she pulled back from him as if guessing his intent. "Don't think to scold me as if I am a child."

"I would be a fool to think that you would listen." His voice roared with anger and even Seera cringed at the sound. Joka did not. She stood her ground, eyes flaring. It was all he could do not to grab her and throw her over his shoulder, but he knew that she would never forgive such an act.

"Perhaps I am the fool for believing that you trust me." It had not been so long ago she had lain wrapped in his arms. Now all she wanted to do was strangle him.

"You are the one with issues of trust," he lowered his voice but it was still tight with irritation.

Seera looked miserable watching them fight. Rafn took her arm and said to the others, "Let us find something to drink."

Feeling uncomfortable they disappeared into the great hall, leaving the angry couple alone. Rakel looked over her shoulder one last time at the woman who had done what she had so many times wished to do. It even pleased her that she was standing up to Peder.

"I would do it again," Joka said. "Kale deserved it and more."

"You have made an enemy." Peder tried to make her understand. What did she expect the outcome of her actions to be?

"He was already my enemy. It is not the first time I've brought him to his knees." A smile of pleasure came to her face and Peder frowned in suspicion.

"Tell me," he demanded. Joka stared at him trying to decide if she should confide in this man. Sensing her indecision he grabbed her hand before she could stop him and led her to his lodge.

Once safely out of earshot of anyone inclined to listen Peder waited for her to answer. He was still angry and he expected an answer from her.

"We grew up in the same village." She finally spoke, though her words were forced. She was still unsure if she should trust him. "He is what all men of my village are."

"And what would that be Joka?" His eyes flared with frustration and hurt that she refused to trust him.

She screamed at him. "Cruel men who treated the women no better than cattle. The men could take any woman whenever they wanted. No one would stop them and the women were too weak to prevent it. I would not allow that happen to me. Kale…he tried but a good kick to his manhood was all I needed to render him useless for some time."

"Damn it Joka." He shook his head in disbelief. "Did you not think what he would do to you?"

"I know what he tried to do. Did I not have the right to defend myself?"

"And what was today about? That had nothing to do with defending yourself. You were purposely humiliating him." His head pounded with frustration. He wanted to shake some sense into her.

"He needed to know that all women are not weak." Her eyes gleamed with triumph. She saw nothing wrong with her actions, and she wouldn't allow Peder to tell her otherwise.

"He will come after you for what you have done."

She could feel the excitement coursing through her veins. "He will find me ready!"

They stood facing each other, each running through a series of emotions that started with anger and ended with a desperate need to be in the other's arms. Their melding was fast and furious.

Their mouths met in a wild frenzy that had them tearing at each other's clothes in a sudden onslaught of madness. Their actions were not gentle or tender, but fulfilled a raw desire that needed to be brought to a satisfying conclusion. It was what both of them wanted and they would not stop until their desperation was sated.

II

Dagstyrr instructed Hachet and Leikr to keep to Kale's trail to make sure he did not attempt to circle back. Not that he believed that the man would. He was alone and no match for any warrior and would need to retreat so that he could find reinforcements.

He had failed to bring home the daughter of his leader. Dagstyrr didn't believe for a minute that this thing was over. Rakel's father would likely send many men for her next time.

As for the other matter, Kale was not likely to forget how he was humiliated by Joka. Dagstyrr didn't doubt that she could take this man in battle. But a man who was not strong with the sword would turn to less honorable means of meeting his goal. He would hire men to fight for him.

He was sure that Peder had understood that. The man had not looked happy. Not that he could blame him. If it had been Kata he would have been fiercely protective. He was not sure he would have had the will not to interfere. He gave Peder credit for staying out of it as long as he had.

Dagstyrr had left Hachet and Leikr a short time before and he was now headed back to the area that Rakel had described to him. She had said that a man had traveled with her and she'd made him hide so that he was not caught and punished because of her.

"Hadde," Dagstyrr called when he came to the right spot. He climbed down from his horse. "My name is Dagstyrr. Rakel has sent me."

He waited for a reply but when none came he realized the man might not trust his words. "My village, Ragnarr, is close. Rakel is there now, she is safe. My men are making sure Kale returns to Skahi. He will not hurt you."

"How do I know I can trust you?" A voice came from within the bushes.

"You have only my word," Dagstyrr said.

There was some rustling before someone stepped from the bushes. At first Dagstyrr thought he was looking at a child before he realized he was just a very short man. This took him by surprise.

"You are Hadde?" He stared down at the little man.

"I am." The dwarf's mouth was defensively set.

"Rakel will be relieved." Dagstyrr jumped up on his horse and pulled Hadde up behind him. The small man hung on tightly as Dagstyrr urged the horse forward. He kept a steady pace as they rode for Ragnarr.

As soon as they crossed through the gates into the town, Rakel was there. She helped Hadde down and dropped down on her knees to give him a hug. The little man looked flustered by the attention.

Rafn appeared beside him and looked at him in wonder. "This is Hadde," Dagstyrr said. The dwarf turned without fear to meet the famed warlord's curious gaze. This caused Rafn to smile.

"Welcome to Ragnarr," Rafn said.

"Thank you," Hadde replied. They continued to study each other for a moment before Rakel broke the silence.

"Are you alright, I was so worried." Hadde faced Rakel before answering.

"I am unharmed. They remained unaware of me."

"That is good." Relief washed through her and for the first time in many days she felt at ease.

"Come," Rafn said. "You must be hungry. Please join us in the great hall and we shall drink some ale and talk of all that has happened."

Hadde considered this for a moment before following the men to the great hall. He glanced over his shoulder once to look at Rakel. She nodded her head in encouragement. Dagstyrr had the sense that Hadde was perhaps not used to being included in men's conversations.

After they had finished their first mug of ale, Dagstyrr understood why. Hadde had relayed his story of how Rakel had helped him escape when he was still a child and how he had lived alone in the mountains. His solitary life had continued until Rakel had need of his help to escape from her village.

III

Hadde was stunned by the men's willingness to include him at their table. They spoke to him as a man, not a child and this made him feel good. Or perhaps it was just the ale that was clouding his mind. He couldn't seem to care which it was, just that he had never felt such a feeling of acceptance.

"What of this Bekan, what is he like?" Rafn was asking him.

"He cares more for power than his own people. Though he was elected to his position, he keeps the people in fear so they dare not replace him. The men listen to him. He keeps them happy by giving them many gifts." Hadde was telling them when Danr walked into the room. He was just about to take a drink of his ale when the large man appeared beside him. Hadde's eyes opened wide when he looked up into his face.

"Hadde," Danr said. "It has been a long time."

"Aye," Hadde said, though he wasn't sure if he said it aloud or not. He felt a bit of fear looking up into the face of the man who had once been a boy in Skahi when Hadde still lived in the village. Even then Danr had been large for his age. "Why are you here?"

Danr took a seat beside Hadde and accepted a mug of ale from Dagstyrr. Hadde noticed at once that he was accepted by the other two men. This made him uneasy and he lost the good feeling that had come to him. Suddenly his stomach felt sick and he placed his mug back on the table.

"I have chosen not to return to Skahi," Danr said. "Lord Rafn has been kind enough to allow me to stay here in Ragnarr."

"Why?" Hadde asked.

"How could I find fault in Rakel's actions," he said. "Were I to be told that I was to marry Kale, I'd have run away too. No woman should be forced to become that cruel one's wife."

"You really believe what you say?"

"Aye. Kale isn't much of a man. He hides behind the power that Bekan has given him, but he knows that the men have no respect for him. This makes him angry because he believes he deserves it. I have seen how he has left the slave women after he has forced them into his bed. They are beaten and bruised. I would not want that for Rakel."

"Then perhaps I will reconsider my opinion of you." Danr raised his mug to him and Hadde obliged by raising his own and taking a deep drink of the amber liquid. It warmed his throat and with it his concerns disappeared.

A tingling feeling rose on his neck that set his nerves on fire. On impulse he turned to find a woman walking towards him. She was short, but taller than he. Her hair was almost white and her eyes were…

Hadde chocked suddenly. "The silver eyed woman," he said. Her gaze met his and a knowing smile came to her lips.

"Been waiting for you, have I," she said. Her statement caused the others to stare at her.

"You have been in my dreams." Hadde spoke to her, forgetting for a moment that they were not alone.

"Twined our minds together within the night." Hadde saw from the corner of his eye that Danr had narrowed his eyes. The other two did not, which told the dwarf that they didn't find the woman's words odd.

"This is Systa," Dagstyrr offered. "She is a Seer."

"A Seer?" Danr was shocked.

"Not heard of one as I?" She snarled as her gaze shifted to the large man. "Seid magic is not known to thee?"

"Magic users are executed in my village," Danr said. "Bekan believes them sinners of the one true God. He has converted all within the walls of Skahi to Christianity."

"You not believe, warrior?" She sneered. For a moment Hadde thought he saw a glowing in her eyes, but the others did not react so he brushed it off as an illusion.

"I do not say that," Danr answered carefully. "I am one who never gave up the old gods. Unlike the other men of my village, I didn't follow

Bekan blindly, but kept to my own path." He stared at her a moment longer before adding, "On our trail here we met some odd weather. It had the feel of magic."

Systa smiled and moved closer to him. To his credit he didn't move away. She brought her face so close to his their noses almost touched. She searched his eyes and he held her gaze unflinchingly.

"The gods have you in their sights," she whispered. "Into woods you must go. Sacrifice to the god Tyr and all will be clear."

"Tyr?" Danr was surprised. "Not Odin."

"Nay," she hissed almost climbing into his lap.

Hadde watched uneasily from where he sat. He didn't know much about the Norse gods, but neither had he been allowed to be baptized. The priest had claimed he was an abomination and did not belong in the kingdom of heaven. The witch had laughed at the monk and taken Hadde into her care. She had taught him of magic, but nothing of the gods and thinking back he thought that was rather odd.

Systa pushed away from Danr to look back at Hadde. He felt as if she had heard his thoughts she stared at him so thoroughly. He took a drink of his ale to keep himself from shaking.

"Across the ocean I have come," she said to him. "It is you I was to find."

"I thought it was I who was supposed to come here?" Rafn's nostrils flared as he stared at her. Hadde had the sense that he was angry.

"Thor himself guides you warlord." She swung around to face him. "Here is where you are meant to be, for here the raven will reawaken."

Rafn's eyes narrowed at her words. Hadde was too afraid to ask of what she meant by waking a raven. Somehow he didn't want to know. Rafn and Systa continued to stare at each other, each unwilling to be the first to look away.

Systa suddenly laughed. It was not a sound of joy but one that brought a chill down Hadde's spine.

IV

Joka lay in Peder's arms, her fingers twined with his. She held them in front of her studying how they fit together. He on the other hand watched the expressions on her face. Many questions warred within his mind.

Her mentioning of the village she grew up in, the way that the men were, caused him to remember the old man and his declaration that Joka had killed her father.

Peder couldn't help but wonder.

"Just tell me what is on your mind," Joka said. "Whatever it is that troubles you is better said."

"I am not so sure it is. Perhaps you prefer to keep your secrets."

Joka glanced up at him a little surprised. "If there is something you want to know then ask." She snapped in irritation. He almost let the subject lay to rest. Did it really matter what had happened in her past. Yet, he could not let it go.

"The night before I left Skiringssal, I was approached by an old man. Something about him made me wary of him. But he told me things," Peder said.

"What things?" Joka sat up in the bed to face him. Her eyes had narrowed and her teeth were now clenched as if she were expecting something foul.

"He spoke of you and Systa. He accused your sister of being a witch."

"That should not come as a surprise to you. Many have spoken such words because they fear her gifts."

"I understand that." Peder rose to a sitting position as well and lightly touched her face. She eased, but did not fully yield to him. Her suspicion was still strong.

"And what did he say of me?" She prompted him to say what it was that lay heavily on his mind. He met her icy blue eyes and felt only love for her.

"He said that you killed your father." He watched her closely as he spoke and saw a shadow move across her face. She seemed to stare inside herself for a moment before she replied.

"I did." There was no remorse in her declaration. "I would do it again."

"I see," Peder kept his voice even.

"No you don't. You don't know anything about what my life was like. You have no idea the pain my father caused. The prison he kept us locked in. He drove my mother to take her own life rather than have to bear one more moment with him."

Joka climbed from the bed and went to grab her clothes where they still lay on the floor. Peder was instantly behind her and wrapped her in his embrace. She stiffened at his touch, which only caused him to hug her harder.

"You are right I don't know how things were for you or your sister." He spoke into her hair. "I have come to know you. I don't believe you would have taken the life of your father if it were not warranted."

Joka turned in his arms and met his tender gaze. "You really mean that?"

"I do."

CHAPTER 20

Kale was angry. He had been aware of the men who had followed him all the way home. He was sure they had meant for him to see them and it made him furious. When Skahi came into view, he kicked his horse to a gallop and raced into the village.

People had to jump out of the way to keep from colliding with his horse. Some even scowled at him in irritation, but what did he care. He pushed the reins of his horse into the hands of the first boy he saw and stomped off to Bekan's dwelling.

He was met at the door by the man. "You have not found her?"

"I found her, but she was helped by some warriors and they would not return her to me."

Bekan looked behind Kale as if searching for something or someone. "Where is Danr?"

"He has betrayed us." Kale pushed past Bekan into the man's home and ordered the servant girl who was within to fetch him some mead. Bekan narrowed his eyes on Kale, expecting more of an explanation so Kale continued his story.

"He has been caught in the Raven's snare," Kale said.

"The Lord of Skiringssal?" Bekan was shocked at the familiar name. When he was a simple blacksmith back in Vestfold, the warlord's name was forever on everyone's lips. The man who had been chosen by Thor when he was only a boy! Bekan forced himself not to shiver.

"Aye, he is here. He has built a new village and named it Ragnarr."

"Has he." Bekan scowled. "And this is where my daughter is?"

"She wouldn't leave with me and I was forced from the village at the point of a spear. They followed me all the way through the mountains to make sure I did not turn back."

"And Danr?"

"Once he learned that Rafn Vakrson led the village he became a blithering idiot trying to impress him and his men. He chose to stay."

"We will deal with him later," Bekan said. "First I demand my daughter back." His eyes narrowed on Kale. "Select two men and return to Ragnarr. Do not let yourself be seen. Watch and learn what goes on and find a weakness in their routine."

"My pleasure," Kale said. "I will take Onnar and Vikkar. I will leave in a few days, once I have had a chance to get some supplies together."

Bekan nodded in agreement and showed his future son-in law to the door. Kale went out into the cold night thinking of what he most wished to do. His thoughts did not include Rakel, she had all but been forgotten by the time he had reached Skahi. It was Joka who would receive his wrath. He would enjoy making her suffer.

II

Joka was sitting outside her longhouse sharpening her sword on a whetstone when Rakel sat down beside her. The woman looked nervous and Joka allowed her to just sit there watching her until she was ready to speak. Meanwhile, from the corner of her eye, Joka studied her.

Rakel had the most beautiful hair that Joka had ever seen. It was a copper red color that shone when the sun reflected off it. She had a trail of freckles across her nose and her golden brown eyes sparkled with the same copper tones as her hair. Joka sensed that she had a spirit to match.

"You are very brave," Rakel finally said.

Joka placed her sword across her lap to look up to the woman beside her. "You have courage as well."

"Nay, not like you." Joka held up a hand to stop her.

"It took courage to leave your home instead of allowing yourself to be forced into marriage to that man."

"It was not bravery, but fear that sent me running," Rakel said. "It was fear of what Kale would do to me once I was his wife that made up my mind. My mother and grandmother both encouraged me to leave."

"Even so, a lesser woman would have been more afraid to run. She would have feared the punishment she would receive if she were caught."

"Yet, I would never have had the courage to stand up to Kale the way you did." Rakel smiled. "If it is not so bold for me to say, I enjoyed watching you bring him to his knees."

The scowl eased from Joka's face into a smile. "I found much joy in humiliating him." The two women stared at each other in understanding.

"Could I make a request?" Rakel looked away from the warrior woman as she spoke. Her fingers played with the edge of her apron in a nervous gesture.

"You can ask and if I think it reasonable I will do my best to fulfill it."

"Would you teach me to use a sword the way you do?" She asked quickly before she lost the nerve. "I have heard the men speak of your skill when they did not know I was listening."

"If you can promise me that you will be committed to your teachings, then I will show you what I know."

"I will not let you down."

"Good," Joka said. "I have always believed that a woman should be able to defend herself. It is not a view that is met favorably by most."

"I would know how for Kale and my father will not give up. They will come for me and I wish to be ready when they do."

"First I will have the blacksmith forge a new sword for you. One that is light and easy to wield. Then I will teach you."

"Thank you."

III

Joka found her way to the blacksmiths forge soon after. She could feel the heat even before she reached the doorway that led inside. Two sides of the building had windows to allow in a fresh breeze, but Joka thought it did little good. The steam choked her as soon as she stepped inside.

Berthor was pounding the hot iron of what would likely be an axe head. He turned and was startled to see Joka standing there. He put down his tools and greeted her.

"What can I do for you?"

"I have need of a sword," she said.

"You have found fault with the one I made for you?" He was alarmed because he'd put great care into the sword requested by his lord for this

BITTER PASSAGE

woman of fierce beauty. He had seen her wield the sword and had felt great pride in his work.

"Nay," she replied putting him at ease. "It is not for me, but for the woman Rakel."

"Really!" He raised his eyebrows. He had come to think of Joka as unique. Who would have thought he would need to make another woman a sword.

"You have talent," she said. "The sword I carry is both light and sharp. Only an expert could have created a sword to so perfectly fit a woman's hand. I ask only that you do the same again. It need not have a gold handle, but I would like the same quality in the blade."

"I could not refuse you." Berthor smiled as her eyes lit with excitement. She was incredibly beautiful. If she were not his lord's woman, he would most likely dream of her during the long cold nights of this northern country.

"I appreciate your willingness." Joka allowed a smile to touch the corners of her mouth. Berthor had to clear his throat at the unwanted effect that had on him.

"I will deliver it to you when it is done." He looked away from her so that he would not get lost in those stunning blue eyes that held such strength and wondered what making love to such a woman would be like. Certainly Lord Peder would skewer him for such a thought.

Joka nodded and returned to the fresh air outside. She welcomed the cold wind that blew through the village and she knew the snows would come soon.

IV

Two days later Berthor found Joka outside of Peder's dwelling. The two of them were readying their hunting weapons. Peder glanced up as he approached. He smiled in acknowledgement of the blacksmith.

"What can I do for you Berthor?"

Berthor glanced over at Joka before replying. "I have the sword ready that Joka ordered." Peder turned to Joka in surprise.

"What need do you have of another sword?" He asked a little harshly causing Berthor to shift his gaze away from the two.

"It is not for myself." She replied without looking at him.

"Who then?" Why such a thing should upset him he didn't know, but he felt a bit defensive.

"It is for Rakel." She narrowed her eyes in anger. "Must you always question what I do?"

Peder turned to Berthor, aware that he was trying very hard not to listen to their argument. "Let us see the sword my friend."

Berthor pulled back the cloth covering and handed the sword to Joka. She gripped it in her hand and tested it by swinging it through the air. A smile of satisfaction spread across her face and Berthor breathed easier.

"It is perfect. I will deliver the payment to you."

"I can pay him now," Peder said.

"Nay, I can pay my own debts."

Peder threw up his hands in defeat. "I didn't mean to imply that you could not."

Berthor looked from one to the other and decided that Joka was not an easy woman to understand and it took a man like Peder to be able to deal with her. He still thought her beautiful, but much too volatile for him. He preferred a woman that would look at him with warmth and tenderness.

"You know where to find me," he said. Peder watched him rapidly walk away. He had to contain a smile. Certainly the blacksmith was wondering what Peder saw in such a strong and fiercely independent woman.

Then Berthor had not seen how she had softened beneath his touch. How she loved with the same fierce passion that she wielded her sword. It was not something he wanted known of his warrior woman.

"Why does Rakel need a sword?"

"She has a wish to use one." Joka turned to him with a spark in her eyes that challenged him to fight her on this.

"And she has asked you to teach her?"

"Aye." Joka smiled and it transformed her face into one of such savage beauty that Peder forgot about their plans to go hunting and reached for her hand instead.

He instinctually thought that she would try and pull away from him, but she surprised him. She slipped her hand into his and led him to the door that was but inches away.

V

Rakel met Joka on the training field the next day. For a moment she wondered what the men would say. Certainly they would argue against it being used to train a woman. Joka boldly stood in the center of the practice field and Rakel followed the woman she had come to admire.

She was not sure that she could copy Joka's fierceness. Joka's face was as hard set as any of the warriors she had ever met, as fierce as the Viking warlord who had led his people here to Iceland. She had come to learn in the short time she had been there that the men greatly respected Rafn and those he held in his closest confidence.

She had even seen Danr bow in respect to the man. Danr who had always refused to give his loyalty to her father and kept his will his own. The awe that sprung into Danr's eyes when he was around Rafn surprised her even though she had heard whispered accounts of Rafn's legendary skill with the sword.

Rakel had seen the Frankish sword that he carried and saw how the men stared at it in envy. She had spoken to Seera of what she'd heard said about her husband. Seera told her that the stories were true. Rafn had been able to call armies to him and enemies had come to fear him, but what his men did not see was the other side of him. The one that made Seera feel safe and loved. The man who held her tenderly in the night and spoke words meant only for her ears.

Rakel had felt envious of Seera's words. To be so loved by a man…to love him in return. Such romantic thoughts had often been in her dreams, but she had never thought to meet anyone to fulfill them.

She hurried to join Joka. Joka had given her a sword the night before, causing a curious stir amongst the others who shared the longhouse with them. Rakel had felt self conscious at being the center of attention as everyone stared at her. Then she held the sword in her hands and it gave her a sense of power she had never known before.

Joka kept their first lessons simple, letting Rakel learn the feel of the sword and how to apply her strength to it. A few people wandered by and stopped to watch, but mostly they were undisturbed.

When they had been practicing for about a week, Seera showed up carrying a sword. A look of mischief crossed her face as she looked from Joka to her. "I decided that Rakel shouldn't be the only one benefiting from Joka's wisdom."

"You wish to be taught as well?" Joka was pleasantly surprised.

"You once taught me how to shoot an arrow with accuracy. Why not learn to use a sword as well."

"I would teach all the women if they so desired." Joka laughed.

"Then after Kata has had her baby I will have her join us."

Rakel welcomed Seera's company and Joka continued the lesson. It was about midday when Rafn came storming up and pulled his wife aside.

"What are you doing?"

"Joka is showing me how to handle a sword." Seera remained calm, but firm and confident in her reply.

Rakel understood for a moment why the men thought Rafn fierce and she feared for Seera. But, Seera stood her ground and her husband's scowl didn't intimidate her. She had admired Joka for her strength, but she could see now that she was not the only one who possessed it.

Peder came up beside Rafn and raised an eyebrow at Joka as if silently asking her what trouble she was causing now. Yet there was love in his gaze that was returned by the warrior woman. Again being faced with two people who loved each other made her ache to find such happiness for herself.

Rafn stared at his wife in frustration before turning to face Peder. "Can you talk some sense into her?"

Seera turned her anger on him and he started to laugh. "I think it is best if I stay out of this one."

"Then talk to her." Rafn flicked a hand toward Joka whose face hardened.

Peder met her gaze and for a moment he contemplated saying something. "That would not be a wise move."

Rafn growled. "We will talk of this later." He snapped at his wife and stormed off into the compound.

"You are determined to make every man's life a little more difficult?" Peder said to Joka and this earned him a smile.

"As much as possible my love."

"Well, at least I won't be the only one," Peder shook his head and followed Rafn back to the village.

Seera laughed. "Come girls. We won't let them ruin our fun."

Rakel wasn't sure what had just happened, but she saw clearly that these women were not cowed by their men. She envied them and wished she could be just like them.

Would she ever find a man who loved her enough to allow such freedom?

VI

Seera was in their dwelling when Rafn found her. She had been expecting him and the objections he would voice. She would be patient she told herself. He only meant well, she would just have to convince him it was in her best interest.

He joined her in front of the hearth, pulling forward one of the wooden chairs that Seera had made a cushion for. He sat watching Seera for a time before speaking. She could see many emotions cross his face as he searched for the right words.

"Why Seera?' he asked.

"Why do I want to learn how to use a sword?" She placed a hand against the stubble on his jaw. "Because I think it is a wise thing."

"To be like Joka? That woman enjoys seeking out danger. She looks for trouble." He shook his head as Seera looked at him and smiled tenderly.

"I don't wish to be like Joka," she said. "I want only to learn from her. I have no interest in looking for a fight. I just want to be prepared if one finds me, to be able to defend myself when you are not there to do it for me."

"I will always be there for you Seera."

"You want to be, but things happen." Seera reminded him. "Twice I have been taken by men that I was powerless against. My back still bears the scars from that last beating. I don't ever wish for it to happen again and I won't allow anyone to get that close again, to me or our son. Can you understand that?"

Rafn's face smoothed as he thought over her words. He took her hand and held it to his lips. He remembered all too well how he had felt when he'd lost her and never wanted to feel that way again. Could he blame her from wanting to protect herself?

"Alright," he said. "I will not stop you from learning. I ask only that you do not use your weapon unless you have to."

"I promise my love." She leaned forward and replaced her hand with her mouth. He reacted immediately to her touch as she hoped he would.

"Don't think to distract me." He pulled away but was smiling.

"I would do no such thing."

Rafn laughed softly and the sound warmed her heart. It was not something he had done often when they first met. He had been so serious in his fight against the world. He'd also been filled with grief over the loss of his brother Orn.

It was good to see him happy and at peace with himself.

CHAPTER 21

Joka and Peder headed out into the mountains to see who would prove to be the better hunter. They were competitive in every way. Joka was determined to show him that they were equals. His pride would not allow him to be less than her, so they pushed themselves in every way until they had the whole village whispering behind their backs.

Despite her need to be as good as Peder, she enjoyed every moment they spent together. Often they would argue, but just as often they would fall into each other's arms and make love until they were both worn out.

They raced across the field as fast as their horses would take them, trying to be first to reach the tree line that hid the path which would take them into the mountains. The guards on the wall shook their heads in amusement at what was becoming a common sight. They had come to the conclusion that the two were evenly matched. Joka won just as often as Peder did.

Their horses ran neck in neck and only at the last did Peder push his horse into the lead. He pulled his horse to a sudden stop and Joka stopped beside him. An expression that could only be described as half smile half scowl was planted on her face.

"You were lucky my lord," she said. She pulled in closer to him.

"Luck had nothing to do with it." Peder brought his nose close to hers. She thought he meant to kiss her but he sat back on his horse and grinned.

"We have yet to hunt," she challenged.

"I look forward to it."

They moved down the trail until they found another that led off the main path and higher into the hills. As he guided his horse up the track Peder saw a good place ahead from which to see the village.

He was not disappointed to find that he was correct and that they had a clear view of the village and the ocean beyond. They jumped from their horses and tied their reins to a bush to keep them from wandering off.

"This is beautiful country." Peder stared in awe at the vista before him.

"It is." Joka said as she slipped her hand into his. The reaction to her touch was immediate and he turned her so that he could kiss her.

"We won't get much hunting done if we linger," she said. He continued kissing her despite her protests.

"Right...hunting." He made no attempt to move away from her. Instead he pulled her more securely into his embrace.

II

Hidden within the trees Kale watched what the lovers thought was a private moment. He sneered in contempt at the woman who had humiliated him as no woman had a right to do. He vowed he would pay for that.

He had sent Onnar and Vikkar away that morning to do some hunting, telling them he was quite capable of watching on his own. They had scowled at him but obeyed his command. Bekan had given them strict instructions to get his daughter back and that they were to listen to Kale as if the orders came directly from him. He knew they resented him but he was not of a mind to care.

Kale recognized the man with Joka as the one who had stopped her before she managed to push her sword through him. He would have done better to prevent her from humiliating him in the first place.

The couple were lost in each other's embrace and Kale was very aware of the passion that sprang between them. He felt himself harden as he thought of Joka naked beneath him. He imagined that she would not wield to him as she obviously did for this blond haired man. She would cower beneath him while he taught her exactly who was in control. She would not have her sword to protect her then.

He smiled in contemplation of how this would take place.

III

"Enough." Joka laughed as she pushed away from Peder. "If you are trying to distract me so I don't best you on the hunt, it will not work. I plan on winning."

"As do I." He reached to grab her back but she had stepped further away and he was unable to reach her.

She collected her spear from her horse. They had agreed that it would be their only weapon that day. They would see who would be the first to bring down prey. Besides the spear they each had a knife attached to their belts, but swore to each other that they would not touch them. It was to be used only for protection.

"Do not think to follow my trail and steal my kill." She glared at him with warning.

"I would not think of it." He grinned and she was almost seduced by his smile. He wouldn't use that ploy on her. She was a stronger woman than that.

"The first one to make it back here wins," Peder said. He turned and took off down a trail that ran opposite to hers.

Joka watched until he disappeared from her sight before heading down her own trail. She knelt to study the tracks she came upon. She found signs of a deer, but they were old. She continued on and stopped when the next tracks she found were clearly made by two men.

She looked back over her shoulder uneasily. All her senses came alert and she knew someone was out there watching her. She gripped her spear tighter and tried to figure out which direction the threat came from.

IV

Peder came to a split in the trail that led back down the hill. He was still thinking of Joka and was not fully concentrating on his surroundings. He almost missed the obvious tracks of three men leading up the hill. He bent to examine them and decided they were fresh and probably been made within the last day.

Peder knew of no others that were away from the village. His suspicions grew and he didn't like where he thoughts were leading. There was a threat nearby, he was sure of it.

He had left Joka alone.

Peder turned and ran back the way he had come.

V

Kale hid behind a tree watching Joka. He held a bow and arrow in his hand. He fingered the feathers on the end of the arrow and thought how easy killing her would be. She wouldn't see it coming.

She didn't have her sword, but she still had a spear. Could he take her? Certainly he could if he met her face to face. She was alone with no one around to defend her. The man had left in the other direction and was long gone by now.

It would be so easy.

His mind whirled with indecision. Finish her quickly and safely from a distance, or prove that he was a man and that no woman could stand against him. Pride was a fault of most warriors he had observed. They were so bent on proving their manhood when they could win so much easier from the shadows.

Would he fall prey to that same pride?

So tempted was he to step from his cover and meet her face to face. The thought of bringing her to her knees as she had done him was so seducing that he almost moved forward, but the flight of a nearby bird stopped him.

That was when he noticed the large dagger strapped to her belt. It could prove as deadly as her sword. There was a small chance that she would use it before he had a chance to kill her.

He lifted his arm instead and pulled back on the arrow. He heard it whistle through the leaves, but so did she. He had not counted on her having such good hearing. She moved at the last second and the arrow struck her shoulder instead of her heart.

She screamed in fury and threw the spear in his direction. It stuck in the ground directly beside him. Too damn close! She grabbed the dagger and came for him. He was too slow to see the danger.

He drew the sword from his back and held it ready as she charged him. She did not seem surprised to see that it was him. She faced him with eyes reddened in madness as blood ran from her left shoulder and he cringed at the pain that she must feel.

It did not slow her. She faced him like a feral beast ready to rip his throat out. Her lips were pulled back to show her teeth as an animal would do when attacking. Kale swallowed in sudden fear and that made him mad.

He would not fear her, not this woman.

"Fight me coward." She screamed at him and smiled in pleasure as he raised his sword.

Kale swung at her clumsily and she easily deflected his attempts with the blade of her knife. She danced away from him each time he swung his sword. She laughed at him as they fought.

"You will die for what you did to me."

Joka began to weaken from the loss of blood. Kale was quick to notice how she began to lose her balance. She managed to fight the desire to collapse and remained on her feet. Damn she was tough.

He took his chance when her defenses dropped and lunged forward. His sword managed to catch her side, but she had expected his move so the cut did not go deep. She hit his sword away with her dagger and brought it back just as quickly to cut a deep gash along his arm. The sudden pain caused him to loosen his grip on his sword, but he managed to grab it before it fell.

"You won't win Joka. You can barely stand on your feet." The blood quickly soaked the arm of his tunic. He grabbed the corner of his cloak and held it to his injury and realized he wouldn't be able to lift the sword again.

"Don't think that makes you a man," she snarled. "Only a coward injures his opponent first before facing them."

"Your injury was an accident," he said. "I was meaning to kill you."

Kale thought he heard something in the bushes and looked up as if searching. He glared back at Joka and said, "This is not over."

Kale slipped into the trees. Joka would have gone after him, but she staggered backwards. Just as he disappeared from view, she collapsed...

...and was caught by Peder. He had not seen Kale and his focus remained on the unconscious woman in his arms. Fear lit his eyes and he gently lay her down so that he could check her wounds.

Peder sighed in relief that she was still breathing. He glanced around briefly but saw no immediate sign of the attacker. He couldn't think of him now. He quickly checked her over and found a second wound in her side.

He ripped strips from the bottom of her tunic to staunch the blood. He knew not to remove the arrow from her shoulder until he had her safely in the care of a healer. His heart pounded as he tended to her.

He shouldn't have left her. He had known that Kale would return and want revenge. That Kale was a weak fighter shouldn't have mattered. He was a coward and had obviously shot from cover before Joka was aware of him.

He wrapped the second wound and knew it had been made by a blade. His warrior woman had fought him. Even injured she had stood her ground, and defended herself with only her knife. He had found it still clutched in her hand, wet with blood. Kale had not escaped unscathed.

He didn't know whether she was brave or stubborn. A bit of both he figured. She should have tried to run or hide once she was injured, but not Joka, she would never run from anyone.

He got her back to the horses and sat her in front of him, leaving the other horse to follow. He held her in his arms and rode for the village as quick as the mountain path would allow.

As soon as he crossed the gates he slowed and turned for his dwelling. As he did this he shouted for the two healers they had.

"Kata, Systa come now." His command caused many to stop to see what was wrong. Kata and Seera appeared from his sister's lodge, and Systa came running from one of the longhouses.

He didn't wait for them. He brought Joka inside and placed her on his bed. She looked so pale that he was close to panicking. Seera was beside him somehow, her hand reached out to touch his shoulder in comfort. He closed his hand over hers.

"What has happened?" Kata asked. She leaned over Joka to start examining her wounds.

"I didn't know," Peder replied as if he were far away. Shock was setting in and he was beginning to feel numb. "She was attacked. By the time I reached her the culprit had vanished."

Systa pushed her way into the room then. A look of disbelief was on her face. "I did not see this," she said to no one in particular. She was beside Kata the next instant and the two women began working together.

"You need to leave." Kata looked over her shoulder at him.

"No." Peder shook his head. "I will stay."

"Nay brother." Seera spoke calmly to him. "It is best if you did not.

She is in good hands. Her sister will not allow harm to come to her. You know this."

Peder gazed down at Seera and saw the concern in her eyes. He knew that he should heed her words, but how was he to walk from this room not knowing if the woman he loved would be alright?

"The chapel has been completed." Seera reminded him and he nodded his head in understanding.

"I will be there." Peder turned his back on Joka and went outside. Flakes of snow began to fall. He was met by Rafn and Dagstyrr as he began to cross the courtyard to the chapel whose construction he had overseen.

"What has happened?" Rafn was asking and he found he had to focus on the other man's words.

"I think it was Kale." Peder replied with more calm than he felt. The anger was returning and if he did not control it, it would explode from him. "Joka has an arrow through her shoulder. He must have shot her while he hid like a coward in the trees."

"We will find him," Rafn said. He called Hachet and gave him orders to take some men and search the trees. If they found Kale or any others from Skahi, they were to bring them back alive. Hachet left to carry out the warlord's orders.

"How is Joka?" Dagstyrr asked.

"I don't know, she lost a lot of blood." He looked back at his dwelling. "They would not let me stay."

"That is the way of all healers," Rafn said. "Come let us find some mead and wait for word in the great hall."

"I will come later. First I must go to the chapel."

"It is a time to speak to one's god," Rafn agreed. "We will seek you there if you are needed."

Peder nodded and continued on to the new chapel. They didn't have a priest to deliver them sermons, but it was a comfort just the same to step within its stone walls and sit on one of the wooden benches. A large wooden cross had been hung from the wall and candles had been set on a table before it.

Peder lit one of the candles before he sat and stared at the cross. "Almighty God, creator of all. I ache with the need for understanding. I love Joka so, I can't lose her. Give her your mercy…"

Words were lost to him. How could he explain the depths of his feelings? He knew instinctually that she would not die. The arrow had not struck any vital organs and the other wound was not so deep. It was just that she had lost so much blood. A person could go into shock if they lost too much, he remembered seeing it happen.

Systa and Kata would see her safe. They were both skilled healers. She would live, she would.

VI

Hadde sat with Rakel on a low bench in the courtyard. It was still strange for Hadde who had spent so many years alone, to be once again in the company of others. He had a hard time sleeping in the longhouse. The snores of the other men drifted too easily to him and kept him awake.

He had not thought he would miss his cave. He had spent so many years being lonely and longing for another's companionship. Why then was it so difficult? These people were so unlike those that he'd grown up around in Skahi. They did not judge him or condemn him for being different. They did not care that he was a dwarf.

Such an acceptance should please him more than it did. He shouldn't be missing the quiet of his cave. He shouldn't be dreaming of it in the night with such hope of once again sleeping within its cold walls.

Rakel told him these feelings would pass. He had to believe her. He just needed time to adjust. He turned to glance at Rakel who stared at Lord Peder's dwelling with a tightness of worry on her face.

"You are concerned about the warrior woman?"

"I am. We have become friends," she said. He already knew that as he had seen them spending time on the training field. He had thought it rather odd at first, but then he was pleased for Rakel. She was able to do something that he would never be capable of. His short arms could never support the heaviness of a sword.

His thoughts retraced to the moment that Peder had returned with Joka. He had taken her from his horse and even from a distance he had seen that she was covered in blood. Peder had called out and the witch had come running. There was a wildness about her as she'd raced across the compound, her hair trailing behind her.

Why did the woman make him so uneasy?

"Have you gotten to know her sister?" Hadde found himself asking.

"Nay, I have spoken very little to her. She keeps to herself. Though, I have caught her watching me often as if she knows something that I don't. I have heard the others talk about her Seer powers and though I am not sure if they are real, it makes me wonder what she has seen."

"She watches me also," Hadde said. "I am not sure I like it."

Rakel looked at him. "I have noticed her interest in you."

"She claims she came to Iceland to find me." Hadde tried not to shiver at the thought.

"You have not asked her what she means."

"I am too afraid to ask."

"When you are ready to know, you will not be." Hadde just nodded and hoped that she was right. He didn't mention the witch's invasions into his dreams. These dreams had not occurred often, as if Systa sensed that he was not comfortable with them. But he sensed her there all the same.

Why was he so scared of her?

CHAPTER 22

Systa franticly worked at Kata's side. She welcomed the presence of the other woman for she was finding it hard to focus. Joka still lay unconscious. Systa was nervous and upset and she was having a hard time not showing it. It bothered her that she had not seen this.

Why had the goddess not shown her that her sister would be injured? Had she known, she could have stopped her from going out that day. Worse still, she did not believe this was the vision of Joka that foretold of a battle whose outcome was not yet set. It was how she knew that her sister would not die. The vision still rang true and the battle was in the future.

But why had she not seen the danger that Joka had faced that day? It disturbed her and made her mind whirl in many different directions as she tried to focus on Joka.

Systa and Kata had removed the arrow and managed to get the bleeding to stop. The other wound was minor and it would heal without much assistance. Systa had cleaned and cauterized it and had securely placed a cloth bandage over the wound.

"The arrow struck cleanly. She will heal nicely," Kata said. Systa nodded in agreement.

"Free of infection she will be."

"You are tired, you should rest." Kata placed a hand on her arm, but Systa shook her head.

"With child are you. Need you rest more than I."

"I will tell the others that she will be alright." Kata decided what Systa needed was to be alone with her sister.

Systa stared with worry at Joka. She should have been able to prevent this. What use was her gift if she couldn't help the ones closest to her? She brushed the hair away from Joka's face with a tenderness not seen by many.

So beautiful was her sister. She was the one with strength, the one who had saved them from their father. Her hand began to tremble as she touched her sister's face and was pleased that it was not hot.

"What is it you fear sister?" Joka spoke even though her eyes remained closed. It took only a moment longer before her gaze fell with concern on Systa.

"I did not see."

"You are only human, same as I. The goddess has blessed us, but even she does not reveal all. Perhaps she does not know all."

"Wisdom you speak, but fear I still," Systa grabbed Joka's hand and held it tightly in her small hand.

"Fear not, for I will never let anything harm you."

"Myself I worry not," Systa said. "You I cannot protect."

"I do not need you to protect me. I can protect myself."

"But see I did not," she said again. Why did it bother her so?

"Then I shall watch with my own eyes. You can't prevent the harshness of our world from touching me. Know that I do not fear it for I will face it head on and I will not falter."

"Live I not without you." She spoke the truth of her heart.

"I am not going anywhere." Joka promised and gave her sister's hand a squeeze and felt how it trembled.

"Get Peder I shall." Systa rose before Joka saw the tears in her eyes. She went for the door and disappeared through it.

II

Seera found Peder silently sitting in the chapel, staring at the large wooden cross. He was so lost in the torment of his thoughts that he did not hear his sister approach until she was beside him. Their eyes met and a quiet message of understanding passed between the siblings.

"She is awake." Seera laid a hand on his arm. "Systa says she will be fine."

Peder closed his eyes and drew in a sigh of relief. His heart seemed to be beating normally again instead of clenched in fear. A shiver went through him that dispelled his worry, but not his anger.

"I want him to suffer for what he has done." Peder looked at Seera.

"I know."

"I have been sitting here begging God to take such hate from my soul." Peder ran his hands through his hair. "Yet I still want to see him dead."

"It is a natural reaction when the one you love is hurt by another."

"I saw what such a feeling did to Rafn when you were taken." Peder took her hand in his and held it. "I pray that I don't become so lost."

"This is not the same," Seera said. "Rafn did not know if I and our unborn son were alive. He didn't know where we were. Joka is alive and she is here."

"I know." He looked deep into her eyes. "She will live this time, but I don't believe for a moment that this is over. Kale will come again and we already know he is not a man of honor. He will attack from the shadows."

"Then you will watch the shadows brother," she said. Peder knew that she was right. He wouldn't for a moment let his guard down. Joka would not welcome it but she would have to suffer his vigilance. To lose her would be much worse.

"I will keep her safe, whether she wants me to or not."

III

Joka stirred from her precarious sleep when the door to the lodge opened. She watched him warily. His blue eyes pierced her with such intense concern it caused her to tense.

"How are you?" He came and sat beside her on the bed. He grabbed her hand and brought it to his face as if needing to feel that she was still warm.

"I will heal. There is no need for you to look at me as if I am about to die." She shifted to ease the pain in her shoulder.

"You almost did die." Peder dropped her hand and got to his feet. He walked across the room with his fists clenched at his sides. He breathed in deeply and said something under his breath. She suspected it was a prayer.

"He didn't kill me." Joka tried to sit up but Peder was suddenly beside her, helping her into a more comfortable position.

"Joka..." His eyes pleaded with her.

"I love you Peder," She tried to find patience through her irritation. It wasn't as easy as Seera made it look.

"And I you," he said. "I don't want to lose you."

"I don't intend on dying."

"Nobody intends to die." Peder snapped. "You are as human as the next person Joka. You bleed when you are cut and you are not immune to death."

"I don't claim to be immortal," Joka's voice hardened in anger.

"Then don't take what has happened lightly."

"I do not. I was caught unprepared and it will not happen again." Patience was far beyond her reach now, but her anger sharpened.

"I will not allow him to get close to you again." He informed her and there was a challenge in his voice that would not be denied.

"I don't need you to protect me. I am as capable as you."

"I don't doubt your skills Joka, but I do not trust Kale. He will come at you anyway he can."

"And I will be watching."

"You are only one person. You can accept that I will not let you out of my sight, or not. Make no mistake, I won't leave you unguarded."

"Whether I welcome it or not." Joka stared at him in disbelief.

"Makes no difference to me."

She was still weak from the loss of blood and she struggled to keep her eyes fixed on him. They shut for a moment all the same and this made Peder realize how weak she still was and she hated that.

"Let us not fight." Peder lay down beside her and pulled her close to him, cautious of her injuries.

Joka gave in to the need for sleep and let her eyes remain close. Peder stroked her hair from her face and it was hard for her to deny that she enjoyed it. He kissed her forehead and the warmth of his lips made her relax and she let sleep claim her.

IV

Kale turned feverish and his arm became infected. The skin around the cut was beginning to swell and it was tender to the touch. Onnar and

Vikkar were not healers and had no idea what to do for Kale. It had been days since he was injured and he was only getting worse.

He had complained at first of the pain, but they had ignored him as they always did. Neither of them had ever liked Kale and would gladly leave him there in the mountains to die, but he was a favored of Bekan.

They had hid within a concealed cave they had found as the Raven's men scoured the area. Luck was on their side when the snow began as it hindered the warrior's search. The three men kept within the cave for days, eating what dried food they had and denying themselves the warmth of a fire.

They kept as silent as they could, talking only when necessary. When Kale's complaints had started Onnar had pierced him with a vicious look that warned him to be quiet.

Kale was not forthcoming with the truth of what had happened and why Rafn had sent his men after them. He would tell them only that he'd run into one of the warlord's warriors and injured him, likely killing him, which of course neither man believed. It was obvious that whoever the man was had enough fight in him to wound Kale.

Kale obviously started something he couldn't finish. That morning Kale had not woken. At first Onnar thought it was a blessing not to have to listen to his whining, but then he realized that Kale was burning with fever.

Begrudgingly Onnar gave the order to gather their belongings and head back to Skahi. They had not brought horses with them so that they could hide more effectively from sight. It was left up to the two men to take turns carrying Kale along the trail.

They arrived back in Skahi amidst a snowstorm. Bekan met them at the edge of the village and was not pleased that they had returned once again without his daughter. He ordered that Kale be brought to his dwelling and called for the healer.

"What happened?" Bekan demanded.

"Kale was not too eager to relay the story," Onnar said. "We were gone hunting and he was left to watch the village. When we returned he was injured. His only claim was that one of Rafn's men chanced upon him and they fought."

"Did he kill the man?" Bekan snapped and Onnar had to fight not to laugh. Truly he didn't think that Kale was capable of bringing down one of the Raven's warriors. Anyone trained by that man would not be so easy to fight. That Kale lived at all was a mystery that Onnar had yet to figure out.

"Nay," Onnar said. "We had to stay for a few days in a cave to hide from Rafn's men. Kale became worse so we took our chances and fled."

"It was wise." Bekan had to agree, even if it angered him. "Rafn will be on the alert, it is best to wait until he has lowered his defenses again."

Bekan walked to the window and stared out at the falling snow. "Damn Rakel for the trouble she has caused."

V

Bekan paced back and forth across the main living space in his lodge. His wife and mother sat at the table watching him. He was angry. Winter had come with force and snow had closed the mountain passes. The frigid winds would make the ocean route too dangerous to attempt.

Who did this lord think he was to come to this new land and take his daughter from him? The Raven wouldn't scare him. He claimed to receive his power from Thor, the god of thunder and storms. Bekan had set aside his beliefs of the Norse gods and taken up Christianity.

The teachings of the Priest told that there was only one true God. Those gods he had falsely worshipped as a young man became nothing but memories. There was a time he had feared them so much they made him weary of everything that he did. Every time there was a storm when he was a boy he had hidden beneath his covers, sure that he had angered Thor and he was coming for him.

Even now he felt nervous whenever lightning streaked across the sky and thunder echoed in the heavens. Thor was not real, he would have to remind himself. It was almost too much of a coincidence that a son of Thor had come to his land and stolen his daughter.

He refused to feel fear. Rafn Vakrson would not shame him into revealing his childhood fear of the Aesir god. Instead Bekan turned to anger. He would meet this lordly man and prove him false.

He would have his daughter back. When spring came to steal the land back from winter's grip, he would face Rafn. The warlord would need to be sworn into the council of men. By the laws set for this new land he would have to return Bekan's daughter.

"Why would your daughter dishonor me so?" He turned his wrath on his wife and she met his gaze with fear in her eyes. Good. She should be afraid.

"She is scared of Kale." His mother answered instead. Amma stared at her son with disapproval. She had been against giving Rakel to Kale in marriage. She had not understood that it was an act of faith, rewarding Kale for being the most loyal of them all.

Bekan knew that the other men didn't respect Kale, but Kale served him well, as he always followed his orders without question.

He had heard the rumors that Kale was rough with the women, but he believed them to be just embellished stories. Rakel had no right to fear him. A wife was to obey her husband. If he had to discipline her when she stepped out of line, it was his right. Why did his mother question this?

Bekan grumbled. "That girl is too headstrong. Mother, you fill her head with too many foolish things."

"Bah," his mother spat. "She is a strong woman. You have failed to see her worth and would give her to such dog scum as Kale."

His mother had always been challenging. His father had liked her spirit, but Bekan had thought that his weakness. He allowed her too much freedom. Bekan had sworn not to make the same mistake with his own wife.

Marina sat silent and watchful as she always did. He had selected a quiet wife from among those available to him as the son of a blacksmith. She had quickly come to understand that she was never to disobey him.

Then his father had died and Bekan decided to take his wife and mother to this new land in search of a better life than that of a blacksmith. He hated working in the heat of the forge.

In Iceland he started his own village and the people came from all over to join Skahi. He was elected to the council of men and enjoyed the role of a leader. He had always envied the Jarls and warlords that had ruled throughout the Viking world. He couldn't claim the title, but he strove to rule with an iron fist.

Christianity had been the tool that he used to bring his people under his rule. The priest that had come to him had given him the perfect opportunity. It had not been so hard to sway the villagers from their old gods with the promises of the new. All but Danr had converted.

He sneered at thoughts of the warrior. He had been his strongest warrior and therefore he had not pushed him too hard. Had allowed him more freedom then he gave the others.

It had been his mistake. Danr never feared him. Without fear to hold a person's loyalty, how could you trust in it?

In the early days of the village, he had given demonstrations of what happened to those who disobeyed. He'd burned those accused of witchcraft at the stake in the name of God.

To secure the warriors he had given them much land and goods. With the men under his rule, the women were forced to obey. Still Danr had held to his faith and his convictions.

His disloyalty was proven when he sided with the Raven. He would pay for that and for failing to return his daughter.

VI

Danr sat with the other warriors in the great hall. The bitter cold outside kept the people locked within. He glanced discreetly across the room to where Rakel was sitting with Hadde. The remnants of supper had been cleared away and a skald seated by the hearth was telling stories. His voice rang out loud and boisterous.

Rakel leaned over to say something to Hadde, but Danr was too far away to hear any of their conversation. Whatever the dwarf said in return caused her to smile and the warrior realized it was the first time he had seen her so happy. Back in Skahi she was always so serious.

He had always thought her beautiful. Perhaps when he'd grown to be a man it had become the real reason he had stayed in Skahi. He had watched her grow from a lanky girl to a woman of rare beauty.

Danr would never have admitted having feelings for Bekan's daughter. He knew they would not be welcomed by the man. How she would feel he had never known, as she ignored him as she had all the others. Not once had her gaze lingered on him.

It had been alright. He had always known that he would never have her. It had given him enough joy just living beside her, watching her. That is until it was announced that she would be given to Kale in marriage. He had gone out into the mountains alone that day and sacrificed a deer to Odin and begged the god to prevent such a thing from happening.

He had been furious that Bekan would give his only daughter to a man like Kale. He had never thought much of the man who had shown up two years ago in Skahi. The man had no skill with a blade and thought too highly of himself. It had amazed him how quickly Bekan had taken Kale into his confidence and given him authority over the others.

It shouldn't have happened. The other warriors should never have accepted it so easily. Danr never understood what power Bekan held over them. Was it because they were so used to wielding under the leadership of another man that they couldn't think for themselves?

They never questioned Bekan's rule over them. They never wondered for a moment how a man who was once a blacksmith deserved to be their leader. True he'd been elected by the people to the position, so it was their own doing. But he would never understand how this had happened.

Since coming to Ragnarr he'd come to learn what a true leader really was. Rafn Vakrson was of lordly rank and yet he didn't boast the way Bekan always did. Rafn's men admired him, trusted him and even befriended him. Rafn welcomed these things and gave them in return.

He is what a leader was supposed to be. Though Rafn was the greatest of all warriors, he did not use his strength to keep his people in line. He valued them. It was an awe inspiring revelation that made Danr regret spending so long in Skahi.

If it hadn't been for Rakel, he wouldn't have stayed so long.

He took a drink of his mead and once again turned his attention to the copper haired woman that had him wondering about so many things. He had always believed she was beautiful, but only in the last few weeks had he learned who she really was. He had come to admire her spirit. That she'd stood up and not accepted her fate had made him take a closer look at her.

He had been so happy when she'd run. He'd not wanted to see her married to Kale. He had not wanted to watch as that weasel beat the spirit from her. Danr had even thought to take her away from Skahi himself, but she did not know him, did not trust him, and so doubted she would have left with him.

That she had taken it upon herself to fight for her freedom had impressed him. He had gone with Kale, yet the whole time he had known that he would not allow the man to catch her. It had pleased him when Rafn had stepped in and prevented Kale from acting.

"Your thoughts are heavy." Hachet punched Danr in the arm bringing the warrior out of his heavy contemplations.

"You are right." Danr raised his mug to bang it against that of the other man. "It is a night to get drunk."

"I will agree to that." Hachet laughed and the two men did their best to render themselves unconscious.

CHAPTER 23

Joka soon became annoyed with Peder as her shadow. When he had said that he was not going to let her out of his sight he meant it. It put a strain on their relationship. She wanted him to leave her alone and was constantly cursing under her breath, but her foul mood did not deter him.

She was finding it hard to give him the slip, now that winter had locked them in its embrace and the mountain passes were under snow. They were trapped into their new home and to Joka it was a prison.

The others welcomed this time as a chance to relax and celebrate. People stayed late in the great hall drinking, and listening to the skald weave his tales, as he often did after the evening meal had been cleared away.

Kata glowing in her advancing pregnancy sat across the table from Joka. Peder sat beside her as he always did, but his attention was given to Dagstyrr and Rafn as they discussed their plans for turning Ragnarr into a trading post.

Joka grew tired of the talk and decided it was time to slip off to the longhouse and her bed. When she was on her feet, Peder turned abruptly to her and she had the sense that he intended to follow her.

"Stay," she said. "I only go to sleep. Certainly I will be safe from here to the longhouse."

Peder scowled but wisely chose not to argue with her. "Goodnight then." He watched her as she crossed the room and out the door.

At once Joka felt relief. She drew in a breath of the cold air and let it refresh her senses. As she let the breath out it formed visibly on the air before her. She pulled her cloak closed around her to protect her from the sharp bite of the wind as she walked to the closest longhouse.

No one else was outside except for the guards as she stepped silently through the snow. The wind suddenly howled and picked up as it snatched at her long woolen cloak. It caught her braids and threw them out behind her.

She pulled open the door to the longhouse and had to fight the wind to shut it again. A fire burned in the central hearth and she went to stand before it. She held her hands to the flames and welcomed the warmth.

Her sister had retired long before and Joka had assumed her asleep, but she was mistaken. Systa came to stand next to her. Her hair was a mess as if she'd been wrestling someone in her sleep. Her eyes were wide and Joka saw a touch of fear in their silvery glow.

"What is it sister?"

"Wind has shaken me from sleep," Systa said.

"The wind has put fear into you?" Joka questioned with a sharp edge to her voice. It was merely concern that had caused it but Systa met her gaze with surprise.

"Dreams troubled is all." She shook her head as if to dispel some bad image that lay before her.

"You wish to talk about it?"

"Not yet ready. Must first understand its meaning."

"Then let us sit and watch the fire for a time before we seek our rest." Joka motioned to two wooden chairs that sat close to the hearth.

Systa joined her and they sat for awhile enjoying the warmth as the fierce wind blew up against the side of the longhouse. Joka added wood to the fire and sat back to watch the flames catch at it. Systa stared blankly into the orange fingers that licked at the wood and Joka grew concerned at her silence.

A shutter blew open and Joka went to the window to secure it. Before pulling it back into place she noticed that the snow had begun to fall. It twirled and danced in the wind's embrace. It seeped through to touch the warmth of Joka's cheek. She secured the shutter and turned to find Systa gone.

Joka stared down the hall to their sleeping area just in time to see her slip behind the thin wall that was used to secure their privacy.

II

Hadde sat on his bed in the longhouse that housed the single men. The wind screamed in the darkness and shook the outside wall of his sleeping area, though it was not the storm that kept him awake, but the noises coming from the other side of the thin partition that separated him from his neighbor.

The warrior named Hachet occupied the space and he was not spending his night alone. Soft feminine giggles reached him as did more intimate sounds of their lovemaking. It had surprised Hadde the first time he'd been woken in the night to the grunting sounds of male pleasure and the answering mews of the woman who shared his bed.

Hadde had been a child when he'd been cast out on his own and had not been given the knowledge of what men and women did together in the dark. It had at once made him uncomfortable and aroused unknown feelings inside of him. An urge to understand what they did kept him restless and awake each time Hachet had brought a woman to his bed.

He couldn't stand to hear any more. He crept silently from his bed and went out to the communal area to seek some kind of peace from the torment of his beating heart and the sweat that had come to his hands.

He reached the hearth to find the man Berthor already there. He turned and smiled as the dwarf approached. He had been nothing but kind to the short man since his arrival and they were fast becoming friends. This was new for Hadde who had never enjoyed the bond of camaraderie with anyone other than Rakel.

It was not just Berthor either. Many of the men, including the warriors, treated Hadde as a man. They did not tease him about his size or his lack of strength to raise a sword.

"They keeping you awake too?" Berthor laughed. He had the sleeping area attached to the other side of Hachet's.

"It is not the first time," Hadde admitted.

"Hachet has a healthy appetite." The Christian man joked. Hadde only smiled in reply, afraid to ask what he meant.

"I should have found myself a wife to bring with me." Berthor's tone was wishful.

"Are there no unmarried women here?" Hadde wondered at the gleam that had come to Berthor's eyes.

"Some, but not many," Berthor said.

"Is there not one among them that you could marry?"

"A couple have caught my eye, but none have held my interest. I am not sure what it is I seek. I was in love once and perhaps she still holds too much of my heart."

"Why did you not marry her?"

"She never knew of my feelings," Berthor said. "She was given in marriage to a man of her father's choosing."

"I am sorry." The flames sputtered and crackled as Hadde watched them. He noticed at the center of the orange and red fire burned a blue flame.

"It doesn't matter." Berthor smiled. "She found happiness with her husband and that is all that I care about."

"I hope you will find another." The dwarf told him and for a moment he was clutched by a sadness that threatened to overwhelm him. This talk of love and marriage sounded so wonderful, but it was not something that he would ever find for himself. What woman would marry one such as him? Berthor must have understood his sudden quietness for his next comment took Hadde by surprise.

"There must be a girl that would not care about your size," Berthor said. Surprised Hadde attempted to smile.

"It is alright." Hadde shrugged. He had never expected such things for himself.

"You have a big heart my friend," Berthor said. "There is a girl who will notice that and love you for it."

"Thank you, for your kind words. I appreciate it, but don't feel sad for me. I have come to accept who and what I am."

Leikr, carrying an ewer, pushed his way in from outside. Snow coated his hair and cloak and he paused long enough to brush it off. He stopped when he saw the two men and smiled. "Good I will not have to drink alone."

"What is it you have?" Berthor asked.

"Honey mead," Leikr said. "I brought it from Skiringssal and it is almost gone. Please share it with me."

Leikr found some drinking horns and poured them each some mead. They drank in relative silence and let the fermented drink warm them from the inside out. The drink numbed Hadde's mind and his troubled thoughts so that when finally he returned to his bed he fell deeply asleep and nothing disturbed him.

III

Rafn walked the walls checking on his men. The sun would soon rise and the next shift would take over. The storm that had blown only hours before had stilled and the sky had cleared to produce a wide unmarred expanse that had turned from black to grey with the promise of the coming day.

The rough ocean beyond was stark in its beauty that caught the first rays of the sun as it crept over the mountains. Rafn felt at once a part of this new and quiet land. He could almost imagine the port they would build and the village that would expand past the current compound to the area that had been left between it and the dock they had already built. People would come from all over to the new trading center. It would become as large as Skiringssal, yet no Jarl would rule it.

When the snows melted he would be forced to meet with the council of men and be made a part of it. It was this council that ruled Iceland in a diplomatic way. No Jarl or King to dictate how things should be.

Still a leader was needed to keep the order. He had been appointed as such, but truth be told he would have been just as happy if someone else had filled the role. The men looked to him as their warlord, a position that he had thought to leave behind. Yet it was still needed. He was taking on both the responsibility of the defense of the village and their lands, as well as keeping those within his community justly treated and satisfied.

Without Peder's help he would have grown frustrated long ago. Rafn had been feeling restless of late. A feeling he had hoped would settle once they reached Iceland. It had for a time, until the cold had set in. He tried to tell himself that it was simply the boredom of winter that was getting to him, but he knew that was not true.

He felt the first stirrings of the storm that had been dormant inside of him all these long months since he'd found his wife and son. It was only a faint prickling of sensation that centered down deep, but he feared that it meant that the god was not yet finished with him.

Mighty Thor, god of thunder and storms, and charged with the order of chaos. What more could he give of himself than he already had. Was it not enough hundreds of men had been killed by his sword as well as those of his men, all in Thor's name as he sought to still the violence within? Had he not already earned his right to the peace he had found.

The storm would awaken. He didn't need Systa to tell him it would be so. Even before she had spoken the words, he had known. It was inside of him and he did not welcome it waking from its slumber.

He walked the outer stretch of the circular enclosure, nodding to his men as he passed. They each bid him good morning and returned to their duty of keeping watch. Not that he expected any trouble at this time of year, when travel through the mountains was impossible, but still he was watchful of all that went on around him. He wouldn't be the man he was if he allowed his guard to drop. It would not happen, not even under the illusion of peace.

Rafn glanced down from the wall to see the woman Rakel crossing to the kitchen. His eyes narrowed on her as she pulled the hood of her cloak over her red mane of hair. There would be trouble because of her. He knew that when the snow melted into spring waters, his peace would be shattered and the raven would come again to haunt him.

He would make Ragnarr into a place that held people's hearts the way Skiringssal had once done for him. It was a new hope, a new beginning and he would see that people were not wrong in trusting him.

"My lord." Hachet climbed the ladder to stand next to Rafn. "All is well?"

"The world sleeps around us," Rafn said. "Nothing much is moving beyond the boundaries of our lands."

"That is good."

"You seem content."

"I am my lord." His face beamed with excitement. "It was a most pleasant night."

Rafn raised an eyebrow for the wind had howled and the snow had blown through most of the night, having kept everyone from venturing too far outside. The gleam in Hachet's eyes made the warlord laugh.

"It would seem that I will be hearing complaints from my other men about being kept awake all night."

"Not all night." Hachet grinned.

"I leave the men in your capable care," Rafn said. He disappeared down the same ladder that Hachet had just ascended.

Rafn caught sight of Dagstyrr and hurried to catch up with him. The two walked to the great hall where they would sit and discuss the division of work that would need to be done once the winter came to an end.

IV

Systa watched with wonder as Hadde made his way across the compound. If it wasn't for Rafn's insistence about keeping the snow cleared away to make walking easier, the dwarf would have gotten stuck. She had heard of such men as he, but had never met one before.

It was true that he had entered her dreams before they had actually met, but seeing him in person was quite a different experience than the vague image her mind had conjured. She had seen into his soul and knew the purity of his heart. In the dream they had touched and he left an imprint on her.

Though his life had been a sad one, he remained true to the goodness inside. He had not turned to violence or hate. It was an oddity that confused her. All men had it in them to be ruthless and violent. Even those she knew to be good men, such as Peder and Rafn, would use their strength against another when it was called for. They had learned to control the savagery in their souls, but it still existed. Yet she had not sensed such a need in Hadde.

He had a great deal of love within, and she had understood his fear, his sadness and the loneliness, that matched her own. There had been no wish for death or to kill. He had the use of magic. She had known that at once by the aroma such use left on a person. Only one familiar with it would smell it and understand the meaning.

It was another thing they shared. It made her ever more curious about the short man who had not so long ago entered her dreams.

It had come first as knowledge that there was another like her somewhere. She had felt his presence, felt the truth of the person he was. Through chants and prayers to the goddess she had been given the knowledge of him.

When it became clear that she was to lead Rafn to Iceland, she knew that she would find him. It had not been until they were almost to the new land that she had her first sense of what he looked like. That he was a dwarf had come as a surprise at first but something that she had since become comfortable with.

One such as he was favored by the gods. She had felt her excitement grow when first she became aware of his flight through the mountains. She had become so nervous that she would meet him at last. It was almost too much to contain, but she told no one of him. He was hers and hers alone. Not even Joka would understand the attachment she had for the dwarf.

She had finally come face to face with the man who had touched her dreams with hope and a promise for the end to her loneliness. Her heart clenched in pain as memory of their first encounter sharpened in her mind.

He had feared her. He had backed away from her as if she were evil. He had looked at her as so many before him had. Her dwarf, who had the purest heart that ever existed, was scared of her.

Tears threatened as he came closer and noticed her in the shadows. His eyes widened in shock and he was reluctant to walk any closer. He met her gaze and for a moment they stared at each other before he veered widely around her and ducked inside the hall.

He did not feel their connection the way she did. He didn't understand in the whole of this cruel world that it was only he that she would give her trust to. She would give it to no other man.

The hurt and humiliation of those times that her father forced her into strange men's beds was buried deep within her. Brutal and cruel men whose strength she could not fight. She had been so afraid. That fear had taken hold of her and threatened to overcome her. Only her magic had allowed her to free herself, but not before she'd been scarred in a place that only she could see.

Her dreams had promised her another that would understand. Not in the way that Joka did, as woman to woman, sister to sister, but as a man who cared for the woman he loved. A tear broke free and trickled down her cold cheek.

Hadde feared her as so many before him had. Forever she was cast the witch. It was a safe haven where she had hid for so long. The haven had become like a prison. Even as she would allow no one in, neither could she let herself out.

She had wanted only for someone to understand her isolation. She had thought that the dwarf in her dreams would be the answer to her loneliness.

How wrong she had been.

CHAPTER 24

Almost every morning Joka was on the training field. She preferred to do her practicing when the warriors were not around. If she practiced later in the day, Rakel and Seera would join her. They were each becoming quite adept at the handling of their swords. She was a proud teacher.

Sometimes she had a need to quietly practice alone before the others tumbled from their beds to begin the day. Only those that stood guard were witness to her early morning workout. At times she caught them watching, at other times Peder would join her after she had spent the night in his bed.

Those times had become less frequent. Whenever possible she avoided intimacy with Peder. Her moods had been swinging wildly one way then the other and more often than not she was irritable and in need of her solitude.

Peder sensed her withdrawing from him and they often fought. He had not let up on his hovering and this was the main problem between them. It caused resentment that she had not wanted to feel towards him. She longed to open her soul to him with the same ease she had her body.

She held back, not allowing him to claim too much of her. She wouldn't allow him to consume her too completely. She feared what that would mean. She had worked so hard to become the woman she was and she would not throw that away so he could feel like a man. He had to accept that she was fiercely protective of herself.

She saw him hardening towards her of late. When they sat together at meals, they didn't speak to one another. He always watched her, but rarely approached her during the day. Even in the desperate moments to satisfy their hunger for each other, there was not much said.

A part of her knew that driving them apart was her own doing. That her inability to completely trust him hurt him in some fundamental way that she could not fully understand.

There were moments when she would catch him staring at her with such misery reflected in his eyes that she almost let her guard down. She didn't know how to make that step that would seal her fate. It was far easier to step in the opposite direction and place more distance between them.

It was at those times that she needed to find the calmness within. She sought to work with her sword in a dance that separated her from all else except the movements of the blade and the placing of her feet.

The wind brushed past with warmth that had not been there a few days ago. It carried the scent of spring and rebirth. It was a time of year that usually brought Joka happiness, but she was now unable to find the joy in watching the earth come back to life.

She pivoted on her left foot and stopped dead. Rafn was standing just past the reach of her arm. He stood with his arms crossed in front of him as if he'd been there for some time studying her. She lowered her sword to face him.

"I think it is time warrior woman," he challenged.

"For what my lord?"

"To show me what you are made of." His voice deepened and carried the power she knew he possessed. His voice rumbled as if it was the thunder god speaking and not the man himself. He saw her hesitation. "If you think you are up for it."

"I welcome it," Joka's jaw hardened as she raised her sword in front of her. She felt the sword's power flow up her arm and she seized hold of it.

Rafn's sword appeared in his hand, though she had not seen him reach for it. It seemed oddly surreal. It was his Frankish sword, the one he called the Serpent and had carried into many battles. There was a fire in his eyes and she knew that he had no intention of being easy on her.

He waited for her to come to him. She stepped and swung. Metal vibrated against metal. Again and again they were brought together in a perfectly timed display. He came at her with strength and she found herself working hard to keep up with him.

He wielded his sword as if it were an extension of his arm which he had supreme control over. As she marveled at his strength and agility, she would not allow him to see her weaken.

The men on the walls watched in silent amazement as their warlord and the warrior woman, who had shown them such courage and strength, practiced in the field. Rafn didn't go easy on her because she was a woman, but pressed her as relentlessly as he would any of them.

If they had been impressed by Joka's skill before, they found a new level of awe as they watched her fighting to maintain her control against a man feared by many.

II

Peder stood in the shadows watching with a grim expression pinched on his face. His eyes had narrowed in an attempt to maintain the jealousy that threatened him. It was a foolish reaction. Rafn was in love with his sister. Yet it had always been Peder that had practiced with Joka.

He saw the fierce excitement in her eyes as she faced Rafn and stopped his blade with hers. There was a challenge set on Rafn's face that he was pushing her to meet. Rafn was enjoying it and it angered Peder. It was not a rational thought he knew. That Rafn had come to respect Joka enough to test her in front of his men was something that she deserved, but it had always been Peder who had practiced with her, taught her.

He was not jealous that the other man's skills surpassed his own. He was the Raven of legend and it was not something he strived to live up to. What irked him was that Joka danced with him in their mock battle as she had once done with him. She was being challenged to her limit and it brought something alive in her that Peder had been failing to do through these long winter months.

Their relationship was becoming strained to the point where it was about to break and Peder was desperate not to lose her. His jaw clenched in fury as he continued to observe their sparring match.

He watched Rafn trick her and when she went to block his sword he changed its swing and brought it back up and under her arm. She almost lost her grip on her own sword and had to steady her balance to keep from falling.

Rafn did not smile, but kept his eyes deadly serious as he stepped back and waited for her to resume her stance. She growled in frustration fueling her energy to continue.

Peder felt a moment of pride at her determination. All those that had crept over to watch had grown quiet as they waited with anxious anticipation for the action to resume on the practice field.

Joka's gaze met his for a brief moment. A spark of irritation glinted in the blue of her eyes before she turned from him.

III

Joka was not surprised to see Peder watching from the shadows. What irritated her was the look on his face that told her plainly that he disapproved of what she was doing. Damn him. Did he think her too weak to train with a warrior such as Rafn?

Was he angry that the warlord had found her worthy enough to cross blades in a display of strength and skill?

Joka didn't care what he thought. Excitement bubbled up from that place that sought to prove her worth. Rafn had come to her and challenged her. She wouldn't back down from such a request. Peder had no right to expect her to.

Rafn's sword blurred slightly in front of her and she almost failed to stop its descent. The contact of their swords vibrated up her arm and she had to fight to steady herself.

Rafn pulled his sword back and anticipated her next swing. Again metal met metal and knocked her off balance. This time her vision blurred and she lost focus on more than her opponent's sword.

She staggered back as if drunk and reached to steady herself. She caught a glimpse of worry on Rafn's face before darkness claimed her.

IV

Peder raced forward the moment he saw her falling. He reached for her just as she collapsed onto the ground. Rafn was at his side, his sword already gone from his hands. Joka lay unconscious in Peder's arms.

"Joka," Peder called to her and touched her face, but she didn't respond. He lifted her into his arms and made for the gates with Rafn following at his heels.

"I did not mean to push her so hard," Rafn said.

"Yes you did." Peder answered but he was not angry at his brother-in law. "She would have been furious if you had gone easy on her."

"Still…"

"Get Systa." Peder ordered him before Rafn could say anymore. Rafn veered off and headed for the longhouse while Peder kept to his course and brought Joka to his dwelling.

Joka stirred as he crossed the threshold into the lodge. Her eyes fluttered open and for a moment she stared at him in confusion before she became angry. "Put me down," she ordered.

"Nay." Peder continued to his bed. Only once she was safely lowered onto it did he step away from her.

Systa pushed her way in without knocking and went to Joka's side. A look crossed the Seer's face that he couldn't decipher. Her silver eyes met his and he had to prevent himself from shivering from their iciness.

"Must go, speak with Joka alone will I," Systa said. Peder wanted to argue but he knew the futility of it. He left the sisters alone and found his way back outside where Rafn waited with Seera.

"How is she?" Seera asked.

"She is awake. Systa wouldn't let me stay." Peder knew he sounded like a sulking boy but he did not care. He was once again being kept from the woman he loved.

V

Systa pushed Joka gently back down when she tried to sit up. Joka scowled in response to her sister's concern. She was fine. She had just gotten a bit dizzy for a moment. She didn't need to be treated like there was something wrong with her. She was not a child.

"Need a moment you do," Systa said. "You have pushed too hard. Not good for the life within."

Joka looked at her in confusion. "I am fine. My life is in no peril from a momentary weakness. I have yet to eat and that is all."

"Sister, strong are you, but foolish."

Joka scowled in reaction to Systa's words. She would not apologize for wanting to better herself with a sword. Men strove to do so, why not her? She met her sister's sharp intruding eyes.

"Disapprove I not of use with sword. Save us you did with your courage to use such a weapon."

"Then why do you carry such a look of disapproval on your face."

"Concern sister, not disapproval."

"You need not feel concern for me, I can take care of myself," she said. Why couldn't those around her understand that?

"But can you care for child?" Systa's eyes pierced her and she felt a sudden trembling shutter through her. For a long moment they remained locked in each other's searching gaze.

"Child?" Joka almost choked to get the question out. Goosebumps rose on her flesh from the chill that seized her.

Systa reached out to place a hand on Joka's abdomen and as she did she closed her eyes and concentrated on something that only she could feel, could see. Joka watched her face for any sign that she had misunderstood what her sister was trying to tell her. Systa opened her eyes and Joka saw in that silvery look what she needed to know.

"A pulsing energy brews within. Life has sparked in you sister. Child of your blood and his…to bond you together forever."

"I am not with child." Joka tried to dismiss Systa's words. She couldn't be… she couldn't. Yet in this very bed she had lain with Peder time and again. It took only once for a woman to ripen with life, and she had been with Peder often. She felt a sick tightening in her stomach as she accepted the truth of it.

"I don't know how to be a mother," Joka said in a whisper that she doubted even Systa could hear, but her sister nodded in understanding.

Systa took her hand and held in tightly. "Aye, learn you will."

VI

Peder pushed his way into his dwelling. He wouldn't be kept locked out of his own lodge. The door swung open harder than he had intended. Joka and Systa were deep in conversation and both looked at him in shock. Something passed across Joka's face that he did not understand.

He recognized it immediately as vulnerability. He frowned in a need to understand. Joka had never shown any hint of frailty in all the time he had known her. As their eyes met he saw a deep seeded fear in them. It was there only an instant before her eyes clouded over and the veil of her independence shielded her susceptibility.

Still she did not trust him to help her. Even as her face hardened against his inquisitive stare, she closed herself off from him.

Damn her for not allowing him in.

"I demand to know what goes on here?" His anger flared in desperation.

"Demand?" Joka growled. "You have no right to make demands of me my lord."

"Don't I? Are we not lovers Joka? Have you not lain in my bed of your own willingness?"

He was aware of Systa's steady gaze on him, but he ignored the Seer. This was between the two of them. He turned with a vicious scowl on his face to look at the small silver eyed woman, who met his fierceness with bared teeth.

"Wise you not to challenge me," she said. The sharpness in her voice took him off guard. He didn't doubt she would fight as viciously as a viper if cornered. He nodded in understanding and her expression eased.

Systa rose from her perch by Joka's side and moved past him as swiftly and soundlessly as a ghost might travel in the wind. He watched her until she slipped out through the door into the compound beyond.

He turned back to find Joka's anger had risen. He steeled himself for the full impact of her fury. Something had triggered her defenses and she was not about to let him get too close. The pain of that clenched inside of him, killing something vital that was between them.

He had known for a long time that she would never really be his. Why did he fight against it? What perverse destruction in his nature kept him battling against this woman?

Dear God, why did he love her so much?

He let his anger go and felt the sad inevitability settle deep inside his soul. From the moment she had refused to marry him, he should have walked away. He shouldn't have dwelled on the hope that she would come to love him in the same way he loved her. It was beyond her capability to trust any man and he had known that from the start.

He had loved her anyway.

"Alright Joka." He met the question in her eyes. "You win. It is ended. I will not push you to trust me, to love me. You can live alone with your misery, but I can't."

Peder searched her face for any sign of pain at his words, but instead she closed herself more completely than she ever had before. He could almost see that invisible wall rising around her as she held herself emotionless.

He wanted her to scream at him. He wanted her to fight to keep him as fiercely as she fought with her sword. He wanted her to tell him he was wrong.

She didn't and he knew beyond doubt that she never would.

CHAPTER 25

Spring had come and the snow was quickly melting. Peder took advantage of this warm day to take a ride along the shoreline. Many others were outside but he chose to avoid them. Since he had ended his relationship with Joka, he had become somewhat of a loner.

A deep sadness filled him that he couldn't shake. He had begun to think often of Dun'O'Tir and how he missed it. He had not thought it would be so, but he did. At first it had been just a small ache of homesickness, but since this land had failed to deliver the hopes he'd had for it, he longed for home.

It was a fierce and desperate need that grew each day. There was nothing left to hold his heart in Iceland. What had started as an exciting adventure and a quest to win Joka's heart had gone wrong. He had been foolish at best and he knew he could not stay.

To see her each day and remember how she felt in his arms. How her lips had felt beneath his. It was too much for any sane man to be forced to deal with. He would leave when the winter seas became calmer and travel would be less risky.

The wind picked up as he pulled his horse to a stop and jumped down from it. He walked to the stone littered beach that he had come upon and bent to pick up a stone. He tossed it and watched it disappear beneath the choppy water.

The sun slid from behind a cloud to wash over him. He closed his eyes and welcomed the heat of it on his face. It brought such promise.

It spoke of rebirth of the land and he hoped to his soul as well. Once he was gone from this place, back within the comforting walls of Dun'O'Tir he could forget. It would all become just a dream.

He turned at the sound of another horse and looked up to see Dagstyrr. The man smiled in greeting and stopped beside his stallion. Jumping from his own horse he came to join Peder.

"The day is beautiful, is it not," Dagstyrr said.

Peder glanced around as if seeing for the first time what Dagstyrr did. "Aye, it is," he replied, but no joy reached him. Dagstyrr studied him for a moment.

"Do you need to talk my friend?"

"There is nothing to talk about." Peder shrugged his shoulders. It had not gone unnoticed by others that Peder and Joka's relationship had changed.

"Kata tells me that Joka no longer goes to the training field, or teaches the other women."

Peder didn't meet Dagstyrr's gaze but continued to stare out at the water. He had realized at once that Joka no longer trained. He assumed that she had found a more private place to practice.

"Kata tells me also that Joka is not herself. That she avoids everyone but her sister."

"And you think this is my fault?" He turned to Dagstyrr in anger. "She has made her own choices."

"I don't look to lay blame." Dagstyrr had much practice dealing with Rafn's anger over the years, so he did not react to Peder's outburst. "I am just concerned about you both."

"You need not be." Peder lost the edge to his voice. "What is done is done."

"I will not push." Dagstyrr relented.

"Thank you." Peder clenched his jaw to keep from admitting just how much his heart had been damaged. It was not something that men shared with each other.

"Are you up for some hunting?" Dagstyrr's smile returned. He pointed to some hills to the south. "I plan on exploring those."

"Kata does not need you at home this close to her time?"

"Nay, she kicked me out. She was feeling ill this morning and I told her to stay in bed. Still she would not let me hover."

"Women do not like that sort of thing," Peder finally allowed a smile to cross his face.

"I need something to keep me busy or I will go crazy with worry." Dagstyrr climbed back on his horse. "You coming?"

"Absolutely." Peder mounted and raced with Dagstyrr toward the distant hills.

II

"This argument is getting old sister," Joka said. "I will not tell him and that is final."

"When belly grows large, you think he not notice," Systa tried to reason with the same words she had spoken many times over the past few weeks. They sat together outside of the longhouse enjoying the pleasant spring weather.

"Let him notice. I will not crawl to him and beg for his forgiveness. I will not ask him to take me back."

"Love him still you do, yet you fight against it."

"Love is not enough when there is no trust between us. We will each go our own way and that will be that."

"You deny the child."

"The child is mine. I will raise her to be strong and independent. She will know no fear and feel no pain. That is what I will give her."

"Deny her love you will. A soul needs it as much."

"She needs only us."

"Peder will not forsake her. To expect such a thing will not be good for her. Shadows will haunt her life if she knows not the fulfillment of her father," Systa warned.

"We survived without a father's love." Joka's face tightened with her anger, but Systa could also see the hurt.

"Wounded us he did, for not offering us love. Peder not such a man, but has good soul. Wrong you are not to tell him."

Joka met Systa's angry stare. She knew that her sister was right. She knew that Peder would be a good father, caring and gentle. She couldn't go to him. Her pride kept her from seeking him out and giving him such hope. How he would react she didn't know. That he would want the child was not a question that needed to be answered. He would.

Joka didn't fit into his life anymore. Would he take the child from her and leave her with nothing? She couldn't believe that he would, but a child would bind them together forever. He would always be there to haunt her with the way things might have been. With the mistakes that she had made that could not be undone. She didn't know if he would accept her now that she had wounded him so badly.

He avoided her as strongly as she avoided him. He would not so easily forgive her lack of trust in him, or her unwillingness to be what he wanted. She could not change, could not.

He had no right to expect her to.

"Wrong are you," Systa shattered her thoughts. "Change is not what he seeks. Wants only that you and he share heart and soul with no fear."

"He asks too much?"

"Believe you so?"

"Yes." Joka shouted drawing the attention of those that worked close by.

"Scarred are you, worse than I had believed."

III

Systa remained alone beside the longhouse. Lost was she in thoughts so deep that she had trouble making sense of all that she felt and believed. The vision had become more intense lately, keeping her locked in its embrace far into the night.

She could no longer focus on anything but Joka and the fear that something terrible was going to happen to her. Searching for answers, that would not come, only made her feel more desperate.

It had been so long since she had felt such vulnerability. She was once again that frightened little girl that could only hide and watch her mother's torment and pain. She had been unable to prevent that inevitable day when her mother had sunk so deeply into despair that she had taken her own life.

Systa had not been able to save her mother, or herself. It had been Joka who had the strength to stand up to their father and change their lives forever.

Her heart tightened in anguish as images of the vision flashed before her. Dark it was and at its center was Joka, fighting a deadly battle. She would die. That knowledge clenched her suddenly. She had never been

BITTER PASSAGE

able to make out that event clearly, though she had a deep sense that it would end badly.

Systa was helpless to save her. Her powers were working against her. Love for her sister was clouding her vision. She was not being given what she needed.

Gripped in the powerful arms of fear she looked up to see Hadde coming out of his longhouse. He stopped the moment he saw her.

A single tear rolled down Systa's face at his need to escape. He was about to turn as he always did when he stopped. Their eyes locked and he seemed confused. Instead of fleeing he came towards her and she felt her heart pounding in response to his presence.

"Something is wrong."

"Please, fear me not." She pleaded and her eyes filled with tears.

Hadde was stunned at the fear in the witch's eyes. When a tear fell from her silver eyes he stopped. He looked at her then, really looked at her as he'd been afraid to do since he had come to Ragnarr.

What he saw was a scared, vulnerable woman who was perhaps as lonely as he was. It made no sense. It didn't fit with everything he had learned about her. Some had a reluctant respect for her powers, while others like him had simply feared her. Had he judged her prematurely?

Had he reacted with prejudice as quickly as people had always treated him? The sudden thought caused him to question his previous actions towards the woman.

She asked him not to fear her, as if it hurt her deeply that he did. That didn't make sense. Why would she care?

"Came for you I did," she told him in a trembling voice as if she had sensed his confusion, "Came for you."

Hadde seated himself beside Systa and met her teary eyes. "Why?" he found himself asking.

"Want only what all others want," she said.

"What is that?"

"To be loved."

He was shocked by her answer, but he saw the truth betrayed in the expression on her face. She wanted him to love her. She was one of the most beautiful women that Hadde had ever seen, why would she want him?

Certainly there was a man, a warrior more worthy of her. One that would not fear her the way he had. The way she was looking at him made him feel warm inside. It was a feeling that he had never experienced before. Somebody wanted him.

"Why me?"

"Pure are you. Hurt me you would not." She told him and waited with abated breath for his response.

Hadde seemed to understand. Someone had hurt her badly. Some man must have used her. He saw it deep in her eyes, that this man, or was it men, had not been gentle or kind. He was sensing the grief of her past in his own mind as if she were allowing access to her feelings. For a moment it unnerved him that she had the power to will such a thing, but then he understood her need to make another understand.

"I would not," he answered her and took her hand and heard her let out her breath.

They stared at each other in bewilderment. Her with relief and him with a wonder at being offered something he believed he would never possess.

He felt the intimacy of the moment and wondered at its power over him. It touched the loneliness that had always been a part of him and promised to replace it with something beyond his understanding.

The fear in Systa eased as Hadde's hand clasped hers. He had the kindest eyes she had ever seen. She felt safe with him. It was a wonderful feeling, one she hoped she could hold onto forever.

IV

Kale had recovered from his injury and over the winter his arm had strengthened, but he was left with a nasty scar. Each time he tried to overdo using his arm it ached and this only deepened his anger towards Joka.

He lay naked in his bed and felt himself harden at thoughts of her. It would be ecstasy to bring her down. That she lived he had no doubts. She was too stubborn to have succumbed to the wounds she had sustained. They had not been severe enough to stop her.

He ground his teeth in an attempt to settle his fury. The sun streamed through a crack in the shutters to his room and he pushed back the furs that covered him. He found his clothes and pulled them on.

He grabbed up his red cloak and secured it with an oval shaped silver broach. His eye twitched angrily that the maid had not brought him his breakfast. That he would have to go to the building that was used as a kitchen made him mad.

He flung open the door to find a scared young slave girl looking at him with a tray in her hand.

"You are late," he screamed at her.

"Sorry sir." She began to tremble.

"Bring it in." She scooted past him to deposit the tray on the barren table.

"Bring me a bath," he said. She moved to step back outside. Fear shone in her eyes and it empowered him.

"Aye." She nodded and scurried away from his dwelling.

Kale seated himself at the wooden table and tore apart the warm bread. He loved it steaming as it did, straight out of the oven, when it came. If it had been cold the young girl would have felt the back of his hand. Fruit, cheese and cold cuts of boar meat were also on the platter.

He was hungry and he ate with greed. The warm mead that accompanied the meal was welcomed and burned its way down his throat. He felt the effects immediately. By the time the girl and two others returned with the hardened leather tub he was on his way to being drunk.

He watched them lustily as they brought in the heated water. The two women quickly left, but the girl had stayed a moment longer to lay out a drying sheet and some soap for washing.

When she turned to go, Kale rose to his feet. He grabbed her arm in a bruising grip. The girl turned her scared brown eyes up to him and shivered as she saw the drunken look on his face.

"You will wash me." He dropped his clothes before she could even respond.

Kale stepped into the warm water and lay back. When the girl did not move immediately he turned a sharp glance her way. She moved forward and crouched down beside him.

She reluctantly picked up the soap and he leaned forward so that she could scrub it across his back. When she moved to wash his chest he lay back with his eyes closed and just enjoyed the feel of her fingers on his skin.

Lust took control of him and it was most obvious to the girl where his thoughts were. He forced her to wash his hardened manhood and found pleasure in her fear.

Without warning he stood and climbed from the tub. Ignoring the water that dripped on the floor he grabbed the girl. She knew better than to fight him as he was known to beat those who didn't obey and sometimes even when they did.

"Take your clothes off." He growled barely in control. She stripped with trembling fingers before he threw her on the bed. He climbed on top of her and quickly found satisfaction in her body and his control of it.

Even as his climax hit him, his thoughts clung to Joka.

V

Rakel stood facing a target that had been set up on the far side of the training field. She held a bow in her hand and was attempting to fit an arrow into it. Joka had given a few instructions on the use of a bow, but the warrior woman was not speaking to anyone of late. Rakel had not wanted to bother her with such a request when it was so obvious her heart was breaking.

She didn't know what had happened between Joka and Peder, but it must have been bad because both of them were seeking solitude. Rakel thought perhaps she should be friendly and see if she was alright, but Seera whom she was close to had said that Joka just needed time to be alone.

Rakel's training had simply stopped. Seera had come a few times to spar with her, but she was often busy with other things, so Rakel had decided perhaps she could learn to use the bow on her own. It shouldn't be so difficult. Joka had shown her how to hold it and how to fit the arrow and aim.

She just needed practice.

Rakel smiled when she managed to fit the arrow without it falling out. She lifted it like she'd been shown and sighted the target. Easing the string of the bow back while holding onto the arrow, she kept her eye on the center of the target.

The arrow popped out of the bow and the string stung her hand.

"Ouch." She stuck her offended finger into her mouth. A small cut appeared when she inspected it.

"Would you like me to show you how it is done?"

Rakel turned to find Danr behind her. She reddened in embarrassment at her unsuccessful attempt. He smiled, but he didn't laugh and it immediately put her at ease.

"You would not mind?"

"It would be my pleasure." Danr nodded and she thought for a moment that he looked a bit nervous, which of course couldn't be, not this large warrior. What did he have to be nervous about?

Danr stood behind her and she felt a fluttering in her stomach as he moved in close to her so that they were touching. He placed his arms around hers and held her hands in the correct position on the bow. With his right hand he helped her to pull the string back and gave her instructions on how to hold the arrow in place so that it would not fall off.

Rakel felt her heart beat faster and couldn't understand why.

Together they pulled the string back a little farther. She felt his breath on the back of her head and the strength of his muscles against her back.

Breathe Rakel, just breathe.

"Now," he said. She released the arrow with his help. Even then he did not step away from her, not until the arrow struck the target. When he did move back she almost regretted it.

What nonsense.

"Now you try it on your own," he said.

Rakel tried to copy exactly what he had shown her and the arrow stayed in place. Keeping a level eye on the target she let the arrow fly and held her breath until it hit. Not in the center, not even close for that matter, but it had struck. It quivered still from the impact and she couldn't contain a feeling of relief.

"Very good." She turned to see Danr staring at her rather oddly. She had to clear her throat before she could speak.

"You instruct well," she said. He seemed pleased by her words.

"Keep trying." He motioned to the target and coaxed her to fit another arrow into the bow.

For the next couple of hours Rakel worked on her aim while Danr offered encouragement and instruction. She was improving, but her arm was becoming tired and she didn't think she could continue.

"I think perhaps I need to rest." She turned to him as she rubbed the muscle in her arm.

"It is enough for now," Danr said. "Practice often and your arm will get used to it. Did you not ache after the first time you trained with your sword?"

"I did," she admitted. "You have seen me?" She found herself asking for she suddenly wanted to know if he had noticed her.

"I have." He leaned in closer to her. "I think you have done well." Rakel felt the blush returning.

"Danr," someone called and they both turned to see who it was. Hachet was headed their way and seeing his approached Danr stepped away from her.

"I was beginning to wonder if you remembered your promise to spar with me this afternoon." Hachet smiled and winked at Rakel.

"I was just helping Rakel first," Danr said. If he'd forgotten he offered no apology to Hachet.

"We are done," Rakel said.

"Then let us go my friend," Hachet hit Danr on the back and for some reason Danr frowned at him. Was he angry? Hachet continued to smile despite the reaction from his friend.

"Remind me not to take it easy on you." Danr growled which caused Hachet to laugh. Rakel figured it was just something between friends.

"Thank you for your help," Rakel said to Danr and left the men to their practicing.

Just as she reached the gates she turned to glance back over her shoulder long enough to see Danr and Hachet start their sparring. Danr had removed his tunic, and for a moment her eyes lingered on his muscular body, before she turned away.

CHAPTER 26

Rafn and Dagstyrr stood on the compound wall looking out at the ocean. A tinge of green was beginning to show in the fields and the trees had the start of buds on them. Birds had been spotted returning from the south.

The animals in the mountains would be searching out places to birth their young as life was returning to the land. Rafn felt anxious to continue with the building. He wanted shops built close to the docks and he would encourage families to begin building homes beyond the compound walls.

Each family would be responsible for the plot of land given them and when the ground beneath was no longer frozen they would begin to cultivate and plant seeds. He would see that the town prospered.

Still, he could not ignore the wakening storm. His sense that he would need it soon plagued him with a negative feeling in a time when he wanted to feel only the simple joys of life.

Systa and Hadde walked across the compound and out through the gates. With their fingers twined together they made their way down to the river just behind the village. It was their closest source of freshwater. Though she was a small woman, Hadde only came up to her shoulders. He frowned at the oddity they made.

"They are a strange couple." Dagstyrr spoke as if he'd heard his thoughts. Rafn turned to see that his friend was also watching the newest couple amongst them.

"There has been much talk about them. Many of the warriors wonder what she sees in the dwarf. Though she is strange, her beauty has not gone unnoticed. Many of the single men have certainly dreamt about her."

Dagstyrr turned to Rafn. "Until recently I had thought she had no interest at all in men. She has never looked at them with any more pleasure than her sister has."

"Seera tells me that Systa suffered at the hands of more than one man at a young age and it has left its mark on her."

"She looks with love at the dwarf. She is obviously not against having a relationship with a man," Dagstyrr said.

"Look at the man she has chosen my friend." Rafn raised an eyebrow, "One that can't physically overpower her."

"That is true. I have spoken with Hadde often enough to know even if he could, he would not. He is one such as your brother was. One that is still pure even after suffering the cruelties of the world."

Rafn stared at Dagstyrr's assessment of the little man. That he had not made the comparison before surprised Rafn, for with Dagstyrr's words he clearly saw it. He felt a moment's pain at the reminder of the brother that had been taken so cruelly from him. He doubted that he would ever stop missing Orn. That Seera had named their son after his little brother had helped, but his absence was still painfully felt.

They turned at a sudden movement from further into the compound. Rafn caught sight of his wife as she ran toward the gate. Her unbraided hair flew out behind her and Rafn realized her feet were bare as if she'd not had time to stop and put her boots on.

Rafn stiffened. What had his wife behaving so oddly? "Come," he said to Dagstyrr who had also noticed Seera's strange flight.

They made their way down the closest ladder and had just approached the gate when Seera was returning with Systa in tow. Both women stopped in shock to see the men suddenly in front of them.

"What is it?" Rafn asked a little too sharply, bringing a smile to Seera's face at his concern. Instead of answering him she turned to Dagstyrr.

"Kata's time has come." Her eyes twinkled with excitement.

"The baby!" Dagstyrr was at a loss for words.

"Aye." Seera reached back to grab Systa's hand. "We must go to her." To Rafn she said, "Keep him from worrying too much."

The women continued on to Kata's dwelling and disappeared inside. Dagstyrr stood frozen to the spot unsure what he should do.

"These things take time," Rafn slapped him on the back. "Let us head to the training field. A good workout will ease your mind."

Dagstyrr only nodded and followed Rafn out through the gate.

II

As in the old days, Systa had wanted to build a special hut for Kata to give birth in, as they had in the mountains for Seera, but Kata had refused. She had laughed at the suggestion and told her she would be more comfortable in her own bed.

In the grips of another contraction she realized comfort was beyond her. The pain gripped her in an iron fist. She clenched her teeth and bit back a scream. Days must have passed since her labor had started, though trapped in an endless wave of pain she knew that it had only been hours.

She was hot, incredibly hot. Sweat beaded on her forehead and trickled down her back. Systa and Seera were close beside her, speaking encouraging words. The door opened letting in a refreshing breeze and for a moment she felt some relief.

She looked up to see Joka at the end of the bed beside Systa. The woman seemed visibly pale when their eyes met. That she was concerned was obvious to Kata and she felt oddly touched by it.

Kata wore a light shift which Systa had pushed up to her waist so that she could examine the progress of the labor. She felt with her fingers to determine if the path of birth was ready.

Another contraction…the most intense yet…struck. Despite her best efforts she let out a muffled scream. She felt the tears of frustration fighting for release. Her abdomen felt like it was ready to rip apart and she was slick with sweat.

Would it not end?

"You are brave my friend, my sister." Seera took her hand and met her eyes. "I know your strength is almost gone, but you must not give up. It will not be so long now, I promise you that."

"I can't…" she gasped through the torment.

"Yes you can." Seera smiled warmly. "I can tell you from experience that it is possible. You will survive this."

A sudden image flashed in Kata's mind, a memory of another who struggled as she did now. The thoughts came unbidden of Geira's pain, the stillborn babe, the woman's death. Fear seized her and she panicked in desperation.

Seera must have understood the direction of her thoughts for she squeezed her hand harder. "It will not be thus for you. Systa has seen and she is never wrong." She looked from her sister-in law to the Seer.

Systa was watching them, listening to all that had been said. Her face held only pleasure, no concern. "Truth she speaks."

Kata felt herself relaxing, letting go of the worry that had plagued her from the onset of labor. With the burden of its weight gone she found a last reserve of strength and the ability to go on.

Clenched in one contraction after another, the time seemed to slowly pass. She was barely able to breathe between them. A new sensation washed through her, one that felt like a trail of fire leading down the birth canal and she got the overwhelming urge to push.

"Ready you are," Systa said. She ordered Seera and Joka to help Kata into a squatting position on the bed. To help the baby come faster Systa explained and Seera assured her that it worked.

With Joka and Seera holding her steady from either side as she squatted, Systa moved behind Kata and positioned herself to catch the baby.

Each time her muscles tightened in pain, Kata bore down. It was hard, so hard to get this baby to come out. Systa spoke softly to her, telling her not to stop. Finally with one last intense contraction, Kata pushed her muscles and a scream tore from her that was surely heard throughout the village. She didn't care. She refused to stop until she felt the head between her legs.

"Enough." Systa's voice penetrated her veil of agony. Systa took hold of the baby's shoulders and eased it out the rest of the way. Once safely placed on the bed beneath Kata, Systa cut and tied the cord. The baby let out a sudden wail that shocked the women and made each of them laugh in relief.

Systa wrapped the baby in a blanket she had set aside earlier as Joka and Seera eased Kata back down on the bed. Once lying comfortably, Kata tried to see her child. Systa met her inquisitive gaze.

"Boy he is." Systa smiled and placed the bundle in Kata's arms.

Kata's eyes filled with tears of joy at seeing her son for the first time. He was so like his father; pale skinned and just a hint of reddish hair on his smooth head. "He is perfect."

III

Joka was overwhelmed. She watched Kata and the baby closely as Systa finished cleaning up the afterbirth and washing her. She had been there when Seera had birthed Orn. Had witnessed her struggle to birth her son, but it had not had the effect that Kata's labor did.

She had come to understand the true bravery a woman possessed. Joka had always believed for a woman to have such strength she needed to do so through the sword. A weapon of death!

What she saw before her now, lying in Kata's arms was life. Something fluttered inside of her at the knowledge that she too was creating life in her body. She had tried not to think too much about the baby that was growing within her.

It was a strange and enlightening kind of power as she realized its significance. Perhaps in her quest to prove herself as good as any man, she had given up that part of her which made her a woman.

Her belief that to be a woman was to be weak was wrong. Joka had not wanted to accept that weakness. She had pushed until she was strong and independent and in doing so she had failed to see that women were stronger than she had believed. She had proved their potential, but only in part.

She had proven that she could take a life as easily as a man. That she could feel the blood of anger swell inside of her until she could send that rage into the sword she wielded. She had thrilled at the power it had given her.

It had been a two sided victory. She had become a warrior, but lost the woman. Her hand moved to touch her stomach in anticipation. It offered life instead of death to heal her pain.

Systa glanced at her and held her eyes. Joka had to keep herself from trembling. Until that moment she had not thought of the final outcome of her situation. She had accepted that she was pregnant, but only now realized she would have a child who would depend on her. That shock hit her as she watched Kata beaming with pride as she stared down at her new son.

Joka needed to breathe. She turned to find the door that would take her outside into the fresh air. She couldn't stay whether the other women might notice that something was wrong. The control that she was so good at maintaining was threatening to shatter. She had to escape before they saw.

"Find this one's father," Systa said. "Excited he will be to know that he has a son."

Yes, Joka nodded. The other women would not question her disappearance if she was gone to get Dagstyrr. It gave her an excuse to bolt out the door and breathe deeply of the spring air. She felt the beating of her heart quicken.

Outside the dwelling she stood for a moment to calm down. When she felt her control snapping back into place she headed towards the hall. It was dark and supper would have ended some time ago but it was where the men would be.

She entered the hall and all eyes turned to her in anticipation. Ignoring their expectant stares she made her way to the head table. Dagstyrr stood immediately and met her just before she reached it.

"You have a son."

"A son." Dagstyrr whooped loudly and cheers rose around the room.

Rafn appeared beside Dagstyrr and clapped him on the back, "A friend and cousin for Orn."

"They wait," Joka said. Dagstyrr did not hesitate. Rafn followed him out and Joka was left to face Peder alone.

He sat watching her closely and she was suddenly afraid that he could see through her thinly veiled control to the turmoil that had seized her. As if by some force that she could not fight, she turned to meet his gaze. His face was unreadable, gone was the love that had once reflected in his eyes.

She was surprised at how much its absence hurt her. She wanted to reach for him, to tell him to hold her. Memories of being in each other's arms threatened to unbalance her. She couldn't let that happen in front of him.

She turned quickly so that he would not see too much. It took all her will not to run for the door at the far end of the hall.

Once outside she gasped for breath. Tears tugged at her and she was scared that she would cry. It was not something she had done in a very long time and it definitely was not something that she wanted to do now.

She barely made it into the confines of her sleeping compartment within the longhouse before the first tear fell. She muffled her sobs by burying her face in her blanket.

A well of grief and regret poured from her and she was afraid that she would never stop crying.

IV

Hadde was sleeping when Systa snuck into his sleeping area in his longhouse. He was surprised when her hand reached out to touch his face. He suddenly came awake and was amazed once again at how beautiful she was. He opened his mouth to speak, but she held a finger to it to keep him silent.

She drew back his blanket and crawled beneath it. He was startled by her actions for they had never been intimate. The most they had done was hold hands. Though he had to admit he thought about her in the night while he tried to sleep. These feelings were new for him.

It was only once she lay up next to him did he realize she was naked. This sparked an immediate and sudden excitement in him.

"Love you I do." She kissed him. He had never been kissed before and he felt a bit awkward. Systa understood and led him slowly.

What she showed him in the dark underneath his blanket was something that was both beautiful and fulfilling. As he stared into her silver eyes he knew love for the first time in his life.

V

Beneath a star filled sky in the vast empty space far from seeing eyes, was set a fire. It burned bright and hot, a sweet scent rising on its smoke. It was both refreshing and necessary to the ritual.

Systa was alone with Joka. A mountain sheep lay slain beside them, an offering to Freyja. It was that time of year when the goddess must be remembered. Another slain animal, this time a deer lay close to the first. This one would be offered to the god Freyr the goddess' twin brother.

Systa had ordered a feast to be made for the annual spring celebration of rebirth and fertility. She would see that the sacrifices were made. She had wanted only Joka to be present. Her sister was needed to find the animals as Systa had no skill in killing.

The sound of an ancient song rose on her lips as she danced around the fire. She closed her eyes and raised her arms to the sky above. Far beyond their view were the worlds of the gods. It was there that the branches of the world tree reached.

Systa's feet hit the ground in soft steps and she knew that beneath that ground was the roots of the world tree that reached to the underworlds. Systa allowed herself to be connected to the energy that flowed between these worlds.

Many times she had felt this connection. She encouraged Joka to join her and her sister began to move in time with her. Joka spoke the words more quietly, but she knew the song as well as Systa.

They stayed until the ritual was done before returning to the courtyard where the feast had been set out. It was such a beautiful night and the celebration lasted into the early morning before the people began to disappear to find their beds.

CHAPTER 27

Rakel knelt by the stream used for washing clothes and bent to the task of scrubbing the soiled wool tunics and dresses that filled her basket. She had offered to help a woman who had four kids with her laundry. The woman looked all but worn out from chasing after the children.

The woman had accepted Rakel's offer with gratitude and had given her the basket of clothes she was intending on washing that morning. Rakel added her own dresses to the pile and had gone down to join the women already at work.

Life had changed for Rakel since coming to Ragnarr and being taken in by people she had come to truly care about. She enjoyed her time on the training field learning both the sword and the bow, though Joka was still absent. Seera told her she still needed more time.

Rakel could understand. She knew that Joka had been Lord Peder's lover, but their relationship had ended badly. Joka was not the only one who absented herself from the things that went on around the village. Peder also went on his horse daily and did not return until late in the evening.

Rafn and Dagstyrr were busy with organizing the new construction down by the dock. Seera was spending much of her time helping Kata with the new baby. Even Hadde no longer spent time with her, but chose instead to spend his days with Systa. It had shocked Rakel at first when she'd noticed their relationship blossoming, but then she had seen the joy in his eyes and she could only feel happiness for him.

Rakel helped the other women when she could. She had developed a friendship with the girl Yrsa who was nursemaid to Seera's son Orn.

The girl was younger than her, but she seemed so much older. Rakel had come to understand that Yrsa had survived a traumatic captivity as a slave.

Rakel found that Yrsa preferred to spend her free time with the boy Fox. The two were obviously in love and she couldn't blame them for seeking time together when demands were not being made of them.

It seemed everyone kept busy with their families and their chores, so Rakel was finding herself spending a lot of time alone. She would visit with Seera and Kata and marvel at their sons, but she was not a mother or a wife and did not share much in common with them.

She had enjoyed her time with Joka in training, but the warrior woman's need for solitude left Rakel without an outlet for her restlessness. So she busied herself wherever she was needed. Sometimes she would help in the kitchens, or with the laundry, even with cleaning out the stables. No work was too good for her.

The others were kind and welcomed her readily and none suspected that she had never done such chores before. Her father had always kept her from such labor. As his daughter he expected the others to treat her as if she were nobility, even though she did not have noble blood within her. Her parents both came from humble beginnings and she had been meant to do such work as the common folk. It was who she was supposed to be, not placed in a position of cosseting and ease.

Rakel had been given a life of plentitude. She had not wanted for anything. Never felt the ache of hunger. She had the best clothes, servants to do her bidding and yet she had been unhappy. A prisoner locked into the confines of the life her father expected her to live.

As her hands learned the hardness of labor she felt a freedom that she hadn't expected to find. She was just another woman among many. It pleased her greatly to be so at ease among these genuinely good people.

She smiled often those days. It was easy to forget that her father was still out there on the other side of the mountains. That as spring brought rebirth to the land around them and opened up the passes, so did it bring an inevitable threat.

As the last of the ice had disappeared, Rakel began to feel a tension building in her. Her father would send his warriors, and Kale would want her back so that she could be forced into marriage.

But she would not go.

She worried about her mother and grandmother back in Skahi. She missed them each day they were apart, but she could never return. She could never live again in bonds that held her down and did not allow her to soar to the sky. As Kale's wife it would be even worse than that. It would be a terrible life of pain and humiliation. In the end her soul would die.

She had tasted freedom, and it wouldn't be so easy to give it up.

Rakel squeezed out the last tunic and placed it atop the rest of the clean clothes. She would take them back to the longhouse and hang them from the clothes line that had been built outside. With no clouds to hide the hot sun, it shouldn't take long to dry them.

She hefted the basket under her arm and stretched the kinks out of her legs before she headed back toward the gates. She was almost to them when a man stepped up beside her.

"Allow me to carry that for you," Danr said.

Rakel was surprised by his appearance. She had not spoken to him since that day on the training field. She had seen him in the great hall among the warriors who had accepted him so easily. She had wanted to approach him when she saw him at the feast the other night, but she had been too scared to be so bold.

"It is not necessary," she said. She tried to quicken her pace, but he matched her step for step.

"You need not have fear of me." She slowed her steps at his words and stopped to stare at him.

"I am not."

"I never agreed with how your father ruled."

"You followed him." She accused without thinking and his eyes betrayed the fact that he was ashamed of it.

"I had nowhere else to go." He attempted to explain. "It was only my reputation as a warrior of strength that kept him from pushing me too hard. He wanted my loyalty, but I insisted it had to be on my terms."

"You still did his bidding."

"And for that I will always be ashamed. I can see more clearly now how wrong it was. Lord Rafn and his men are the most honorable men I have ever met. They have taught me a valuable lesson."

"I shall not hold it against you. You have never done anything to harm me. When it mattered most you chose to defy my father and for that you have earned my gratitude."

He smiled at her words and she was startled to realize how attractive he was. Not with the roguishly wild strength of Rafn, or the dashing handsomeness of Peder, but when he smiled he was quite appealing.

She let him take the basket from her on his second request and they walked together back to the longhouse that she shared with the other single women and some of the families.

Danr kept silently glancing at her. Even after placing the basket on the ground beside the clothes line, he seemed reluctant to leave. She wasn't sure how to react to such attention. Her father had always kept her separated from the men so they would not have a chance to make such advances on her.

She admitted she liked the way he stared at her and the interest in his eyes. She once again felt the freedom she had achieved and it was her choice whether or not to accept the invitation. What her father might think was not a concern. She couldn't stop herself from remembering how it had felt to stand within the strength of Danr's arms.

"Thank you," she said.

"Anytime," Danr replied. The warmth of his smile was still on his face. He had blue eyes that reflected the sunlight above and she marveled at her body's reaction to what she saw in them.

She was still a maiden and had no knowledge in the ways of men. He must have understood this for he simply nodded and melted away behind the longhouse. Some mischievous part of her wanted to follow him and the other was too scared to be so bold.

II

The boar snuffled around in the foliage that carpeted the forest floor. Peder watched silently from where he was concealed by a bush. The boar snorted and pawed at the ground as if something was irritating him.

The pig's grunts of annoyance did not deter Peder. He would make his kill. He kept still and gripped his spear as he waited for the boar to present him with a perfect target.

Peder's muscles bunched in anticipation as the boar swiveled around on his stumpy legs. The pig raised its big snout and sniffed at the air. He was facing Peder now and he could not give up the chance of a kill.

The spear flew through the air and pierced the boar's eye. The pig dropped before it even had a chance to squeal in panic. It was a clean and quick kill, just how Peder preferred it.

He stood over the animal and stared down at it. Its brown dirty hide bore many scratches. One of its tusks had its tip broken off and part of one ear was missing. It was a sorry looking thing, but its meat would be welcomed at the supper table.

He retrieved his stallion from where he'd left it a short distance away and led it to the kill site. The horse was well trained and didn't shy from the smell of blood or the weight of the dead pig when it was tied onto his back.

Peder took up the reins and began to head back down the same path he'd taken earlier. He had not gone far when he heard a noise from a nearby clearing. He crept upon it slowly, stopping only long enough to tie his horse.

He saw her at once sitting on a large boulder. Her sword was strapped to her back and her bow held in her hand, but she did not appear to be hunting. Instead Joka simply sat there staring at something of interest in the dirt, or more likely she was lost in such deep thoughts that she was not looking at anything at all.

As a bee to a flower, Peder was drawn to her. She heard his approach and looked up at him as he neared her. He stopped at what he saw in her eyes. If he was not mistaken, she had been crying as they were still red and slightly swollen, and this surprised him.

"Joka," he said with tenderness and concern. In all the time he'd known this warrior woman, she had never cried. What would cause her to do so now?

He saw her jaw harden in an attempt to gain control of her emotions. Her body stiffened when he touched a hand to her shoulder and he instantly drew it away.

There was so much he wanted to say, but things were never easy with this woman. The words that he should have said did not come and the ones that did were all wrong.

"You take a chance being here alone," he said sharper than he'd intended. He watched her defenses flare up in response.

"I am fine." She stared back at him and the edge to her voice cut as deep as any knife.

"There is still a threat against you." He snapped back before he could stop himself. "Kale caught you once before in these woods when you were unprepared. Do you think he would not do so again?"

Joka was on her feet and facing him by the time he had finished his rant. He felt his heart race at the fury he saw in her. He saw her fighting an internal battle as she stared at him.

"I will meet Kale again, of that I am sure." Her jaw remained clenched as she spoke out the words.

"Then why take unnecessary risks?"

"I do not," she said.

"Joka…" he responded to the shine of moisture that came to her eyes. She blinked desperately to rid the tears before she shed them. He reached out a hand to her, but she stepped back.

"Don't," she said in a half choked whisper.

"What is it," he pleaded.

"I…" her face softened and for a moment he thought she would tell him, but she stepped further away. "It is nothing."

"You can trust me." He attempted to tell her but he saw clearly that she did not believe him.

"You left me," she accused and he saw for the first time how much that truly hurt her. He had not expected that. He thought he had been the only one to mourn the loss of what they shared.

"You gave me no choice."

She scowled in anger. "There are always choices. You made yours, now leave me be."

Peder saw his mistake too late. In ending their relationship he had proven to her what she had always feared. That he couldn't be trusted. That he would fail her.

He had failed her. That sudden knowledge was like a knife twisting in his gut. The damage had been made and could not be repaired. He had done this. He had not given her his faith.

Peder backed up one step at a time. His feet felt like they were made of iron. As the distance opened up between them he somehow knew that it would never close again.

Damn him for the fool he was.

III

Systa had found a cave while out with Hadde. It was small but would serve her needs well. The dreams had become more intense and she knew that their unfolding would be soon. Still the shadows remained cloaked and in her desperation she sought Hadde's help.

He knew magic. Had used it himself when he'd had the need of it. He didn't have her Seer abilities but that didn't matter. She only needed him to help her call out to the goddess in a plea for answers. Perhaps two voices would be stronger than one.

Hadde sat next to her arranging the plants and animal parts that she needed. She stirred the boiling water in a cauldron suspended on a tripod over a fire. In the night she had shared with him her fears about the dream that plagued her.

He had listened with understanding and concern. He did not judge or condemn her strange ability as many in the past had done. Instead he'd offered to help her in any way that he could.

Their eyes connected and she drew comfort from the warmth that radiated from within him. It soothed the icy fear that had taken a hold of her. Hadde smiled in encouragement and she felt the corners of her lips raise in reply.

Taking a deep breath she turned towards the cauldron and began to whisper the familiar words she used to speak to the goddess. She promised her continued loyalty as Freyja's servant. Her hands moved one at a time to the ingredients she would need to invoke her power.

Hadde began to chant beside her and a yellowish steam rose to surround them. Systa breathed in the sharp scent and kept her voice steady in its continued song of praise. When the time was right and Hadde had helped her to invoke a cloak of protection he opened up a final leather bound package.

It held desiccated mushrooms that had been dried with special care and chants. She hoped that they would help her push past the barrier that stood in her way and was preventing her from proceeding past the shadows into the light that would shed the truth.

She took them from his offered hand and placed them on her tongue. Syste did not chew them, but swallowed them with a cup of water that easily washed them down her throat.

The effects were immediate and she felt a disconnection from the physical bonds of her body. She reached out beyond her limits and found her way into the shadows. She was not aware of how her body slumped forward or Hadde's tender touch as he eased her down onto a fur. She didn't feel him touch her slack face in concern and love.

Darkness formed thick walls around her and she fought not to give into the fear. Systa found her courage. She had to rely on it. Joka would not hesitate if it were Systa whose life was threatened. Joka would charge head long into the fight and hack away at the enemy with her sword until he lay dead.

Systa could do no less with her own weapon. It was not of cold metal, but one that she plucked from the very essence of the world around them. On the threads that held it together was a power that could be borrowed and wielded in the right hands.

Her hands!

Strange images formed within the shadows that circled her. She did not fear their distorted faces or their spindly limbs. With thoughts of the goddess' love she reached past the shadows that tried to seize her.

She did not fear them!

With the freedom that such a revelation brought, she was able to step into the light that lay beyond the shadow's reach. It was warm and welcoming and it filled her.

It came then, the vision that had been haunting her dreams for many months now. It came so sharply it felt real. Only that sense of disconnection kept her from believing that what she saw was happening.

Rain fell from the sky above as warriors fought warriors. Rafn led them to the fight as the power of Thor shone fully in his eyes and rumbled in the sky above him. Men flocked to the raven because they were unafraid of the fury of the god.

The men that met them were blurred and unimportant, all but one. Kale rode in the center and fought desperately.

Joka met him face to face. Sword to sword, feet slipping on the mud beneath their feet. The rain did not let up as they battled.

Her pregnancy made her weak, but she faced him unafraid and furious. The shadows crept in around her and threatened to claim Systa once again, but she screamed to be heard.

"Stay where you are," she demanded and searched out her sister in desperation.

Joka faltered on the slick mud. Kale's eyes were red with viciousness and a deep seeded need for revenge.

He raised his sword to strike a killing blow.

Fear gripped Systa suddenly and she screamed as the shadows reached out with misty fingers and grabbed her. They clouded her view and the vision slipped away.

Systa bolted awake and gasped anxiously for breath. Panic kept hold of her as the memory rang strong. She met Hadde's worried expression and shivered uncontrollably.

"Be here soon he will," she managed to say.

CHAPTER 28

Kale along with the other warriors that traveled both in front and behind him, wound through the mountains. Tomorrow they would reach the village of Ragnarr and then he would finally fulfill his need for revenge. He would kill Joka and he would claim Rakel. Both women would pay dearly for disgracing him.

Bekan's patience had worn thin by the time the mountain passes had become passable. He didn't want to wait, giving the warlord time to realize what he was doing. He would strike before they were ready for him and hopefully take them off guard when their minds were still turned to the spring planting.

Rafn would not expect him to arrive so early. Bekan had called Kale to him and told him he was to lead the men. That the men were displeased by this decision was obvious, but Kale ignored them. He would not be kept from this battle. He had been practicing through the long winter months under the tutelage of Onnar and he was anxious to use his new found skill with the sword.

At first the man had looked at him in disbelief when Kale had made the request to be trained. Onnar was the lead warrior now that Danr was gone and he rose to the challenge. He was a relentless teacher. Kale cursed his name at the day's end but soon realized that his efforts were paying off.

Kale became more confident with his sword and had even won a few nods of approval from the other men. They still did not like him, but he had earned their reluctant respect.

Onnar was pleased with his student's accomplishments by the time the snow had disappeared and Bekan had called them forth. They would go into battle and Kale knew that he was ready for what lay ahead.

II

A rumbling filtered through his dreams causing Rafn to suddenly waken with dread. Seera still slept soundly beside him and he watched her for a moment and tried to keep himself centered. Again he felt a rippling effect go through his whole body and this time he knew that it was not a dream. The storm was brewing…it was waking.

He steeled himself to become the warrior he'd always been and crept from his wife's side to find his clothes. A curious sensation spread through his arms and his fingers twitched in anticipation of the coming storm. The time had come….

The sun was already up when Rafn found Dagstyrr chopping wood down by the dock. Even then the fire was spreading through him as the storm came alive. Something was going to happen and soon. He didn't need the Seer's powers to tell him so. The first black clouds travelling in the distance appeared over the water and he felt the power reach out and seize him.

He gasped at the sharpness of the fingers that had pierced him.

Rafn didn't have to call Dagstyrr's name. His second in command, his best friend had known him forever. When he recognized the look in Rafn's eyes, Dagstyrr lost his smile and grew serious.

"What has happened?"

"Nothing yet." Rafn looked to the mountains across the pasture lands that the men had already begun to plow. "But it will."

"What is it you see?"

"It is not what I see, but what I feel." He pointed to the blackening sky. "A storm gathers there, plain for all to see. But also does it form here," he indicated as he touched his chest.

"Your power awakens." Dagstyrr understood what the significance of that meant. "What needs to be done?"

"Prepare the men for battle," he ordered. "They must be ready."

"And you?"

"I must seek out Systa and find out what she has seen if anything." Rafn turned and the two men ran back to the village gates.

Dagstyrr went to organize the men for the upcoming battle. They responded immediately, having lost none of their training through the long winter months. Rafn went to the longhouse closest to the great hall. He ducked inside and found that it was mostly empty.

"Systa." He called out for he didn't know which area was hers.

Joka stepped out into the communal area of the longhouse and met Rafn. "Systa is not here."

"Where is she?" The sharpness in his voice made Joka suspicious.

"I have not seen her. Her and Hadde left for the mountains this morning and have yet to return."

Rafn growled in frustration causing Joka to stiffen. "What goes on here my lord?"

Rafn studied her for a long moment deciding whether or not to answer her question. She had proven to him that she was good with a sword. Her arm would be useful in the coming battle. He knew that she could handle herself, but he knew also that Peder would kill him for placing her in danger.

Joka was her own woman and would be displeased if Rafn kept her from the fight because of a man whose bed she no longer shared. The decision had to be hers. He owed her that much.

"We prepare for battle. If you need armor, see Berthor and he will fit you with some." Rafn saw a gleam of excitement come to her eyes.

Rafn turned to go. His hand was on the door when she replied, "Thank you." He paused only long enough to nod and he was back outside.

He saw Seera outside their dwelling and raced towards it. Yrsa was with her and she handed Orn to the girl when she saw Rafn. Worry showed in her eyes as she said something to Yrsa who turned and left with his son.

"Something goes on," Seera said. She met his eyes. "The men are racing around as if they prepare for battle."

"They do." Rafn dragged her into his arms. He hugged her to him in an attempt to center himself. He fought against the storm that threatened to overpower him. He could not let it loose until it was needed.

"Is it Kale?"

"I believe so." Rafn stepped from her. He touched a hand to her face and felt the love that was between them, feeling the calming effect it had on him. "Gather the women and children and have them stay in the hall. I put you in charge of their safety."

"You are not going to assign us a strong man?" She chuckled to ease the tension she felt growing around Rafn, but his face remained hard and distant.

"We will not let this enemy penetrate the walls, but I have seen you and Rakel practicing. You both have some skill. Joka has taught you well."

"Is that praise my lord?" She smiled.

"I will not allow you in the battle as I have Joka," he warned her. "Your son and I can't afford to lose you."

She was startled. "You would let Joka fight?"

"Aye."

"Peder will not like that." Seera raised her eyebrows.

"No he won't, but she would have liked it even less if I'd ordered her to stay with the women. She is a warrior and I have to respect that."

"I love you." Seera's smile returned.

"And I you." Rafn kissed her lightly. "Go now, there is not much time."

Seera nodded and quickly headed for Kata's dwelling. She disappeared inside and Rafn headed for his men. Dagstyrr had already managed to bring them all together and they were putting on their breastplates and helmets, cleaning and sharpening their swords and offering up prayers to the gods.

III

Joka had just come from Berthor's forge where he'd given her armor and a shield. He had admitted to privately working on them for her. He hadn't known that she would need them so soon, but had realized if she were ever to go into battle, the men's armor would be much too big on her.

She had spontaneously hugged him in thanks leaving the man a little flustered, but she had barely noticed his discomfort. She had retreated to the confines of her longhouse to dress. She was not sure if the men would welcome her among them at such a time as this.

She sat on her bed and said a prayer to the goddess that had always watched over her.

Where was Systa? She hadn't returned and Joka had begun to worry that she would not make it back before the enemy arrived.

Kale was coming. She knew this without Systa having to tell her it was so. Anger flared within her. He came to kill her, but she would not let that happen. A power of excitement surged through her in anticipation of their swords locking.

It would not be much of a battle. A child had more skill than Kale, but that would not stop her, for she would see him dead. By her hand he would crumble and bleed into the earth.

She could barely wait.

The metal armor conformed perfectly to her body and Joka marveled at how much movement she still had with it on. She picked up the helmet and noticed that it too was lighter than those the men wore. Berthor had been working on a new way of folding metal and he had obviously used his new technique on her armor.

She was placing the helmet on her head when the first shouts went up outside. The enemy had been spotted.

She smiled.

IV

"They have just broken the tree line." Peder and Rafn stood together on the wall. Each man wore his armor and was loaded down with weapons.

The gate opened and Peder watched as Systa and Hadde slipped through it. Systa looked wild with fear. Hadde gripped her hand and glanced at her in worry as Peder narrowed his eyes on them.

"They outnumber us, at least three to one," Rafn said.

"Certainly you have met greater odds than that."

"I have," Rafn admitted.

"They will not make it past our defenses," Dagstyrr said as he joined them.

Peder glanced behind him just in time to see Joka crossing the courtyard. A moment of surprise left him speechless before he turned angrily to Rafn. "Certainly you will not allow her to fight."

Rafn glanced briefly over his shoulder at the warrior woman and shrugged. "I would not have been able to stop her."

"She is going to get herself killed." Peder tensed as he watched her.

"She knows how to fight. Do not doubt her. We will need her on our side."

"She has never faced such odds." Peder stared at Rafn. He clenched his fists at his side in an attempt to prevent himself from hitting his brother-in law.

"My friend," Dagstyrr said. "Rafn is right. She would not have forgiven any of us if we tried to keep her behind with the other women. She would have found a way to join the battle. At least this way she goes prepared."

Peder shot him a look of disbelief. "She…" he lost his argument as the men's words sank in. They were right. She would fight with or without Rafn's approval. No one would stop her.

"Fine, let her fight."

V

Onnar moved his horse up next to Kale. "They look ready for us. How can that be?"

Kale scowled in anger. He should have known that a man with the reputation of the raven would be prepared. "He must have spies watching."

"We kept a watchful eye and we saw no one," Onnar said.

A sudden thought clenched Kale's gut. It must have been the witch. He did not share his beliefs with Onnar as the men had all turned from the old beliefs. They would not put much credence in the so called powers of the Seer.

"It matters not how they found out," Kale said. "They are ready for us. I say we don't delay and allow them any more time to set up their defenses."

"I see wisdom in your words," Onnar agreed.

"We outnumber them."

"Aye." Onnar nodded then moved among the men to relay his orders.

As a group they moved quickly. He sent forward the archers first. When they were in range they sent up a volley of arrows with fiery tips, which they shot over the wall, but they did not seem to catch. Rafn's men had been prepared for such an attempt and the fires were quickly snuffed out.

The large gates to the compound opened and out poured fierce looking men, eyes staring with fury beneath their helmets.

Kale felt a lump form in his throat. These were no ordinary warriors. They were trained Vikings and they'd been taught by the fiercest man of all.

Lord Rafn Vakrson rode out on dark colored stallion and the horse seemed as wild as its master. That he was seeing the Raven unleashed he did not doubt as Rafn bellowed out an order and his men spread out and the gate snapped closed behind them.

He remembered to feel fear at the sight.

Kale knew better than to show the men under his command such a feeling. Grabbing the slim threads of courage to him, he yelled out to his men to charge. As one they ran towards the waiting men.

VI

Systa had raced to stop Joka at the last moment before she followed the warriors out through the gate, but she had not listened. Systa had been unable to tell her what she had seen or the fear that she felt.

Joka had brushed her off with her impatience. There was no reasoning with her sister. This was a moment she had waited far too long for and there was no denying it. She had been accepted as a warrior and allowed amongst them.

Systa had not failed to see the pride reflected in her determined eyes. It worried her, the chances that her sister would take.

Hadde had followed at her heals trying to offer his support, but when she looked back at him he had no better idea of what to do than she.

VII

Rakel raced to the ladder that led up to the heights of the circular wall. The men ignored her as she stepped among them, her bow clenched in her hands and a quiver of arrows strapped onto her back.

Joka was being allowed to fight among the men, why couldn't she. She didn't believe they would allow her out amongst them, but there was no reason that she couldn't use her bow from the relative safety of the wall.

Berthor saw her approach and she saw him struggle to contain a smile of amusement as she stepped up next to him. "Joka would be so proud."

Rakel shrugged casually. "She has taught me well."

"Then you can keep me company and the two of us can pick off those vermin one at a time with our well placed arrows."

"It will be my pleasure." She smiled.

Rafn raced back and forth in front of his men on his stallion. The rest waited on foot. From what she could see her father's men were mostly without horses. Just a few that stayed near the back row.

Rakel spotted Kale at once and it fueled her anger.

"Be sure to take out that one." She pointed to Kale and heard Berthor laugh beside her.

"Is he not the one you are to marry," he teased.

"Please help me make sure that will no longer be an option."

"I will do what I can," he said.

Rakel peered down among Rafn's men. They all stood still and silent waiting for their warlord to unleash their fury. It was an impressive sight and Rakel felt a thrill of excitement course through her.

What foul creature lived inside of her that welcomed the blood bath that was about to take place.

She spotted Joka and wished she had the courage to be standing next to the woman. She preferred her perch on the wall as it gave her a measure of protection. It was a cowardly thought, but she did not have the strength that the warrior woman did. As much as she admired the woman and wanted to follow her example, she was a long way from being her equal.

Somehow that was alright with Rakel. Each of them had their own path to follow and Joka's was not hers.

Rakel's gaze shifted to the man standing to Joka's left. His sandy hair stuck out from beneath his helmet. He clutched a shield in his left hand and a spear in his right. His sword was visible in the sheath on his back.

Memories of the previous day came to mind and the attraction she had seen in Danr's eyes had surprised and excited her. Seeing him standing there ready to do battle made her suddenly regret that she had not answered his invitation and gone to him.

When the fighting was over and they had sent her father's men chasing their tails back into the mountain that had spit them out, she would see if he still felt the same.

Would she be bold enough to keep that promise?

VIII

Seera had hurried through the village collecting all the women and children and sent them to the hall. Each moved with hurried steps as they glanced to their men and understood the seriousness of the situation that had befallen them. Even the children were oddly quiet as they kept to their mother's side.

They crowded into the hall and silently sat wherever they could find room. They believed their men would protect them, keep the enemy from the gates. The fear that shone in the women's eyes was not for them but for those they loved who stood ready to defend them with their lives. Each was scared that it would be their husband, their brother, their son that would fall in battle that day.

Seera turned to Kata where she sat clutching her newborn babe to her. He was still so small and unaware of the threat that was descending upon them. He let out a cry of displeasure and Kata fumbled with her dress so she could quiet him with a breast. Tannr, for that is the name that Dagstyrr had chosen for his son, sucked contently. A bit of milk formed at the corners of his mouth and Seera wished she could be so easily soothed.

Yrsa, with Orn in her lap, stayed nearby. Her son did not sleep but stared in wide eyed wonder at the crowd that sat together. A slight frown had formed between his brows as if he sensed something was out of place, but was not sure what it was.

The women stared at each other and Seera could see evidence of panic forming on their faces. Seera had no words of encouragement, for she too was scared. She was Rafn's wife and it fell to her to keep these women strong, to keep their courage from failing them.

"Come my sisters," she said and all eyes turned to her. "Our men need our prayers."

Seera prayed to God and the Lord Jesus Christ who had died on the cross almost nine hundred years before. She asked for their mercy and the safety of all those who fought outside the walls. She repeated the words she'd heard from the monk in Skiringssal. She spoke the words loudly so that all could hear, even though all of them were not Christians.

It did not matter. Her words brought them comfort as each one listened and clung to hope.

CHAPTER 29

Rafn's voice boomed out above his men to the archers that lined the wall above him. "Fire," he yelled and a volley of arrows flew over his head. A few men fell to the deadly missiles.

Joka stood by the warrior Danr and wondered how he felt facing the men he used to fight beside. Certainly there were friends among those he would battle this day. Perhaps there were none who had earned his loyalty.

She hoped that he would not hesitate when he stared into the eyes of a man he once shared a drink of ale with.

She spared a quick glance at the man and saw only a hard set to his strong features. His eyes remained sharp and deadly and it was all she needed to see to set her mind at ease.

Joka had not been able to find Peder. She knew he was out there somewhere, she could feel his presence, but he kept his distance from her. It both saddened and pleased her. She would hate it if he fought only to protect her instead of allowing her to protect herself, but she was also sad that he obviously did not feel the same towards her that he used to. That he didn't worry over her safety.

What a contrary woman she was. She blamed the pregnancy for her emotional highs and lows, for her uncertain feelings.

She couldn't think of the baby now, not if she were to keep her mind focused on the warriors who were now bearing down on them. She saw Kale on his horse. He stayed to the back, further from harm. So like him.

He would die by her spear or sword that day. She didn't care which, but he would die.

II

Bekan's archers aimed and fired. Arrows shot towards Ragnarr's warriors, but many were rendered useless as Rafn's archers sent arrows to interrupt their flight. It appeared as two walls of arrows colliding with one another in mid air. The men's shields were able to stop the one's that made it through the wall. Only a couple of minor injuries had come from the rain of arrows.

Before the Skahi warriors had a chance to send another volley, the archers on the wall sent another shower of sharp pointed missiles into their midst.

A few found flesh, but Bekan's warriors did not stop. Spears were thrown at those in the lead, while others were used to thrust out at the men who began to penetrate their barrier.

The archers had become useless. Now they were just as likely to hit their own men as they were the enemy.

Thunder rumbled through the clouds above and Rafn felt it deep within him. He answered the call of the god and released the storm. His men saw and responded. The sky darkened further and lightning filled the sky behind the enemy.

A few had the good sense to be nervous, but most ignored the impending storm in both the heavens and the famous warlord.

Spears cracked and became useless as men from both sides moved in closer. Swords were raised and metal clanged to echo the rolling crescendo that boomed in the threatening clouds.

Rafn abandoned his horse so that he could fight one on one. Rafn met a man and growled in warning, but the man kept coming and he felt the power surge down his arm into the Serpent. With a will of its own the sword struck out and could not be stopped. The man fell in a pool of his own blood, eyes wide with disbelief at having so easily fallen.

Rafn did not hesitate and eagerly met the next man. Rain began to fall as the storm descended on them, but it did not stop the Raven. He welcomed the god into him and fought as always, with the strength to equal ten men.

Many stepped back from the sight of the legendary Viking as he wielded a sword that men envied. Too late they realized that the stories told of Rafn Vakrson were true.

III

Joka swung and sliced with her sword. It met metal and she stepped back to disconnect her blade from her opponents. The man had laughed when he'd first faced her. That he did not fear her was apparent, but she would make him regret it.

It didn't take long before the man lost his smile and realized that she was skilled. It had become a challenge between them and it was one that Joka met gladly and with confidence.

The rain had started and lightning lit the sky in a magical display of power. Not far off she could see Rafn fighting and was awed by his display on the battlefield. She couldn't allow her focus to waver so she looked away from the warlord and concentrated on the man before her.

He sneered and his eyes narrowed. Joka spotted a scar underneath one of his eyes. It was small but must have been cut deep. This man was a trained and experienced warrior. Certainly he had fought more than Joka had, but that would not stop her.

She hissed in answer to his certainty that he would win. She bent her knees and watched his movements very closely as she circled him. She saw his knuckles go white as he clenched his sword.

He watched her as closely and they continued their circular dance until she bellowed and spun and broke the continuous motion by slicing her sword through the air with supreme control and forced it down into a deadly descent. He was taken off balance for a moment and as the sky flashed suddenly above them, he saw the fierceness in her eyes.

It shocked him long enough for her to find him vulnerable. She caught him underneath his arm, beneath the protection of his breastplate. She pushed the sword deep and ignored the blood that sprayed her face.

As the warrior died he was sure he was looking at one of the battle-maidens, called the Valkyries who came to battlefields to choose from the slain, and that she'd come to claim his soul.

IV

Peder fought two men at once. In one hand he held his sword, in the other he deflected with his shield, which was becoming more difficult to use effectively under the heavy assault.

The men fought together in a perfectly timed team. One after the other they brought their swords towards him. He had barely deflected one before he had to hit the other away.

He had lost sight of Joka. He had placed himself close enough to her so that he could watch her and rush forward in defense if needed, but so that she would not see him. But the Skahi warrior's had filled in and he'd been continuously pushed further from her position. More and more distance had been placed between them as he brought down one warrior after another in his desperation to make his way back to her.

His aggressive display had not gone unnoticed. The two men he faced now were determined to bring him down and stop his luck, but he could not let them.

So the fight continued and he felt a moment of panic as he realized he'd been forced back so far he was almost at the gate.

It stopped here!

He threw his shield to the side and grabbed the dagger from his belt. Doubly armed now he went at the two men with every ounce of strength he possessed.

His opponents' eyes widened with respect as they witnessed his courage. They expected him to use his dagger as he did his sword, but before the man to his left could bring his sword down he threw the dagger at him, and stopped the second man's sword with his own.

The contact sent a vibration up his arm. His dagger flew true and was embedded through the warrior's throat. The man gagged as he grasped at its handle before he toppled backwards and died.

Surprise flashed across the other's face and he almost missed Peder's sword whistling through the air towards him. He stopped it just before the tip found his flesh. The man dropped his own shield to gain better momentum.

The warrior aimed for a vulnerable spot beneath Peder's arm but his action was anticipated and Peder hit the man's hand with the side of his sword, causing his opponent's weapon to fly from his grasp.

Without a moment's hesitation Peder pushed his sword beneath the man's armor and through his chest. He yanked the blade back out and prepared to plunge it in again, but it wasn't necessary. The man died at his feet.

V

Dagstyrr would not allow himself to give into the fatigue that threatened to take over. It was nothing, inconsequential and unworthy of notice. He kept a firm grip on both his sword and knife. He'd lost his helmet at some point, but he didn't care. It allowed him better sight and he took advantage of it.

Rafn fought close to him but he paid the other warrior no heed. He had his own problems as warriors that fought with skill and strength kept coming at him. That they were still greatly outnumbered did not go unnoticed.

These Skahi warriors were not so easily disposed of as they had hoped. More than one of their men already lay dead and others fought viciously to remain alive. The storm continued overhead, making the fighting that much more dangerous.

It distorted the vision and made the mud slick beneath his feet. A few times now he'd almost slipped and given his opponent an opportunity to kill him. He fought for balance. He would not make a widow of Kata, or an orphan of his son. Never!

He killed the man he fought, but not before receiving a deep cut across his left arm. He ignored the stinging pain and the blood that was washed away by the rain. It just made him angrier and he used that anger to call up his reserve of strength as he met yet another warrior.

They kept coming, one after another. He had no time to breathe between opponents.

He vaguely heard a call from somewhere on the wall, but the words were drowned by a sudden crash of thunder. He sent a silent prayer to Thor.

VI

Kale fought with luck more than anything. He stayed close to Onnar and kept within his shadow so that the other warrior was the one faced with the worst attacks. Kale did not go unscathed as he'd been forced to fight two men that must have been half animal they snarled so much.

He had to force himself not to panic as he held his shield close to him and let his sword meet the first man's assault. It had only been a thickening of the rain and a misplaced foot by the warrior that had given

Kale a lucky thrust, not with his sword, but with the spear he'd still had gripped in his hand.

The spear penetrated the man's flesh and he fell away, but he was not dead. He managed to get back on his feet to continue his fight, regardless of the shaft of wood that was stuck in him. The man howled and removed the spear. He broke it in half and threw it at Kale's feet. Only then did Kale realize he'd failed to place another weapon into his hands.

Onnar saw and took a moment to end the man's life before turning back to his own battle. Kale quickly grabbed the sword from his back and met the next man who came at him. This time the man was relentless. The warrior was as strong as an enraged boar and Kale had to fight desperately to maintain his balance and his life.

Vikkar closed in on the man's other side and Kale yelled to him for help. The man looked at him in distain that he would make such a request. The Ragnarr warrior kept beating him down until he'd sunk to his knees, his shield held up for protection.

Vikkar tripped the man and he fell into the mud and knocked his head on the ground so hard that he lost his focus and was momentarily disoriented. Vikkar glared at Kale as he stumbled to his feet.

"Finish him off." Vikkar snarled and pushed his way back into the thick of the battle.

Kale quickly followed his command before the warrior regained himself. He raised the sword in both hands, pointing it straight down and aimed at the warrior's abdomen. He screamed in fury and used all his strength to push the sword down through the warrior.

The man's eyes met his as he did and despite the fact he knew he was dying, Kale saw no fear in them. By the warrior's beliefs he was on his way to Vahalla, Odin's hall for warriors who died in battle. Kale shivered when the man smiled as death came to claim him.

He turned suddenly to find that Onnar was still close by. He looked beyond him and spotted Danr. As he moved in closer to Onnar, he scowled at the sight of the man who had betrayed them.

"I command you to finish him off." He yelled to the warrior under his command and pointed to where Danr fought. Onnar, in disbelief, stared at him before turning his gaze toward the man who had always been a friend. "Do as you are ordered. The request comes straight from Bekan,"

Kale screamed at the other man's hesitation.

Onnar growled in reply and moved towards his prey. Kale kept close to him to ensure that his orders were successfully carried out.

VII

Rakel felt useless standing beside Berthor on the wall. Many of the other archers had grabbed up their swords and joined the fight below, but Berthor had been ordered to remain at his position. Enough men had to be left on the wall to shoot down any that tried to climb its heights or reach the gate.

So far the Ragnarr warriors had not allowed them to get close enough. So Rakel, now soaked from the rain, waited in misery. Berthor had tried to make her leave but she'd adamantly refused, wanting…needing to remain on the wall.

She knew that men were dying because of her. If she had remained at home and married Kale then this battle would not be taking place. As she saw men from both sides fall, deep and guilty thoughts clenched her stomach like a fist. She had to keep from vomiting at the sight of such violence.

It was her due to stay and watch. It was her punishment. She spent a good deal of the time watching Danr fight one man then another. Fear seized hold of her and would not let go as she waited for the moment when he would fall.

Pride had touched her when she first witnessed how well he fought, but that had long been replaced by sheer terror as she watched him.

What she had imagined a battle would be was so far from the reality. She had earned a new respect for the men who fought, even as her mind reeled from the horror of what she was witnessing.

"Ships," Berthor yelled beside her and others on the wall turned to see through the muted light of the day to the sails that rose on the water close to the dock.

New fear washed through her as she imaged that her father had sent a second wave of attack upon them. She wanted to scream, but the warrior Hachet, smiled as he looked out at the harbor.

"The lead ship bears the mark of the Jarl of Skiringssal," he told Berthor. "Lord Valr has come."

"Who is he?" she asked Berthor.

"Rafn's brother." He smiled at her. "On those three ships are enough men to turn this fight in our favor."

Rakel understood and allowed his words to bring her hope. She looked back down at Danr.

"Do not falter now," she said.

VIII

Hachet climbed down the side wall and made his way to the dock from a direction that would not lead him close to the fighting. He needed to warn Valr what was happening here.

The rain continued in thick sheets and helped to conceal his movements. He was on the pier by the time the lead ship pulled up. He saw Valr standing at the rail and waved him in. He rushed to grab the rope that was thrown him and secured the knarr.

A plank was dropped and Valr was the first off the vessel. He met Hachet's haggard and anxious appearance with suspicion.

"Where is my brother?" he demanded, but even as he asked he became aware of the commotion that took place before the compound.

"He fights as do the others. We are outnumbered, but not without hope. Your arrival could not have been better timed."

The other two vessels pulled as close to the dock as they could and were tied down. Valr called out a sharp command that had warriors spilling over the sides of all three ships.

"Our warlord needs us." His deep voice matched the strength of the thunder that echoed towards them.

The men didn't stop to grab their armor, but each carried a sword in his hand. They flocked to Valr and on his command they charged forth in a commanding power through the rain. Hachet felt relief surge through him.

Not wanting to return to the safety of the walls, he ran after Valr, clutching his own sword.

IX

Rakel's eyes shifted between Danr below and the men that had poured from the ships. A large dark haired man was the first off the knarr and had spoken briefly with Hachet.

It was not long before he'd called many men to him and headed to join the fight. As he neared she felt her hope growing. Again she glanced down at Danr and watched as he fought a man with a pinched face and dark eyes. She recognized him as Onnar and next to Danr he was her father's most skilled warrior.

They were evenly matched in their battle and her heart clenched in worry. The fight could go either way. Onnar could fall, or Danr. If she'd had a clear shot of the man's back she would be tempted to put an arrow through him.

She knew that Danr would not want to win in such a way.

She held her breath as the fight grew more violent. Danr scowled fiercely as he brought his sword towards his opponent again and again, trying to wear down his strength. His technique worked for Onnar staggered suddenly as he slipped. He reached for the air in an attempt to balance himself, but instead he received the long blade of Danr's sword through his gut.

Danr drew the sword out and the warrior toppled sideways. Blood frothed from Onnar's mouth as he lay there in anticipation of his death.

Danr's eyes lit with victory one moment, then shock the next as the blade of a sword emerged from his chest where his armor had been knocked away. Its sudden appearance was surreal. Danr dropped to his knees and Rakel was stunned at the sight of Kale. There was blood on his brow where he'd been injured, but a vicious scowl gripped his face.

"Danr!" Rakel screamed loudly causing Berthor to jump beside her. Danr must have her heard her because over the distance their eyes met.

She looked like a goddess to Danr as he stared up at her on the wall. Even with her hair plastered to her head, she was the most beautiful woman he'd ever seen. His only regret as he died was that he'd not had a chance to see what passion she possessed.

Rakel stared at him in disbelief as he fell forward into the mud. Kale noticed her and when she looked towards him he was staring at her and the look he gave her convinced her that he was touched with insanity.

CHAPTER 30

Systa was near to panicking as she leaned against the gate. The nightmare that had been haunting her these long months was unfolding outside the walls of the compound. She could hear the terrible sounds of the battle; the angry cries, the weapons clanging against each other and the howls that penetrated the wooden gate.

Hadde stood close by, silently watching her agony as she feared what she could not see. She had failed to stop Joka. She couldn't see what took place on the battlefield but she could feel every pulse vibrating through her.

She leaned against the wood and tried to peer out through a small crack between the boards. She could not see much of anything. Thunder boomed and made her jump, but she pressed herself closer and tried her best to tell what was going on.

Her wet clothes clung to her and she had to clench her teeth against the chill that was threatening to take over her body. Then she sensed something, someone on the other side.

This was her hope.

"Systa no," she heard Hadde plead, but it did not stop her.

II

Peder was at the gate now. He had but to step back and swing it open to disappear to safety behind it. He did not consider this an option. What he wanted was to be back to where he had started, close to Joka.

Worry for her was grating on him, but in the few glimpses he'd caught of her she was holding her own. He needed her to continue her furious fight until he could get to her.

Peder heard the gate creep open behind him just as he killed the man he was fighting. Before another could engage him someone lightly touched his arm. He turned to find Systa.

"What are you doing here?" he asked. "Return inside where it is safe."

"Save her you must." Systa pleaded ignoring his order. Fear shone brightly in her silver eyes and Peder felt a sudden cold seize him.

"I am trying to get back to her."

"Listen she would not." She trembled as she spoke as if some inner torment had taken hold of her and would not let her go.

"She is fighting well." Peder told her to ease her mind as much as his own. "She has killed many."

"Seen not has she what I have." Systa clutched desperately at his arm, "Does not understand that the child weakens her."

"Child?" Peder froze at the Seer's words. "What child?" he demanded to know at once.

"Her child," she said in a whisper, "Your child."

Fury like none other Peder had ever known clutched him in its grip. Systa saw the anger and stepped back from him. "Go," he snapped at her.

He didn't watch to make sure she made it back through the gate but turned with fierce determination to the mob that kept him from Joka. He stabbed his sword through a man who dared to step in front of him.

He couldn't be stopped from his course. Those who tried met a grisly end for he did not care how much blood he shed.

He became vaguely aware of new warriors joining the fight. He met Valr's curious speculation of him, but did not so much as spare the man a nod of welcome. He did not question where he'd come from or the men who fought without armor. What mattered was getting to Joka.

III

Rafn met two men head on. They circled him, and despite the wet ground, Rafn's feet danced surely beneath him. The thunder sounded now in the distance, no longer overhead. At first he wondered why the god was retreating until he brought his sword up to stop the swing of one of the men. As he raised the axe in his left hand to stop the second another sword beat him to it.

The Skahi warrior's sword was hit aside and his body became impaled at the end of a blade that had yet to be bloodied. Rafn twisted to see who had come to his aid and stopped in shock to see his brother.

"Valr," he said as he put a quick finish to the other man.

"I thought perhaps you could use my help." He smiled in greeting.

"It is most welcome." He glanced around and saw others he knew, swarming out to overwhelm the enemy.

"It is not the greeting I had expected." Valr chuckled. He and Rafn were left with no one to fight, "But with you what else could I expect."

"Let us finish this, and then we will feast." Rafn promised and the brothers dove back into the thickest part of the battle.

The Skahi warriors were startled by the new arrivals. They began to fight desperately and fiercely in an attempt to save their lives. That they would lose was no longer a question. It was inevitable.

They waited for Kale to call them back, to order them to retreat, but he did not, so they were forced to fight on.

IV

Rakel watched from the heights the large dark haired man that was said to be Rafn's brother. He was certainly the most powerful looking man she had ever seen. His dark eyes were hard as iron as he met the enemy.

Where Rafn fought with a wild fury, this man charged head on with a force of will and strength. Valr was the name she had heard him called. She barely remembered to blink as she watched him.

Why was her heart beating so rapidly?

She glanced away in time to see Kale find Joka. She was about to scream a warning when Joka turned to face him. Excitement flashed across her face in anticipation as she brought up her sword.

Kale sneered in answer and started the battle that would end with one of them dead.

Systa appeared beside her and to Rakel she seemed trapped in fear. She had heard of the woman's ability as a Seer and not knowing if it was true or not, she wondered if the woman had seen something.

Had she seen how this battle would end? If so, the look on her face could only mean that it would not end well.

V

"I have waited a long time for this Joka." Kale spat as their swords rang together.

"I was expecting you," she replied with eagerness.

She started the dance she had played in her mind many times, one that had started when she was still young. It had become clearer through the past winter while she waited for this inevitable moment between them.

"You thought you could insult me and live." Kale spoke through clenched teeth. His anger was barely contained.

"You were not much of a man," Joka taunted. "You need no help from me to humiliate yourself."

"No woman speaks thus to me," he screamed and came at her, but she was anticipating his foolishness and easily sidestepped his attack. He fought for balance and finding it he turned in time to stop her sword.

Back and forth the dance between them continued towards its deadly conclusion. Joka had to work hard at keeping Kale's sword from breaking through her defensive moves. She had not expected this.

"It would seem that you have been practicing." Joka watched the sheer pleasure her comment brought to Kale's face.

"I am more than prepared to end your life Joka." Kale laughed. "Do not doubt me on that."

"You may try." Joka challenged him and the fight became more intense.

The rain was suddenly sucked back up into the sky. Joka realized when a stream of sunlight shone down upon her that the thunder was gone. Sweat stung her eyes and in annoyance she ripped off her helmet and tossed it aside.

She was now able to see more easily as she faced the man she had dared to insult. She did not regret her actions and if necessary would repeat them again if she were forced. He deserved to be put in his place because he thought too highly of himself, and too poorly of women.

It would be his undoing to misjudge her now.

From the corner of her eye she became aware that the battle was coming to an end. That somehow their numbers had swelled. As if she were dreaming she spotted Valr in the crowd to her left and couldn't understand how he'd gotten there.

BITTER PASSAGE

She had no time to contemplate such an anomaly. She screamed her rage and threw all her strength behind her sword. She even went so far as to grip it with both hands to lend her extra momentum. Her shield was long shattered and forgotten.

"Come to your death Joka," Kale invited. "My blade will be empowered by your blood when I stand over your dead body and celebrate."

Joka ignored his boasting words and did not relent. More than once she saw the strain on his face as he fought to keep from falling to her blade. It would be the ultimate humiliation to die in battle at the hand of a woman. She knew that he believed this. Had not all the men of her village thought that women were nothing more than inferior beings that they could humiliate?

It would not be so with her.

Again and again they danced around each other, moving in grotesque movements as they jumped first towards each other then away. He was weakening and it gave her the power to continue.

She was beating him down by the sheer will to do so. She saw the rage flare up in his eyes as they met hers. He had not expected the fight to last so long. Many were now watching their brutal battle. She saw Valr step closer with his sword raised, ready to enter the fight if needed.

She screamed in fury at the action and went at Kale like one of the legendary Valkyries. She saw the fear take him, saw him realize that he was no match for her. She only needed one good swing and he was dead. He knew this and turned to desperation.

Her vision blurred as a dizzy spell claimed her. She staggered slightly and slipped on the mud beneath her feet. She fought for balance but felt the loss of support from her legs and the ground rose up to meet her. As she landed hard on her bottom lights sparkled before her eyes then cleared enough for her to see Kale glaring down at her.

From the corner of her eye she spotted a fallen shield and grabbed it in time to stop the deadly blade that descended on her. She brought up her own blade to bring it beneath Kale's armor, but before she could do this his body jerked in a sudden spasm.

Blood appeared on his lips and his eyes widened in pain. His body went limp as he fell to the ground.

Joka looked up to see a very furious Peder standing above her. She had never seen him this mad before.

Joka scrambled to her feet and met him face to face, her own anger fueling her words. "He was my kill," she screamed at him. "How dare you!"

"I dare," he lifted his bloody sword to point it at her, "Because that is my child you carry." She heard a murmur of shock travel through those who heard.

"She had no right to tell you." Joka snapped in realization of what Systa had done.

"You should have told me," he accused and she felt a knot form in her gut at the truth of his words.

Unable to find a good reply, Joka turned and left him standing there fuming.

VI

Valr watched the couple in amusement. He had known that Joka had caught Peder's attention even before he left Skiringssal. That she had undone him so completely since they had last met was obvious. He met Peder's gaze and could not help but chuckle at the obvious dissention between them.

"I am glad to see that you children are getting along so well."

Peder stared at him as if he'd gone mad. Perhaps he had, but he saw the man visibly relax and even award him with a smile. "Much has happened."

"What have I walked into?" Valr swept his hand to encompass the many dead bodies around them. In the distance the remaining Skahi warriors were just now reaching the tree line and disappearing back into the mountains.

"We have hit a few snags," Peder said. His gaze moved to the gate which was now opened and realized that Joka had already disappeared through it.

"Go to her," Valr said.

"I had better wait." He answered with a shrug. "I am bound to wring her neck if I tried to speak with her just now."

Valr laughed. "Loving a woman like her is bound to be a challenge."

"That is an understatement if I ever heard one." Peder seemed to deflate before him, but without another word he left.

Rafn and Dagstyrr were checking through the bodies for anyone that was injured. A dozen men were being supported and helped back into the village compound.

Valr noticed a woman that looked half drowned, duck out through the gate and head towards the carnage. A quiver of arrows was held to her back by a strap and in her hand she absently carried a bow that judging by its dimensions had been made for her hand. Joka's influence he surmised.

The dress she wore was soaked and on her face was set a look of grim determination. Though her hair was wet, it did not hide the fact that when dry it would be a deep coppery red.

With curiosity he watched her as she stepped around the bodies and made her way to one of the fallen young men.

Someone she loved?

With no concern for soiling her dress, she fell to her knees in the mud. Dropping the bow, she struggled to roll the warrior onto his back then reached to pull off the man's helmet and lay it to the side. She brushed the hair from his face and wiped off the mud with the bottom of her dress.

She seemed in shock as she stared down into the man's face.

Valr didn't know what possessed him but he found himself approaching her. His shadow moved across the man's body causing her to look up. She had tears in her eyes as they met his.

"Is he your husband?" he asked, prompted by the misery he saw on her face.

"Nay." She shook her head. "Though I have known him my whole life, we barely knew each other."

Valr wondered at her reaction to the man's death. Had she hoped for a relationship with this man and was now denied it?

"He died because of me." He was caught off guard by her torment as she looked around at the bloody bodies around them. "All of this was because of me, all their deaths."

"You can't mean that." He did not know her, but certainly she was not responsible.

"I do." She half choked on a sob that she fought to suppress. "If I had not run away...my father would not have sent his men. This is my punishment. These men paid for my sins."

She was a Christian.

"Dear God, what have I done?" She brought her muddy hands to her face and would have hid her face within them if Valr hadn't suddenly knelt down and grabbed them in his own.

She looked at him as if she were just now seeing him. She seemed to study him for a moment before she spoke again.

"I saw you fighting," she said with a puzzled look on her face.

"Rafn is my brother," Valr said. "I am Valr Vakrson. I have just arrived from Skiringssal."

She looked down at his hands still wrapped around her own. He thought that she was about to cry, but she managed to stop herself. Her lip stiffened and as she looked up with new resolve, she replied. "I am Rakel."

CHAPTER 31

Peder retreated to the one place where he found comfort, the little chapel. He sat on the front bench and stared up at the simple wooden cross he had made with his own hands. Because he found his way there straight from the battlefield, his hands and clothing were still stained with blood.

He opened up his hands and studied them as if they belonged to someone else. He shuddered in remembrance of the all consuming rage that had taken hold of him. From the moment Systa told him that Joka was pregnant to the moment he had ended Kale's life, a fire had consumed him.

He had come to the chapel to beg for God's forgiveness, but he could not find the proper words. Anger had directed his hand. It claimed him still as he thought of Joka and how she'd lied to him.

He understood that she had not directly spoken words that were not true, but she had lied by omission. Many times she could have come to him and told him of the child. He would not have forsaken her.

She knew that, didn't she?

He clenched his fists in an attempt to keep the anger in. She had placed her life at risk as well as the child's. How could she have done that?

Movement startled Peder from his deep thoughts and he glanced up to see Father Duncun from Skiringssal before him. He was confused at first but realized that he must have been on Valr's ship.

"What brings you here Father?"

"So many were anxious to head to this new land." He took a seat beside Peder. "I thought perhaps I would be needed here."

"It is good that you have come." Peder made an attempt at a smile. "This chapel has need of someone to deliver the sermons."

"I had not thought to find a chapel waiting for me when I arrived." Father Duncun glanced around the building that was still so new.

"It has brought me comfort even without a monk to serve it."

"Something troubles you? I am here to listen."

Peder once again stared at the blood on his hands. "I accepted my duty today to protect Ragnarr," Peder said.

"I did not shy from the killing. My training and honor would not let me do so. It had to be done," Peder explained and the monk nodded in understanding. "But when I feared for the life of the woman I love, when I learned that she had placed our child in danger, I lost control. I let rage enter my soul."

"Fear is an irrational emotion and we often do things, or feel things that we otherwise would not."

"Does God understand that?"

"I believe he does."

"What of the anger I have for her?" Peder asked. "How do I come to terms with the hurt I feel about what she has done."

"Have you spoken to the woman?"

"Nay, I have not been able to bring myself to confront her. I am afraid of what I will say."

"You have done the right thing, by coming here."

"What should I do Father?"

"Let God's peace back into your soul and find a way to talk to her."

"You are right." Peder nodded, feeling a bit better than he had moments before. He needed God's patience now more than ever.

"I will leave you to your prayers." The monk rose from the wooden bench. "Come speak with me whenever a need should arise."

"Thank you Father."

Peder took a deep breath and considered carefully how to do the most difficult thing he had ever been faced with; Forcing the most stubborn woman in the world to open up to him.

II

Joka hid from Peder in the most cowardly way possible. She had seen him enter the chapel and quickly crossed the courtyard to seek a hiding place at Seera's. Seera was just returning from the hall, where she had stayed with the other women during the battle.

Seera met her and was instantly concerned at the look on Joka's face. "Come." She beckoned her to enter and Joka followed.

Orn was asleep in Seera's arms and she took a moment to settle him into his bed before returning to sit at the table with Joka.

Joka realized how she must look. Blood and mud still soiled her clothes and her hands desperately needed washing. She didn't even want to know what kind of tangled mess her hair was in as half of it had escaped the braids she had made earlier.

Noticing a basin of water on a stand beneath the window, Joka washed her hands. As the water turned red, Joka grabbed the soap that sat beside the basin and furiously began to scrub. Even once the blood was gone they felt stained. She could not wash the hurt and the self hate from them.

She scrubbed until her hands were almost raw before Seera stepped up behind her and told her to stop. Seera handed her a drying sheet and Joka took it unaware that someone else was directing her actions.

"The battle was bad?" Seera asked as they returned to the table.

"I fought like I always imagined I would."

"Were you hurt?" Seera visually searched Joka for signs of a wound.

"Nay," Joka answered without looking at her.

"What is it then?" Seera encouraged, "Tell me."

"The look on his face will haunt me always." Joka had to fight the tears that pooled in her eyes. It was the sight of these tears that had Seera most concerned. She had never seen Joka come close to crying.

"You faced Kale?" Seera thought she understood.

"He is dead." Joka answered as tears left streaks through the dirt on her face.

"You killed him?"

"Nay." Joka looked up to meet Seera's eyes. "Peder did."

"He saved you?" Seera realized.

"He was so mad, that I had not told him."

"Told him what?"

"That I carry his child," Joka said. The words caused Seera to sit up straighter.

"You are pregnant?"

"Aye."

"Why did you not tell Peder?" Seera reached for Joka's hands and squeezed them in support. It was obvious that Joka was really upset by what had happened.

"He ended our relationship," Joka tried to make Seera understand. "After that I did not know how to tell him."

"You thought he failed you?"

"At first," Joka said. "But the truth is I failed him. I did not know how to ask for forgiveness."

"What are you going to do now?"

"I don't know." Joka shook her head. She was so confused about everything. From the start she had made such a mess of it all. Peder had never been anything but a good man and she had been stupid in not trusting him.

"First we must clean you up." Seera put a hand on her shoulder. "You stay here and I will go and get you some clean clothes and send one of the women with a bath. I will tell Rafn to stay away so you can have your privacy."

"He won't mind that?"

Seera smiled. "He will be busy with Valr for some time yet."

III

Rafn paced the length of the great hall while Valr patiently stood by. The storm had been released and it was not so easily quieted again. Rafn fumed with anger as he thought about the battle that had just occurred.

"This is not over." Rafn turned to look at his brother. "It is just the beginning. This man Bekan is going to have to be dealt with."

"What kind of man is he?" Valr asked.

"I don't know much about him," Rafn said. "I have not met the man personally, but he makes this fight personal when he brings it to my door."

"What have you done brother, to anger him?" Valr raised his eyebrows.

"He wants his daughter back." Rafn flicked his hand as if the reason was inconsequential.

"You have kidnapped his daughter?" Valr was surprised.

"Of course I haven't." Rafn scowled. "She came here of her own free will. She asked for my protection, what was I to do? Send her back to marry that foul creature her father had intended to be her husband."

"Foul creature?" Valr questioned with a trace of amusement.

"That man that Joka fought, that Peder killed." Rafn grabbed a chair from the closest table and took a seat. Valr took another and sat to join his brother.

"Who was he?"

"His name was Kale. He is someone that grew up in the same village as Joka. She was not happy to see him again. She made a point of insulting him in front of all the men," Rafn explained. "She tells me that he had no respect for women and he beat those he brought to his bed. Could I condemn Rakel to such a fate?"

"Rakel?"

"Bekan's daughter." Rafn wondered at the strange look that had come to Valr's face.

"You did the right thing," Valr said.

"I would do it again. That still leaves me with this problem of Bekan. He does not know who he deals with, but he will soon find out."

"I will be by your side when he does." Valr smiled.

"It is good to have you here." Rafn beckoned over a servant and requested ale before continuing. "Now tell me your story. Why do you show up here with three ships full of people?"

"The King's arrogance turned his sights on my land. With you gone, he found the courage to strike. He began to attack the outer settlements where good people who were nothing more than farmers lived. He was sending a message, telling me that he did not fear me."

"You fought back?" Rafn was shocked by this news, though he should have expected it. Even before he left Skiringssal the King's greed had grown. He demanded too much tribute.

"Of course I did," Valr growled. "In my heart though, I missed my family. I took it as a sign that I was to follow you and thankfully many wished to join me."

"You didn't take long to build the ships."

"Nay." Valr's smile returned. "I did not have the desire or the patience to build ships. I simply traded for them. Your old drekar was highly prized."

"You traded my ship?" Rafn pretended to be shocked before he burst out laughing.

"I did." Valr chuckled.

"Things are different here brother. There are no Kings. Men do not hold the titles of Jarl and Warlord."

"Yes, I know. I stopped at a village on my way here. They told me where to find you and also explained things to me."

The servant returned with a ewer of ale and two drinking horns. Rafn nodded in thanks when she placed them on the table before the brothers.

Valr took a drink and then became serious. "I stopped at Dun'O'Tir before heading here. I have an important message to deliver to Peder and your wife."

Rafn set down his drinking horn and met the worry in Valr's eyes. "Then I shall get them."

IV

Seera found Peder in the chapel. He looked up and saw the concern on her face as she came to sit next to him. She took his hand in hers and for a moment seemed to be trying to find the right words to say.

"She has told me," Seera said.

"I wish she had been so honest with me." Peder looked away so that Seera would not see the full extent of his misery.

"It will work out as it should"

"Perhaps."

"Valr summons us." She changed the subject for which he was glad. "He has news from Dun'O'Tir."

Peder followed her outside and was stunned by how bright the sun had become. It did not match his misery. Somehow he had expected it to still be overcast. They made their way to the hall where they found Valr and Rafn waiting for them.

Both men rose from where they sat. "You have word from my father?"

"Aye." A frown formed on Valr's face. Peder's chest tightened in sudden worry. "The Eorl is very ill. The healer that has seen to him does not believe he will live much longer."

Seera gasped and Rafn's arm went around her in comfort. "You have seen him?" she asked.

"He beckoned me to his room. He can no longer get out of his bed and he wanted to meet me. He has great respect for Rafn and admitted to having a desire to make my acquaintance. He apologized for having to meet under such circumstances, but he wanted me to bring a message to you both."

"And what is that?" Peder's voice tightened in grief. He had not thought in leaving that he would leave Dun'O'Tir vulnerable. He had not considered his father would fall ill, for he had always been such a strong and healthy man.

"He misses you both very much. He had hoped to see you again, but he knows that God has other plans. He wanted me to pass on his love."

Peder glanced at Seera. Tears spilled down her face. She was as shocked as he was.

"I will be leaving at once." Peder told them and was about to turn when Rafn's voice stopped him.

"My wife and I will be joining you." Seera looked up at him with surprise and gratitude. "I will assemble a crew willing to take us."

"Thank you," Peder said.

Rafn turned to Valr. "Brother, will you watch over Ragnarr in my absence?"

"Of course I will."

Rafn led Seera out of the hall. Peder watched them go and only once they were through the door and out of earshot did he turn back to Valr.

"In your opinion, will we make it in time?"

"I don't know my friend."

Peder made a decision, one he had been playing with in his mind for a long time. One which suddenly seemed like the only one left to him. He knew where his place was, where he was needed most.

It was not here.

"I give you my dwelling." Valr stared at him in sudden understanding.

V

Seera went to search for Agata and Esja. When she had first seen them among the people who had disembarked from the three knarrs her mood had lightened considerably. They were her friends and she had missed them. She went out beyond the gates to find them both among the many who were setting up temporary tents.

"Mistress, it is good to see you." Agata rushed forward and gave Seera a hug.

"As it is to see you."

"Esja." Seera turned to the older woman and hugged her as well. "I have missed your company."

Esja fought to maintain her composure and not show how much the younger woman's words affected her. She straightened her apron-dress and took a glance around before she spoke.

"I have heard that Kata has had a child," Esja said.

"Aye, she has had a boy. Dagstyrr has named him Tannr after an uncle he was fond of."

"I remember the one named Tannr. He was a prankster. Let us hope that his namesake does not inherit that quality. He was forever causing mischief." There was a twinkle in her eye when she spoke.

"You knew this Tannr well, did you?" Seera chuckled.

"I had my dealings with him." Esja did not elaborate but she failed to hide a smile that told Seera exactly what kind of dealings the older woman was remembering.

Seera's expression became serious as she glanced between the two women. "I am sorry our reunion has to be short, as I must leave at once for Dun'O'Tir."

"There was talk about your father's illness when we stopped at the Fortress by the Sea," Agata said. "I wish that you may quickly get to his side."

Seera stayed only a short time longer with the women before she made her way back into the compound and saw to her packing. Rafn was off with Valr showing him around and leaving him with instructions regarding the building of their port.

She knew that Rafn worried about leaving when Bekan had yet to be dwelt with, and she loved him all the more for taking her to Dun'O'Tir in hopes that she would make it in time to say goodbye to her father.

She felt the grief welling up and the fear that gripped her heart. What if she didn't make it in time?

CHAPTER 32

Joka sat on the bed in her sleeping area. Seera had come rushing into her dwelling a short time ago and told her that they were going to Dun'O'Tir. She babbled on in a panic about her father being ill and that he might already be dead. They had to leave at once if they were to have even the slightest chance of making it in time.

Seera had been wild with worry as she began to pack for the journey. She had called for Yrsa and the girl had come to her aid. Helping not just with Orn but with what needed to be done so they could leave.

Joka did not know what to say. She had left her friend and retreated to the longhouse. She sat now on her bed, her thoughts on Peder. She knew of his closeness to his father. He would be worried sick and desperate to get to his father's side. She wanted to go to him, to offer her comfort and support.

So much lay between them. It was not so easy to just walk up to him and take him into her arms.

"Go you must." Joka was startled by Systa's voice for she had not heard her sister approach. She met Systa's steady gaze and a frown formed between her sister's brows. Silently she sat on the bed beside Joka and took her hand in her own.

Joka speculated on the contrast between the two hands. Hers was darkened by the sun and rough to the touch. Systa's was pale and smooth, delicate, what a woman's hand was meant to be.

She could not shake the sadness that filled her. Systa touched her other hand to Joka's face as a mother might do for a daughter before speaking.

"Needs you he does," Systa said.

"Perhaps it would be best to wait for his return. By then we will both have had time to think and to work through our feelings." It was a good idea. Distance between them might be what was best.

"Nay sister." Systa shook her head. "Stay he will at the Fortress by the Sea."

"He will not come back?" Joka was shocked. She had not thought that he would choose to remain at Dun'O'Tir.

"It holds his heart. Come here for you. Lost you he has. No reason left to stay."

"I…" Joka choked on the feelings that engulfed her.

"Love him still," Systa finished for her.

"Yes." A simple declaration that lay her whole heart open even as it threatened to break.

"Go you must," her sister said again.

Joka panicked. "What of you?" They had never been apart. They had helped each other survive through the worst pain. They had fled together in hopes of finding something better. No two sisters could be as close as they.

"Fine will I be." Systa smiled. "Hadde have I. Happy I am."

Joka looked at her in surprise. What others had noticed, she had failed to. That Systa had found something special and she had not even realized it.

"Hadde? The dwarf?"

"Good man is he." Systa beamed with delight and Joka felt her happiness. It warmed her wounded heart. She grabbed for her sister's hand and held tight.

"Will Peder have me?" Joka was frightened. She had been wrong in so many things she had done. Could Peder forgive her? Would he still want her? Still love her?

"Only he can say."

II

Things moved quickly. Forty men volunteered to take Peder and Rafn to Dun'O'Tir. Peder left the details to Rafn. It was enough for him to pack up his things from his dwelling, even though all he owned fit into two trunks.

He stared down at the trunks where they had been placed beside his door, ready to be taken to the ship. It did not seem like much. He glanced around the lodge that he had built himself. It seemed suddenly so bare.

Somehow it was fitting. It was exactly how he felt inside. That everything that had made him happy had been stripped away until there was nothing left. He'd had such hopes when he had decided to join Rafn's quest to Iceland.

He stared at the bed and forced the memories of the woman whose arms had wrapped around him, deep down where they would not choke him. He had not dealt with the fact that she carried his child.

He could not.

He would not deny the child once he or she was born. He would return to Ragnarr someday to visit his sister. He'd make sure that Joka allowed him to be a father. It was not ideal. He would not be the kind of father that his had always been to him.

His absence from the child's life would not go unnoticed by either of them. He was gripped with many regrets. Worry about his father kept him from dealing with them.

He had many lonely years ahead of him in which to replay the moments of happiness that he'd so briefly shared with the woman whose soul he had failed to capture. Someday perhaps he would be able to remember her without being consumed by pain.

A knock on the door drew his attention. A moment's hope was dashed when he opened the door to Valr instead of Joka.

What had he expected?

"I thought you could use some help," Valr said.

"This is all I have." Peder motioned to the trunks. "You are most welcome to carry one of them."

"Indeed." Valr replied as he bent down to scoop up the closest one.

"That one contains my weapons, be careful." Peder attempted to lighten the mood but Valr saw right through it.

"You can trust me." Valr smiled.

The men joined the others already gathered at the docks. Peder and Valr passed the trunks off to a couple of the men, who brought them to one of the sleeping compartments below deck.

BITTER PASSAGE

They joined Rafn and Dagstyrr. Dagstyrr would be staying to help Valr with things in Ragnarr. Seera and Orn were already on the ship. It was just Rafn and Peder who needed to board the knarr and then they would be off.

"Have a safe voyage brother." Valr clasped hands to arms with Rafn. "Worry not of things here. Dagstyrr and I will not fail you."

"I leave with things unsettled."

"We will handle it." Valr turned then to Peder and clasped hands to arms with him. "I wish you luck."

"Thank you." Peder accepted a similar wish from Dagstyrr. He found it hard to move his feet, to leave behind all his dreams.

It had to be done. Duty called him home.

All three of the other men looked up at the same time to focus on something just over his shoulder. He turned to see what had drawn their attention. Joka stood there, her eyes on him. He met them and suddenly his resolve to leave her behind faltered.

"I would go with you," she said. He could only stare at her as if she were speaking an unknown language. The shield that had always kept her hidden from him was gone. She looked at him with such vulnerability and fear.

And love.

"I will not be returning to Iceland. I must claim my title and my birthright."

She motioned to the trunk that lay at her feet. "I know, as I know there is much between us that has not been settled."

"And how would you like it to be settled Joka." He felt his chest tightened as he waited for her response.

"To be with you, to raise our child together."

He reacted suddenly and desperately. He grabbed her to him and kissed her, uncaring that others watched. She responded to his touch and her arms went around him. It was not something he had expected and the receiving of it was more satisfying than anything he could have imagined.

Peder did not see the other three men smile and exchange looks of amusement. He could only feel the beating of his heart and the heat of the woman pressed against him.

"Um, I believe it is time we go." Rafn chuckled and Peder was forced to acknowledge his words.

Reluctantly he stepped from Joka and saw tears in her eyes. He grabbed her hand and squeezed it tight. "Let us go then," he replied without dragging his eyes from Joka. Rafn bent to grab her trunk.

Dagstyrr stepped forward. He spontaneously hugged Joka. "You will be missed around here."

"Thank you," she said.

"Take care of each other." Valr came forward and hugged her as well, but more formally than had Dagstyrr.

"We will." She glanced back at Peder as if she were still not sure what had just happened.

III

The ship was rowed from port out into the bay. Joka stood with Peder watching Ragnarr disappear from sight. Systa had stood on the wall with Hadde. The sisters stared at each as long as they could until they were too far away to been seen.

Joka felt sad that she was leaving her. Peder grabbed her hand as if sensing her thoughts. "This is what you want?" he asked her. Perhaps he was as aware of the fragility between them as she was.

They kept glancing at each other in confusion. The wounds that each felt were not yet healed. It would take much effort on both their part to work past them. Joka had taken the first step in trusting this man who had claimed her heart, but she was not fooled into believing that she would not have more to take.

"It is what I want." She saw the relief in his eyes. He was as unsure as she. Somehow that comforted her. She understood that they both had to give of themselves.

"I love you Joka." He touched her face to turn it towards him. He bent to kiss her lightly to emphasize just how much. She automatically leaned into him, deepening the kiss.

"And I love you as well."

Peder's hand moved to lay flat on the small bulge of her stomach. She felt the heat of his hand through her tunic. She saw the wonder on his face.

"You are not displeased?" she asked. He looked up and a smile transformed his face, taking with it the worry that had been on it since he'd heard of his father's illness.

"I am not," he said. "Perhaps it is a son."

"It is a daughter," she said matter-of-factly, causing him to laugh at her bold statement.

"That would make me just as happy"

IV

The sky remained clear as they followed the coastline east until they reached the end and had to turn south. They passed by Seyois, not wanting to stop traveling even for a short time. They worked in shifts. One directed the sails and rudder oar through the long night, and then another group took over to keep the knarr on course during the day.

Peder had insisted that Joka share his sleeping compartment with him, and they lay together each night wrapped in each other's arms, but they did not make love. Joka wanted to question why, but she was too afraid to ask.

During the day he was usually with Rafn keeping everything in order. They did not travel with animals this time, except for Peder's stallion, as he would not be returning to Ragnarr and he didn't want to leave him behind.

Peder often checked on the horse to make sure he was traveling well. She had seen Peder talking in whispers meant to soothe the animal.

He would smile at her when she would glance his way, but he kept from her except for the nights. It was not what she had expected. It was almost too formal between them, too pleasant.

What had happened to the passion that had burned between them? Why did she fail to spark such a response in him now? What was she still doing wrong?

Seera came up on deck and joined Joka at the rail. They were traveling across the open water now and there was no land in sight. It was still a bit unnerving to Joka to be so far from land.

"How are you feeling?" Seera asked her. "The ships motion is not making you sick." Both women remembered how Kata had suffered with morning sickness on the voyage over.

"I have not felt ill. When I do too much I have had dizzy spells, but that has been the worst of it." It still felt unreal to her that she carried a child.

Her pregnancy was starting to become quite evident, especially with the stretching of her tunic. It was a marvel that she had not expected to experience in her lifetime.

Then again she had not expected to find love.

"And things with Peder?"

"He is different with me." Joka found herself needing to share her concerns with someone. Seera's question had cut straight to the problem.

"How so?"

"He keeps himself distant. He smiles, tells me he loves me, kisses me… but he doesn't touch me."

"You have not made love." Seera immediately understood her concern.

"He lies chastely beside me each night."

"Have you spoken with him about it?"

Joka looked at her in shock. "I have not dared. We have much to heal between us. It is still far too delicate a subject to broach."

"Has he asked you to marry him?"

"No," Joka shook her head. "Once long ago he did. That first night we made love, but I told him that I wouldn't marry him."

"Why is that?" Seera's gaze held understanding, making her feel safe enough to explain.

"I was too afraid if I married, I would lose who I was."

"And now?"

Joka felt her heart clench. "He has not asked again."

"Do you want him to?"

Joka thought very carefully how she would answer. She had opened herself up to him. She was willing to take whatever chances she needed to, for them to be together. She would marry him, she was not sure that is what he still wanted. Perhaps he had believed her when she said she would never marry.

Why would he doubt that her words had been true? She had meant them.

"I don't think the idea scares me like it once did," she said.

"Then tell him."

"I don't know if I can." Joka shook her head. She was already feeling more vulnerable than ever before. She was losing that hard determined shield that in the past had always kept her safe.

Even her anger was gone. She no longer felt like she had to fight the whole world just to find a place in it. She didn't know how to be a normal woman. Didn't know how to make Peder believe she would be a good wife.

She wasn't sure herself that she could be what would be expected of her.

"Perhaps you should take some time." Seera touched her shoulder. "I ask only that you not give up. Peder will come around."

Joka glanced over her shoulder to find Peder. He was with Hachet on the far side of the ship. They were adjusting the sails, trying to catch the wind from the right angle to increase the speed.

She would wait. She could give him that much.

CHAPTER 33

Peder felt his anxiety growing as soon as they reached Pictland and began to follow its shores to Dun'O'Tir. Seera stood beside him with the same fear etched on her face. Each asked the silent question.

Had they made it in time?

The ship would not move fast enough, but eventually the fortress walls of home finally appeared and once again Peder began to pace. The knarr sat too deep in the water and therefore could not be pulled up to the beach. Instead a boat was lowered to take them to shore. Rafn helped Seera and Yrsa into the boat. Orn was being carried by Yrsa as they both settled down beside Seera.

Joka climbed in next and Peder descended last. The others would follow shortly and, as they had before, they would set up camp outside the gates of Dun'O'Tir.

Peder raced on ahead, not able to wait a moment longer to find out if his father still lived. He was met at the gate by Jakob and the man looked relieved to see him.

"I am glad you have returned, my lord," Jakob said.

"My father?" Peder asked sharply but Jakob did not seem to mind.

"He is still with us." Peder felt a weight lift from his shoulders. The others were just now catching up to him.

"We have made it." He turned to Seera who shared his relief.

They followed Jakob to the Keep and Peder refused to be kept from his father any longer. Seera joined him and they together went to their father's bed chamber. Rafn told them that they would wait in the hall.

Peder met Joka's concerned gaze for only a moment before charging up the stairs. He didn't announce their arrival but pushed his way into the bed chamber. A middle aged man stood by his father's bed.

"Who are you?" Peder demanded. Seera touched his arm to calm him and he realized he had been rude.

"I am Issac, the healer brought in to care for the Eorl."

Issac studied him and Peder could see that he wanted to ask who they were, but somehow sensed that it would not be proper to do so.

"I am Seera." She stepped forward. "Forgive Peder. He is only worried for our father."

"It is good that you have come." Issac stepped back to allow Seera to take his place by Airic's side.

Their father looked pale and had lost much weight. His eyes flicked up to lock on Seera's and Peder saw confusion in them. Airic reached out with a shaky hand to touch his daughter's face.

"Do my eyes deceive me?"

"No papa." Seera's voice trembled. "Peder is here also." She looked back at him and he stepped closer to the bed.

Airic looked from Seera to his son. His mouth quivered in emotion. "I had not thought to see either of you again."

"Did you think we would not come the moment Valr told us you were sick." Peder sat on the edge of the bed.

"I had not expected you to."

"Then you do not know us as well as you think." Peder tried to smile.

"My heart sings with joy that you are here." Airic choked and began to cough. Peder noticed the blood left on his hand when the coughing ceased.

Issac came forward with a cloth and wiped clean Airic's hand and the corners of his mouth. Seera's face had become pinched in grief. Peder could see that she was fighting back tears as he placed a hand on her shoulder in understanding.

"Tell me of your new home." Airic looked to Seera and she began to tell him of how beautiful it was. How the village they were building was going to be wonderful when it was complete.

Peder met his father's eyes and answered the question that he saw in them. "This is my home father. I will be staying."

This news brought comfort to Airic. He had wanted his son to find his own future, but when he realized he was going to die, the future of Dun'O'Tir worried him more than he had thought it would.

""Is it what you want son?"

"I have missed home, more than I thought I would. I know now that it is my place to be here."

"Have you found what you searched for then?" He searched his son's eyes and saw that he had aged, matured.

"I have," Peder said. "I have brought her home with me."

Airic returned his son's smile. "Her? You have married."

"Not yet, but nothing will stop me from doing so."

"That is good." Airic began coughing while everyone watched in silence until the episode passed and he was able to speak again. "Then may I ask that you do it soon so that I may see it happen."

"I don't think you should leave this bed," Issac said. He moved closer, ready to do battle with his patient.

Airic met the healers gaze and spoke plainly. "I am dying. What difference will it make if I sat for a while in the chapel and watch my son get married?"

"None I suppose." The healer relented, but he was not happy about it.

"I will make it happen." Peder met Seera's amused expression.

"Perhaps you should propose first."

"Certainly she knows. She carries my child, she can't deny me now."

"I did not say she would deny you, but maybe she is not so confident in where she stands with you."

Peder stared at her as if he didn't understand what she was saying to him. Joka knew that he loved her. What was his sister going on about?

"Talk to her Peder."

Peder looked between his sister and father and realized that she was right. He had left many things unsaid since they had gotten back together.

II

Peder found her in the hall. The others had left and she was sitting alone by the hearth staring into the fire. She glanced back at his approach but did not rise to meet him. There was weariness on her face and he wondered if the voyage had been too hard on her in her condition.

He had tried to be considerate of the fact that she carried his babe.

He had kept his distance, not forcing himself upon her. It had been hard, especially in the nights as she lay beside him. He had wanted so desperately to make love to her, but wasn't sure if that was good for the baby.

Perhaps he should insist that she rest.

"I wasn't sure if you would still be here," he said as he went to stand before her. She met his eyes and again he thought that she looked tired.

"I was not sure where I was to go." He saw the look of confusion on her face and realized that Seera had been right. That Joka didn't know what Peder was feeling or what he wanted.

He would need to change that.

He dropped to his knees in front of her and took both her hands in his. Their eyes met and he saw that she waited expectantly. Truly she was the most beautiful woman in all of creation.

"I love you so much Joka. The time we spent apart nearly killed me. I had come to accept that I would remain dead inside without you."

"Peder..."

"Let me finish," he cut her off. "I want nothing more than for us to spend the rest of our lives together. To raise our baby in these same walls that I grew up in...Marry me Joka. Please don't say no this time."

He saw the tension leave her and a smile transform her face with happiness. Even her eyes seemed to sparkle with excitement. "I can ask for nothing more, my love. I want to be your wife, to share each moment with you until we are old. I had feared that things had changed too much between us."

"Why?" He was startled by her admission.

"Because you do not touch me in the night."

"Only because I did not want to hurt the child." He brought her hands to his lips.

"Women have been having babies forever. There is nothing wrong with us sharing our bodies while I am with child. Ask your sister if you do not believe me."

"I will never doubt you again" He softly laughed. On their wedding night he would join with her again.

"That is good, and I will not fail to place my trust in you again." He saw the truth of her words in her eyes. It was good to finally hear and know that she meant it.

"Tomorrow we will wed. If you have no objections I would like to be married by Father Robert in the chapel. I know you are not Christian but it is where my parents and my sister were both married and I would also like to marry in the walls of the church."

"I am honored that you find me worthy." She leaned down to kiss him.

III

Neither saw the woman who hid in the shadows behind one of the Eorl's banners. A look of horror and disbelief contorted her face.

Isibel had known that he would come home when he received word of his father's illness. It was what kept her from rashly boarding one of the Viking vessels and going to Iceland in search of him.

She had missed him these months that he had been gone. She had dreamed of him in the night and remembered how it felt to lie in his arms. Their passion had been real and though he had ended it with her, she believed it was only because she was not a Lady and he could not marry beneath his station.

She had vowed to change his mind when he returned. She had inadvertently walked in on him with Joka. She couldn't believe her ears when he'd declared his love and asked for her hand in marriage. How could he prefer a woman, who despite her obvious beauty, preferred to be a warrior, to act like a man.

When Joka had been there before, she had misjudged things greatly. She had come to the conclusion that Peder did not see her as a woman.

Apparently she was the reason Peder left his duties and his home to sail off to some unknown land. She had been shocked when he had done that, but had not guessed the reason why. She had assumed he was just young and in need of an adventure.

She believed in the end that he would return home, but she had thought he would return alone.

He had told Joka that they would marry tomorrow. She could not stand by and watch that happen.

She had to do something.

IV

Joka's things were brought up to Peder's room. She was nervous. Tomorrow she would marry despite her claim to never do so. It was cause for great excitement. She didn't realize how happy it would make her to become his wife.

In all ways she had already become his partner. Proclaiming so in front of his God would only make it official. She believed the goddess wouldn't mind her marrying in a Christian ceremony. It truly did not matter to Joka but it did to Peder and it was something that she wanted to do for him.

She lifted the lid to her trunk and suddenly laughed in amusement. Lying on top was a dress. Joka lifted it and shook it out. It was of a blue to match her eyes and Joka had to shake her head at Systa's foresight.

"You had known I would have need of it," she spoke aloud even though she was alone in the room. There was a knock on the door.

"Come in" She turned in time to see Seera come into the room.

"You have a dress." Seera was surprised.

"Systa must have slipped it into my trunk when I wasn't looking." She studied the dress further. "It even has some extra room around the waist."

"Her foresight is a benefit," Seera said. "I had hoped to convince you not to get married in one of your tunics."

"I suppose that would not be proper," Joka agreed. "It has been so long since I have worn a dress, especially one so beautiful."

"It will surprise Peder and I look forward to seeing his reaction," Seera said.

"Perhaps I should allow you to help me purchase more dresses." This won a soft laugh from Seera.

"It would mean long hours of standing and being pricked by a seamstress." Seera felt she had best warn her.

"It would be for Peder."

"I don't think he cares if you wear a dress or a tunic," Seera said.

"I know, but he will take up his birth right and become the Eorl of Dun'O'Tir. I should at least make an attempt to fit the part of his wife."

"He will be amazed at your willingness." Seera chuckled as she ran a hand over the soft material of the dress.

"He had better appreciate the sacrifice." Joka grinned. What did it matter if she wore a dress? She would still be strong and self reliant. She would still teach her daughter such strength.

Seera helped her hang the dress up on the dressing screen and smooth out the wrinkles. "You will need new boots." Seera beckoned to the tattered ones on Joka's feet. "And, a necklace to highlight the colors of the dress."

"I have no jewelry." Joka shook her head at Seera's enthusiasm.

Seera's hand reached for the necklace she wore, the very one that Rafn had gifted her long ago. "I will lend you mine. Tomorrow when I come to help you dress, you can borrow it for the day and I hope it will bring you luck as it has me."

"You are a good friend," Joka said. "Tell me truthfully. Will I disappoint Peder?"

"You never could." Seera turned back for the door. "I promised my father I would bring Orn to see him. If you need anything send the maid to fetch me from his bed chamber."

"How does he feel about me marrying his son? I am not of noble blood."

"He wants only to see Peder happy. My brother has convinced him that he is and that is all my father wishes for."

"I am sorry that he is so ill." Joka happiness faded as her thoughts turned to her future father-in law.

"I know. Peder would not be rushing the marriage if it was not for my father's wish to attend the wedding. He would take the time to make it more lavish."

"I have no need for a large wedding."

"You don't mind that there is no time to send for your sister and your friends back in Ragnarr?"

She reached again to touch the dress. "My sister will understand as I believe she knows. Why else hide a dress in my trunk."

"Perhaps she already sees the happiness you will find."

Joka pushed her towards the open door. "I am sure she does. Now go, your father needs you far more than I."

"Get some rest. I will see you in the morning." Seera closed the door behind her.

Joka was feeling so overwhelmed. Peder had gone off who knows where to make some preparations. He said to hold with tradition he would not share her bed that night, but find somewhere else to sleep. He would see her tomorrow when she walked down the aisle to join with him in wedlock.

How was she to sleep?

She went over to the corner of the room and picked up her sword. She pulled it from its sheath and remembered the night Peder had sent it to her. They had come a long way since that day. She had come to trust him, and the feelings that he had awakened in her.

She no longer doubted that the future held great things for them.

V

Peder was on the fortress wall. He had just finished checking with the guards on duty and making sure that in his absence everything continued to run smoothly. He was greeted with warm welcomes and much relief that he had returned. If the Eorl had died before his heir had returned it would have been a time of unrest within the castle.

Peder found that his soldiers had not believed that he was gone for good. They'd had complete faith that he would not fail in his duty to them all. He had been touched by their loyalty and trust that he would make the right decision. How could he have doubted that he belonged at Dun'O'Tir?

He turned at the approach of another and smiled in recognition of his friend Iver. The two men clasped hands to arms in greeting. "It is good to see you, my lord," Iver said. He wore a smile that bespoke his pleasure.

"I have been gone too long."

"Just a few moments ago I heard of your return. I myself have just returned from the King and I could not wait a second longer to find you."

"I am glad." It was very good to see him again. "How fares David?"

"The King is well," Iver told him. "He has been most impatient awaiting your return."

"And how is it that everyone knew that I would come back?" Peder laughed. Did everyone know his heart better than he did himself?

"Not one of us had our doubts." Iver's expression became serious.

Peder glanced down into the courtyard at the many people milling around. His eyes trailed over the training area, the forge, the small chapel and finally to the keep. It was all so familiar, so comfortable. It was home.

"How do things go for you my good friend?" Peder asked.

Iver's smiled returned. "Very well, my wife has given me a daughter just two weeks past."

"I am glad to hear" Peder felt pleasure at the news. "She deserves no less. She has already given you a son, now she needs a daughter to dote on."

"I fear it is I who will be spoiling that one." Iver laughed. "She is the most precious little thing I have ever seen."

"A daughter would be a treasure." Peder's thoughts turned to the child that would soon grace his life. A daughter of his own if Joka got her way and somehow he knew that she would.

"Now, about the other bit of news that was passed to me." Iver grinned at the contentment that had come to his lord's face. "Is it true that you are getting married and tomorrow no less?"

"You have heard correctly."

"I did not think that you would ever find one that you would take as a wife." Iver watched him carefully. "Yet from your smile, she is one you have come to love."

"From the moment I first saw her." Peder was unafraid to admit this to his oldest friend.

"Who is she?" Iver asked at the same moment that Joka walked from the keep to stand on the steps and look around the courtyard as if she were looking for someone. Her eyes moved over the fortress wall until they came to rest on Peder.

Iver did not miss the way Peder's eyes lit at the sight of her. In sudden understanding he looked from his lord to the warrior woman. He chuckled in amusement at the fact that it took a woman so fiercely independent to win Peder's heart. He had been witness to their sword play on that long ago day before Peder had left. It was suddenly clear what had led him away from this place that was his home.

"Her name is Joka." Peder told him without taking his eyes from the woman that was walking towards them.

When she was just below them Iver noticed the bulge beneath her tunic and was once again surprised. He met Peder's gaze as it shifted to him. Iver could see at once that he was a very proud man.

"You are to be a father as well?"

"Aye," Peder nodded, his gaze never leaving Joka. "Our daughters shall grow up and play together."

Iver smiled at his promise of a daughter, not a son. He roared in laughter and slapped Peder on the back. "We shall grow grey together with worry watching over them."

"If she is anything like her mother, it will not take long."

CHAPTER 34

Joka woke early and needed to clear her head before all the excitement began. She glanced at her dress still hanging on the changing screen. She couldn't believe that this was the day she would marry. Flowers filled the room and from what Seera told her they had been used to decorate the chapel as well.

She found her tunic and trousers and slipped them on. She felt a small kick within her abdomen. It was the first and it caused her heart to fill with wonder and joy. She placed a hand on her rounded stomach and smiled.

She would have a family, a child and a husband.

Breathe, she really needed to breathe. She found her way down the stairs to the main floor. Servants already scurried around in preparation for the wedding feast. A few nodded in greeting as she walked by.

Joka went out into the courtyard. The air was already warm, despite the early hour and promised to be a beautiful day. The sky was clear, but for a few small puffy white clouds. She walked around the courtyard and found her way to the training area. She smiled in memory of the first time Peder had invited her to spar with him.

Her sword rested on her back as it always did, but she made no move to grab for it. She passed the training area and went out through the gates. She had to walk through the tents Rafn's warriors had set up to reach a path that she knew led down to a small ledge. She had seen it the last time she was here, but had not had the chance to explore it.

It would serve her need for solitude. The climb was steeper than she thought but not so far down. A flat topped ledge that could sit maybe four people was soon beneath her feet.

She sat with her back against the smooth stone wall and stared out at the waves that rode the ocean. Far below, where she had no clear view, she could hear the water crashing up against the large rock that held Dun'O'Tir on its top.

Faint noises from the fortress castle reached her, but she ignored them. Instead she felt the peace that had come to live within her. She was almost a stranger to herself. So different were her thoughts from a few weeks ago.

She opened up her hands and stared down at them. They were still rough from the battle back at Ragnarr that she had fought with an unleashed fury. She marveled at the savagery of the sword fights she had engaged in.

When finally she had met Kale she had been consumed with the need for his death. In that moment she had been seized with all the memories of her childhood and the men who controlled the village. Kale had been the living representation of all the pain and suffering that she and her sister had lived through.

There was no question he had to die.

It was an all consuming rage that had directed her sword and begged for release from the torment of her soul. She would have to kill him to see it gone, to avenge the past crimes against her.

But Peder had been the one to take his life.

She now realized that he had been right to do so. She could have died that day. She had pushed herself too far, not knowing the baby would sap her strength so quickly. Just one mistake and she had left herself vulnerable.

She would have died and her child with her.

A sudden chill swept through her. Systa had told Peder of the child and sent him to save her. What had her sister seen? Had she seen her death?

Why had she been so selfish?

The sun had climbed higher bringing Joka back to the present. The wedding was to take place in the afternoon. She should head back and start getting ready. She also needed to eat as this child made her hungry all the time.

She was just reaching the Keep when Seera met her. She had come from the kitchen where she had been checking the progress of the feast.

"We need to get you bathed and dressed." Seera grabbed her arm and gently urged her inside.

They climbed the stairs to Peder's bed chamber. The very one she had spent the night alone in. She wanted to ask Seera where Peder was but decided they would see each other soon enough.

Seera pushed the heavy wooden door open and both women stepped inside. Seera squealed in shock, her hands flying to her mouth. Joka stared in disbelief at the ruins of the room.

The flowers had been ripped apart and strewn everywhere. The bedding looked like a knife had been taken to it and cut until it was rendered useless. Even the beautiful banners that hung on the walls had been destroyed.

But what Joka focused on and brought her the greatest anger, was her dress that had been left in shreds. There was nothing left of it that could be salvaged.

Who would have done such a thing?

Joka clenched her hands at her sides in an attempt to quiet the rage that was swelling within her. She wanted to kill the person responsible for this atrocity.

II

Peder was mad. He stood in the doorway to the chapel. The flowers that had so beautifully decorated the inside had been destroyed. All the candles had been chopped into pieces and left in a crumbled mess.

Father Robert was shocked by such a desecration to a house of the Lord. Thankfully the wooden cross had been left untouched. In fact if Peder looked more closely, it was only the things that were to have been used for the wedding that had been damaged.

Who would do such a thing?

Seera appeared behind him and gasped. "Not here too," she said.

Peder turned to her in suspicion. "What do you know sister?"

"I have just come from your bed chamber. It has been destroyed far more than this I am afraid. The covers on your bed and your personal banners have been cut into pieces, the flowers strewn everywhere and sadly Joka's dress has been shredded."

"What!" Peder's anger grew. That someone had deliberately set out to ruin his day was obvious. Who would do so and why?

"You have no idea who the culprit might be?"

"Nay," he answered, "But when I do, I will string him up by his neck."

"Someone is trying to stop the wedding," Seera said.

"Why?" Peder met her concerned gaze.

"We will find the answer to that soon enough. I will send the servants to clean up this mess and set out fresh flowers."

"You are right," Peder said. "This wedding will take place as planned. I have waited too long for this day and I will not let anyone stop it."

"I will see to it then."

Peder would see to finding out who did this. He ordered guards to be stationed at the chapel so a second attempt at destroying it would not be possible.

He would get married and nothing on earth or in the heavens would stop him from marrying the woman he loved.

III

Peder didn't notice Isibel skulking around in the shadows. She had waited anxiously to see his reaction. She was close enough to hear the conversation with his sister. She waited to hear that the wedding would be called off, but Seera had encouraged him to go ahead with it.

Damn her. After all the trouble she had gone to so that the wedding would not take place.

A tight expression had warped her face into something ugly. She turned back to the Keep with the intention of sneaking inside. Maybe there was something she could do to destroy the feast.

Seera was quick to notice her, and was instantly suspicious. She turned back to her brother who was just making his way across the courtyard. She hurried to his side.

"Brother," she called and he turned to face her.

"What is it?" he asked sharply and she couldn't blame his anger.

"I must ask you a personal question," she said.

He was out of patience. He gestured with his hand for her to speak. "Just ask."

"Have you ever had a relationship with the maid Isibel?"

Peder frowned for a moment as if he didn't understand where Seera's thoughts were leading. "A small tryst, nothing more."

"Could she have developed an attachment to you?"

"I was afraid that she would and that is why I ended it." Seera saw the moment he understood what she was saying.

"Isibel did this?" He growled.

"It is possible. I just saw her sneaking around by the chapel."

"I will kill her!"

Seera placed a hand on his chest to stop him. "Let me deal with her brother."

"I would throw her in a dark cell for the night and see that she can do no more harm."

"I suggest just placing a guard on her door and keeping her from leaving her room."

Peder worked through a whole range of facial expressions before he finally conceded to allow Seera to deal with the woman.

"You have a wedding to get ready for."

"How is Joka?"

"As angry as you," she said. "I have her soaking in a bath to relax her and to quiet her temper."

"Perhaps you should not tell her."

"A marriage should not be started with secrets," she said. "I will find an easy way to explain things to her. You go and ready yourself and leave the rest to me."

Seera spotted Rafn coming towards them and quickly pulled him over. "Make sure this groom gets ready. I am leaving you in charge of him."

"I don't need a babysitter." Peder grumbled.

"Yes you do." Seera shook her head. To Rafn she added, "Do not allow him near the woman who has tried to destroy the wedding."

"Woman?" Rafn raised an eyebrow at his brother-in law, "One not so pleased with your upcoming nuptials.

"Apparently not." Peder was forced to face the amusement in Rafn's eyes.

Seera hurried off in search of Isibel before the woman could get herself into more mischief. She cornered her just outside the kitchen.

She was waiting patiently for the others to give her an opportunity to sneak in unseen.

"Isibel." The woman jumped at Seera's sharp voice.

"My lady." She bowed slightly in a gesture of respect.

"What do you know of the sabotage done to foil my brother's wedding?" Seera asked and watched closely for Isibel's reaction.

"I know nothing." Her mouth pinched in an effort to control her sudden fear at having been found out.

"I don't know what your thoughts are. Perhaps you have feelings for Peder? Many women have. He did not choose you and this has made you angry. That he fell in love with another doesn't please you."

"What kind of woman is she?"

"She is one who is unique." Seera stepped closer to the girl. "One that could skewer you on the end of her sword if that is what she wanted."

Seera was pleased to see Isibel's eyes widen in understanding. She had failed to fear the warrior woman and Seera found great delight in placing that fear in her. Not that Joka would waste her time on someone so petty, but Isibel didn't know that.

"Guard," Seera called to a man who had been waiting for her command. "See that Isibel doesn't leave the maid's quarters."

"Aye, my lady." Isibel had no choice but to be escorted away by the fierce looking man.

Now, Seera needed to make sure that the wedding took place.

IV

Joka was just wrapping the drying sheet around her when Seera returned. The bath had soothed her somewhat. Maids had come and cleared away all the destruction and new furs had been draped over the bed.

She had insisted they leave the dress. They had thought such a request was strange but they left the shredded material in a pile on the bed.

Joka picked it up and let it run through her fingers. "What should I do now?" she said to Seera.

"I have another." Seera held up a dress in her arms. It was a cream colored silk dress with beadwork along the hem and arms. The bodice was not form fitting around the waist but held tight by a ribbon.

"It was my mother's," Seera said. Joka stared at her in surprise.

"I could not." She reached to touch the dress even as she objected. It was so smooth. She had never seen anything so exquisite in her life.

"She would want you to wear it," Seera said. "I have spoken to my father about what has happened and he has agreed with me. It would please him to see you in it."

"Will it fit?" Her hand went to her stomach.

"It is made loose, meant to be cinched with the ribbon. If you don't use the ribbon it should flow on you beautifully."

Seera helped her dress. First in a thin shift that was almost transparent and made Joka wonder what it was made of. Next the dress was lowered over Joka's head and she marveled at the feeling of the silk against her skin.

Two maids returned and Seera had them arrange Joka's hair so that it was partly pinned up on top and the rest flowing down her back. Somehow they attached small flowers so they would not fall out of her hair.

Lastly Seera clasped her necklace around Joka's neck. When a full length mirror was brought in front of Joka she did not recognize the woman staring back at her. She looked like a goddess from the stories told by the skalds. She thought of Freyja, the goddess of love. Perhaps finally the goddess looked down on her with approval.

Seera sent the maids away and Joka sat on the edge of the bed. Her nerves were a tangled mess and her stomach full of flutters. What bizarre creature had come to live within her skin?

"I heard the flowers in the chapel were also destroyed," Joka said to Seera.

"It is true," Seera said. "Peder has placed guards on it, but they will not be necessary."

Joka turned to stare at Seera. "What is it you know?"

"I discovered the one who caused the mess." Seera flicked her hand as if it were simply a minor nuisance.

"Do you intend to tell me?" Joka's voice betrayed her frustration.

"It was only a maid who is smitten with my brother and jealous that he has found love with another." Seera smiled to make light of it.

"Isibel," Joka replied bringing a look of shock to Seera's face.

"You knew that they were once lovers?"

"Isibel made a point of letting me know the last time we were here and when I questioned Peder he told me it had ended."

"You asked him?" Seera was amused. "Even though, back then you still hated him."

"I did, but I was also relieved to hear that he did not continue to share that woman's bed."

"You are a contrary woman." Seera chuckled.

"You have no idea." Joka replied with a smile.

There was a knock on the door and Seera went to answer it. It was Jakob and as he tentatively stepped into the room, Joka rose at once.

"My lady, you look…" Jakob searched for the right words, but failed to find them. This articulate educated man was speechless.

"She is beautiful," Seera finished for him.

"Aye," he agreed. "They are ready for you."

"Tell them we will be right there." Seera pushed Jakob out the door. She smoothed out the green dress she had chosen to wear and checked in the mirror to make sure the pins that held up her hair were still secure.

"Are you ready?"

"I am," Joka answered and knew that she truly meant it.

CHAPTER 35

Peder turned from where he stood at the altar. He had been speaking with his father who sat in a high back chair to Peder's left. A smile touched Airic's face at the stunned look on his son's. Indeed the woman standing just inside the doorway was an image out of a dream.

Peder stared in amazement at the transformation that had come over Joka. He searched to find the woman he knew beneath the stunning beauty that walked towards him. Their eyes met and he felt the sense of relief to see that it was indeed Joka.

She smiled radiantly as he reached out to take her hand. He was vaguely aware of Seera moving to stand at Joka's side. Father Robert came before them and began to speak of the sanctity of marriage.

He heard each word but still felt as if he were not truly there. So unreal was it all. Happiness infused him so completely that this day was really happening. That this woman who had challenged him and denied him, had shown him such passion and screamed at him in fury, had turned him so inside out that he had nearly walked away was really going to be his wife.

Thankfully she had finally accepted his love and his loyalty, and agreed to marry him.

They spoke words of promise to each other, stared at each other as if no one else existed, held each other's hands in support and with no reservations bound themselves to one another.

Father Robert pronounced them man and wife and it was all Peder needed to lean towards his wife and kiss her. The kiss said everything that he ever needed to know, that Joka was truly and finally his, body and soul.

II

They moved from the chapel to the hall, where a feast meant for a King was brought before them. His father was taken back to his room and Peder promised that they would come visit him later.

When the night grew late, Peder took his bride's hand and led her from the hall. They were followed by cheers and innuendos from the bolder among their guests.

"It is done wife." Peder smiled as he squeezed her hand in his and started up the stairs.

"We should go and see your father first," Joka said. "You promised him you would."

"I did." They followed the stairs to the top and entered the large bed chamber that belonged to Airic.

He was alone, but not asleep. He attempted to sit when his son entered, but Peder hurried to his side to put extra support behind him allowing Airic to see better. He held out his hand to Joka.

"Come my new daughter," he invited. Joka moved to sit on the stool by the Eorl's bedside. He was a pale shadow of the man she had met many months ago. It was hard to look at him and not feel sadness. She carried this man's grandchild inside of her and she was saddened to realize that he would never know her.

"My son surprised me. I had not guessed that you would be the one. It makes his eagerness to join Rafn more understandable."

"Your son is the best man I have ever met."

"He tells me you are with child." Airic looked between the couple and Peder smiled with pride. "I wish I could have seen whether you have a son or daughter." His words echoed her thoughts from a moment before.

"It is a daughter." Her bold declaration caused Airic to laugh.

"So she keeps telling me," Peder said.

"A woman knows these things," Joka smiled at him. "I do not need my sister's Seer powers to tell me it is so."

"A granddaughter." Airic looked wistful. "With your spirit I hope. You are a woman of great courage and spunk."

Joka was touched by his words. She had not been as confident in the Eorl's approval of his son's choose of a bride as had Peder. She should have known the one that had sired such a man as Peder would be just as wonderful.

"That dress looks beautiful on you," Airic said. "My wife would have been overjoyed to have seen you in it."

"I am honored that you allowed me to wear it."

Airic started coughing and Joka moved from the seat to allow Peder to take it. He stared at his father with such grief that spoke to Joka of the strong bond between father and son.

"You must rest father. I will come in the morning to see you again."

Airic reached for his son's hand before he could move away. "I am proud of you my son and glad that you have found such happiness."

III

They went to their bed chamber to find it had once again been filled with flowers. Petals were sprinkled on the bed and in a path on the floor. The sconces on the wall had been lit and many candles placed around the room. Someone must have come and lit them all while they were in with Airic. Peder swept her to him and found her mouth.

"I love you woman," he said. "My wife."

"I like how you say that." She reached up to wrap her arms around his neck. Once again they locked in a kiss that made her feel weak in the knees. It had been so long since she'd been in his arms.

Peder pushed her from him so his eyes could roam over her in approval. "You are so beautiful."

"It's the dress."

"It is you.'" He very delicately removed the dress from her. He smiled in delight to see the filmy shift that barely hid the shape of her body. He reached to caress the swell that held their child.

With urgency she peeled his tunic over his head and tossed it somewhere on the floor behind her. "It is enough. Tonight you touch me."

Peder's smile widened in amusement of her boldness and his eyes reflected the passion that she invoked in him. Yes, tonight he would lay her beneath him and claim her for the first time as his wife.

Well, maybe not claim, but join together as equals.

It was perhaps the most honest lovemaking that they had ever shared. All walls had been broken down, nothing was held back. No lies or mistrust lay between them. No anger or resentment, no regret.

They lay naked together, not just in body, but with their souls completely exposed.

IV

Peder woke to the pounding on the door of the bed chamber. He was still wrapped around Joka and reluctantly peeled himself away from her. His new wife opened her eyes in confusion and watched as he pulled on his trousers and went to the door.

"I am sorry to bother you my lord," Jakob said. "Seera sent me for you. It is the Eorl."

"I am coming." He closed the door and reached for his tunic. Joka sat up in bed and with concern watched him. "I have to go."

"I know."

He didn't stop to put on his boots but ran barefoot up the stairs and forced opened the heavy door to his father's chamber. Seera was already by his bed, tears streaming down her face.

He went to her side at once and met the glazed eyes of his father. He reached a shaky hand out to his son. "I love you both." His scratchy and weak voice was barely heard.

"We love you." Peder grabbed his father's frail hand.

Airic closed his eyes and his face smoothed as the pain left him. His hand went slack and Peder placed it back on the bed. He looked down at his father and he looked so peaceful.

"Oh papa," Seera cried and Peder dragged her into his arms and tightly held her.

A funeral was held that day. A fresh grave was dug beside that of their mother. Father Robert spoke the words of the Lord, asking him to accept his child into heaven. Peder stood numbly holding Joka's hand. Seera was on his other side with Rafn's arm around her to keep her from falling.

Both Peder and Rafn helped refill the grave with dirt. A simple cross was pounded in the ground to mark the site.

"If it was not for Valr's decision to stop here on his way to Iceland," Peder said to Rafn. "We would not have been here in his final days."

"What are your plans now?" Rafn asked. "You now hold his title and his lands."

"I will take my father's place as it was always meant for me to do." He looked over at Joka.

"You will not be alone," she said. He raised her hand to his lips.

V

It was just yesterday that the castle celebrated and everyone was so happy. Only yesterday there was dancing and joy. Just last night Peder had spent the entire night wrapped in the arms of the woman he loved. He'd felt so complete.

Even though he had known that his father was dying he'd been full of joy. Pain gripped him at the image of how his father had looked in the end. He had grown pale and scrawny. Even breathing had become painful for him.

It was a hard blow to know that his father was gone forever. The wind picked up and a thin veil of rain fell. He had sent the others away. He needed time alone by his father's grave. Joka had wanted to stay, but he'd insisted she leave.

There would be a feast to honor the life of the Eorl. Those who loved and respected him would not let his death go by without remembering his life.

Peder felt a sudden peace as if his father's soul had brushed up against him. He was connected to Dun'O'Tir as strongly as his father had been. He was now the Eorl of Dun'O'Tir and he would not let his father down. He was no stranger to duty and he would not fail it now.

The wind picked up even as the rain began to disperse. Peder closed his eyes and took a deep breath. He smelled the rich pine of the forest and the deep loamy scent of the earth and wet mud. A faint saltier smell rode the wind up from the ocean.

It was the smell of his childhood. He had left his home in search of something new. His dreams had led him far from Dun'O'Tir only to have them lead him back again. What he had learned over the past months when he had been away was that everything that he ever wanted was right here.

Would he have felt the same if Joka had not returned with him. He would never know the answer to that question and in truth he didn't wish to dwell on such thoughts. Things had turned out as they were meant to.

He stared back at the castle and smiled. The daughter Joka promised him would be born within those walls. She would race barefoot down the halls and sneak into the kitchen for a snack when no one was looking, as he and Seera had done. She would come to know every corner of the castle, learn the feel of the land around it.

It would be her birthright.

Peder turned and walked back to the Keep and his waiting wife. He found her in the hall with Seera and Rafn. Orn toddled around on his feet close to them and Peder picked him up and tossed him in the air. Orn giggled in delight at the game.

Peder smiled in answer to his nephew's laughter.

"I have just one last thing to take care of," Peder said to his wife. "Then I am all yours."

"I will hold you to that."

VI

Peder found Isibel still in the maid's chamber. She was sitting on her bed sulking because she'd been ordered to stay within the confines of the room. The stern looking guard remained outside her door. When she noticed Peder enter she immediately stood to face him.

"Why did you do it Isibel?"

"I love you my lord," she whined and it caused him to wonder why he'd ever brought her to his bed in the first place.

"You knew that I did not love you. I made it quite clear that there was no future for us."

"I had thought it was because you had to marry a Lady. Yet you chose a common woman. One that dresses like a man." Tears came to her eyes and she did nothing to try and hide them.

"Joka is my wife. Through marriage to me she receives the title of Lady and as such you will show her respect."

"My lord," she cried.

"It is enough Isibel. In the morning I am sending you to work for King David. He will understand and assign you a place to live. You will no longer be welcomed here at Dun'O'Tir."

"My lord…" she tried to protest but he stopped her.

"I will not have you here."

Isibel lowered her head in submission. He turned his back on her and left her to curl up on her bed and cry. It wouldn't be a bad life for her in the King's castle. Perhaps leaving for somewhere new will help the girl to grow up.

He raced up the stairs to find Joka waiting for him in their bed. They were still newlyweds and had time before they were expected downstairs. He shut the door behind him and went to her.

VII

Seera found Rafn on the fortress wall staring out at the sea. He had a determined expression on his face and she knew instantly what was on his mind as she went to stand next to him.

"You worry about what goes on at home."

"This thing with Bekan is not finished. He has awakened the storm in me and he will force my hand. It is just a matter of time."

"You left Valr in charge."

"I know that he is more than capable of handling any situation, but it was of my making and I would prefer to be there."

"We will leave soon," she promised.

"When you are ready." His face softened. "I do not want to rush you. Take what time you need for I will be fine."

"I love you," she said and walked into his arms.

"As I do you."

VIII

Far to the north in the village of Ragnarr, Rakel stood on the wall looking down at the same ground that had raged with battle not so long ago. She stood in the same spot she had on that day when men had died because of her.

Rakel imagined that Danr's blood still stained the dirt where his life had ended. She choked on the tears that threatened. A feeling of numbness had settled inside of her since the battle had ended and life in the compound had returned to normal.

She had forced herself to watch as the bodies had been burned. The pungent scent of the smoke still stung her senses. Blood and death haunted her when she was awake, and the images took over her dreams.

Danr's warm arms around her were a memory that she tried desperately to cling to, one good memory in the center of the nightmares. As hard as she tried to clutch to that one happy moment they'd shared on the training field when he'd helped her with her archery, it was quickly fading in her mind.

Fear of the knowledge that her father would come again kept the remorse strongly alive within.

It was far from over...

PREVIEW OF

THUNDER FROM ABOVE BOOK 3:

STORMY FREEDOM

CHAPTER 1

Far to the north in the village of Ragnarr, Rakel stood on the wall looking down at the same ground that had raged with battle not so long ago. She stood in the same spot she had on that day when men had died because of her.

Rakel imagined that Danr's blood still stained the dirt where his life had ended. She choked on the tears that threatened. A feeling of numbness had settled inside of her since the battle had ended and life in the compound had returned to normal.

She had forced herself to watch as the bodies had been burned. The pungent scent of the smoke still stung her senses. Blood and death haunted her when she was awake, and the images took over her dreams.

Danr's warm arms around her were a memory that she tried desperately to cling to, one good memory in the center of the nightmares. As hard as she tried to clutch to that one happy moment they'd shared on the training field when he'd helped her with her archery, it was quickly fading in her mind.

Fear of the knowledge that her father would come again kept the remorse strongly alive within.

It was far from over.

She knew that as surely as she knew that the sun would rise each morning and set each night. Kale's death was but one small step towards her freedom. She still needed to weather the storm…and she was not sure she had the strength to endure anymore.

An image flashed in front of her, a vivid memory of the moment that Kale had driven a spear through Danr's body. Of the instant that Danr had dropped to his knees and looked up at her standing on this very wall. He knew he was about to die, she had seen that stark reality reflected in his eyes.

She had seen his regret and something inside of her had mourned for the memories they had not yet made with one another. It wasn't that she had loved him. It had been too soon for that. It was that she had not been given the chance to know him, to learn to love him.

He had felt it too, in those final moments before he had collapsed in the mud and she had cried out his name in anguish.

He had died because of her…were words that echoed through her thoughts time and again. They had become a daily litany that she could not shed. Her penance demanded that she not forget. That she understand what exactly she had brought down upon all of them.

Rakel stared though the imagined turmoil until she was once again in the present. The sun shone brightly in the sky above her. Its heat strong enough that she had no need of a cloak, yet she could not feel it, could not see the beauty of the day. What she saw were shadows that stood before her and wouldn't disappear.

Rakel thought perhaps that she should return to Skahi. Kale was dead and the threat of a marriage to him was gone, yet she had trouble believing that she could live within her father's prison once again. She knew that were she to return to her father that it would take away the threat that she'd brought against the people of Ragnarr…but then Danr would have died for nothing and she felt that it would be dishonoring the warrior if she didn't accept the sacrifice of his life to save her.

So her torment continued.

II

Valr was standing outside the forge talking with Berthor when he glanced up and noticed the woman Rakel was on the wall again. He had often seen her there and wondered what it was that kept bringing her to that spot. Berthor noticed the direction of his gaze.

"It is where she stood during the battle," Berthor said. "She would not leave even when the rain had soaked her."

"Why does she keep returning there?" Valr wondered not really expecting an answer.

"What she saw that night has traumatized her. She wanted so much to be brave, to prove she was of use that night, but I don't think she understood the reality of battle. She saw men die in hideous ways."

"She blames herself." Valr said. He understood something the blacksmith didn't. He turned to see the confusion on Berthor's face.

"Why would she do that?"

"In her mind if she had not come here to Ragnarr, but stayed in Skahi and married the man her father had chosen for her, then the battle wouldn't have happened. She believes it her fault so many died."

Berthor scowled. "She was right to run from that man. No one should accept such a fate, even from one's own father."

"One should honor their father." Valr looked at him with a stern expression as he schooled the younger man about duty.

"It is so. But in her case I don't think it was the right choice."

"Even though she is right, that the battle would not have happened?" Valr questioned him.

"Each man that died was a trained warrior. It was what they lived for. How they all expected to die," Berthor said. "None would blame a woman."

"No, they wouldn't." Valr looked up at Rakel, "But she does not know that."

"Someone should explain it to her then."

"In time," Valr said. "She is not yet ready to hear it."

III

Kata lifted her son, Tannr, from her breast where he'd fallen asleep and placed him in the wooden cradle she kept beside her bed. The sun had set long before and she was tired. She waited for Dagstyrr wanting him to hold her in the still night when all other duties had been laid to rest.

She missed Seera and hoped that her and Rafn would return from Dun'O'Tir soon. She understood that Seera's father, the Eorl of Dun'O'Tir was dying and Seera and her brother Peder both needed to be with him. She also knew that Peder wouldn't be returning to Ragnarr with his sister, that he would take up his duties as the new Eorl of the fortress by the sea.

Joka would remain with him, the warrior woman who had stolen his heart from the first and had made him work hard to earn hers in return. In the end, pregnant with his child she had chosen to go with him to Pictland.

She prayed for their happiness and hoped they would visit often. Kata had come to respect and admire the woman who could wield a sword as good as any warrior she had ever known.

Seera and Rakel had both received training from Joka. Kata had hoped that when she was no longer with child that she too would be able to benefit from Joka's teaching, but was not to be. Perhaps Seera would give her instructions, or maybe Rakel.

It was a thought for another time. The door opened and Dagstyrr came in with a blast of wind that threatened to take the door off the hinges. He wrestled the door closed and secured the latch. His reddish hair had become a tangled mess that fell to his shoulders.

Kata smiled when he turned to her and opened her arms in invitation. He came to her in three long strides and eased down on the bed beside her, careful not to wake the baby. He kissed her tenderly and whispered words of love that she never got tired of hearing.

The wind continued to pick up outside, blowing the cold out of the north. Shutters rattled and dirt blew across the open courtyard as people hurried indoors to find shelter from the wind storm.

Somewhere off in the hills a wolf howled.

IV

A four legged creature with fur a deep gray color wandered down from the heights of the mountain that lay behind Ragnarr. He stopped on a high summit and stared down at the town which consisted of a compound with a fortified circular wall and buildings within, docks down at the water that held three knarr and beyond that the shops and the newer dwellings with their thatched roofs that would house the new arrivals to the village.

The creatures yellow eyes stared down at the land that had once been bare of human existence. It was curious of the activity of the men that walked the walls in defense of the village.

A wild wind blew through its shaggy hair but it didn't seem to mind.

It watched for some time before slinking back into the trees and the shelter of its den.

V

Rakel still lived within one of the longhouses within the compound. Most of the families had chosen to move out and build private dwellings outside the walls. With so many new arrivals from Skiringssal there was not enough room in the longhouses for everyone.

There were some single women that had arrived on Valr's ships who moved into the places vacated by the families. She had a met a few. There was Agata who had been maid to Seera in Skiringssal. She had also spoken a few times to Esja, who had been head servant of the trading village back in Vestfold.

Both women had been pleasant and cheerful, yet Rakel had not struck an immediate friendship with either women. She tended to stay by herself most of the time. Her old friend Hadde had moved outside the walls with Systa into a small dwelling set far apart from the others. She saw him rarely.

Seera had yet to return and Joka would not. She missed both women. It was just as well as she was not good company for anyone.

Rakel rose early as she often did, finding it hard to sleep. She went out to the river to bathe before the other women wandered down to the section of stream set aside for them.

The water was cold as it came directly from the high passes of the mountains. Rakel quickly washed and wrapped a drying cloth around her shivering body. She had brought a clean smock and apron dress with her that she dressed in. She tied a kerchief in her hair to keep it back from her face. She slipped her feet back into her soft leather boots and collected her dirty clothes into a pile along with the drying cloth.

She headed back towards the compound and the duties she would find waiting there, that would keep her mind busy.

She went through the gates as she had so many times before, so familiar with the path she took that she no longer paid much attention to her surroundings. So she was surprised when a large shadow fell across her, startling her as she jumped back.

"I did not mean to frighten you." Valr reached out a hand to steady her. His hand upon her arm, so innocently placed caused an even more unnerving reaction inside of her.

"It was I who was not paying attention." Rakel flicked her eyes up to meet his only briefly. He made her nervous, this brother of Rafn's who was said to be as deadly with a weapon in his hands as was the man known through the Viking world as the Raven. She didn't doubt that was so. She had seen him that night charge into the battle and pick off men as if they were nothing but flies buzzing around him.

He had done so with no expression on his face. He had been so cold and hard that he had left an impression upon her. This man of iron would not suffer nights of remorse and regret. He would not question his actions when it was too late to make a difference. He would hold onto his resolve and plunge forward through life with no looking back.

It was a quality that she both envied and feared. For certainly a man void of such emotions would not feel love. And still his people looked upon him with respect.

Valr stood so still watching her that she had to keep herself from shaking. She was afraid to meet his hard stare and kept her eyes to the ground as she bid him good day.

VI

Valr watched her go but made no move to stop her. What was it about her that drew his gaze whenever she was around? She was a beautiful woman, but that was not it. He lived beside many beautiful women and had not been lured by them. Yet this red-haired maiden, for surely there was no doubt of that, had him daydreaming like a boy who had just hit puberty.

Perhaps it was simply the look of sorrow he saw reflected in her hazel eyes. He understood such grief and he wanted to be able to tell her that it wouldn't last, that one day she would be able to look forward instead of back, but his words would be lies. He had yet to find such solace in himself.

A flutter of activity drew his attention to the changing of the guards. Men were scrambling up the wooden ladders that led to the upper wall that was made of logs and mortar. Watch towers were placed each forty feet. As men switched off, they all looked alert and ready to spring into action, even those that had been awake all night. Such was the strength of the warrior.

Valr could not help but feel pride in all the men that had come to serve his brother in Ragnarr. They were loyal and strong men. When he had made the decision to leave Skiringssal he had called to him the finest of the men to venture forth to the new land. Many still remained behind to follow Hamr, the Jarl of their choosing. Valr felt that he had left the trading village in good hands otherwise he would have had a harder time walking away from the only home he had ever known.

Though after Rafn had left, he found that a home without a family was not the same. It had become a hollow place of memories that he had to fight against daily. Most strongly were those of Geira and Orn, for they were gone from this world and his heart ached at the knowledge. There had been other ghosts to haunt him however, those of his family that still lived but no longer shared his life.

He had turned every corner expecting to hear Rafn shouting to his men in training, to hear Kata's soft laughter as she gossiped with the other women. Even his extended family members, Dagstyrr and Seera were sorely missed for what they had brought into his life.

The head table had become oddly silent in those first few weeks after they had gone. Had Geira still been by his side, perhaps he would have been able to bear it. He had come to realize he had no wish to remain alone. Though he made sure such feelings were not seen by his men, for such weakness in a leader was not welcomed.

Nothing of value remained for him in Skiringssal except for those memories that stretched back to his childhood. He could not live with only the past for comfort.

King Harald's greed grew and it had become Valr's excuse to leave. He left Skiringssal's fate to those who still felt passionate about the place and all it stood for. It was time for Valr to follow Rafn's path, words that the Seer herself had spoken to him when she had left on Rafn's ship.

Valr continued walking around the compound making sure everything was in order and stopping at the forge when he was finished. Billows of steam were already pouring out from the hot fires and the open side of the forge.

As if sensing his presence Berthor stepped from beneath the shelters roof. He caught sight of his friend and smiled. "What has your thoughts so heavy today, my friend?"

Not wanting the smith to know the waywardness of his mind he quickly thought of a reply. "I am only envisioning the sword that you shall make me. One made using that new technique of yours. I have seen the weapon you made Joka and your talent has impressed me."

"You flatter me lord." Berthor's face reddened at such praise.

"Your work flatters you. I have merely stated the obvious."

"I will make you a sword worthy of a king."

"I have no need to be a king." Valr leveled him a stern gaze. He'd had enough of Kings with greedy ambitions.

"That doesn't mean you can't carry a sword envied by one."

Valr smiled. "So true, see it done."

Berthor disappeared back into the steam and Valr searched for something more productive than wandering aimlessly with his heavy thoughts to pass his time. He headed for the docks and thought to help with the building that was still taking place, to create a trading center to rival that of Skiringssal's.

Rafn wanted an area where all traders could meet and barter. He wanted an open market for all to display their wares. Circling that would be the shops that were already being built. Further away was the town where several dwellings had also been started. Valr knew that his brother would be pleased upon his return to see how much had been accomplished in his absence.

When the Raven took it upon himself to finally fly home!